KAI

The World on the Brink of Darkness

Alison Hill

Michael Terence Publishing

First published in paperback by
Michael Terence Publishing in 2019
www.mtp.agency

ISBN 9781913289119

For my little bookworms, Anna, Eden and Lyla.

The only thing better than reading a good book

Is writing a good story…

THE IMMORTAL BUTTERFLY

A Native American Apache Story

In our world there was no colour. Everything was grey and the people were very sad and no longer smiled.

Twice a week the Apache Elders would dance to the Creator to beg him to bring back colour to the world. Months went by and nothing happened, then one night they heard a loud buzz of flying insects coming from the horizon. They stood still and watched as an enormous cloud of flies flew towards them in a huge sphere. The grey flies flew into the shape of a dark and scary face and shouted down to the stunned Apaches.

"I know what you seek and I know where you must go," roared the Face of Flies. "You must stand below the sun and follow me."

The Apaches desperately wanted their colour back, so they followed the great face of flies for many weeks through treacherous terrain. Eventually the flies stopped as they had finally reached their destination and the face turned to them and said, "I have brought you to where the sun shines. When I created your world, I made the sun to give you light and beautiful colour. But the colour has been stolen by a greedy creature. You must get it back, but to do this you must obey his every command and then he will give you back the colour."

Before anyone could speak, the great face of flies vanished. The people slept where the Sun had been and during the night a huge Butterfly appeared. He was 1000 feet tall and 5000 feet wide and his luminescent wings were covered in every colour you could imagine. The people fell to their knees and begged for their colour to be returned. But the Butterfly did not answer, instead he flew to show them what he wanted.

The followed him to the lake to give him water. They followed him to the forest to give him wood. The followed him to a Bee's nest and they gave him honey. Then the Butterfly flew to his resting place and ignored them. He stayed there for months and still there was no colour.

His resting place was an island and as time went by the Apaches became despondent and angry. Eventually one brave Apache swam across to the Island to confront the Butterfly.

"How did you take the all the colour?" he asked the Butterfly.

"At night, when no one could guard it," replied the Butterfly.

"But we cannot live without our beauty, life means nothing without it," cried the Apache.

"If I give the colour back, I will die, for I am nothing but a fragile mortal" replied the Butterfly.

The Apache left the Island with his head hung low. He and his people returned to their village and resumed their sad lives without colour.

Then one day the Butterfly came to them. Afraid they hid away from him, but he called to them. He said he was sorry and he wanted to return their colour to them.

"But you will die," said the Apache who had visited him before.

"Yes, I will die, but living my life while others suffer is not worth my existence. I would rather sacrifice my life than have others live in grief, I understand that now."

The Butterfly then flew to the highest peak of the great mountains and spread his enormous wings. Taking a deep breath, he began to flap them and the colour flew off spreading huge splats of colour to every living and non-living object in the world. Then the Butterfly shrivelled away to a grey coil.

The Face of Flies returned to the Apaches and shouted down at them, "No, look what you have done! The Butterfly is dead! He gave the almighty sacrifice and now he is gone!"

The Apaches were confused as to why the creator should be angry with them. Then he spoke again.

"No one should ever have to suffer for eternity for giving up their life for others. I can not bring back the Butterfly, but I can give you something to remember him by."

The Creator then vanished and the Apaches never saw him again.

The next morning, they awoke to the sound of rapid fluttering. There were thousands of small Butterflies spread throughout the valley. The beautiful wings every colour you could imagine and they flew from bush to bush and flower to flower.

As the days went by the world became a happier place. The Creator made the moon to guard over the colour at night and that is where the spirit of the giant Butterfly lives.

The Apaches will never forget that the Butterfly gave his life to preserve their happiness on Earth. Sometimes, on a really dark night if you look to the highest peak, you can still see his light. He may have died before his time, but to the Apaches, he will always be 'The Immortal Butterfly'.

The Apache name for Butterfly is Neshusuhaw.

PROLOGUE

The Ne'Shuwa flew down to land in the trees close to where his bonded had fallen. The men were everywhere, their quivers were full of deadly arrows and their jovial voices rang out through the trees. The Ne'Shuwa folded its magnificent wings to stay hidden in the canopies praying that his bonded was alive still.

She had been hit by an arrow and he had seen her tumble into the branches below, but could not see where she landed. He reached out for her with his antenna and felt her fear, she was still alive but in pain and too scared to move on. He would have to find her and help her escape, then they, like the other Ne'Shuwa would leave this world for good.

Satiren had been their home for centuries and they had once been worshipped by the inhabitants of this beautiful planet. They flourished in the rich, lush landscape and flew freely over the mountain peaks and rain forests, but now the newcomers had arrived, they were no longer revered, instead they were hunted for their wings that the newcomers wore as trophies.

The men walked underneath the canopy he was hiding in and he waited until he could no longer hear them, then he reached out again to his bonded. This time he could feel her pain and he used it to lead him to where she was hiding. He swung down the branches using his huge muscular arms swinging from tree to tree until he saw finally her. She was crying and frightened, they had only been bonded a few months but he loved her like she had been his for his whole life. He landed on the branch next to her and pulled her into his arms, his antenna clicking away to reassure her she was now safe.

Now he had to get them to the portal, the others had gone on before them but he had no idea how many of them made it. He coaxed her gently and she lifted her beautiful head then reached up to put her arms around his neck. They had to leave now, or they would lose the others and they could not survive on their own in the portal tunnels.

He opened his wings, their luminescent aquamarine glistened in the sunlight and he lifted her up with him and flew high above the canopies. The other Ne'Shuwa had gone to the mountains to enter the portal and he flew as high as he could to reach them, but carrying the weight of his bonded made it difficult. The men had climbed to the top of the canopies and they lay in wait for the creatures to fly over them.

He felt her pain as he held her close, at first not realising he had been struck and four arrows were embedded into his body. He tried to gain altitude to escape the flying missiles, but his bonded was a dead weight and he couldn't climb fast enough. He could hear the men whooping with joy as more arrows struck him and he knew now his bonded was dead, but his heart would not allow him to drop her. They wouldn't take her beautiful wings he wouldn't allow it so he flew towards the great lake knowing the men would not be able to take her from the water.

A last arrow struck him but his determination battled the pain and his loss of blood as he flew over the coast line and out across the blue waves.

His life was draining away as he pulled her perfect face towards his for the last time and lay his own head against it. He outstretched his wings letting them glide gracefully down into the water and then they sunk together below the waves, his last hope was that the others had survived.

BOOK ONE

KAI'S ARRIVAL

CHAPTER ONE

Solitaire padded silently on four paws into the Dome of Glass, but as quiet as he was, his feline form was reflected by the thousands of mirrors that covered the walls, announcing his arrival to the occupant of the Crystal throne positioned at the centre of the Dome.

She was still as captivating as he remembered, he had not set eyes on her for nearly eleven years and his heart fluttered slightly at the sight of her.

She sat with her knees pulled up lazily to her chest whilst she read a large book. Her white hair was piled untidily on top of her head, with long stray strands falling loosely over her slender shoulders and almost swamping her pale face.

She sat upright, pretending she had only just noticed him, and smiled a little sadly, "Solitaire, you came quickly. It's so good to see you again my old friend."

As soon as she said 'old friend' Solitaire winced. Is that what it had come to now, after a millennium together, they were just simply 'old friends'?

He shook his shaggy white head and stretched out his large, white feline body and then a blue light sphere cloaked him, obscuring him from view. The sphere grew as the woman on the throne watched on calmly and out of the light stepped a man, stretching his limbs and flexing his over-sized muscles.

"Still handsome after all these years," he announced looking at himself proudly in the mirrors that surrounded him. "It's been too long, there are only so many hairballs a man can cough up in his lifetime!"

"I see you haven't lost your sense of humour, or your vanity," laughed the woman.

Solitaire stretched out his muscular arms again. He was tall, with long white hair that was braided, beaded and decorated with blue and gold Razorbird feathers. He wore grey deerskin trousers and soft leather boots of the same colour but his enormous muscular chest remained bare, apart from the battle scars that he wore with pride. Around his waist a magnificent belt held a collection of deadly looking knives along with a huge silver sword, whilst draped over his wide shoulders was a magnificent silver-grey cloak.

He walked over to the throne, his corn blue eyes shining as he grinned into the face of the woman he had loved for a millennium. "It's about time Sirena, I have been a cat for too long now."

Sirena got up from the throne and swept herself into his arms. He was right of course it had been too long. Neither of them had expected things to turn out the way they had.

Solitaire lowered his mouth to kiss her, not wanting to let her go again. She returned his kiss willingly, but then pulled away too soon, "Not yet my love. We have much to discuss, things have got complicated."

He scrutinized her face and noticed the lines of strain around her eyes and sighed, "things are always complicated with you Sirena so why have you not summoned me before? I did not expect to be exiled for so long."

"It was out of my hands, I wouldn't have chosen this path, and now I fear that more damage may have been done because of it," replied Sirena sadly.

***

Sirena's official title was Overlord of Satiren, one of the worlds in the Odysseus Galaxy, but unofficially, she was known as the White Witch, the Ice Queen of the Heavens. She and Solitaire were both eternal beings, confidants of the God Odysseus and he used their skills to police the Universe. Solitaire was a powerful warrior for Odysseus and he had met Sirena over a millennium ago and their love had endured.

Sirena was not the only Overlord, there were many throughout the Galaxy and they all took their individual power from the elements of the Universe. Twelve thousand years ago the Fire Gods and the Ice Gods battled for ultimate power, but then Odysseus came and showed them they needed each other to exist. He split the Universe into Galaxies and created worlds within these Galaxies. Odysseus gave the Gods their own planets to nurture and grow, hoping that their creativity would supress their need for ultimate power. The Gods worked together creating worlds using both fire and ice, shaping them to their own desires and fantasies and then they created life to live upon these worlds.

Humans were created, they were made in the likeness of the gods and given intelligence and magic, but they were also given rules to abide by. As a result, the humans both feared and honoured their Gods in equal measure. But Gods have egos bigger than any human could possibly comprehend and they bickered amongst themselves constantly, challenging each other for ruling power over the worlds. They fought and argued throughout the heavens, eventually enraging Odysseus.

The Gods used mankind as tools and weapons in their wars, unaware that in the midst of all these battles, mankind was growing powerful itself, learning from the Gods and creating their own world.

Odysseus finally lost patience and once again intervened, this time allocating one world to each God so they would become the sole Overlord of that planet. On their own world they could rule as they saw fit, unencumbered by the other gods. And so, the Universe remained peaceful for a time.

One such planet was Earth, the most beautiful world in the Odysseus Galaxy. The great God Odysseus himself had made this planet and sent his magical Ne'Shuwa to bring life to his creation. The Earth was lush and green, huge waterfalls tumbled into pristine aqua marine oceans, whilst birds and animals lived unencumbered in rich grasslands and forests. When he had finished Odysseus gifted Earth to Zebulon, a mild natured Ice God who preferred to live a solitary life, and tended to steer clear of the constant bickering's between the other Gods. Earth was without doubt the jewel in the crown of the universe.

To travel between the different worlds in the Galaxies, the Gods used a magical gateway of portals that could transport them to other worlds in minutes. Sirena, the White Witch, and Solitaire served Odysseus as his eyes and ears across the Universe, and travelled between worlds to report back to him. They spent a lot of time on Earth, staying at the poles in giant ice caves, enjoying the bounty of this beautiful planet and playing with the creatures that Odysseus had created.

Time past and mankind evolved and became a powerful force in their own right. Zebulon was not a forceful Overlord and the humans on Earth began to forget about him as the centuries rolled by. They started to fight and argue amongst themselves, mirroring the battles of the Gods that had once raged in the heavens.

The humans created great machines that could fly and sail across the oceans. They developed weapons that could even kill a God, and Odysseus's world was soon over-run with huge ugly cities of stone and steel. It seemed the whole world had forgotten about the beautiful, natural planet that had once been gifted to them. At first no one noticed as many animal species died out, then there were famines and people began to starve. This made them angry and wars broke out between the great nation of Earth.

Soon the void between those who had and those who had not, became too huge to comprehend, and people began killing one another over something as simple as a loaf of bread.

Zebulon begged Sirena for help, he had let his world get out of control and he had no idea how to save it. Sirena and Solitaire travelled around the planet, but they saw death and destruction almost everywhere they went, the once lush and fertile planet was totally unrecognisable. There was nothing they could do. The wars and famine now covered the globe, the ice caps had almost completely melted, flooding huge territories of once fertile land. The planet itself seemed to know it was dying, and giant Volcanoes erupted sending deadly clouds of poisonous gases into the atmosphere. Rivers of lava spilled out and destroyed everything in their path and soon the colour was gone from the world.

Sirena knew it was too late for Earth, but she had found a small pocket of people who still lived by the old ways and who still worshiped the gods. They called themselves the Mavaho Tribe and they were hunters and gatherers, riding horses and living off the land, but they were struggling to grow anything and the animals they had once hunted for food had long since died out.

Odysseus had given Sirena a small world of her own to nurture, and she named it Satiren. It was only a few centuries old but was already growing to be a beautiful planet. Odysseus sent his beloved Ne'Shuwa to help her create it and the Ne'Shuwa remained there, making the planet their home. The White Witch took pity on the few remaining survivors of the Mavaho Tribe on Earth and she, with Zebulon's help, led them through the gateway into the portals and brought them to Satiren, allowing them to set up a new home.

Odysseus watched on with great sadness as his greatest ever creation destroyed itself and eventually, he could stomach it no longer. He blacked out the sun that was the source of all life on Earth and the planet was consumed in eternal darkness. Then the Dark Lord himself, Draconan, swept in to claim the souls of those who were left to die. The planet Earth died and became nothing but a toxic dead star in the Galaxy, a reminder to the other Overlords of what could happen if a firm hand was not taken.

Satiren was once a dead star of ice but the Ne'Shuwa had changed it all to almost a mirror image of how Earth had first been. It was a lush green paradise with snow covered peaks, inhabited by many different races that had been brought from other planets around the Universe. Magic on Satiren was common place and the Ne'Shuwa lived there in their hundreds, bringing life and abundance to the small planet.

Odysseus did not know that Sirena had brought a group of survivors from Earth. She had taken that decision herself, feeling that they did not deserve to be punished as they had always lived the way the Gods had wished them to.

There were nearly five hundred Mavaho men, women and children that she led through the portal to Satiren. At first it went well and the Mavaho's settled well on the planet, befriending the other occupants whilst they built a new home for themselves and Sirena watched on closely from within her mirrored Dome in the heavens. As time passed, she stopped being concerned about her decision and got bored watching the Mavaho's so she and Solitaire started exploring the Universe once again. She never told Solitaire that it was she who had saved the Earth people, he would have been angry with her for disobeying Odysseus, so it was easier for her not to involve him.

When the Mavaho's started hunting the Ne'shuwa for their wings, Sirena and Solitaire were on the other side of the Universe unaware that the people of Satiren were furious with the newcomers. But the other inhabitants were not warriors and were no match for the trained bowmen of the Mavaho's, and so they could only stand back and watch in horror as these beautiful creatures were shot from the Skies.

Satiren was about to change, and not for the better.

***

"I need you to take Kai back to Satiren," said Sirena and she saw a hundred different emotions sweep across his face almost at once.

"What in the name of Draconan are you talking about? We agreed I can never take Kai back there!" Solitaire replied not hiding his irritation at her request. "You haven't seen me for eleven years and that's all you have to say! Take Kai back, back to the world that tried to destroy her!"

Sirena stood abruptly, her demeanour changed as she revealed the Goddess and powerful Overlord that she was. Solitaire may be immortal, but he was a warrior, a tool for the Gods, he did not have the right to question her orders. "Did you think I enjoyed being apart from you all this time Sol? I have been watched you both closely and I did not dare reveal your whereabouts. Now, our beloved Satiren is to be destroyed, and I have been banished from setting foot there. I cannot interfere with the will of Odysseus, but I can get Kai to return. I gave her the power of my magic on the day she was born. I didn't know then that she would have to leave Satiren, but I do know now that she is the only one who can save it."

"I don't think I even want to ask what's happened to make Odysseus decide to destroy your world. Surely things settled down there after we left? I believed that was the only way back then but now you're telling me it made no difference. More to the point, you're actually asking me to disobey Odysseus and put myself and my ward in danger, all to save a planet that forgot about us long ago," replied Solitaire strolling over to a table that held a bowl of fruit. He picked up some grapes and popped a couple in his mouth, smiling to himself as the sweet juice of the fruit trickled down his throat. It had been a while since he had been able to enjoy the taste of fruit.

"It's not as if it's the first time you've disobeyed Odysseus, stop playing the victim. There is nothing you like more than a good adventure, especially one fraught with danger. Remember it's me your talking to," snapped Sirena walking over to join him at the table. She slipped her arms around his waist and reached up to kiss him gently.

Solitaire raised his eyebrows in mock disbelief, but couldn't maintain it for long. He dropped the grapes and pulled her into his body, crushing his mouth down on hers, his desire taking control. Sirena's passion mirrored his, she had missed him dreadfully over the years, she needed Sol in her life no matter what Odysseus had to say about it. Eventually she pulled away, catching her breath, "We haven't time Sol, I have to tell you about Satiren."

Ignoring her Solitaire went to kiss her again but she pushed him away. He shrugged and picked up another handful of grapes from the bowl, then went and plonked himself on her throne, "Go on then. I'm not going to stop you, I can see that," he conceded.

Sirena grimaced as Solitaire made himself comfortable, hanging his thigh sloppily over the side of the arm and lowering the bunch of grapes to his mouth to bite one off. He was furious at Sirena's suggestion and he was doing his best not to show it. Kai was his ward, and he loved her like a daughter.

"Do you remember Satiren when the Mavaho's first came, how beautiful and alive it was?" asked Sirena.

"I remember, that Odysseus brought these Earth people, and they destroyed his precious Ne'Shuwa. They almost destroyed Satiren, had it not been for Wigholt," replied Solitaire.

"That isn't strictly true my love," said Sirena softly. "It wasn't Odysseus that brought the Mavaho people to Satiren. He never knew about it, it was me," she said waiting for a reaction that never came.

Solitaire bit off another grape, then turned to look at her without that faintest trace of surprise in his eyes. "I guessed that a while ago, Odysseus would not have forgiven the Earth people so easily, they had destroyed his precious creation and he wanted them all wiped out. Sirena did you really think I didn't know what you had done?"

"Why didn't you say anything before?" she asked him feeling a little irritated.

"I agreed with you, so there was no point. And when you discovered they had hunted the Ne'Shuwa, I could see the guilt was too much for you to bear. There was no point in me adding to it, and to be honest I expected Odysseus to destroy Satiren then," he replied. "But what has Kai got to do with this. It all happened centuries before she was born."

"Let me finish Sol," interrupted Sirena. "Odysseus allowed Satiren to survive as a favour to me back then, but I am all out of favours. We both know what happened on Satiren and why Kai had to leave. I managed to keep it hidden from Odysseus and the other Overlords, and so for a while, things calmed down on the planet. The Crystalite King Atolin returned to rule in the mountains, and Tokala, the Mavaho Chief kept his people safe and happy in the Silversands. The two races never mixed and peace once again came to Satiren, but now things have changed, there is a darkness seeping back into the world and taking hold of certain individuals," explained the White Witch.

"But surely Tokala has learned from last time what could happen if evil is allowed to take hold on Satiren. I cannot believe that he of all people would let that happen," said Solitaire looking puzzled.

"It's not Tokala that's the problem, it's Atolin. When he was rescued from Mount Gloom he had changed, but none of us guessed by how much. His wickedness and cruelty to his own people has not gone unnoticed and Draconan is hovering, awaiting in the shadows for his chance to turn the world to darkness and claim the souls of Satiren for his own. He has already gone to Odysseus demanding that Satiren be given over to him, and I have just seven days to argue my case and save my world from extinction. If things have not changed by then, I will have to hand the world over to the Dark Lord" she told him. "Odysseus has still not forgiven the people of Satiren for what they did to the Ne'Shuwa, he has little patience for my world now."

"For the love of the Gods Sirena, what can Kai do? Very few will even remember her name, and from the sounds of it I'm sure Atolin won't be happy to see her," replied Solitaire frowning. "Though I'm finding it hard to imagine that the kind, loving boy I once knew could have turned to darkness."

"Kai can find the Ne'Shuwa and bring them back to Satiren. If the Ne'Shuwa return then Odysseus will have no choice but to let Satiren survive," said Sirena.

Solitaire got up from the throne and walked over to Sirena, looking at her as if she were a confused child, "the Ne'Shuwa are dead my love, you know that, they are not returning," he said gently.

Sirena turned and waved her hand across her huge crystal ball that was nestled in the arm of her throne. A pale blue light shone and Solitaire found himself looking into the portal tunnels that separated the worlds. As he watched he saw a flash of something in the tunnel, he looked closer and then he saw them. The Ne'Shuwa, there were two of them flying through the magical blue light, their great metallic blue wings charged by the potent energy in the portals.

"How? I don't understand?" whispered Solitaire.

"They escaped, and now the last five Ne'Shuwa live in the Portals, away from the worlds that seek to use and destroy them. They feel safe in the light, but they do not trust me as I was the one who brought their murderer's to Satiren. Kai's magic, although she doesn't know of it yet, can set the balance right on Satiren and then she can try to persuade the Ne'Shuwa to come home. It's our only chance Sol, we must try," Sirena was begging him now and it made him uncomfortable.

She once again waved her hand over the Crystal Ball and the scene inside changed and Solitaire could see his ward lying on top of one of the hills that surrounded her village. He frowned, Kai should have been helping to repair the fishing nets, she was constantly flaunting the rules.

"Look at her. She is miserable on Balon, she struggles every day with her identity," Sirena only succeeded in pointing out what he already knew.

"Then why did you send us there?" snapped Solitaire. "It hasn't exactly been a walk in the park for me either."

"I know, I'm sorry," she said. Solitaire was speechless, he hadn't expected an apology, especially not from Sirena. She had always been so strong, so determined in her choices and decisions, so to hear regret in her voice was uncomfortable for him. He looked at Kai again, her white hair blowing wildly in the wind, she definitely did not belong on Balon.

"Very well, how do you want me to do this?" he asked.

"If you could reveal your true self to her and then take her into the portals, I will meet you there," said Sirena. "I will explain to her who she is and her task, while you go on ahead to meetup with Tokala and Catori. Kai will need their help if she is going to succeed."

"And you think it is going to be that easy, do you? Kai will be furious when she realises she's been duped all these years. I will be lucky to get her to the gateway let alone the portals when she discovers who I am. You don't know her Sirena, she is as head strong as you are," replied Solitaire knowing this was a bad idea already. He loved Kai, he would not willingly put her in danger, but if what Sirena had told him was true, then there was no other way. Knowing Kai, he would have to duck for cover when she found out and he wasn't sure what Sirena would make of her, life was about to become very interesting.

"That spell you put on her to block her memories, are you going to lift it?" he asked. Perhaps if Sirena did that first, then seeing him change from a cat into a man would not be so alarming for Kai.

"Not until I'm sure she's prepared to do this task," replied Sirena then saw his raised eyebrow. "I will restore her memories in the portal if everything goes to plan."

He swore under his breath, he was not looking forward to this, but he was sick of remaining in his cat form for so long, it was time that Solitaire the warrior re-emerged.

CHAPTER TWO

He downed his umpteenth Sandfire Ale and noticed Catori rolling her eyes at him in mock disgust from across the room.

"I'm not drunk," he insisted and then managed to hiccup as if he had done it on purpose. Paco roared with laughter and Tokala decided his best friend was drunker than he was. Catori left them to it, it was a day of celebration and her brother deserved a day off. He was young to be the Chief of the entire Mavaho nation, a role he had taken on since he was a small boy and the annual games event was something he really enjoyed.

The games decided who were the bravest, quickest and strongest of the Mavaho warriors and they all competed on a range of different events. Tokala had been the overall winner for the last two years and this was his third in a row victory.

There were four main events that all the competitors had to compete in, the first was an agility test. A diamond was hidden at the top of the tower that overlooked the city and it could only be reached from climbing the outside of the smooth sand stone walls without ropes or climbing aids. Both Tokala and Paco were beaten by Chooli, she was a tall, lithe warrior and her climbing skills were second to none. No one had expected to beat her, but Tokala came second. Paco had got half way up, but as usual his fear of heights got the better of him and he conceded defeat.

The second event was archery and Tokala won easily with his bow, he was a bow master, no one could out match him. Then came the hand to hand combat, something Paco had trained for relentlessly in secret over the last few months. Tokala had humiliated him last year, and that was not going to happen to him again.

They rounded on each other with Tokala grinning widely just before he sprung, but Paco was ready for him and Tokala found himself hitting the floor and getting a mouthful of sand.

"A lucky throw!" he shouted to the amused crowd as he spluttered and spat.

The crowd loved it, they loved their Chief and life was good for the Mavaho's of Burning Towers.

Tokala was floored for a second time and then a third before he realised that Paco had been training and he may well be out matched. If he was put on the ground again, he would have to concede defeat. Paco's face was grim, watching every move Tokala made, expecting the unexpected, but it did not save him from his Chief's deceptive next move and he found his legs swept out from under him and down he went. The battle was on. Paco went down again, Tokala only had to get him down once more to even the score board, then it would be sudden death. But Paco swept in suddenly, they clung to each other, wrestling to get the upper hand, but Paco managed to twist out of Tokala's grip, spun around and using the whole of his weight, he brought the Chief down hard.

Tokala lay there winded as the crowd went wild and Paco did a victory dance around his bewildered friend. As Tokala got his breath back he kicked the back of Paco's legs and the dancing warrior toppled down on top of him. Still it did not dampen the grin from Paco's victorious face and Tokala couldn't help but laugh as he pulled himself and then Paco, back up to their feet.

The final event was a forgone conclusion, it was a horse race and there was no horse in the Silversands that could beat Chaser. The Chief's magnificent black stallion was stamping the ground impatiently with his hooves, eagerly awaiting to get going. As the starter arrow flew into the air Chaser left the other riders behind in a cloud of red dust, the race for them was always about second place. Paco's grin dropped from his face as Chooli overtook him in the last minute to come an overall second in the games.

Tokala and Chaser did their lap of honour in a faster time than they had actually run the race, and eventually the stable master came out to take hold of Chaser's reins.

"Let him rest now Tokala, enough is enough," said Yumi firmly. The stable master had no time for these antics on his beloved horses. Tokala leapt off Chaser's back to the roar of the crowd, he had won for a third year running and the feasting was about to start. The Mavaho's sat down to a night of celebration, safely within the city walls of Burning Towers as darkness approached and the desert sands surrounding them transformed.

Tokala's mother, Sisika, named him after a great warrior chief from the old Mavaho legends. His father, Black Eagle, had been a legend also, but a legend many on Satiren wished to forget, most of all Tokala and his sister, Catori. There were still many who remembered the tortures and the terror of living under the rule of Black Eagle and his vicious power-hungry warriors. That was many years ago now, and people no longer mentioned the old Chief's name, it had become synonymous with evil and dark memories.

Burning Towers, the city of the Mavaho's, glistened like a red ruby in the vast Silversands desert of Satiren. The desert covered a third of the world and for those who did not understand the ways of the desert they would be amiss to think that there was nothing alive in these red desert sands. There was no water, no living plants, and seemingly no life, just endless sand and the charred twisted remains of what had once been great forests. But underneath the dried-up terrain were huge underground lakes and caverns that the Mavahos used as an endless water supply, allowing them to irrigate crops and grow all the food they needed as well as keeping a herd of Gappins for milk. The Gappins were a cross between a goat and a sheep, and provided the tribe well with milk, cheese and clothing.

Mavaho hunters knew the desert well, their black skin did not burn from the sun's rays and their golden eagle eyes allowed them to see through the shimmer of the rising heat across the desert planes.

The hunters rode out daily, they were quite a spectacular sight, armed with bows and quivers of arrows; they wore deadly long knives hanging from their belts and their long black hair was braided and decorated with feathers and small animal bones. They were tasked with keeping the giant Kroll lizards from the city walls. The lizards were vicious and constantly after the Gappin herd, one Kroll would devour at least two Gappins, but they would kill many more just for the fun of it if they got to the herd.

Killing a Kroll would bring in enough meat to feed half the city, but the beasts had lethal teeth and claws and they could spit venom over fifty feet making them not easy to kill. Their hides were as tough as old leather and the Mavaho arrows could not pierce their skin, so the hunters had to get close enough to stab the beast in its soft vulnerable spot behind its ears. This meant mounting the lizard and so the hunters worked in teams. The first team tried to distract the beast, while the second attempted to leap on its back. It was dangerous and there had been many deaths over the years; there was no antidote for the Kroll venom.

In the centre of Burning Towers stood a castle with a spectacular tower that gave its name to the city. The castle was the only sand stone structure within the walls, it had been built by Black Eagle, but the Mavaho's preferred to live in their Cabana's, light round structures made from the un-limited supply of old dead wood, canvas and Kroll skins. The Cabana kept them cool during the hot sun of the day, and warm in the cold night air.

Tokala had toyed with the idea of tearing down the castle, but eventually decided against it. It was a sturdy building and it had its uses, and so the Mavaho's set up a school in the upper floors of the castle, while the lower floor became stables for their prized desert horses. However, the great hall was still used as a feasting hall on special occasions such as today.

The desert was extremely hot during the day, not for the faint hearted, but the Mavaho people could endure the heat and worked easily outside. It was when the night set in that things changed. At the same time each day the sun set rapidly; by then all the tribe would be safely within the city walls just in time for the three blue moons of Satiren to rise and transform the desert. There were diamond crystals in the red sands and at night they reflected the light of the blue moons causing a strange glimmer over the entire desert, hence the reason it was named the Silversands. The desert danced and sparkled, strange eerie shapes and shadows loomed from the the twisted tree stumps and the night creatures ventured out from their underground hideaways to roam and hunt in the sands, it was not a safe place to be and even the Krolls hid away at night. Stories and legends of horrific beasts and magical demons had grown up around the Silversands over the centuries, and so no one, but a mad man would dare enter the desert after dark.

Tokala was not afraid of the Silversands, nor the darkness. He had been in the desert at night many times, he knew about the acid scorpions and the crater spiders; he knew about the long- toothed leopards and the small singing devils that would eat your foot before you realised; but he also knew how to avoid them. Tokala kept that part of his life tucked away, only Catori knew what they had lived through and it was safer that it remained that way. Tokala had no need to travel into the Silversands at night any longer, yet there was a part of him that missed the adventure and his old friends in the mountains, but he had promised the White Witch to stay away, and so he had. He had been Chief of the Mavaho's since he was eight years old, but there was a part of him that wished he could be free.

The feast was in full swing, Catori was dancing with Paco's brother, Tuari, her long golden hair cascading down her back while her green eyes were filled with laughter. Tokala was watching with interest, he made a note to self that he would find out Tuari's intentions towards his sister. Paco slapped him hard on the back making him wince, his body was beginning to ache after the day's events.

"So, when are you going to allow me to breed my mare with Chaser?" asked

Paco. "You need some competition in that race."

Tokala grinned at his drunken friend, "Chaser is very picky, I can't just present him with any old nag."

"My mare is from the best breeding stock in town, he'll not find one better," cried Paco drunkenly outraged.

"I tell you Paco, I might be chief, but Chaser has refined tastes, I have to let him choose his own mare," argued Tokala.

"If he's anything like his master, no one will be good enough," growled Paco then staggered off in the direction of Willow, a beautiful young female hunter he had been pursuing for weeks.

It was a fair observation, Tokala knew it, it wasn't as if he hadn't had his fair share of women. He just struggled with connecting with them on a more personal level. He couldn't share his secrets with anyone except Catori, so he deliberately remained aloof when it came to relationships.

The feast went on most of the night and Tokala had some vague recollection of returning to his cabana sometime before sunrise and collapsing on his bed letting blackness take over. It seemed like only minutes later when Catori was shaking him roughly awake. He automatically reached for his knife his fuzzy brain telling him there must be trouble. Catori slapped his hand away from it, "No! Wake up Tokala, we have a visitor."

Tokala's eyes opened painfully, there was bright sunlight shining through the open flap and his mouth felt like he had been eating the desert sand. Squinting through the brightness he could see Catori's beautiful face, her green eyes alert and full of excitement.

"What hour is it? Have I over slept?" he mumbled as he sat up with his head pounding at the effort.

"Tokala, please wake up. You need to come with me now, he's in the castle forecourt," replied Catori.

Tokala looked down to see he was still wearing the winner colours in his hair He groaned and stood up, his stomach lurched slightly, but apart from that, he guessed he'd got off lightly considering the amount of Sandfire ale he had drunk. He picked up the bucket of water by his bed and poured its contents over his head, shaking off the drips he followed Catori out into the hot sun and through the quiet streets of Cabanas leading to the castle. No one was up and he realised it must still be early. The day after the games was always a tribal rest day, which probably explained why everyone was still asleep, yet there was something strange about today and Tokala realised suddenly that there were usually watchmen on duty by the wall, where were they?

As he stepped into the castle forecourt his question was answered, there were at least seven of his Mavaho warriors standing stock still with their bows aimed at a stranger slightly hidden in the shadows of the castle entrance. Tokala heard Catori order the warriors to disarm, but they ignored her, waiting to hear the order from their Chief. Tokala stepped towards the man who was leaning comfortable against the doorway to the castle, unfettered by all the attention he had brought.

"Step out so I can see you," Tokala demanded.

The stranger slowly peeled himself away from the wall and ambled out into the sunlight, his eyes squinting in the brightness. He was a powerful looking man, well-muscled with striking long white hair that had many braids threaded through it. His skin was white and his ice blue eyes were filled with humour as he looked at the Mavaho Chief. It had been eleven years since Tokala had seen Solitaire and the ancient warrior hadn't changed.

"Solitaire!" he cried his astonishment clear to all those who watched. "I can't believe your back."

Solitaire smiled, but before he could reply Catori ran forward and threw her arms around his neck. "It is you, Solitaire, I knew it was you!" she cried. "Is Kai with you?"

"Heavens above, this can't be Catori, look at you! You're a vison of beauty, just like a warm sunrise," laughed the ancient warrior holding her at arms-reach so he could get a better look at her.

Catori blushed knowing he was being kind. The tribe loved her, but she was so different to them, with her green eyes, golden hair and olive skin, she certainly never considered herself beautiful.

She often wondered if the Mavahos would have accepted her if she had not been Tokala's sister. They were are a superstitious race at best, and a suspicious, hostile race at worst. She remembered the fearful look in many of their eyes when Tokala had first brought her to Burning Towers and it had taken a while before they truly accepted her. But as she got older, she found she had the power to heal small ailments and alleviate the more serious conditions, and now she was the tribe's healer, earning their respect in her own right.

"Please lower your weapons," said Tokala to the bemused warriors. "Solitaire is an old friend of the Mavaho's and of the White Witch." The puzzled warriors reluctantly lowered their bows," Chooli can you organise someone to bring us some refreshments? We'll be in the great hall of the castle. Oh, and can you please go and awaken Paco, I want him to meet Solitaire."

"Yes, some of that delicious Sandfire Ale would be very pleasurable, I haven't tasted it in years," piped in Solitaire and winked at Chooli's bewildered face as Tokala's stomach lurched at the thought of more ale.

The great hall was quiet, it was usually had children running through it as the school was on the next level, but it was closed for the day due to the games. Solitaire made himself comfortable at one of the large tables and the others joined him. Tokala was torn between being pleased to see his friend, and irritated that Solitaire had not contacted them sooner. At the very least to let them know that he and Kai were safe.

A tray of food and more of the Sandfire Ale was brought up to them, followed shortly afterwards by an extremely bleary-eyed Paco, who looked just like Tokala felt.

"Sit down Paco, you need to meet Solitaire," said the Chief.

Paco stumbled onto the bench at the table and stared across at Solitaire, "You mean 'the Solitaire'?" he asked frowning. "I thought he was a cat."

"Long story," replied Solitaire sliding a cup of Sandfire Ale over to the hungover warrior. Paco grimaced as he looked down at it. "Trust me, a little taster of the snake that stung you will heal your wounded head."

Paco and Tokala gingerly picked up their ale mugs and both gulped down a little of the sweet brew. Solitaire was right, it did settle their stomachs and clear their heads almost immediately.

"So, everyone fighting fit now?" he chuckled. "Where will I begin?"

"You could tell us if Kai is still alive," said Catori. "I'm almost scared to ask."

"My apologies sweet girl, yes Kai is still alive. She has been living on another world known as Balon for the last eleven years, and she is the reason for my visit," Solitaire told them taking another swig of his ale.

"Is she alright? I think of her often and pray to Odysseus that she is alive and safe," replied Catori.

"She has been safe on Balon, but it's not her world and I think she suspects that now. I need to bring her back to Satiren and I'm going to need your help."

"Of course we'll help, but does she not wish to see her brother?" asked Tokala.

"Kai knows nothing of Satiren. The White Witch cast a spell on her when we left, so she has no memories of her home. The thing is Kai feels like an outcast on Balon, the differences between her and the people of that world are more apparent every day and it has been hard for her to fit in there. She doesn't understand why she is so different from the others," explained Solitaire.

"That's horrible, surely you could explain to her?" said Catori. "Or even just brought her to us. She could have stayed with us here at Burning Towers."

"No, that wouldn't work, Kai is a Crystalite so she would not fare well in the desert, she belongs in the cool of the mountains. And the other problem is that Kai does not know me in my human form. She thinks of me as her cat," explained Solitaire and then he grimaced. "She's not going to be happy when she finds out that she has been lied to all these years."

"I don't understand why you never brought her back sooner. Surely her brother would have protected her, he is the Crystalite King now, things must have changed in the mountains," said Tokala chewing on a piece of dried meat whilst kicking Paco under the table at the same time. His friend's head had slumped down and he looked like he was about to fall asleep on the table.

"Things have changed in the mountains, but not for the better. By all accounts Atolin is a cruel and evil King; his people live in fear for their lives if they dare to speak out against him. The Wizard Council has been disbanded, many of them imprisoned or they have just simply vanished with no explanation. If he were to hear his sister, Kai, was still alive, he would do everything in his power to destroy her," said Solitaire sadly as he saw the shocked look in their faces.

"But Atolin, he was my best friend. Is this true what you're telling me, the Atolin I remember would never hurt a soul," argued Tokala. He and Atolin had spent years together as small boys and the Atolin did not have a speck of cruelty in his body.

"I don't know all the details yet, but we will undoubtably find out how things in the mountains have changed for ourselves over the next few days. The White Witch has requested that we accompany Kai to the mountains to try to put right the damage that Atolin has done and bring peace and balance back to Satiren. Odysseus and the Overlords are growing impatient and Sirena has been given seven days to change things here or Satiren will be destroyed. The Gods will not allow the evil on Satiren to spread to other worlds."

"Is this a joke?" said Paco not sure if he had heard right.

"I wish it were, believe me, I did not want to return to you all this way," replied Solitaire.

Silence filled the great hall as Solitaires words started to sink in. Their world, their lives, everything that Tokala had worked for in trying to fix the wrongs of his father, all to be wiped out in a matter of days. "Why Kai?" he found himself asking. "What has she got to do with this? She would be safer staying on Balon."

"Kai has more power than she realises, gifted to her from the White Witch years ago on the day she was born. Sirena saw danger in her future and wanted to protect her. Once Kai's memories are restored, she will be able to use her powers to defeat Atolin and then find a way to bring the Ne'Shuwa back to the world. If Odysseus knows the Ne'Shuwa have returned, he will spare Satiren from its destruction."

Paco looked completely baffled, he had no idea what this stranger was talking about and was beginning to wish he had remained in his bed. Catori had got to her feet and was pacing around nervously, "I remember Wigholt telling us stories of the Ne'Shuwa when we stayed with him, but he told us that they were all destroyed centuries ago," said Catori.

"Wigholt was correct, the Ne'Shuwa were mostly destroyed, but what he didn't know was that a few managed to escape into the portals, and there they have existed in the realms of time and space, awaiting a new home. Their home could be Satiren again, but it will take a lot of persuasion to get them to return," said Solitaire.

"So, what now?" sighed Tokala, not bothering to hide his frustration.

"Now, I go and get Kai. I will be no more than a couple of hours and in that time, I ask you to prepare for a journey to the mountains. We will need good horses, ones that are not easily spooked by the dark and are able to climb the rocky pathways of the mountains. We will leave as soon as I return," replied Solitaire.

"How do you think Kai will take this news?" asked Catori.

"That's going to be the fun part," replied Solitaire rolling his eyes. "She's not exactly the easiest person to get along with, and she still thinks I'm a cat. I would hazard a guess that she is going to be very angry."

CHAPTER THREE

The fire flower's swayed in the strong breeze, they bloomed even in the middle of winter here on Balon, making the hills that surrounded Lake Runo look as if they were ablaze when the sun shone on them. If she could, Kai would stay up here in the hills, away from the prying eyes of the priests that ran the orphanage she grew up in. But Lake Runo parish would not allow it, they had an obligation as far as they saw it, to make sure she had every opportunity to make a good life for herself. That did not involve helping her to live like a hermit alone in the hills.

Kai sighed deeply, it was cold up here, but she loved that. She thrived in the cold, winter was her favourite season, she felt more alive than at any other time of year. The other children at the orphanage had attempted to make friends with her and for her part she had tried also, but as she got older their differences became more apparent and that was when the bullying started. That was also when Kai discovered how much stronger she was than the other children in the orphanage. She had always stood at least a head taller than the tallest boy, but now they knew she had the strength to match it and the children were afraid of her. Kai told herself that she liked it that way, but truthfully, she felt alone and miserable.

Cleric Roth had found her on the steps of his church when she was just four years old. Seated next to her was a huge white cat, the likes of which he had never seen before. The child had such strange colouring, brilliant white hair tinged with blue streaks running through it and pale, almost translucent violet eyes, nothing like he had ever come across before. The people of Lake Runo and the surrounding regions were all short and stocky, with dark curling hair and dark brown eyes, a complete contrast to this child. The Cleric believed she must have been a gift from Kutumi, their God and creator. So, he decided without hesitation that they should keep her, but when his wife cast her eyes on the strange child, she refused to have Kai near her other children.

The other Clerics debated at length about where she had come from, the only thing the child could tell them was that her name was Kai and the cats name was Solitaire. As none of them could agree on what should be done with her, she was eventually sent to the orphanage. Throughout the years Solitaire had remained her only friend, though she could never understand how she knew his name, nor where he went when he disappeared for days on end. Animals were not allowed at the orphanage, but it soon became apparent that Solitaire was not going to abide by these rules and eventually they relented and allowed him to remain with her.

Kai lay back in amongst the fire-flowers and wondered where Solitaire was, he normally accompanied her on her walks in the hills, but today he was nowhere to be seen. In some ways it was a relief, this was the only place she didn't feel trapped and she loved being alone. Kai hated her life, trapped in this small town of people who feared her and she often toyed with the idea of running away. But then Solitaire would come and calm her and these thoughts would leave her for a time. However today he was not here and she got to her feet, she felt like she could just keep walking, there had to be something at the other side of these hills, something better than her life in the orphanage. She was soon to be sixteen, too old to be trapped there fixing fishing nets any longer, it was time she found her own way.

She continued on, climbing hill after hill without Solitaire, now more certain than ever that she would not be going back, yet she had a strong feeling that the cat would find her, no matter where she went. He would not change her mind today, she was resilient in her decision, she was not going back. Feeling exhilarated Kai continued her journey, the hills were now getting higher and some of them had snow on their summits. This was much further than she had ever been before and it was turning into the most exciting day of her life, but then she stopped dead in her tracks. In front of her the air seemed to be rippling, as if she were staring through a curtain of water and she couldn't see anything beyond the strange anomaly. As she stared unsure what to do, the ripple widened and started to glow with a pale blue light the Solitaire leapt out of it.

Kai stared at her cat for a second, then looked back to where he had come from. The air was once again clear and she could see far into the distance. "How the hell did you do that?" she asked the cat as she sunk down onto her knees next to him.

"It's easier than it looks," replied Solitaire.

Kai squealed and jumped backwards in shock. Solitaire had just spoken to her, surely not, had she imagined it?

"Did you just speak?" she asked him feeling stupid.

"Yes, I just spoke. I've been looking for you, why are you so far away from home?" replied Solitaire sitting there calmly looking at her.

"Wait… just a minute, back up a bit! YOU CAN SPEAK!... You have been able to speak all this time and you're only just letting me know this now!" cried Kai her mind now ravished with questions. "You've left me alone for all these years, when you could have told me who I was and why I was so different!"

"That was not my decision to make Kai, I was following orders to keep you safe," said the cat moving slightly away from her for his own safety.

"Safe, or just a prisoner? You knew I didn't belong here! I have been miserable for years and you decide it's time to speak to me now. I should strangle you!" hissed Kai through gritted teeth, tears of frustration beginning to form in her eyes.

"If you promise not to throw a rock at me, I have something else to show you. But it might be a bit of a shock," replied her cat.

"More of a shock than having a talking cat?" Bring it on!" she hissed sarcastically.

The air around Solitaire begin to ripple once more and the cat stood on its hind legs, then seemed to be getting bigger in front of her eyes. Kai found herself staring open mouthed at a huge man with similar colouring to her own. "Solitaire?" she said.

"This is my true form," said the man taking a step towards her. Kai backed away as if stung, she couldn't get her brain to focus properly. Was she dreaming?

"I know this is a lot to take in, but you need to take it in, and quickly. I've been asked to bring you back to Satiren, back to where you came from," said Solitaire hoping it hadn't all been too much for her to cope with.

"All this time, and you have watched me struggle. I don't know whether to hate you or hit you," whispered Kai quietly.

"I understand but…" replied the ancient warrior shifting uncomfortably under her stare.

"Do you?... Do you really understand?... There have been times when I could have just swum out into the lake and let myself drown! No one would have missed me, no one cared. You saw how unhappy I was, you saw my tears and my loneliness and you let me suffer! Why should I listen to anything you have to say now?" her fury reaching a peak.

"Because Kai, neither of us had a choice in this, you are the daughter of a Crystalite Queen. When she died, we had to take you to safety, your life was in danger and if anyone had discovered where you were, they would have hunted you down. I can't explain it all now, we have no time, but you must know that I have loved you as I would have my own child,"he tried to explain.

"How would I know that? How can I believe anything you are telling me? You have lied to me my whole life!"

"I watched over you and it broke my heart to see your unhappiness, but I had to weigh that against your survival. Now I can take you back, but things are still dangerous for you. There is so much for you to know in such a short time, and I cannot explain it all in the time we have. I have never abandoned you Kai and I'm asking you to trust me now. Please come with me," begged Solitaire.

Kai's anger subsided a little, she stood there blinking at him, feeling strangely absolved from all the fury she had carried throughout her time in Lake Runo. It was as if she were suddenly free, wasn't that what she always wanted? Yet lingering in the back of her mind was a deep sense of betrayal that she could not forgive. She didn't know this Solitaire who stood before her, asking her to trust him. Why should she?

Aware Kai had been silent now for a few minutes, Solitaire was getting nervous. "I know you think you have no reason to trust me Kai, but if you want your questions answered then come with me. What have you got to lose?" he asked trying a different approach.

Kai thought about it for a minute before answering, "I will come, as you say what have I got to lose, it's not as if anyone will miss me, but just so we're clear, I have not forgiven you."

Solitaire looked at her sadly for a second then waved his arm and once again the air behind him started to ripple, there was no point in trying to ask her forgiveness now, they had no time and Sirena was waiting. He held out his hand towards her indicating she should take it, and Kai did so reluctantly. He pulled her forward and the pair of them stepped through the ripple, out of Balon and into the portal tunnels.

"Kai, get control!" she could hear Solitaire shouting from somewhere distant, but it wasn't important. She felt wonderful, like she was floating in a blissful dream, the cold blue light washing over her. She could fly, it was such a rush, the ground blurring beneath her as she sped through euphoric electric blue light.

"SIRENA!" Kai heard Solitaire's panicked call and she giggled to herself. Then someone grabbed her arm, stopping her in mid-flight and pulled her down towards the ground, her head was instantly clear.

"The magic in these portals is more powerful than you realise, you'll have to learn to control it if you're to travel safely," said the stunning woman who held onto her firmly. "I am Sirena, The White Witch of Satiren, and it was me that sent you to Balon."

Sirena was dressed casually in a white tunic tied at the waist, under a deep blue cloak with soft grey legging and knee length grey boots. She wore a silver circlet on her head and her white hair hung loose over her shoulders. She resembled Kai more than anyone else Kai had ever met in her life, and she could feel the powerful magic aura that surrounded her.

"So, you're the person I have to thank for taking me from my home and imprisoning me on a world that hated me," said Kai spitefully, now directing all her frustration at Sirena. She suddenly became aware that she was standing in what looked like a long tunnel, with electric blue ribbons of light dancing all around her, inviting her to be consumed by its potent magic once again. She had to struggle to keep focused and not lose herself.

Sirena ignored the hostility coming from Kai, "I am the reason, but I heard Solitaire explain to you that it was for your own good, so I will not try to justify my actions. I will however, ask you to forgive the sudden nature of this journey, it was not intended to be so urgent but we have very little time and I believe you are the only one who can help us." Sirena's stern eyes left Kai's face for a moment as she glanced over at Solitaire who had just found them both.

"Thank the Gods, I thought I'd lost her, she just took off before I could get hold of her" he announced looking slightly stressed.

"I have her now my love, you may go on to Tokala and help him prepare, whilst I prepare Kai for what she will encounter. Be ready within the hour," said Sirena and Kai watched open-mouthed as Solitaire bowed low and did what he was bade. Sirena then turned to her again and smiled kindly, "this is going to be difficult, but you need to understand a little more before I send you onwards."

"This is all beginning to sound dangerous, do I have a choice in this?" Kai asked.

"There is always a choice," replied the White Witch, but she offered no more explanation than that. She pulled a large crystal from her pocket, it shimmered as it reflected the dancing light of the portal. This will help you understand a little, then you may make your choice," said Sirena as she placed the crystal in Kai's hand.

As soon as Kai took hold of it, she was pulled into a world she did not recognise. She found herself flying in a cloudless sky over a never-ending desert landscape, with dark red sand dotted with blackened, twisted and decayed trees alongside giant rocks and boulders. It seemed so flat and empty, completely barren and seemingly devoid of any life, and she continued to fly with speed across the vastness beneath her. Then she felt herself slow and up ahead she saw a lone figure. As she drew closer, she could see a girl around her own age, kneeling in the sand. There was something familiar about the girl but Kai could not understand why. The girl had rich golden hair and huge deep emerald eyes, which were presently filled with tears and her face was etched in pain. She was staring at a tiny yellow flower, the only living thing that seemed to be growing in the desert sand and she was attempting to water it. As Kai watched she saw the flower petals fall one by one, then its stalk shrivelled, curled then crumbled away to dust.

Kai was whisked away from the scene before she saw anymore with the memory of the girl's face etched into her mind. She was now leaving the desert and flying over hills of jagged, grey rocks. They looked treacherous and uninviting and as she sped onwards, she found she was climbing higher and was soon flying through enormous mountains. These mountains were much higher than any of the hills she had climbed on Balon, and like the desert there was no signs of life here either. As she climbed higher Kai noticed small shrubs and the occasional tree fighting for life in amongst the rocky terrain. She felt herself slow once again and this time she was looking at the figure of a very old man standing on a rocky ledge. He was leaning on a staff almost bent double with arthritis and his clothes looked dirty and ragged while his wild hair and beard were long and matted. As she got closer, he turned to look in her direction and she gasped with shock. This was not the face of an old man, but of someone much younger, his face was unlined, but heavily burdened with pain and his eyes shone brightly with the same violet hue as her own. Before she could make sense as to what had happened to him, she was flying again, slower this time, moving through the mountain tracks as if she were looking for something.

Then she saw it, up ahead, it was the entrance to a cave, set back and almost hidden from the path. Kai felt herself being drawn to it and she had an overwhelming urge to find out what was inside that cave but once again she was being pulled away to continue her journey through the mountains. Soon there was snow and ice everywhere, more than she had ever seen in her life and just as she got used to the snow-covered slopes, she rounded the peak of a vast mountain to see a breath-taking city sparkling beneath her.

The city was carved from the same rock as the mountains, except for the magnificent palace in the centre, which seemed to be made entirely of crystals. The people milling about were just like her in appearance, all with the tell-tale white hair and pale purple eyes, but something about them made her uncomfortable. They did not look happy, they looked scared and ill at ease. None of them made eye contact with each other as they went about their business, and she guessed that wherever this was, it was not a happy place to be.

Kai was being pulled away again, she had no control of this journey and once again she was flying at great speed, she broke free from the mountains and found herself over the desert once more, travelling so fast that everything beneath her was becoming a blur. Just as she got used to the speed, she then she slowed abruptly and found herself approaching another city, not quite as spectacular as the one in the mountains. This city was surrounded by a huge red sand stone wall, and inside were neat rows of small round structures made up with animal skins and canvas. In the centre was a red stone castle with one huge tower that stood over two hundred feet high.

The people here seemed happy, in complete contrast to the mountain folk. They were black skinned and had unique golden eyes like those of an eagle. They played and worked in unison and their children ran free and happy around the city. As she approached the castle, she saw a tall, handsome, powerful looking boy maybe a couple of years older than her grooming an equally handsome black horse. He looked up suddenly as if someone had called his name and the same young woman Kai had seen with the dying flower in the desert, appeared at the doorway and strolled over to him. She was laughing at something and the boy laughed also, they were so at ease with one another that it tugged at Kai's heart, there was something so familiar about them but she didn't know why.

The image in front of her started to evaporate and the electric blue light of the portal shone through her vision and she found herself back in the tunnel with Sirena watching her.

"What you saw there is my world Satiren as it is now. It is where you come from, and if you haven't guessed already, you are a Crystalite from the mountains," said the White Witch.

"I didn't recognise any of it," replied Kai.

"That is my fault, I had to put a memory block spell on you when you left. It was for your own good, I could not risk the dark master Draconan finding you," explained Sirena.

"You did what? You stole my memories! Is that why none of this make any sense to me? You're telling me that people have been lying to me my whole life and all these places and names you're throwing are places I should know! Why should I care about your stupid world?" cried Kai furious at this woman in front of her.

"You need to care, you are the only hope that 'stupid' world has of surviving," Sirena snapped back at her. She hadn't expected Kai to be so angry, but then she hadn't really thought about it at all if she were to be honest.

"How can you be putting that responsibility on my shoulders? You are so out of order you don't even see it!" cried Kai her fury taking over. How dare they do this to her, take her memories and then expect her to just do what she was told, no matter what the danger to herself may be.

"No! that's my answer, I'm not going to do it. You said I had a choice and that's my choice!" she cried defiantly.

The White Witch was silent for a minute or two, then she bowed her head slightly, "very well, I will have to find another way. You can wait here until I get Solitaire to take you back to Balon. I'm sorry I've made you so angry, but I haven't time to explain everything to you now. So goodbye and good luck Kai."

Before Kai could say anything else, Sirena vanished, and she found herself standing alone in the portal of dancing light. That was abrupt and unexpected, she had thought Sirena would argue with her a bit longer. Well she wasn't going to stand around and wait for Solitaire to drag her back to the clerics at Lake Runo, she would find her own way now.

Kai started to move through the light and was soon floating above the ground once again. She did her best not to fall under its spell, but it was so inviting and soon she was blissfully floating through the tunnels, not caring where she was headed.

Suddenly she felt something big and hard crash into her, jerking her instantly back to reality. She blinked and looked around to see a giant creature looking at her, tilting its enormous head curiously from side to side. It was twice the size of Kai and had the body of a human, but its head was that of an insect, with oval black shiny discs at the side of its head where its eyes should have been and long, inquisitive antennae reaching out from the top of its head. The wings on the creature were huge, breath-taking, a majestic almost metallic turquoise that reflected brilliantly in the light of the portal.

In a split second it opened its mouth and a piercing scream rang out all around her. Kai put her hands over her ears as the noise was splitting her ear drums. Then it flew at her and hit her again, sending her careering off out of control through the portal. She felt something hit her once again and now she was completely disorientated, spinning wildly and unable to stop, then in a flash she was thrown out of the portal and came crashing down on red desert sand. She landed hard, her head hitting a rock and then everything went black.

CHAPTER FOUR

"What do you mean you left her?" Solitaire paced furiously inside the portal tunnel. Sirena could not set foot on Satiren so she had summoned him to her. Tokala and Catori were prepared and ready to go, it was already an hour later than Sirena had promised.

"I thought I would leave her for a while to gather her thoughts. She was so angry, but I knew she would calm down, there was no way she would allow you to take her back to Balon. I didn't expect her to just leave," said Sirena looking bewildered.

"This is Kai we're talking about. She is not just going to stand there and wait for you, not if she's angry. Have you any idea where she's gone?" he groaned. He should never have left the two of them alone, they didn't know each other well enough.

"The Ne'Shuwa say she's on Satiren, but they have no idea where," replied Sirena.

"The Ne'Shuwa! Dare I ask how they know this?" asked Solitaire.

"They encountered her in the portal and didn't know who she was. They thought she was a threat so they attacked her and forced her out of the tunnels," grimaced Sirena watching Solitaire's face look like it was going to explode.

"What in the Gods does that mean? Have they harmed her?" he shouted.

"No, well, I don't think so. They just forced her out the nearest portal entrance, but they don't know exactly where, only that it leads to Satiren. That was all they would tell me, they still don't trust me" explained Sirena. "You're going to have to find her."

"You don't make things easy, do you?" replied Solitaire putting his head in his hands. "She could be anywhere. Can you not use your power to find her?"

"I'm not allowed to use any magic on Satiren. If I do, Odysseus will destroy it immediately," Sirena sighed then suddenly a thought came to her. "What about

Wigholt? If you could contact him, he will have the power to locate her."

"I could try that, hopefully Tokala will know where he is. It seems like it's our only option just now," agreed Solitaire.

"I'm sorry my love, I should have listened to you. She is far more head strong than I ever imagined, I hope I haven't put her in danger," sighed Sirena.

***

The heat was brutal, it felt as if flames were licking at her bare skin and the pain was almost too much to bear. She moaned slightly then rolled onto her side and tried to open her eyes, it was as if they had dried shut. Eventually, managing to squint around she saw she was in the red desert of her vision, and the burning red sun above her was the culprit that was causing her all this pain.

Kai sat up, and her head started to spin, it was thumping and she felt a dried sticky substance matted into her hair. It was blood, her head had a nasty cut and her tongue felt swollen and dry.

She was not dressed appropriately, the sleeveless shirt she wore was all she needed on Balon as she never felt the cold. Thankfully her legs were covered with leggings but her arms and face that were exposed to the sun were already blistering and Kai knew she had to find some sort of shelter as soon as possible.

Getting unsteadily to her feet feeling sick and dizzy Kai looked around, the desert seemed to be a never-ending flatland in all directions. The heat caused a shimmering haze that prevented her from seeing too far ahead but as far as she could tell there was nowhere shelter. The dead tree stumps and boulders that littered the landscape cast no shadows as the sun blazed down directly above them. Kai started to walk, trying to shield her arms and face from the sun, but it was useless. If she didn't find shelter soon, she would die out here and no one would know what had happened to her.

She wondered if Solitaire would be looking for her by now. What was that creature she had encountered? She had never seen anything like it, and why would Sirena leave her when there were dangerous animals in the portals? All these questions rang around her head as she continued onwards, every step becoming more and more difficult.

The sun was merciless, her throat was dry and her tongue was so swollen it almost filled her entire mouth, she needed water but there was none to be seen. How long could she keep going like this? Her arms were numb, but were a horrible angry red colour, even the blisters had popped now. Exhaustion was taking hold and Kai knew if she carried on, she would eventually pass out. There was no where she could go, everywhere she looked was the same, so giving up she sat down leaning her back against a sizzling hot boulder pulling up her knees and burying her face and arms into them in misery, knowing that she would die here all alone.

It was only a matter of minutes later that a strange phenonium started to happen to the desert around her, she didn't notice at first, but then all at once she realised the heat of the sun was not so intense on her back. She lifted her head to see her tormentor rapidly setting in the horizon, the desert turning bright orange for just a minute as the sun ducked under the horizon and then everything went black.

Kai was grateful to be out of the heat, but the darkness was so intense that she could see nothing at all around her for a minute or two. Then rising into the sky in the opposite direction from where the sun had set, three bright blue moons started to climb. It was strange to watch the speed in which they moved through the sky and soon enough they stopped directly above her where they remained shining their bright blue light down brilliantly onto the desert, changing the entire landscape.

The ground and the rocks were sparkling with what seemed likes millions of tiny lights and Kai guessed there must be millions of tiny crystals reflecting in the moonlight. But stranger than this, as the magical light from the moons shone down on her tortured and burnt skin, it slowly began to heal itself. Kai could feel a coolness spread deliciously over her body, her hair began to tingle and her skin grew back over the burns. The sharp pain from the cut on her head began to feel better and her swollen tongue shrank back to its normal size as her terrible thirst subsided. She lay her head back on the boulder, bathing in the magical light of the moons and a sense of relief flooded into her.

"WHO ARE YOU!" a voice rang out over the desert making Kai jump to her feet. She looked around startled, but could see nothing except for the shadows cast from the twisted tree stumps.

"WHO ARE YOU!" the voice bellowed out again.

"WHO ARE YOU!" Kai yelled back.

"You are trespassing on my land, you will introduce yourself or suffer my wrath!" came the voice again, this time sounding closer. Still Kai could see nothing.

"How would I know this is your land? Do you own the desert?" she shouted out to the night air.

There was a flash behind her and she turned to see a strange sign stuck in the ground, it definitely hadn't been there before.

'THIS IS THE PRIVATE PROPERTY OF WIGHOLT

GRAND WIZARD OF THE SILVERSANDS

TRESPASSER WILL BE PUNISHED'

"That's not very friendly, and you can't just make it appear like that. That's not fair," cried Kai.

"I'm not trying to be friendly. I want you to leave," replied the voice.

"Wigholt, that's your name, right? I'm lost, I need help, please come out so we can talk," she called out again.

"I'm right behind you," replied the voice and Kai spun around then almost toppled over in shock. There in front of her stood the most comical little man she had ever seen. He could not have been more than three-foot high, his skin was a chalky blue colour and he had very long white hair and a beard to match. On his head he wore a dark woollen bobble hat pulled down over his ears. It matched his dark woollen clothing, but his cloak sparkled with the same crystals that were in the sands.

"It's rude to stare!" he snapped at her.

"I'm sorry, I've never met anyone like you before," replied Kai.

"So, the Crystalites have forgotten me already? I don't know why I ever bothered with you all," replied Wigholt.

"I'm not a Crystalite, that is, I am a Crystalite, but I don't know any of them," Kai tried to explain.

"You're talking in riddles girl. You mean to say that neither Atolin nor Arcos have ever mentioned me," said Wigholt clearly offended and not listening to what she was saying. "After all I've done for them, this is the gratitude they show me!"

"I don't know who they are!" cried Kai wishing this strange little man would stop talking for a minute.

"You're not very bright, are you? Atolin is your King, probably too high up for the likes of you, but even a dumb girl like you should know who your King is," huffed Wigholt.

"Are you always this rude?" yelled Kai, now very frustrated. "I have just told you I don't know who the Crystalite's are. Why won't you listen? And just for the record, I AM NOT DUMB!"

"Well there is no need to shout. You wouldn't be very smart if I changed you into a desert lizard," snapped the little Wizard.

"Right now, I don't think I'd care!" yelled Kai, then she sighed. "Look Wigholt I need your help. I need to find Solitaire, do you know him?"

"Solitaire," replied Wigholt looking startled. He stared at the girl in front of him. There was something about her, but it had been so long since he had been to the mountains. It was strange to come across a Crystalite so far away from their home and he had watched her a while before he decided to approach. Now she had mentioned Solitaire, it had shaken him to his core. Surely, she couldn't be, not now, not after all this time.

"What is your name child?" he asked suddenly, his tone much gentler than it had been.

"I'm Kai," she replied and watched his eyes widen in shock. "Do you know who I am?"

The strange little man took a step towards her and stared up at her face for a moment or two. Then he said, "You'd better come with me."

***

"So, you're saying she definitely came to Satiren, but nobody knows where she is. She doesn't know who she is or who we are, and she is the only person that can save the planet," said Tokala stating the obvious but unable to hold back the tone of his frustration.

"I agree it hasn't been handled well, but we don't have time to dwell on that. We should leave now, the only person that can help us is Wigholt. He has a Seeing Crystal and he'll be able to find her," said Solitaire ignoring Tokala's bad mood.

"Wigholt will not speak with us," said Catori. "I've tried for years to speak with him, but he just stays hidden in his underground cavern. I wonder sometimes if he is still alive."

"Since when have you been trying to speak to him? Why haven't you told me what you were doing?" growled Tokala. "I don't like you going out into the desert on your own."

"Catori wasn't on her own," interjected Paco looking slightly sheepish. "I went with her, she asked me."

"Oh, so you both running off behind my back now!" replied Tokala throwing up his hands in despair. "Wigholt told us to let him be. Why would you try to disturb him?"

"Because no one should live alone like that, and after all he did for us. I just wanted to make sure he was alright," cried Catori.

"Can we discuss the ins and outs of this later please. If Catori and Paco know the way they can lead us there, then we can try to persuade Wigholt to help us. You do remember the way, don't you?" asked Solitaire.

"Yes, of course," she replied sullenly avoiding looking at her brother.

Within twenty minutes the small riding party had set off, it would soon be dark and Tokala knew Paco would be nervous being out of the city. He had to rein in Chaser, the black stallion wanted to set the pace but the other horses could not keep up with him.

"We should reach Wigholt's cavern by mid-morning tomorrow," said Catori.

***

Kai followed Wigholt over to some large boulders and jumped back startled as one of them slid along the ground when he clapped his hands together. It revealed the entrance to a stairway that descended down deep into the ground. Wigholt started to climb down the steps, then he stopped and turned back towards her, "Well," he said pointing down. Taking a deep breath Kai followed him down, it went further than she could have imagined. When she had gone about twenty steps or so she heard a loud grinding sound and the boulder above her slid back over the entrance.

The stairway was instantly lit up with strange blue flaming torches that were inserted into the stone walls. When Kai arrived at the bottom she was greeted by a warmly lit cavern, richly furnished and very cosy. Wigholt pointed towards a large chair covered in furs and Kai went over to sit down.

"Are you hungry?" he asked.

She was starving she realised, it had been a very long time since she had eaten. She made herself comfortable as Wigholt fetched some bread and cheese for her, along with some strange looking meat that tasted very peppery. He also gave her some deliciously sweet milk to wash it all down with.

Wigholt picked up his pipe and lit it while she ate ravenously. After a while she looked over at him, a little embarrassed at how greedy she had been. "I'm sorry, it's delicious and it's been a while since I had any food."

"It's good to have company, it's been a long while since I have been able to play host," he replied. "Now Kai, perhaps you could tell me what you're doing here?"

"Nothing is very clear to me, Wigholt. Solitaire brought me through the portal tunnels, and I met the White Witch. She told me that I came from a world called Satiren and I was being sent back there to save it. I didn't understand what she meant and then she told me she had taken my memories from me when I was a small child, I got angry with her, so she left me alone in the tunnel. I was trying to find my way when I collided with a strange creature and the next thing I knew I woke up in this red desert, it's all I can remember," explained Kai.

Wigholt looked at her thoughtfully, "Well you are now on Satiren, so at least you have come to the right planet. It does sounds like we need to find Solitaire, he is probably looking for you. I wonder why Sirena would want you to come back here now?"

"She said I was the only hope for this world, but I don't know what she meant. One minute I was walking in the hills on Balon, and the next I find out Solitaire is not a cat and I am some Crystalite princess from another world. I got so angry with her, she kept throwing names at me as if I should know who they were. When she left me, I didn't know what I was supposed to do."

"I wonder what's happened? I've been away so long I've not kept an eye on things here on Satiren. Mind you it sounds as if Sirena met her match with you, you must have really annoyed her," he chuckled to himself.

"You know the White Witch? Yes, I got really angry with her when she told me she had taken the memories of my childhood from me. I told her she was out of order and that I wouldn't help her, it didn't go down very well," confessed Kai.

"Yes, that would probably do it, however I'm sure she had no intention of you ending up in the Silversands desert alone. It's not safe for a Crystalite here," said Wigholt, he liked this girl's spirit. "I would imagine that they are probably at the Crystal City looking for you."

"The Crystal City?" repeated Kai.

"It was once your home Kai, and I think perhaps you should return there. However, from what you say you have no understanding of our world at all. I agree with you, that doesn't seem fair," said Wigholt thoughtfully.

"Can you help me?" Kai asked, feeling warm and comfortable and a little sleepy now wrapped in the soft furs.

"Yes, I can help you, but first I think you have to understand what happened to Satiren. It was a very different world centuries ago, a magical place full of magical creatures," said Wigholt sadly and he waved his hand in front of her face and Kai felt her eyelid get heavy.

Wigholt started to speak but his voice sounded distant, Kai closed her eyes and soon she felt herself being transported back in time to another world as Wigholt told the story.

CHAPTER FIVE

Five Hundred Years Ago

Satiren was a lush, green world. Dense forests and woodlands, flowing rivers and flower dotted meadows covered what is now the Silversands desert. Lush rainforests teamed with life in the foot hills of the mountains and up in the mountains themselves there were sweet smelling pine trees that made their way up the steep slopes to the snow-covered peaks. There were seas and great lakes fed by lively rivers and cascading waterfalls and they brought life to the entire planet. The different races of people on Satiren lived in harmony, alongside the more magical creatures that also existed there.

My people were called the Jacartans, also known as the dragon riders and we lived in the upper territories just beyond the rain forests. We were the smallest race of people here in this world, but we had the strongest magic. The dragons lived alongside us, they were huge fierce reptiles, but our magic kept them calm and content. The dragons were proud and intelligent beasts, and our bond with them was strong.

We Jacartans kept ourselves to ourselves and did not mingle much with the other races and creatures on Satiren. We kept the dragons at bay and had all we needed to survive comfortably, so we did not attend the annual meetings that the White Witch held for all the inhabitants of Satiren. We were arrogant and did not see the need to converse with others and that was going to be a huge mistake on our part.

I had a wife named Josee, and we had two children of our own. We lived alone, which is the way Jacartans liked to live, only meeting with the others of our kind at certain times during the year.

In the forests on the higher slopes lived the magical Ne'Shuwa. Huge, mysterious creatures, with the torso that resembled a human but with the most beautiful, magical blue wings like those of an enormous butterfly. There were many stories throughout Satiren surrounding the Ne'Shuwa, as they were rarely seen. Legend said they brought life to all things on our world and without them Satiren would die.

Then one day the White Witch came to Satiren and held a meeting, of course we Jacartans once again did not attend. Sirena proposed bringing a group of survivors from another world to Satiren, their own world was dying and these people needed a home. She asked for the approval from the leaders of all the races on Satiren and they agreed to her request. The first we Jacartan's knew of the new arrivals was when the Mavaho leader came to visit us in our forests. I can still see his face now, so strong and sincere he was, ready to be our friend. He wanted to make a home for his people near to where we lived but we were not happy. The Jacartans and the Dragons did not want strangers living amongst us, so we suggested he took his people to the hills beyond the rainforests. No one lived in these hills and there was plenty of good hunting for them. He thanked us and left, and took his people to make their home where we had foolishly suggested.

They were hunters in their own world and they brought all their hunting knowledge with them to ours. What we did not know was we had sent the newcomers to where the Ne'shuwa hunted for food, and before long the Mavaho's began to hunt the Ne'Shuwa. No one had told them about the legend of the Ne'shuwa and so they hunted them for their beautiful wings, unaware of the devastation they were causing.

By the time we Jacartans had any idea of what was happening, it was already too late. The Ne'Shuwa thought that the whole of Satiren had turned against them and as their numbers diminished the rainforest began to die. Not that you would notice at first, the plants would simply shrivel and die as plant do, but no others would grow in their place. The rain stopped falling and soon the exotic perfume of the rainforest flowers faded away and was replaced with the rotten stench of dying vegetation. That was when we noticed.

There had once been such an abundance of life on Satiren, but the small birds and insects died out first, sending out a chain reaction that affected every creature on the planet. The whole forest was dying and the Dragons became restless and angry, we could no longer control them and they took flight and went hunting for food in other parts of the planet. The great lakes and rivers started to dry up, and soon famine and disease had spread to every corner of the world.

With that came war, people blamed the new comers and attacked them. The newcomers fought back and many people were killed, then came a plague. Some say Odysseus sent the plague to punish us, but I think it was of our own doing. There was no sign of the White Witch, no one knew where she was and as the plague spread infecting every creature on the planet, soon there was no one left to care. The Dragons were almost wiped out and my own wife and children fell victim to the disease, and I, the so-called great Wizard Wigholt, could only sit and watch helplessly as the life left their bodies.

I buried my family and set out searching for survivors but soon discovered that I was the last surviving Jacartan. With a broken heart I travelled south to see what had happened to the rest of the world and all I saw drove me to despair, the whole planet stank of death and decay; it had become nothing but a rotting wasteland and I had no desire to help the few pockets of Survivors that I came across.

Eventually I found my way down to this cavern and an underground stream, fed by the snow-capped mountains. I made my home here in the darkness, the crystal-clear water allowing me to survive. I remained alone, drowning in my own self-pity and loathing for ten years. My hatred for those who had caused this was the only thing that kept me going. But, as time went by, my hatred turned to grief and a deep-rooted sadness. Curiosity eventually brought me to the surface, I think part of me thought that perhaps everything would have been restored to the way it was. I was not prepared for what I faced.

I walked out onto the vast sands of a burnt red desert, no sign at all that anything had once existed here, apart from the deformed, burnt and blackened trees that were the remains of the forests. Nothing grew anywhere and the only sign of life I saw were a few nasty looking scorpions. I looked through the heat haze towards the mountains in the distance and could see they were grey and barren and I thought everything and everyone had died.

I travelled onwards and came across people who like me had survived using the underground streams. I took pity on them and set about gathering together the small pockets of survivors that remained and then I helped them build a city here in the desert. They learnt how to irrigate their water supplies and grow crops again. Eventually there were around ten thousand survivors in total, but it took a while before trust was established between them and they constantly bickered amongst themselves.

There were only a few animals left and so they did not use them for meat until they became too old for breeding. Over the years they managed to rebuild herds of Gappins, and the population of the survivors grew. Eventually they became more tolerant of each other and it seemed to me that a good strong community was forming.

Then I began to notice that something strange was happening to me. Jacartan's lived normally for about two hundred years, but I had far surpassed that age. I had watched children being born, growing into adulthood and old age then dying, but I was still as young as I had been when all this had first started. I was not ageing and I didn't know why.

I began to feel very lonely and I craved my underground retreat once more, so one night I left them all without a word and returned here. I lived here alone for another one hundred and fifty years, reading my father's ancient book of magic and becoming more powerful than I had ever been before. My father had told me it took a lifetime to become a great Wizard and I had already lived well over two lifetimes.

One day I used a spell to render myself invisible and I ventured out my home once more and went back to the city. Outside the city gates were huge fields of healthy-looking crops tended to by dark skinned people with golden eyes. They very much resembled the newcomers who had brought the destruction here in the first place. They seemed happy, full of life and well fed.

But when I arrived in the city it was a different story. There were a different group of people, pale skinned with white blonde hair, all dressed in servants clothing with rags covering their faces to protect them from the sun. They were the objects of ridicule, and were spoken to harshly by the others. I discovered that the masters of the city called themselves the Mavahos, the name of their earthly ancestors, they thrived in the sunlight hours but they did not venture at night.

The pale, sickly looking people were known as the Crystalites, they hated the rays of the sun that burnt their skin so harshly, but they felt stronger and more alive during the hours of darkness when the three moons of Satiren would rise.

I spent months watching the plight of the Crystalites before I decided to intervene once more. I had been to the mountains and I believed these people could make their home there, so one night I led the Crystalites away from the Mavaho city up into the mountains. I took them to the highest peak that they eventually named Mount Solomite, and there, about three quarters of the way up was a huge plateau where the Crystalites built homes for themselves. As I had promised they became strong and healthy in the mountain air, I used my magic to help them mine for the shiny granite stones and crystals they could build their city with.

Many animals still lived in the mountains and the Crystalites soon became self-sufficient, living off the milk from mountains goats and meat from the huge Elks. They found mountain horses and trained and bred them to help transport them around the mountain slopes. Life became good for the Crystalites and they prospered greatly. There was an enormous supply of

Crystals in the mountains and they set about building a magnificent Crystal Palace that stood in the centre of their city. It took many decades to finish but it became their pride and joy, a symbol reminding them that they were now a great nation.

I visited the Mavaho's from time to time and they too prospered. They had no idea what had happened to the Crystalites, but they were soon forgotten as time went on and peace reigned once more on Satiren. That is, until the time of Black Eagle, but that's another story and not for me to tell.

"So, I'm a Crystalite," said Kai suddenly opening her eyes.

"Yes, you're not only a Crystalite, but Crystalite royalty. Your brother Atolin is King," replied Wigholt.

Her reaction to that was unexpected, "Yes, I heard that, but I'm sure Sirena told me I had to meet up with someone called Tokala, not Atolin."

"But why would she send you to the Mavaho city?" asked Wigholt frowning.

"I don't know, but if I have a brother then I would like to see him. Can you help me get to the Crystalite city?" she said suddenly feeling full of energy.

"Perhaps we should wait. If Solitaire is trying to find you, he will probably search me out," suggested the little Wizard.

"The White Witch told me there is very little time and I've already wasted so much, I'm sure my brother will help," begged Kai.

"Your probably right, your brother and Tokala were once best friends and I'm sure Tokala will go to him to find you. I can get you close to the city, but I cannot take you all the way. I do not wish to be seen, I have my reasons child," replied Wigholt.

Kai could not hide her disappointment, she liked this funny little man, she felt safe with him and wished he would go with her. Everything she heard so far had a strange ring of familiarity about it, but nothing she could grasp hold of, maybe seeing her brother would trigger her lost memories.

"I'll draw you a map from where the chariot leaves you, the Crystal City will be easy enough to find from there," said Wigholt breaking her thoughts.

"When shall I leave," she asked.

"I have to get my chariot ready it will take a couple of hours to summon my bats. I think perhaps during that time you should learn who you are and why you were taken away. It will help you with your journey to know what happened, follow me," said Wigholt getting to his feet.

Kai followed him into a narrow tunnel that led to another smaller cavern with a sparkling stream running through it. There were strange little trees growing around the edges and on one tree hung a huge silver python with black shiny eyes and a blue diamond shape on its head.

Some rust coloured fox cubs were wrestling with one another under the trees and she could see black bats hanging upside down from the roof of the cavern. "Your pets?" she asked.

"My companions; would you lie down here please," said Wigholt and pointed to a strange looking pallet that was situated right next to the stream.

"I'm not really tired," said Kai not wanting to lie on it. It was made of a strange carved wood and looked hard and uncomfortable.

"This is a magical stream, if you lie on the pallet and let your hand float in the water all your questions will be answered. You wanted to know where you came from, now is as good a time as any," said Wigholt.

Kai did what she was told and sat down on the wooden pallet and laid her head back onto a small cushion. She placed her right hand in the stream and as soon as she did so her body began to tingle and she felt her eyes once again grow heavy, within seconds she was pulled into a world of dreams.

Wigholt looked down at her and wondered to himself what her sudden arrival back here could mean. Something told him that it didn't bode well for Satiren.

BOOK TWO

DARKSTAR

CHAPTER SIX

The Crystal city had become a bustling hive of scientific and magical studies in recent years, due to their new King's fascination with these subjects. King Darkstar had been born on the only day in Satiren's history when the three moons had eclipsed with the red sun. All the planets had aligned, bringing darkness to what should have been the middle of the day. The Crystalites were not usually a superstitious people, but even they could not ignore the significance of his birth, the only child to be born on that day, and so for that reason Darkstar was educated to become their King when he came of age. The Crystalites had never had one leader before, they had always been governed by the Wizard Council, but Darkstar's reign was already proving to be a good one.

The King grew up to be everything they had hoped for, he was tall and strong, he excelled in his studies and had an inquisitive mind, exploring every part of his mountain home, studying the plants that grew and the different rock formations. He sourced where all the water came from and learnt about all the creatures that lived in the mountains. He was fascinated in all creations and actively encouraged scientific lessons, experiments and magic to be taught in the schools. Soon the results of his endeavours started to pay off and the Crystal city became a place of discoveries, growth and on the whole, contentment.

Even so, this was not enough for their restless young King and his curiosity started to wonder about the Silversands desert and what lay in these vast wastelands. As time passed Darkstar's obsession with the Silversands became a fixation and it was not going unnoticed. The Crystalites never ventured into the desert, they had old books and texts that told of the dark times suffered by their ancestors when they were forced to live in the gruelling heat. The blistering sun of the Silversands was deadly for a Crystalite and for that reason alone, they had no desire to explore there.

In the huge Crystal Palace, there was a smoked glass meeting room for the Wizard Council. These fifteen council members were chosen by the people to aid Darkstar in governing the city. They passed laws, settled disputes, made judgements and dealt out punishments if need be. The Wizard Council comprised of teachers, healers and mages, all top of their profession although only a few members of the council had any real magical power.

One council member was very powerful and very ancient, his name was Zebulon. No one knew where he lived or where he came from, and he would only attend the meetings from time to time, never saying much but listening in closely. The aura that surrounded him made the others all bow their heads and fall silent as a mark of respect whenever he entered the glass meeting chamber. Zebulon was ancient but his age was undeterminable, he had sharp black eyes that twinkled with mischief and his hair was long and white although he chose to be beardless. He always had a pleasant smile and greeting for those he met and he especially loved visiting the schools to meet the children. His rich robes were a strange silken sapphire blue, with the three pale blue moons of Satiren embroidered onto the back. He carried a long black staff with a shining silver stone set into the top of it and he radiated powerful magic. Zebulon rarely got involved in the day to day running of the Crystal City, and no one ever questioned this, but having him around always brought a sense of calm to the meetings.

Darkstar would seek Zebulon out as soon as he had word the old Wizard had arrived at the Crystal Palace. He was sure the ancient one knew more about the Silversands desert than the others and he pestered Zebulon relentlessly for information. At first Zebulon had been amused by Darkstar's persistence and he told him very little, but this made Darkstar all the more determined to find out more.

The King began to take his mountain horse down the mountain trails to the lower slopes, which could be dangerous territory for anyone travelling alone. The lower slopes were crawling with Trolls; large, filthy black hairy creatures with long limbs and vicious claws. Their small black eyes were sunken and hidden behind their huge jaws displaying rows of razor-sharp teeth. The Trolls would attack an unarmed Crystalite without hesitation, so Darkstar kept his sword drawn at all times. He only ever encountered two of the stinking creatures that he quickly disposed of, they posed no real threat to him. He knew they were watching him from the rocks and cliff faces, but they were scared of his sword skills and did not dare attack.

Each journey he made he would venture further away from the mountains, collecting samples of the plants and soil to analyse on his return to the city. On the lower slopes there were herds of deer like creatures he had ever seen before. They were a pale silvery grey colour, quite small, about the size of a large goat except they all had a long dangerous looking horn set right in the centre of their heads. They were not afraid of him, but were always on the alert for the wild cats that roamed in these hills. The cats were enormous, a pale orange in colour with narrow black stripes all across their bodies that enabled them to blend into the long dry grass of the lower slopes. Darkstar steered clear of the wild cats, they dwarfed him and even with his sword they would probably tear him apart in seconds.

Zebulon watched Darkstar's journeys through his Seeing Crystal in his home high amongst the clouds and began to feel concerned. He was sure that the Crystalite King would not be satisfied with just these fleeting visits to the edge of the desert and it was likely Darkstar would try to arrange an expedition into the Silversands for scientific purposes. In doing so he would be putting himself and possibly his people in danger. Sirena had decided to keep the Crystalites and the Mavahos separate for good reason and Darkstar's curiosity was threatening that.

Zebulon pondered on this over many months as Darkstar's trips out of the Crystal City became more regular. The Wizard Council had begun to discuss their King's long periods away from the city and were not happy. Darkstar ignored their concerns, something was drawing to the Silversands and he was determined more than ever to find out all he could about the world they lived on.

Making a bold decision that he prayed would not come back to haunt him, Zebulon visited Darkstar in the King's chambers late one night. "I've been thinking over your request for my help in your explorations into the Silversands desert and I have decided that I will aid you in this matter, if only to alleviate your curiosity. Your extended journey's away from your duties are causing the Wizard Council some concerns," he announced with his black eyes twinkling.

"I haven't neglected any of my duties," replied Darkstar defiantly.

"Maybe so, but your absences cause frictions between the council members," replied the old Overlord, unphased by Darkstar's reaction. "However, I am not here to discuss the pointless bickering's of Wizard Egor and his foolish followers, I've something that may help satisfy your desires and keep the council quiet."

Zebulon flicked his hand and a glistening black, hooded cloak appeared on the chair next to Darkstar. The Crystalite King picked it up, it weighed almost nothing yet seemed strong and hung straight. "Put it on," instructed Zebulon and Darkstar obeyed, pulling the cloak around his shoulders. Zebulon pointed to Darkstar's full length mirror and the King stepped in front of it gasping as he did so, all he could see was his head, the rest of his body had been rendered completely invisible. He slipped the hood over his head and disappeared entirely from sight.

"That's incredible! What's it made of?" cried Darkstar absolutely delighted with his gift.

"Nothing from this world," replied Zebulon, amused at the King's reaction. "This cloak will help you visit the Silversands unseen, but wait I have something else for you."

Zebulon handed Darkstar a small bottle filled with tiny dark coloured crystals then spoke to him sternly," these hold a very powerful magic, each tiny crystal when swallowed has the power to give you great speed, you will be able to travel long distances in a matter of minutes."

"You mean I can travel out into the desert," said Darkstar holding up the tiny bottle to get a better look at them.

"You may, but only at night as the magic only works from the power generated by the three moons of Satiren. Each crystal will give you up to eight hours of incredible speed, but you must only take one and be back in the mountains before sunlight," replied Zebulon looking deadly serious.

"I'm eternally grateful Zebulon," said Darkstar desperate to try out the crystals and struggling to maintain his excitement. "How can I thank you for these gifts?"

"I've given you this magic to keep you and your people safe. There are people who live in the desert, people who must never know, or more to the point, reminded of your existence. Every night you travel there, you put yourself at risk and I cannot allow that to continue. Darkstar you must promise me that you will remain hidden from all you witness in the Silversands."

"Of course, I can you promise you that. You've helped me more than you know and I will be eternally grateful. I only wish to understand our world, I've no intention of putting my people at risk," replied the King meaning every word he said.

Zebulon studied him for a moment then smiled, "we'll be the only two that know of this, good luck my boy."

Before Darkstar could reply there was a flash and Zebulon vanished from sight without another word. Darkstar was charged with anticipation, but it was already too late to try out the magic that night. Tomorrow he would leave as soon as it got dark and he began counting the hours.

CHAPTER SEVEN

The next evening Darkstar made sure all his duties were finished long before sunset, and then faking a headache he told his servants that he was having an early night, so they would leave him undisturbed in his chambers. He pulled out the black cloak and threw it over his shoulders while standing in front of the mirror and he felt a rush of excitement as he vanished from sight.

With his heart beating loudly he slipped out his chambers walking unseen amongst the servants in the Crystal Palace. No one noticed him and he grinned to himself as he slipped out into the streets and walked through the city without anyone seeing him. It was almost sunset and by the time Darkstar got to the city limits it was already dark. He pulled out the bottle of tiny crystals and put one on his finger, putting it to his lips he put it on the end of his tongue and swallowed, then he waited.

His limbs began to tingle almost immediately and he felt a surge of energy flow through him. He ran down the path a little to try it out, but the burst of speed shocked him and he went crashing into some bushes missing the end of the path completely. When he staggered to his feet, he saw he had moved at least half a mile in an instant, he was going to have to be more careful. This time he tried again, slowly building up his speed as he went and adjusting to the terrain he was travelling through. He gained more control over his movements and within a few minutes he had arrived at the foothills of the mountains.

Here the landscape was flatter and he found he could move at a greater speed much more safely. Darkstar was soon speeding over the desert sands, the ground a blur beneath his feet as his adrenalin was pumping through his veins. He slowed down then and stopped to get a better look around and he found he was not in the least breathless. The sand surrounding him glistened and sparkled as if it were alive and he knelt down to scrape up some of the sand into a small sample container, Darkstar had never seen anything like it before. There were many dark, twisted shapes protruding from the ground, half buried in the sand and he guessed they were the remains of what looked like an old forest of some sort. He took more samples of the dead bark then once again he took off into the night, covering miles in seconds, stopping from time to time to take more samples and map his journey.

Darkstar was careful to keep a check on the time, and was back in the Crystal city long before sun up feeling elated and desperate to tell someone of his discovery. Of course, he couldn't, he had promised Zebulon and so for now he had to be contented with making secret maps of the desert for his eyes only. One day he hoped to be able to share this knowledge with his people, but for now he could not discuss it with anyone.

As the months went by, people got used to Darkstar's early nights and occasional afternoon naps and they began to wonder if he was ailing. But truth be told, the Crystalite King had never felt more alive and inspired in his whole life. Each night he attempted to go further, exploring valleys and canyons that were completely deserted. He began to wonder if Zebulon had been right when he said there were people who lived on the Silversands as Darkstar had yet to see any signs of life.

Then one night the King travelled further than he had before, pushing the limits of his speed when he noticed a faint orange glow in the sky up ahead. As he got closer, he could make out a structure, some sort of tower casting its shadow over the desert. He had finally stumbled upon Burning Towers, the Mavaho city.

This is what he had been looking for, signs of life in an otherwise barren land and here it was, miles from any water supply as far as he could tell. Yet there were hundreds of fields around the city wall, all yielding healthy crops of food, enough to feed the entire population. Darkstar guessed there must be an underground water source supplying them and feeding the crops, and that made him rethink his findings. He had not considered that there may be life underneath the desert, yet here was proof that there was a definite water supply.

Sneaking quietly to the city perimeter and its huge wall, Darkstar found his way to one of the arrow slits built into the wall and pressed his face against it to see inside. From what he could make out the city inside was brightly lit with fires and torches revealing rows of animal skin structures that must have been their homes. Darkstar was a little surprised, when he had seen the tower and the wall, he assumed they would live in stone buildings, instead of these small but comfortable looking Cabanas.

The people he could see were black skinned, something Darkstar had only ever seen before in old historical picture books written and drawn by their ancestors. The ancient books had made out the desert people to be monsters, yet from what Darkstar saw they were very similar to the Crystalites apart from their skin colour and their startling golden eyes. The men wore animal skin trousers and jerkins, many were simply bare chested and they wore their black hair long, braided and decorated with feathers. The women wore simple tunics and leggings, their arms were decorated with many bangles and bracelets while their hair fell loose and long. Darkstar was so fascinated he didn't notice when a small dog started to growl and bark at where he stood on the other side of the wall. One of the Mavaho men came to the arrow slit and looked out making Darkstar jump backwards in fright, but the man saw nothing.

"Shut that dog up!" came an ugly voice roaring through the street, Darkstar pressed his face back against the slit in the wall to see where it came from, but he couldn't make out anyone. He then heard a pitiful yelp followed by a scuffle, then some nasty laughter from a group of men.

"Please Chief Black Eagle, let the pup come back to me, he meant no harm" came a pleading voice from a woman that Darkstar could only see the back of.

He heard another yelp and a cry of dismay from the woman, more laughter from the men as they walked away from the wall. He could hear the woman sobbing quietly on the other side and wished he could help her. Who was this Chief Black Eagle that would treat his people and a small animal so cruelly?

After that, Darkstar spent many nights returning to the city in the desert trying to find out more about its inhabitants, but none of them ever left the protection of the wall during the night and Darkstar's view inside the wall was limited. He did however sense a feeling of unease and fear from the city dwellers. There were many hushed whispers and he never saw anyone laugh or enjoy themselves as they did in the Crystal City. He was sure that Chief Black Eagle was responsible for their disposition, but he could only guess as to the reason why. Darkstar began to feel frustrated, wishing he could get into the city and truly see what was going on.

***

He was not the only one frustrated, the Wizard Council in the Crystal City were concerned that their King had shown no interest in getting a wife. It was important to them that Darkstar's bloodline was continued and they addressed the subject of an heir with him at the next meeting he attended. He had missed many of their meetings over the last few months which was giving rise to speculation that he had no interest in the throne.

Egor, the Education Wizard was the loudest of those stirring this ugly pot of rumours. He was a thin, spindly man, with a very prominent nose and a nasty, permanent sneer on his lips. Garik, the Wizard of Justice, was the longest established Wizard and he often wondered how Egor had got his position on the council, the oily man was continually disrupting proceedings with complaints and negative observations. Garik had little time for him, which thankfully kept Egor in check for the most part, although it was exhausting for Garik continually having to keep the little man quiet.

Darkstar was summoned to a meeting and he sat silently listening to the Wizard Council's concerns over his lack of interest in finding himself a wife. His eyes flickered over to see his friend Lord Arcos smother laughter when Wizard Egor had the nerve to stand and suggest that the King may not be interested in women. Arcos's title was Lord Warrior, and he was responsible for the security of the Crystal City, he was also Darkstar's closest friend and the pair of them had spent many an evening out enjoying the company of the young ladies in the city.

It was not that Darkstar was against being married, he just had not met anyone who shared his interests, nor his curiosity that stretched far beyond the city and the mountains. The Crystalite women to him were shallow and uninteresting, but he recognised the concerns of the council and eventually agreed to allow them to find him a suitable Queen.

Thinking he had pacified the council, Darkstar went about his business, but to his shock it was only a couple of days later when it was announced that a young woman had been found and the wedding ceremony was already being prepared. Lord Arcos had laughed until his ribs hurt at Darkstar's predicament when heard, guessing his friend had not expected to be rushed into marriage so quickly. Darkstar was not quite so amused but he eventually agreed, his main priority was exploration and if this meant it got the Wizard Council off his back, then he would go ahead with their plans.

***

Lada Tokesen was without a doubt a beauty, chosen from one of the most affluent families in the city, she made a perfect candidate to be Darkstar's Queen. She was also more than willing to take on the role she had set her sights on since she was a young child. Lada was the youngest daughter of Menogi, the now very old Science Wizard. Her mother had died when she was an infant and as her two older sisters were already adults, her father had spoiled Lada, giving her anything her heart desired. As far as she was concerned the word 'No' did not exist in her vocabulary, anything she wanted she got, and now she wanted to be Queen.

As she grew older the servants within the Tokesen household became very wary of Lada. She manipulated her father completely and if any of them dared to complain about her harsh treatment, they would find themselves out on the street with no hope of further employment.

Her eldest sister, Tanja, went to their father one day and told him he had to take a harder line with Lada. Her little sister was getting out of control and he was doing her no favours in giving in to her every demand. Lada had been listening to their conversation through a connecting door and she seethed with rage when she heard her father meekly agree with Tanja.

Tanja was happily married to one of the palace soldiers, second in command to Lord Arcos. She and her husband, Cnut, had two young girls of their own and they were both genuinely worried about Tanja's sister, so it was a pleasant surprise to find that Lada started to visit them frequently, to help Tanja out with her girls. As the weeks went by Tanja didn't notice that Lada would only arrive when her husband was also at home, and then as Lada became more familiar with her sister's routine, she would often visit when Tanja was out.

Lada flirted outrageously with Cnut, but Tanja's husband was not biting, and Lada became even more determined. She slipped a bewitching potion into his drink one evening making him easy to manipulate, so when Tanja and the girls arrived home later, they found Lada with Cnut in Tanja's bed.

Her sister guessed immediately that this was Lada's doing, but Lada managed to convince everyone she was the innocent victim of an older man's obsession, and of course her father believed her. It was all swept under the carpet, but it did not stop the local gossip and once again Lada had got off scot free leaving Tanja and Cnut trying to pick up the pieces of their marriage. After that episode, Tanja refused to visit her father while Lada remained living at his home.

Shortly afterwards Lada set her sights set on Darkstar as her husband and insisted that her father take her along to every council meeting at the palace. While the meetings were in session Lada would become a charming visitor, sharing jokes and helping out with all the servants, gushing over Darkstar's friends and Wizard Council members, making herself well known within the palace walls. She had even been introduced to Darkstar twice before, and although she did her best to captivate him with her beauty, he just smiled politely then dismissed her out of mind.

Now it seemed that Lada's perseverance had paid off and she was at the forefront of the Wizard Council's mind when Darkstar agreed to have them find him a bride.

***

"So, what do you think of her?" Darkstar asked Lord Arcos one evening over some wine. "She pretty, and she seems quite smart, though I can't help but feel it's all a bit of an act. What woman would just agree to marry someone they hardly know?"

"One who is desperate to be Queen I imagine," replied Lord Arcos filling his glass. "Cnut is her brother in law you know, he hasn't a nice word to say about her. He reckons she will hurt anyone who gets in the way of what she wants."

"That's just what I need, still if she's busy playing at Queen with any luck she'll leave me alone," replied Darkstar with a resigned sigh.

"She does seem to have charmed the Wizard Council, mind you I always found her to be quite cold. I can't seem to read her at all, which always make me a bit suspicious," said the Lord Warrior sitting back in a chair and putting his huge booted feet up on another.

"Well thanks for having my back, I can hardly wait, a cold, power hungry wife, sounds delightful," retorted Darkstar getting to his feet and stretching.

"Are you off somewhere?" Lord Arcos asked, he had also been wondering where his friend disappeared to in the night. "Have you another woman stashed away somewhere, a forbidden love that would anger the council?"

"You have a vivid imagination for a warrior. No, no other woman," sighed Darkstar then chucked a cushion at Arcos. "I guess I'll marry Lada, if it means the council will get off my back. She can't be that bad surely? Garik would never set me up with someone who was going to be trouble."

Lord Arcos just shrugged then grinned, "It might be fun watching you trying to manage a wife!"

The wedding took place the following week, it was a huge affair with most of the city out filling the streets for the wedding procession. Unbeknown to Darkstar, there were those who truly knew Lada for what she was and they stayed away, amongst those were her sisters and their families.

For his part, Darkstar played the dutiful husband, he no longer travelled into the desert at night and remained attentive to his new wife, albeit he was bored out his mind. Lada was enamoured with Darkstar, he was handsome and widely popular, making her the object of envy of every young woman in the Crystal City, or so she believed.

Her husband started to confide in her about his trips to the desert and showed her some of the maps he was making, being careful not to mention his magical cloak and speed potion, nor the Mavaho people who lived in the desert. Lada truthfully couldn't care less, but feigned interest to humour him, all the while establishing her place at his side. She convinced herself that Darkstar was now completely besotted with her and would soon be able to refuse her nothing. When she announced she was to have his child, Lada knew then she had complete power over him. As she expected, Darkstar was more than excited by the news, announcing to everyone in the city that the Crystalite Queen was carrying his baby.

However, Lada could not have been more wrong about Darkstar's feelings towards her. He had guessed early on in their relationship that his wife was shallow and only interested in herself; he was not taken in when she pretended to get excited about the Silversands desert. She bored him to the point of exhaustion and he prided himself that he was a better actor than she was. Now that she was pregnant, he had done his duty by his people and his time would once again be his. Lada would have all the attention she wanted lavished on her now she was pregnant, he could take a step back.

Darkstar returned to his nightly adventures, whilst Lada kept the palace servants busy with all her demands. It took her some months to realise that the King was neglecting her, he had not visited her in weeks and it was beginning to irritate her.

Rumours began to fly around the Crystal City that their king was neglecting his young wife whilst she was confined with illness due to her pregnancy. The rumours were of course started by Lada, but the whisperings around the city grew and as they did, they caused many arguments. Lada was no longer the golden girl of the palace, the palace servants had all too often witnessed her dark contemptuous side, and so defended their King with rumours of their own. Many in the city had already come across Lada's selfish cruelness and so it was not long before the city was divided into the King's supporters versus the Queens.

Then out of the blue the old Science Wizard, Menogi, died and Queen Lada and the King were to lead the funeral procession along with Lada's sisters. It was the first time Darkstar had met Lada's sisters, in fact he had not been aware she had any and he recognised immediately the tension between them.

Neither of the Queen's sisters would speak with her, and were obviously disgusted when Lada halted the proceedings in the middle of the service to announce she didn't feel well and should be taken home. King Darkstar knew she was faking, and was determined not to be dragged into her drama, so he instructed a servant to take her home instead of accompanying her himself. He then remained at the funeral, but word soon got out that he had abandoned his very pregnant wife.

Foolishly, perhaps, for Darkstar cared little for the tittle tattle around the city, he continued to ignore his wife. The Wizard Council were more disturbed by the rumours, but by then Darkstar was finding it increasingly difficult to be in her company.

Things changed for a time when Atolin was born. Both Lada and Darkstar were infatuated with their son and for a short time an unspoken truce was endured in the palace. People were excited with the arrival of the new royal baby, and the King and Queen proudly introduced their son around the city together.

Lada was in her element as her new son brought her all the attention she craved and even her husband was being more considerate towards her. Peace reigned in the Crystal palace once more and for the next two or three years Darkstar was content governing the city and watching his son grow.

When Atolin got a little older, Darkstar gave him his first mountain pony, a small white sturdy animal named Icicle. Atolin loved his pony and soon he and his father were riding out regularly into the mountain slopes and up Mount Solomite. There they would visit Ragnar, a mysterious hermit who had the power to connect with all the animals in the mountains. He was also a member of the Wizard Council but he lived in a cave high up in the slopes of the Mount Solomite, and it became Atolin's favourite place to visit. Ragnar had many animal friends who visited him in his cave, moody mountain goats who demanded his attention, mountain horses, wild cats and bears, even the great mountain eagles flew down for food and to have their heads scratched by the strange magical man. Ragnar grew very fond of Atolin, and taught him all about animal life in the mountains and how to survive in the harsh environment.

Darkstar was content spending time with his small son, but when Atolin started school and spent more time with the other children in the city, the King began to get itchy feet once more. He and Lada rarely spoke, she had her own circle of friends now and showed no interest in him. And so, feeling his duty had been done to appease the Wizard Council, Darkstar donned his invisible cloak and once again headed out into the Silversands.

CHAPTER EIGHT

He never felt more alive as he did when he was speeding through the Silversands, and it soon became a regular nightly outing for Darkstar. He avoided the walled city at first, spreading his explorations in other directions, but it was all much of a sameness and curiosity eventually drew him back to the strange people behind the wall. He was fascinated by them, but again could only catch fleeting glimpses of what they were like. However, he began to realise that the people there were much unhappier than they had been on his previous visits, their streets seemed deserted, no one ventured out of their cabanas at night. He wished he could find out what was going on, but he dared not try to enter the city.

Then one night it all changed, Darkstar was approaching the city wall when he heard a voice calling out in distress. He saw a dark figure kneeling over another shape in the sand. As he drew closer, he saw it was one of the women from the other side of the wall and she was crying whilst holding a small unconscious boy in her arms; the child's head was caked in blood. The boy appeared to be the same age as Atolin and Darkstar had to resist the urge to fling off his cloak and help her, he had promised Zebulon to stay hidden.

"Please Tokala, wake up," the woman sobbed holding the child to her chest. She was strikingly beautiful, her shining, long black hair hung over her sculptured face with prominent high cheek bones that gave way to large, intoxicating golden eyes. Darkstar was mesmerised by her and he grimaced to himself as she struggled to her feet lifting the lifeless boy as she did so. She staggered as she carried him in the darkness, then tripped over a gnarled tree stump and would have fallen had Darkstar not stepped in and caught her.

The startled woman squealed in shock looking all around her in bewilderment for the invisible force that had stopped her from falling.

Ignoring Zebulon's warning Darkstar spoke, "Please my lady, don't be alarmed. I mean you no harm, I only wish to help you."

"Who… Where are you?" she cried looking more panicked than before.

"Behind you," said Darkstar and he removed his cloak.

The woman spun around, still holding the boy to her chest, her eyes opened wide when she saw Darkstar standing where he definitely hadn't been before.

"What magic is this? Get away from us demon!" she cried then crouched down to pick up a large rock, holding it aloft as if to strike.

"Please, I'm no demon. I'm just a traveller, I saw your predicament and thought I'd better help," said Darkstar holding both his hands aloft in surrender.

The woman stared at him for what seemed an age then she dropped the rock. "I'm sorry, it's just I've never seen anyone like you before," she said.

"I come from the mountains, I've been exploring these desert sands during the night, making maps and studying the landscape, I promise I'm no threat to you. My name is Aran," said Darkstar, deciding it would be wiser not to tell her who he actually was.

"I'm Sisika, and this is my son Tokala," replied the woman warily.

"If you let me have a look at your boy, I may be able to help," said the King.

Sisika nodded and laid her son on the ground kneeling next to him. Darkstar bent down and examined the cut on the boy's head, there was a huge lump and he would definitely need some stitches, but his breathing was regular which was a good sign. Darkstar tore a strip of cloth from his shirt and wound it around Tokala's head, "I have a boy the same age, don't worry he'll be fine, nothing that a good rest, some stitches and an icepack won't fix," he told her.

"An icepack?" repeated Sisika looking confused.

"Ah, yes perhaps not," replied Darkstar kicking himself for his stupidity. "I'll help you carry him back to the city, but I would ask you to keep our meeting a secret, I'm not sure your people would understand my appearance."

"I won't mention it, my people live in fear as it is, and you would not be safe if you were caught," replied Sisika and then she suddenly added, "I'm the wife of Black Eagle." She seemed to think that would mean something to Darkstar, but he just looked at her blankly, so she went on to explain. "He is the Chief of the Mavaho people, he is cruel and ruthless and I loathe him with all of my being."

If Darkstar was startled at her blunt honesty he didn't show it, he simply lifted Tokala and walked quietly next to her while she talked freely.

"Tokala and his puppy, Nico, were playing in the castle forecourt near to Black Eagles chambers. Their ball went through the window and Tokala thinking his father was out climbed in to retrieve it. Nico followed him through the window and started to explore the chambers as Tokala walked in to catch his father entertaining a lady in his bedroom. Black Eagle lost his temper and flew at Tokala knocking him down, so Nico started to bark and Black Eagle grabbed hold of the pup, kicking the animal and then hurled it across the room.

Tokala screamed bloody murder and attacked his father who simply laughed at his small efforts. I heard the commotion and one of the castle staff came running to warn me that my son was in danger. By the time I got there, Black Eagle was losing his patience with Tokala and had struck him hard across the face. I grabbed Tokala and pulled him back, but Black Eagle grabbed me and started shaking me, saying it was my fault that our son had turned against him. I managed to push him off, I was the daughter of a respected and revered warrior, the people do not tolerate the Chief's cruelty to me. He just laughed in my face and turned back to the poor woman who was forced to endure him.

I picked up Nico, the pup was barely breathing so I took him to the stables and had them put the poor animal out of its misery. Tokala wept, his heart was broken but as time went by I could feel his grief turn to anger. He leapt upon one of his father's stallions before I could stop him, and then he was racing out of the city. The sun was just setting and I begged some of the warriors to go after him. They were about to leave when Black Eagle arrived, he had been told of his son's departure, he would not allow a search party to go out.

I took one of the other horses and followed my son out into the Silversands. Black Eagle did not dare stop me but he ordered them to close the gates as soon as I rode through. Tokala was not strong enough to rein in such a large animal so when darkness fell his horse must have got spooked and thrown him. I saw the horse running back towards the city so I followed the direction it had come from and found my son. As soon as I had dismounted my own horse turned and fled leaving us alone out here."

"I'm sorry this has happened to you and even sorrier to say that your husband sounds like a monster, why would he harm his own child?" said Darkstar who was truly unnerved by her story.

"Don't be sorry, that is a good description of him. I was forced to marry him, but I refuse to play any part in his oppressive rule of my people. I pray that one day we can stand up against him, but he has too many followers, eager for power of their own and he has given them all free reign throughout our city. They terrorise all those that stand up to them, knowing that they have the Chief's backing. My father would never have allowed this to happen if he were alive, but Black Eagle killed him and now we have no one strong enough to challenge him," explained Sisika.

"Perhaps one day your son will take his place, he sounds like he is a brave boy," said Darkstar wishing he could take on Black Eagle himself. "We live peacefully in the mountains our King just wants his people to be content."

"You're lucky, perhaps one day you could tell me more about your home," replied Sisika smiling at him. It made Darkstar's heart flutter, she was the bravest woman he had ever encountered, and also incredibly beautiful.

They walked through the sparkling sands talking as Tokala moaned and stirred a little in Darkstar's arms every now and then. The King told her a little about the mountains, and the ice and snow that were freezing to touch. He told her about the eagles that lived in the high peaks and the sturdy, sure footed mountain horses that knew their way around the mountain tracks. Sisika listened fascinated by his descriptions, she had never imagined such a place existed and she yearned to know more.

Tokala began to wake up, he groaned slightly lifting his head and staring up at Darkstar with groggy golden eyes. "Who are you?" he croaked.

"Just a friend who's helping you," replied Darkstar smiling at the child in his arms.

"It's ok Tokala, I'm here," said Sisika bending over to kiss her son's forehead. Darkstar could smell her musky scent and his heart began to race as she brushed against him; he had never felt this way before.

The wall appeared all too soon and Sisika lifted Tokala from Darkstars arms. "You must go now Aran, before you are seen. People will be looking out for us," she said.

"Will Black Eagle allow you back in?" the King asked frowning.

"He'll no longer be interested, he's probably drinking with his friends by now, the men on the gate will be watching for us they'll let us in, don't worry," reassured Sisika.

"Will you meet me again," Darkstar suddenly asked, knowing he was being reckless, but not wanting to let this woman go from his life.

"I'd like that," she replied and smiled up at him. "I can sneak out at night, I've a way out of the castle into the Silversands, we could meet here."

"Tomorrow night?" he took a chance.

"Yes, if Tokala is well, shall we say tomorrow night three hours after dark," replied Sisika and gave him a brilliant smile when he nodded. Darkstar watched her as she strolled away with Tokala half asleep over her shoulders.

Putting his cloak back on he followed her a short distance behind until she reached the city wall. She called out to the men at the gate and there was a lot of shouting as the gates were opened and men ran out to take Tokala from her. She walked inside but at the last moment she turned and looked back, then smiled her beautiful smile and let the gates close behind her.

Darkstar's heart was pumping with excitment, he was completely captivated by Sisika and his mind was filled with her radiant smile as he sped back to the Crystal City. He could not sleep and the next day dragged as his thoughts turned to her every second. His happiness was infectious and the palace servants had no idea what had come over him, but whatever it was, they liked it. His laughter echoed around the palace as he played with Atolin, he even told Lada she looked beautiful when he passed her by.

When nightfall arrived Darkstar went to his rooms early, saying he had work to catch up on. He left the Crystal City minutes later and was soon on the Silversands heading towards Burning Towers.

He arrived just before Sisika, she came from the city wearing a warm cloak this time and Darkstar kicked himself for not noticing that she may have been cold the night before. He slipped off his invisibility cloak and she gasped, then giggled as he appeared before her. Her smile was every bit as intoxicating as he remembered it had been and he wanted to reach out and hold her, but he kept himself in check.

They strolled through the desert once again, regaling stories from one another's lives, both as infatuated as the other. Darkstar, who Sisika still believed to be Aran, told her of his unhappy marriage, which had also been arranged for him and so they commiserated one another's misfortune together. Time went by too quickly for them and soon they had to say goodbye, so Darkstar took his chance and bent his head kissing her gently on her lips. He pulled back to see her smiling at him coyly, then she reached out her hand and gently touched the side of his face pulling him back towards her. This time their kiss was deep and passionate, neither one of them wanting to let go of the other.

Finally, they broke apart, breathless and desperate for more. Sisika promised she would be there the next night and so their love affair began. For months, night after night they met, finding comfort in one another's arms, sharing their daily lives and stories of their children, neither of them daring to dwell on what the future might hold, especially if they were caught.

Unbeknownst to them, they were being watched, by someone who was very aware of what danger would unfold should they be found out. It happened when one night, Darkstar had carried Sisika far out into the Silversands using his magical speed. When he finally stopped running, they both were laughing loudly unaware they had stumbled close to the underground home of Wigholt, and he heard them. Using his Seeing Crystal he looked to see who was making all the noise and recognised Darkstar immediately. Curious about what the Crystalite King was doing out in the Silversands at night, Wigholt continued to watch wondering who Sisika may be. The little Wizard was concerned for he had heard the rumblings of unrest within Burning Towers, and had seen with his own eyes the cruelty that the Mavaho people endured. What was the Crystalite King doing with one of the Mavaho women?

Wigholt watched them meet night after night in an effort to try to discover who this Mavaho woman was, and soon enough he discovered that she was Sisika, the wife of Chief Black Eagle.

Wigholt cursed his life, he was getting too old these days, death should have taken him years ago, but here he was, having once again to intervene for the sake of this world. He knew of Black Eagle's reputation, and he shuddered when he thought about the repercussions should they ever be found out. He couldn't help to wonder why it had all been left to him to sort, he hated being the bearer of bad news.

CHAPTER NINE

Sisika was finding it more and more difficult to sneak out unnoticed from the castle. There was a secret opening from the grand hall that her father had once shown her when she was a child, it led to the underground stores where there was a narrow opening that she could squeeze through to the other side of the wall. When Sirena was a child, she and her friends would dare each other to sneak out after dark into the desert when their parents thought them in bed. They never stayed out in the desert long, but she had never forgotten the way and the underground storage was hardly ever used so she could get out unseen quite easily.

The trouble was her disappearance from the castle was not going unnoticed and people began to speculate that she may have a lover. No one could blame her for that, but the rumours spread and soon they spread to the wrong people.

When the gossip reached Black Eagle's ears he seethed with rage. He could not believe that Sisika would dare to take a lover, but the rumours alone were enough to warrant his attention. One evening just before Sisika was about to leave he made an impromptu visit to his estranged wife's rooms and he had nothing but cruel menace in his eyes.

Chief Black Eagle had been spoilt by his mother and beaten by his father and he grew into a rebellious, unforgiving child. He was the only nephew to the Mavaho Chief, and as the Chief had no children of his own, Black Eagle was expected to become their next leader. He was larger and stronger than the other boys of his age and by the time he was fifteen he had established his own band of followers who lived to torment the other children in the city. His father often punished him for cruelty and thoughtlessness, but to no avail. Black Eagle was biding his time, waiting for the day when he would become Chief.

Then, out of the blue, his dreams were shattered when his Aunt died leaving the Chief free to remarry a much younger woman. Within months the Chief's new bride was pregnant and the city rejoiced at the coming of the new heir.

Black Eagle's popularity was at an all-time low and the Mavaho's celebrated the forthcoming birth of the new baby with glee, relieved that Black Eagle would not become their leader. He and his friends simmered with rage he was not going to accept this outcome.

The Chief and his Queen were delighted to announce the birth of their baby girl, who would become the next Mavaho ruler. This news sent Black Eagle over the edge, he had been cast aside for a girl, there was no way he would allow this to happen.

The old Chief passed away suddenly one night and the entire city was in shock. He was only in his fifties and in good health, there were many rumours as people suspected foul play. Black Eagle stepped in immediately to take charge, he was a young man now and a baby girl could not run the city yet.

The Mavaho's were disgruntled, but no one stood up to Black Eagle who had too many warrior supporters who were eager to take over the running of Burning Towers. No one dared to speak out against him, except for the Queen who accused him time and time again of overstepping his authority.

Many were concerned for the Queen and the young princess's safety; Sisika's father arranged an armed guard to protect them at all times. Seven warriors escorted the Queen and her young daughter when they went out riding one day, but by nightfall none of them had returned to Burning Towers. A search party was sent out the next day and all their bodies were discovered, along with those of their horses. It seemed as if the water supply they had drunk from was poisoned and Black Eagle declared it an unfortunate accident, these things happened in the desert.

Sisika's father, Hok'ee, was having none of it and he launched his own investigation into the death of the Queen, the princess, his men and his own son. Hok'ee was a well-respected warrior in Burning Towers, his own son, Sisika's older brother, had been given charge of the Queen's protection and had been poisoned alongside her and the princess. A broken hearted Hok'ee knew Black Eagle was behind it and so he challenged him outright to a one on one unarmed combat for the truth.

Sisika was terrified for her father, he was too old now to take this challenge and Black Eagle was a renowned and vicious warrior. As they fought, they seemed equally matched at first, but then Hok'ee got the upper hand holding his opponent in a strangling head lock. The suddenly out of nowhere, Black Eagle had a dagger in his hand and having already lost her brother, Sisika had to watch while her father was brutally stabbed to death in front of her.

No one dared speak out as Black Eagles warriors surrounded the forecourt where Hok'ee lay dead and Black Eagle got to his feet announcing himself Chief of the Mavahos.

Devastated, Sisika swore to herself she would find a way to get revenge, but before she could form a plan, she found herself being dragged before the new murderous Chief. Black Eagle declared that through respect for her father, he would marry her and give her sons to carry on Hok'ee's bloodline. Sisika was horrified and appealed against it, but no one dared to stand against Black Eagle now. She was forced into a marriage with a man she abhorred and who's very presence filled her with disgust.

The Chief, for his part, tried to win Sisika over. She was the most beautiful woman in the city and he had set his sights on her long before he had killed her father. She was a prize as far as he was concerned and he lavished jewels and beautifully embroidered clothing on her. She never wore them, and regarded him at all times with a cold hostility. Eventually after weeks of trying to win her over his anger got the better of him, and he brutally attacked her one night, and then night after night, trying to break her spirit. Sisika stayed strong, still believing that one day she would finally find a way to get her revenge and make Black Eagle pay for what he had done.

After Sisika announced she was pregnant with Tokala, the Chief thankfully left her alone, finding other women to satisfy his desires. Sisika moved into her own room on the other side of the castle away from Black Eagle and they became strangers to each other. When Tokala was born he visited her once and then took his baby out to display him to his friends. Thankfully he then left her alone to raise their son, having little to do with the baby after that.

As Tokala got older, Black Eagle attempted to take more of an interest in his boy, but soon found the child bored him. Sisika was still as beautiful, perhaps even more so and Black Eagle found himself wanting her again. She was so hostile towards him, that it enraged him and so he turned to violence when he did not get his way. He was clever enough to make sure the bruises he dealt her went unseen by others, but he was unaware of how much Tokala had seen and the boy began to hate his father.

Now with the rumours of Sisika's excursions Black Eagle had the excuse he needed to finally knock her off her perch and let the people see how contemptuous she actually was. He was filled with hostility as he turned to face his wife.

"Are you going somewhere woman?" his smile was unnerving.

"Just for my usual evening stroll around the city," relied Sisika unsure of what Black Eagle may have heard.

"Is that what you're doing?" he replied walking around her room and casting his eyes over all her belongings. His eyes fell on a crystal that sat on her dresser, he picked it up and studied it for a minute or two thinking. Sisika held her breath, Darkstar had given her that Crystal, it was from the mountains and she prayed her husband would not ask about it. Black Eagle put the crystal down and turned to face her once more, his eyes cold and hard, "tell me there is no truth in these rumours!"

"I don't know what you're talking about," replied Sisika, her heart hammering in her chest.

"You know exactly what I'm talking about, you have taken a lover and I want to know his name." His tone was unmistakably threatening.

"I have not taken a lover, as if I would dare put someone at risk like that," she replied, now he was making her angry.

Black Eagle walked dangerously close to her and bent to whisper in her ear, "So where do you go at night Sisika? Perhaps Tokala will tell me if I beat it out of him."

Sisika wouldn't rise to his bait, though her blood was boiling at the mention of her son. "I go to cleanse my soul Black Eagle you should try it sometime!"

From the corner of her eye she saw his hand reeling towards her head, she had no time to get out of its path before she was struck. Lights flashed in her vision as she was sent crashing over the floor. She lay for a second or two then pulled herself shakily to her feet, "you think you have power over me but you don't! I will never bend to your will you are no better than an animal!" she hissed at him through gritted teeth.

Black Eagle roared in fury as he came for her, grabbing her by her arms and shaking her violently. "You will tell me who it is you are meeting! I am your husband and your Chief!"

"You are a bully and a murderer! I spit on the ground as you pass me by and I cannot cleanse myself enough after you have touched me with your murderous hands. I am not afraid of you! You are not worthy of my fear!" Sisika screamed at him. She had lost control now and she lashed out with her fists wanting to hurt him as much as he had hurt her.

Black Eagle roared again holding her at arm's length he struck her again and again until everything became a blur and she could hear nothing but ringing in her ears. He let her go and she fell in a heap to the ground. She couldn't focus properly as her eyes were already swollen, she tried to speak but no words would come. Black Eagle left her where she lay, and stormed out of her rooms.

Just before Sisika lost consciousness she could have sworn there was a cloaked figure in the corner of her room, but then everything went black.

When she awoke, she felt something cool pressing on her forehead. Her eyes would not open, but she heard her son breathing next to her. "Tokala?" she croaked through swollen lips.

"Hush mama, I'm here. I'll kill him this time, I promise you," said her small, angry son.

"No, not yet. Tokala go and get some help," she whispered.

"Black Eagle won't allow anyone to attend you," replied Tokala. "That's why I'm here."

"I'm here also," came a voice that Sisika recognised as her best friend Ninia. "For the love of Odysseus, what has he done to you?"

Sisika felt the strong arms of her friend grab hold of her gently helping her to her feet and leading her to her bed. "Tokala we need bandages, medicines and more water. Go to the kitchens and find Doba, tell her what has happened to your mother, she will know what to send," instructed Ninia.

Tokala ran off and Ninia helped Sisika get comfortable, then said, "he has over stepped himself this time, how will he explain this?"

"He gets away with everything Ninia, don't put yourself in danger by helping me," whispered Sisika grateful to have her close friend at her side.

"He will back off for a while, people are already pointing fingers at him, when they hear about this there will be anger. You have a lot more friends that you think Sisika, his cruelty to you and Tokala will not be tolerated much longer," said Ninia.

"I wish I could believe you, but he has a way of twisting things. He'll find a way to blame me for this," said Sisika.

Tokala arrived minutes later, he had a number of herbal ointments, bandages and water, "I have to go back soon, Doba is making a special broth for you," he said.

***

Darkstar was like a bear with a sore head around the Crystal Palace, everyone was steering clear of his dark mood. He had been visiting the desert every night for almost a week, but Sisika did not appear. He was beside himself with worry, had Black Eagle discovered their secret? Darkstar was sure something had happened to her and he couldn't let it go. He told himself that if Sisika had not arrived by the end of the next week he would find a way to get into the city and search for her. He had to be sure she and Tokala were safe.

He stood waiting again in their regular meeting place, it was exactly two weeks since their last meeting and he was ready to enter the city when he saw someone walking towards him. She wore a cloak that shielded her face as she approached, "Arran I'm here."

Darkstar threw his cloak aside and tried to take Sisika in his arms, but she winced with pain. He drew back her hood and recoiled in shock when he saw the bruises and cuts that had still not quite healed.

"Did Black Eagle do this?" Darkstar demanded.

"He heard I was disappearing at night, he wanted to teach me a lesson," replied Sisika.

"I'll kill him for this," said Darkstar, fury coursing through his veins.

"You and Tokala have both said the same," said Sisika sadly. "The truth is, we will have to be more careful, we cannot meet every night. I'm putting my son at risk. Black Eagle knows the only way to truly hurt me is through him."

"Has he hurt Tokala?"

"No, not yet, but I must be careful," she replied.

Darkstar was livid, his blood raged wanting to challenge Black Eagle there and then, but he could not put Sisika, nor his people at risk. He had to agree with her, they were playing a dangerous game and it was time they were more careful. They decided that they would only meet once a week from then on, if it was impossible for one or the other not to come, then they would wait until the following week. Sisika had to make Darkstar promise he would not come and search for her if she did not appear.

The Crystalite King returned to his city with a heavy heart. He could not bear the thought of not being able to spend as much time with Sisika, his love for her over-shadowed almost everything else in his life, apart from Atolin. He had to find a way to get her and Tokala away from Black Eagle before she was hurt again or worse.

CHAPTER TEN

Two months after Black Eagle's vicious attack on her, Sisika was waiting for Darkstar to arrive. They had managed to keep to meeting once a week for the first month, but then it became twice a week and now here she was, meeting him for the third time in just five days. He was a little later than usual, so Sisika sat with her back against a boulder and stared up at the moons. She had some news for Darkstar, something that had been playing on her mind for the last couple of weeks and she was not sure what it would mean for them when she told him.

A strange noise suddenly started to filter into her ears and as it got louder, she realised it was the sound of large wings flapping in the night sky. Sisika jumped to her feet in fright when she saw a large shape in the sky heading towards her. As it hovered above her, she could make out four giant bats carrying a carriage of some sort and she watched as they lowered it to the ground close to where she stood. A small, almost comical looking blue man climbed out of the carriage and onto the desert bowing low to her. Sisika stared at him with her mouth open, yet there was something familiar about his long white hair and beard along with the staff he carried. She suddenly remembered she had seen pictures of him in old books in the Mavaho library at the castle. The books had called him 'The Guider', a magical being who had helped the Mavahos create their home on the Silversands. She had always thought he was nothing more than an old legend, a fairy tale for the children, yet here he was standing in front of her.

"Guider?" she asked nervously.

"Aaah, your people once called me that a long time ago," said the strange blue dwarf. "My name is Wigholt, and I'm a Jacartan Wizard."

"Please forgive my ignorance, I've no idea what that means," replied Sisika feeling a little braver now. Whoever this strange man was, he did not seem threatening.

"That doesn't surprise me," said Wigholt sadly. "I'm the only one of my kind left, and I'm very old. I would not have interrupted your meeting if I did not think it was necessary. Perhaps we should wait for your friend to arrive. This is a serious matter that concerns you both." said Wigholt jumping up onto the boulder and making himself comfortable. He lit a long pipe which made him look even more comical as he puffed great clouds of smoke into the night sky.

"How do you know of Aran?" Sisika asked him seating herself back down where she had before.

"There is not much that goes on within the Silversands that I don't know about, and as for Aran, I'm afraid my dear he has not been altogether truthful with you. His name is not Aran, he is in fact Darkstar, King of the Crystalite people," replied Wigholt.

"You must be mistaken, Aran would not lie to me, why would he not tell me this?" said Sisika feeling confused.

"Because I wanted to keep you safe," said Darkstar stepping out from under his cloak. "Please forgive me, I'm not proud of lying, especially to you, but when we first met, I had to be wary. Then later I toyed with the idea of telling you the truth, but after you told me about Black Eagle, I knew if he ever discovered you were seeing the King of the Crystalites, it would put my people in grave danger."

"I would never have told him!" cried Sisika feeling hurt by Darkstar's betrayal. She had shared everything about her life, believing he had done the same. "How long would it have taken before you did trust me Aran? Darkstar? Whatever your name is!"

"It wasn't a matter of trust Sisika, I trust you with my life, you should know that by now. However, I don't trust Black Eagle and what he is capable of."

"May I speak?" bellowed Wigholt over the two of them. "You have both behaved foolishly and I am here to tell you that these meetings cannot continue."

"Who in the name of Odysseus are you to interfere?" demanded Darkstar angrily.

Wigholt puffed on his pipe and stared at Darkstar thoughtfully before he spoke, "I have lived for centuries and I have stood by and watched as more foolish men than yourself have made foolish decisions that changed the face of this planet. You are no fool Darkstar, but you are blinded by your passion for this woman and your liaisons will bring extreme danger to the people you have sworn to love and protect."

When Wigholt had first seen the pair of them in the desert together he had been a little concerned, but it had been years since he had visited the Mavaho city and he wondered if things had changed. Using an old astral projection magic he had walked through Burning Towers city unseen, but what he saw disturbed him greatly. After the sickening attack on Sisika by her husband, Wigholt knew that he would have to intervene. Men like Black Eagle would cause the complete destruction of Satiren if he were to discover the Crystalites, it would undoubtably lead to war.

"He's right," said Sisika sadly. "We have been foolish and thoughtless.

"He's not right! He is interfering when there is no need, we are more than careful. I cannot lose you Sisika!" growled Darkstar.

"Perhaps it is time you understood the reason there are only two races of people left on Satiren and why they must live apart. I can show you, if you'll let me," suggested Wigholt.

Darkstar reluctantly looked over at Sisika who nodded, "Very well, show us," he said, determined that nothing would change his mind, he was not going to lose Sisika, not now, not ever.

Wigholt lumbered off the boulder and bade them sit in front of him. He lifted his staff muttering a small incantation then touched them both gently on their foreheads with the tip. They both fell into a deep trance and the history of Satiren and the Ne'shuwa played out in their minds.

Hours later Darkstar and Sisika stood together looking towards the lights of Burning Towers in silence, the pain almost too much for either of them to bear. Wigholt watched them sadly through his seeing crystal, he had left them when they awoke from their dream feeling the pain and sadness that washed over them. If there was another way, he would have found it, but now was not the time for a Crystalite Mavaho confrontation. There was an evil darkness hovering over Satiren, Wigholt had felt it over the last few years. He was sure Draconan was watching them from afar, waiting for his chance to find an opening into this world. Until Wigholt had seen Chief Black Eagle with his own eyes, he had not understood how Draconan's darkness was finding a way in, but now he was sure that the Mavaho Chief was Draconan's servant and the cause of it. Darkstar and Sisika risked being the catalyst that would cause great devastation upon Satiren and for this reason they could no longer be together.

Darkstar kissed Sisika for the last time, his heart was breaking and he knew she felt the same. They would carry on with their lives, he would never visit the desert again, the memories would be too painful. He finally let her go and she pulled her cloak around herself and walked away towards the wall, tears poured down her face, but she did not look back. There was something she had not told them, something Wigholt with all his magical powers had not guessed. She would have to face it alone and she was terrified about what it would mean.

***

Over the next few months, Sisika lived fairly peacefully in Burning Towers. The sadness that risked enveloping her was eased by the joy she had with her son, Tokala. After Black Eagle's brutal attack on her he had left her alone, not wanting to anger the Mavaho's anymore than he had done already.

Ninia guessed first, Sisika could no longer hide her swollen stomach and she was becoming more of a recluse.

"Is it Black Eagles?" Ninia asked her directly, already guessing the answer.

"No," replied Sisika.

"Oh Sisika, what are you going to do? He will kill you, you must leave here," begged Ninia.

"I can't, I have not been well with this pregnancy and the baby is only a few weeks off. I will not leave Tokala to the wrath of his father if I run away, and I cannot bring up my children alone in the desert," said Sisika. "I will have to tell Black Eagle and pray he does not kill me or the baby."

"Maybe we could hide you until the baby is born. Then we could sneak it away, find a wet nurse to raise it. What about the father? Will he not want to raise his child?" Ninia had so many questions but she sensed that Sisika was reluctant to divulge much.

"The baby's father is no longer with us," replied Sisika. "We won't be able to hide it, and I'm not letting you put yourself in danger for me. I will send for Black Eagle, tell him the truth and take my chances. Just promise me, if anything happens to me you'll take care of Tokala."

"Of course," replied Ninia but her eyes were filled with fear. She knew that Black Eagle would not let this go, her friend was in terrible danger.

Two weeks later the doors to Sisika's room flew open and Black Eagle marched in, "This better be important!" he said.

Sisika got to her feet watching as his eyes drifted down to her midriff and widened in disbelief. She could see his brain turning as he registered the state she was in and then he started to smile grotesquely. "Do you expect me to say congratulations?"

"I don't know what I expect," she replied keeping her voice level.

"Who is the father?" Black Eagle asked.

"Someone who is far from here. He doesn't know I carry his child, and he's well out of your reach," Sisika told him, she was trembling inside.

The Chief began to pace around her room, he needed time to digest this. She had made a fool out of him and she would pay, his eyes suddenly caught sight of the Crystal again. He went over and picked it up, "I've never seen a rock like this anywhere, did he give you it?"

"It's from the mountains, my father gave me it," she replied, he did not need to know more.

"The mountains," he repeated thoughtfully.

"I only ask that you let me have the baby before you make an example out of me. The child has done nothing wrong," said Sisika.

Black Eagle barked out a laugh, "you dare to ask me that woman. I haven't yet decided what I will do with you, or with the brat you are about to produce. You'll be imprisoned while I decide your fate, but I promise you, you will die. You can pray to Odysseus that your death will be swift."

"I want you to know that I loathe you, I've always loathed you. I knew you would kill me, but I promise you one day you will pay dearly for the cruelty and oppression you have inflicted upon my people. There will be a day of reckoning, and when that day comes, my spirit shall be standing over you as they drag you to Dhurgon," spat Sisika expecting him to strike her.

Instead Black Eagle looked at her and an eerie silence filled the room, then almost triumphantly he called for the guards ordering them to bind and gag her. If they seemed surprised, they did not show it and did what they were asked without question. "Take her to the tower, lock her in, one meal a day."

Sisika was bundled out of her room and marched through the castle. There were many startled faces of people she knew staring in shock at her now obvious condition, as well as her predicament. She was forced to climb the steep spiral staircase of the tower and was taken to the small cramped room right at the top where she had to stoop to get in as the ceiling was so low. They took off her bindings and slammed the door shut on her.

Feeling sick and dizzy, Sisika sat down on a small pallet by an opening that looked directly down onto the castle forecourt and out towards the Siversands. She could see the mountains through the heat haze of the desert and she wept thinking about what she had done to Tokala and her unborn child.

CHAPTER ELEVEN

Darkstar was spending a lot more time with Atolin in the evenings now that his trips to the Silversands had stopped. His son was everything he had hoped for in a boy, clever, brave, curious and kind. The King started to tell Atolin stories about his adventures in the Silversands, showing him all the treasures he had collected from his travels, and describing the desert city and the strange people that lived there, swearing his son to secrecy. Atolin was thrilled to be taken into his father's confidence, he was five years old now and as inquisitive as his father was at that age.

The Crystalite King attempted to put all thoughts of Sisika out of his mind, concentrating on his son and the affairs of running the Crystal City. The Wizard Council had never seen him be so focused and work so hard. He had begun building projects to expand the city, and found the busier he was, the less he thought about her. He missed her so much it hurt to think of her name.

Darkstar's strengthening bond with Atolin did not go down well with the Queen, she completely alienated herself from her husband and her son, finding other interests to keep her occupied. One of those interests happened to be Ragnar. The Animal Wizard, as he was known in the city, rarely visited, preferring his own company high up in Mount Solomite. Yet from time to time he would be summoned to the Wizard Council for expert advice about the creatures who lived in the mountains. On these days he always visited the palace stables and checked on the welfare of the horses, then he would he run a small clinic for people to bring in their injured or sick pets.

Queen Lada visited him one day with a kitten who was ailing, and he had gently chided her for taking the kitten from its mother too early. He then showed Lada how to care for her pet and Lada became infatuated with his gentleness. Ragnar had an intoxicating charisma that had helped him charm most creatures throughout his life, but on this occasion, he had managed to charm the Queen. He was an unassuming but handsome man and Lada began to take trips out on her horse to visit him in his mountain dwelling.

Ragnar's fascination with the Queen grew, he likened her to the proud, vain snow eagles who lived among the mountain peaks preening themselves and demanding his admiration. He tried to ignore her blatant advances, having no desire to start something with Darkstar's wife. But Ragnar was drawn to her, and she would seek solace with him, often crying and telling him of her loneliness in the palace, He pitied her and then one day before he could stop himself, he found he was kissing her.

Everyone in the city knew that Darkstar neglected his wife, but Lada was unpopular, stories of her vicious temper and frequent tantrums had spread throughout the city, so no one blamed him, he had after all been forced into this marriage by the Wizard Council. The Queen was completely disinterested in the needs of her people, she did not understand the concept of charity and had no intention of learning. Over the last few years her unpopularity had grown to such an extent that there was hardly anybody left who had any sympathy for her claims of neglect.

Ragnar, on the other hand found goodness in all creatures and became a regular distraction for Lada. She found the animal Wizard exciting and fascinating, he treated her as he would a playful puppy, spoiling her and telling her how beautiful she was. Most of all, Lada loved the thrill of sneaking around behind Darkstar's back, and the fact that Ragnar was so respected by the King made it all the better.

Darkstar had begun to acknowledge Lada in recent weeks, but he had no idea how much resentment and hatred the Queen harboured for him. She wanted to hurt him and she was going to find a way. If he spoke to her, she was pleasant enough, but she would always make excuses to leave as quickly as possible. If he noticed, he didn't show it and most of the time he behaved as if she didn't exist.

Then her chance to finally humiliate her husband came, and one day, unannounced, she strolled into one of his meetings with the city architects, her smile radiant, "Darkstar, I'm sorry to interrupt but I couldn't wait to tell you the news. We're having a baby! Isn't it wonderful?"

Darkstar stared at her for a few seconds letting the news register in his brain, knowing the child was not his, but more to the point, he wondered why she was being so bold in announcing it this way. She was obviously trying to bait him, and if she wanted a reaction, then he was going to give her one. He became aware of all the surprised congratulations from the people in the room, so putting a beaming smile on his own face to match hers he marched over to her.

Lada looked momentarily confused as he pulled her in to hug her tightly,

"Darling, that's fantastic news, I couldn't be happier!" Then he whispered in her ear, "I don't know what you're playing at but you'll not use me as a pawn in your little games. If you want to tell them the baby isn't mine go ahead, I'm not going to do it for you, as far as I know it's my child."

Lada's eyes widened in shock; she had expected Darkstar to fly off into a rage which would have allowed her to play the victim. She had her speech all prepared, and she had already imagined the whisperings around the city. *'Not only does the King neglect his wife, but now, he wants nothing to do with his own child!'*

His reaction astonished her, but she was unable to do anything about it, unless she was to admit the child wasn't his, and she couldn't do that, they would hate her for it. She glanced over at Darkstar, who was still grinning from ear to ear accepting congratulations and pats on the back, playing the part of the delighted father to be. She hated him now, he would suffer, she promised herself that.

Leaving the meeting room, Lada headed out to the stables and had her mountain horse prepared for her. She needed Ragnar now, he would calm her and she had yet to tell him of the child she was carrying.

The snow clouds were gathering as she left the city, the young stable hand had tried to persuade her to postpone her outing, but she had no intention of doing so. She rode steadily up the track towards Ragnar's cavern as the wind had picked up and the first few flakes began to fall. Lada pulled her cloak tightly around her shoulders, perhaps she should have waited.

By the time she reached Ragnar's cavern the snow was falling thick and fast, her teeth were chattering as she called out to the animal Wizard. Ragnar came running out, and lifted Lada from her horse then led them both into his warm cavern. Her cloak was soaked through and Ragnar took it from her then led her to a warm pile of furs next to the fire. Lada collapsed down next the flames and held her frozen hands out to get warmed, then she noticed Ragnar was not alone. There was a huge white cat sitting at the other side of the fire scrutinising her with ice blue eyes, she had never seen a cat like this before.

"His name is Solitaire, he lives high in the mountains, but comes to visit with me occasionally, especially when the weather is bad," explained Ragnar.

"Is he safe?" asked Lada unsure what to make of the cat.

Ragnar chuckled, "he's safe enough, providing he gets his fair share of meat."

Solitaire continued to stare at them as he remained motionless by the fire, making the Queen a little uncomfortable, however she turned her attention back to Ragnar. "We need to talk."

"Lada, why would you come out when a storm was coming? You could have got stuck in the snow," said Ragnar.

"I'm having your child," she replied and watched his face change from utter bewilderment to abject horror in an instant.

"Does Darkstar know?" he asked glancing over at Solitaire as guilt began to wash over him.

"He knows it's not his, but he doesn't know who the father is. He is pretending to everybody that he is delighted with the news," replied Lada. "There is nothing I can say without exposing us to the people."

"Perhaps that is for the best," said Ragnar quietly staring into the fire.

"How can you say that?" cried Lada. "It's your child!"

"I've betrayed my friend and my King. I need to go and talk with Darkstar, it is the right thing to do," replied Ragnar.

"And say what?" yelled Lada, anger washing over her. "What about me? What about betraying me?"

Ragnar looked at her long and hard, his mind was racing. Lada was right, why would he do that to her now? She was carrying his child it was too late to be sorry now. He knew what he was doing when he had started this affair with the Queen, how would admitting that to Darkstar help anyone? It was a selfish idea, only serving to ease some of the guilt from his own shoulders. He could feel Solitaires eyes on him, and he knew what his old friend was thinking, it was what they had just been talking about before Lada arrived. Solitaire had just made him promise that he would call if off with Lada, before something like this happened.

Ragnar sidled over to Lada, who sat shivering by the fire, "I'm sorry my beauty, you're right, I will not tell Darkstar. But I will find it hard to watch him be the father to my child, perhaps one day we will find a way." He heard Solitaire hiss behind them and turned to see the cat walk away from the fire to the back of the cavern, he was clearly not impressed.

***

"What do you mean you let her go out Erin?" shouted Darkstar at the young stable hand.

"I tried to warn her, but she wouldn't listen," argued Erin, he was only sixteen. "That's why I came to tell you."

Darkstar was still reeling from Lada's news and he knew he was taking it out on the boy. There was no way Erin could argue with the Queen. "Yes, I'm sorry boy, you did right to come and tell me. We'd better get a search party out," he said in a gentler tone.

"I don't think a search party will get very far," said Kaeshia, the Earth Wizard. She had been at the architects meeting when Lada had announced her pregnancy and it hadn't escaped her notice that the Queen had not anticipated Darkstar's reaction. "Lada will find somewhere to shelter, she is probably with Ragnar, I know she visits with him."

"Really? I didn't know she had such interest in the mountain wildlife," replied Darkstar, wondering how he had never known that. He looked out at the sky, the snow was falling thick and fast, Kaeshia was right, they could not search for her until the blizzard subsided. Still guilt washed over him, if anything happened to Lada, he only had himself to blame. He treated her poorly, he knew that, no wonder she had found the arms of another lover. His mind drifted to Sisika, and for a fleeting moment he felt his heart break all over again, but he swallowed hard and shook the image of her beautiful face from his mind. Once the snow stopped, he would find Lada and apologise to her for his neglect, perhaps the arrival of this child, albeit not his bloodline, would mend a rift between them.

CHAPTER TWELVE

The castle turret was hot and oppressive, Sisika had spent two weeks in there, unable to move around properly. No one had been allowed to attend to her, not even Tokala could get to her as there were castle guards outside her door at all times. All the guards were Black Eagle's men and they continuously laughed and tormented her about her pending fate, telling her the whole of Burning Towers knew she was a harlot. The food they served her was barely worth eating, watery soup and hard bread that should have been thrown. Black Eagle's cruelness had no limits and she was getting weaker daily but thankfully she could feel the child kicking inside her. Some days she was overcome with guilt when she thought about the future for this poor baby and her son Tokala, if only Black Eagle would allow him to visit her so she could explain.

Then in the third week of her confinement one of the guards brought her a goblet of wine, "With the Chief's compliments, he'll be visiting you later," he said shoving the goblet towards her. Sisika sat up and blinked at it for a second before grabbing hold of it and flinging it back at the guard as he slammed her door shut. She could hear his laughter but he had left the goblet lying where it was.

Sisika laid back down on the straw mattress and stared down at it, then an idea came to her, it was reckless but due to her current situation it was worth the risk, she sat up and grabbed hold of the heavy goblet. Crouching by the door entrance she cried out to the guard for help. She heard him swear then heavy footsteps came towards the door, Sisika was ready. The guard swung the door open, he had to stoop low to get inside and as he bent, Sisika pounced smashing the metal goblet over the back of his head with every ounce of strength she possessed. He staggered and fell face first to the floor, blood spurting from his nose and mouth, it was all the time she needed and she ran out the door, slamming, then bolting it, trapping him inside.

Without hesitating for a second, she sped down the spiral staircase of the tower, somewhere behind her in the distance she could hear the guard banging on the door shouting angrily. When she finally reached the bottom, she heard a deep growl and turned to see one of Black Eagles vicious dogs, crouched with its teeth bared, ready to spring. She looked desperately around for a weapon, and grabbed one of the flaming torches from the wall. The dog circled her growling viciously, its red eyes fixed on her every move, then without warning it sprung forward but Sisika was ready. She rammed the flaming torch directly into its face as it pounced and the animal howled with pain and fright. Feeling braver Sisika pursued the dog with the hot flames until eventually it ran off. Dropping the torch, she ran to the door leading into the courtyard, but as soon as she reached it, she was grabbed roughly by two strong arms that swung her around to face their owner. Black Eagle smiled grotesquely into her face, "Going so soon?"

Sisika cursed and tried to struggle free but it was useless and she knew it. "LET HER GO" the small voice rang out over the courtyard and Sisika was swung around to look upon her small son, standing with all the authority of a Chief, his hands on his hips and his face filled with cold intent. Even at five years old he commanded respect and Black Eagle could not help but be impressed.

"Leave us Tokala, this is no concern of yours," the Chief barked.

"If you lay another finger on my mother, I'll kill you," replied Tokala with absolute certainty.

Two of Black Eagle's warriors started to approach the boy, but Tokala was ready, as quick as a flash he pulled out his sling shot and fired a jagged rock at one of them hitting the warrior on the side of his head. He dropped to floor and the second warrior hesitated looking bewildered, it was all Tokala needed. He had another lethal rock loaded and fired in a split second and the second warrior went down.

Black Eagle roared in anger, "Come here boy!" He dragged Sisika with him, but was stopped short as Tokala took aim and fired a sharp rock that hit the Chief straight in his eye, blinding him with a searing hot pain. He let go of Sisika as he grabbed hold of his face which was now spraying blood from his eye socket. He screamed in pain and rage and Tokala moved as fast as an arrow. He ran to his mother and grabbed her arm, pulling her away. Sisika ran trying to keep up with her son and they escaped the courtyard and were out into the streets of city before any of Black Eagle's shocked guards could reach them.

The surprised Mavahos watched on as they sprinted through the streets, but no one attempted to stop them. The castle guards came tearing out of the castle forecourt, demanding to know which way they had taken. Most of the people pretended they had seen nothing, whilst others sent the guards in the complete wrong direction.

Sisika was panting with pain, she wasn't sure how much further she could go, when Yumi, one of the stable hands appeared. "Tokala, over here," he hissed.

Tokala dragged his panting mother into Yumi's cabana, Ninia was already waiting there and she helped Sisika over to a bed. Ninia started to cry when she saw the state her friend, "Oh Sisika, what has he done to you?"

"I never thought you'd pull that off boy," said Yumi ruffling Tokala's hair affectionately.

"It didn't go to plan; my mother had already escaped and now I have injured Black Eagle. He will kill me, we will have to leave the city," said Tokala.

An hour later Sisika was beginning to feel a little better. Ninia had given her some herbal tonic to help with the pain and the cramps and Yumi made her eat a little food before he went out to see what was going on in the city. He came back soon after, his face was grim.

Black Eagle has ordered you brought him, anyone found harbouring you will suffer a thousand deaths, he is raging Tokala, you took his eye out. We must get you out the city tonight." Yumi had agreed to help Tokala rescue his mother, but this was much worse than he could have imagined. "They are going to start searching all the cabanas, you can't stay here, I have my own family to think of."

"But where will they go?" cried Ninia. "There is only desert out there, Sisika will not survive."

"Please Ninia, it's fine. If we can make it to the mountains, I have a friend there who will help us," said Sisika, trying to sound positive.

"How far are the mountains?" asked Ninia not convinced for one second this was a good idea.

"I'm not sure, but I can make it with Tokala's help," replied Sisika.

"I'll get us there," said Tokala, his little face set with determination.

Burning Towers was in chaos as Black Eagles warriors continued searching. Yumi left it as late as he could before he went to collect the wagon and horses for his evening pick up of the Mavaho field workers. It was an hour before dark and Yumi tied a couple of extra horses to the back of the wagon, which was not unusual, for sometimes there was not enough room in the wagon for all the workers. As he passed his Cabana, he stopped to collect some supplies from inside and Tokala and his mother sneaked on board the wagon unseen. They lay on the bottom and Hok'ee covered them with blankets then loaded on food and water as he usually did. When he reached the city gates, he could see at least seven of Black Eagle's warriors standing at the entrance. He rode slowly towards them and was relieved to see one of them was his younger brother.

"You've got a load there tonight Yumi," said his brother.

"Yes, there's a lot of them tonight. Any luck finding that young Tokala and his mother?" Yumi asked lazily, praying that his brother would not see through his act.

"Not yet, I feel for the lad, Black Eagle will kill him when he gets his hands on him," replied his brother sadly. "He would have made a great warrior that boy."

Sisika grabbed hold of Tokala's hand as she listened, terrified that they would search the wagon, but a minute later she could feel the wagon trundle onwards and knew they were free.

Yumi drove the wagon away from the city, but far away from the fields also. He could not risk Sisika or Tokala being spotted by the workers. When he knew it was safe, he untied the horses from the back of the wagon and pulled the blankets off them.

They climbed out the wagon and Yumi helped Sisika mount one the horses, she looked dreadful and his heart ached at what he was having to do. In their saddlebags he had packed enough food and water to last them a few days. "I don't know how I will ever repay you," said Sisika.

"Just keep this boy safe," replied Yumi, he felt a terrible guilt leaving them alone out here, but if they went back to the city, they would both be killed. He watched them ride off, the mountains were just faint outlines in the distance, he had no idea how long it would take them.

As he stood watching them go Yumi became aware that it would be dark very soon and he was still a couple of miles away from the fields. The workers would be getting nervous, he would have to come up with a good excuse for being so late, and for the missing horses. Hopefully with everything going on in the city, no one would notice.

The darkness came quickly and the desert changed into a world of sparkling sands and dark dancing shadows. The horses got nervous and Sisika had to calm them, she no longer feared the desert at night but she could see her son was also uneasy, "It's alright Tokala, it's really quite beautiful out here at night."

"Do you really know where we're going?" he asked.

"Yes, I've a friend who lives in the mountains. He'll give us shelter I am sure," replied Sisika, she was sure Darkstar would help them.

"Is he the man who carried me that day I ran away," asked her son.

"Yes, I wasn't sure if you remembered that. Yes, it's him," she replied.

They rode in silence for a while, Ninia's tonic was wearing off and Sisika was beginning to feel cramping sensations across her abdomen and up her back, she bit her lip not wanting to let Tokala know. They carried on a little longer but suddenly Sisika gasped when a spasm shot through her body, she grabbed onto the saddle and slid off the horse.

"I just need a minute," she panted, her legs trembling beneath her.

Tokala jumped down from his horse and was at her side, then helped her to lie down. He pulled a blanket out and laid it under her head. "If anything happens to me, promise me you'll go onto the mountains. Ask to see the King, his name is Darkstar, he will know what to do," she whispered to him.

"I'm not leaving you," cried Tokala, he could not lose his mother now, not after everything.

Sisika lay there trembling with the pain, her son had her head in his lap, she couldn't end this way. She wanted her baby to live and then a thought struck her and she suddenly cried out, "Wigholt, if you can hear me, please help us!"

"I'm here," said the Wizard, he had already seen and was on his way to aid them.

Tokala jumped to his feet and pulled out a knife, "Get away from us demon!" he growled.

"Demon? Well I've been called a lot of things, but never a demon. What's the matter with you boy? I'm here to help," snapped Wigholt.

"Tokala, he's a friend, please," said Sisika weakly. "He'll help us."

Tokala lowered the knife slowly, still suspicious having never seen anything quite like this small, blue man before in his life.

"Dear lady, you have suffered, I am here now, we need to get you inside to the warmth," said Wigholt and he started to speak in a strange tongue. Tokala could not make out any of the words, but a pale blue bubble of light sprung up around his mother and lifted her gently from the ground.

"Follow me, and bring the horses," said Wigholt walking off with the bubble holding Tokala's mother floating alongside him.

Tokala followed on bringing the horses with him and soon enough they reached the large boulder that covered the entrance to Wigholt's underground home. The boulder slid aside and the Wizard walked down the staircase, indicating the Tokala should follow.

"What about the horses?" the boy asked.

"Bring them down, I've a stable for them," replied Wigholt.

An hour later Tokala found himself drifting off to sleep on a bed of furs next to his mother. Wigholt's cavern was safe and warm, he had given them both some hot gappin milk to drink while the horses settled down contentedly eating oats in a hay covered stable. Tokala was exhausted but he finally felt safe as he watched the strange blue man light his pipe allowing the intoxicating aroma from the smoke drift around them, Tokala found he could no longer keep his eyes open.

Wigholt sat and puffed on his pipe looking over at his sleeping guests. Sisika would not have long for this world, he knew that, he could not save her now, but he could save her baby. As for Tokala, he would have to think about what he should do, he could not raise two children hidden away underground. Darkstar would have to know about his child, and about Sisika, but in doing so, Wigholt had no idea what evil forces he may unleash. Something was making the ancient little Wizard feel deeply unsettled, like someone else was pulling the strings here, and causing all this pain.

CHAPTER THIRTEEN

Atolin was allowing Ragnar's huge moon snake to coil herself around his shoulders and neck, it was the first time the creature had allowed Atolin to hold her. He was sitting in the Animal Wizards cave near to the summit of Mount Solomite, the snake was pure white with a blue diamond on its forehead and it was extremely rare, not many Crystalites had come across a moon snake before. Snakes did not live in the mountains generally, it was too cold for them, but a moon snake was different, its magic allowed it to exist in the snow and ice way up in the highest peaks. This snake was named Kai, it visited with Ragnar occasionally and today Ragnar decided to teach Atolin how to handle it.

It would only take the snake a minute to crush the life out of the boy if it wanted to, but Ragnar had taught Atolin soft magical words that mesmerised the animal and made it gentle and submissive.

"I wish my father could see me," said Atolin. "I bet he's never held a moon snake before. It's the most beautiful creature I've ever seen."

"No, I don't think he has. This creature only visits me here occasionally, so this is a rare occasion indeed," replied Ragnar. The snake eventually started to slide out of Atolin's arms and head towards to entrance. "Perhaps it's time I took you back now."

Atolin reluctantly agreed, he would have preferred to stay up in the cave, but his mother did not allow it. They got the mountain horses ready then started making their way down the narrow mountain track, it had not snowed for a while so it was an easy ride. As they approached the city one of the palace horsemen came riding out to meet them, "Prince Atolin, Your father has sent me to fetch you, you must go to the palace at once."

They picked up their speed as they made their way through the streets of the Crystal City to the palace, where the servants were waiting for them. They took Atolin directly to the Queen's chambers and there he found his father, alongside his mother who was sleeping. Next to her was a crib and Atolin could hear the baby inside it.

"Ahh Atolin," said Darkstar looking pleased. "Come and meet your new baby sister."

Atolin went nervously to the crib and peered down at the tiny baby who lay there wide awake and staring back up at him with shining violet eyes. "She's beautiful," he whispered in total awe.

"Yes, she is," replied his father smiling happily. Darkstar was already besotted with the tiny baby, even though he knew she wasn't his. He held no malice, no blame, how could he? He had betrayed Lada in more ways than she would ever know. It would not be difficult for him to love this child as his own.

"May I see the baby?" asked Ragnar from the doorway.

"Yes, of course," said Darkstar standing aside to let the Animal Wizard look at the child.

As Ragnar walked closer to see his baby his heart was pounding so loudly he was frightened he would give himself away. When he drew closer a strange aura began to fill the chamber, Darkstar noticed it first and then Atolin. They both looked puzzled as Ragnar picked up the baby gently just as the cat Solitaire padded into the chamber. No one knew where he had come from, but he sat himself on the floor looking up curiously at Ragnar and the baby.

The Animal Wizard felt himself choking with emotion as he laid the child back down in her crib, but as he did so a strange blue aura started to shine around her. Darkstar tried to move but found he was stuck to the spot unable to move, unnerved he looked to Atolin who was also standing stock still, staring at the crib. The light lingered around the baby for a while, then disbursed into the air and as it did so, Darkstar found he had control of his limbs once again.

"What just happened?" he shouted angrily at Ragnar as he walked over and picked the baby up to see if she had been harmed.

"The baby was just given a gift from the White Witch herself," replied Ragnar. Solitaire was still sitting calmly behind the crib licking his huge paw.

"What sort of nonsense are you talking? Where did that cat come from?" demanded the King feeling irritated. He trusted Ragnar with his life, but this cat had done something to the child's crib and he wanted an explanation.

Ragnar looked embarrassed and flustered, unable to explain properly what had happened, but he was saved as Zebulon strolled into the room. "Calm yourself Darkstar, there is no harm done here, just a special blessing from the White Witch herself. It is a great honour and she has sent her cat Solitaire to watch over the child. This child has been especially blessed by the Gods and for that we must be grateful."

"She is just a tiny baby!" Darkstar was not satisfied although he knew deep down if Zebulon was here, then there was magic involved.

"There are many things in this universe that we don't understand, but I'm sure Sirena has her reasons," replied Zebulon.

Darkstar was still disgruntled, but not wanting to insult the good name of the White Witch he kept quiet instead handing the baby over to Atolin, "What should we name her?"

"What does mother want to call her?" asked Atolin dutifully.

"She asked me to name her, and now I'm asking you?" replied Darkstar smiling at his son's thoughtfulness.

"What about Kai?" suggested Atolin looking over at Ragnar, who smiled approvingly.

"Kai, I think that's perfect," replied Darkstar then kissed the baby's head.

"Solitaire would like to stay with Kai, he is a wise creature and he will protect her," said Ragnar suddenly.

"What do you think Atolin?" asked Darkstar biting his tongue. What he really wanted to say was *'protect her from what?'*

"I think she'll love Solitaire," replied his son who had met the white cat many times before.

"Then we thank you Ragnar, and we thank you Solitaire," said Darkstar, the moment by the crib now almost forgotten as Zebulon guessed it would be.

The old Wizard was puzzled at Sirena's interference with the child, he suspected there was probably trouble heading their way, especially if she had sent Solitaire to guard her.

Shame and sadness engulfed Ragnar as he left the palace, how had he got himself into this situation? He made a promise to himself that he would not come to the city again, for it would break his heart watching his own daughter grow without the knowledge of who her real father was. At least Solitaire would stay close to her, although he had no idea why the White Witch thought this important.

Three weeks after the birth of Kai, Darkstar was in his chambers going over architect plans for the city expansion; it was late at night and suddenly he heard what sounded like the sweeping of great wings from outside his window. He went over to see what the sound was and pulled back the screens only to recoil in horror. There, hanging upside down from his window frame was a giant black bat, it almost filled the entirety of the window. Darkstar had never seen a creature like this before, its huge round black, glassy eyes were staring unblinking at him from what could only be described as a mottled, ugly face. He noticed a pouch tied around one of its legs and he nervously approached the window, carefully pulling it open but thankfully the bat did not move. He reached over and gently unclipped the pouch from its leg then almost immediately the creature spread its great wings and flew off into the night air.

Opening the small leather pouch with shaking hands, Darkstar discovered a note inside. Written on it was a very short message, "Come to me now, Wigholt."

Without hesitating Darkstar grabbed his invisibility cloak and took a small crystal from his bottle. He left the Crystal city heading out into the Silversands for the first time in months. He did not really know the way to Wigholt's, but he continued onwards, suspecting that the little Wizard was already guiding and watching him approach.

He came across Tokala first, the boy was sitting on the top of Wigholt's boulder waiting for his arrival. Puzzled as to why the boy was here, Darkstar removed his cloak and when Tokala saw him he jumped off the boulder, "You are Darkstar?"

"I am, what are you doing here Tokala? Have you run away again?" Darkstar asked.

"Something like that, I've to take you to my mother," replied the boy and Darkstar began to sense the sadness in the child's voice.

"Sisika is here?" he asked.

"Yes, she's here, but she's dying," replied Tokala in a matter of fact tone. He stood aside as the boulder began to rumble then slid aside, revealing the wide staircase down to Wigholt's cavern. The boy started to walk down and Darkstar followed, the last words Tokala had said still ringing in his ears and he prayed it could not be true.

As he arrived in a huge brightly lit cavern, Darkstar saw Wigholt sitting next to a cot. The little Wizard lifted his head, "We have been waiting for you," he said.

Darkstar walked over and saw Sisika lying there with a tiny baby nestled next to her. He froze for a second, trying to take it all in.

"Hallo my love," whispered Sisika, her eyes shone when she saw him.

He collapsed next to the cot and grabbed her hand, his heart was splitting, "How long have you been here?" he asked, kissing her hand.

"A few weeks I think," she replied.

"Why did you not call me sooner? What has happened? The child, is it?" he could not stop his flow of questions as tears began to spill from his eyes.

"Yes, she is your child," said Sisika. "Her name is Catori."

"Black Eagle tried to kill Sisika and Tokala when he discovered that she was carrying a child. They came to me, but Sisika has already suffered a great deal at his hands, I cannot help her now," explained Wigholt.

Darkstar turned on him, anger taking control, "why did you not send for me sooner? I will kill Black Eagle for this!"

"That is exactly why I didn't send for you. Do you think a Mavaho-Crystalite war would solve this? You cannot go to Black Eagle, the most important thing is the future of these children," said Wigholt.

"He's right Darkstar, I made him send for you now that my time to leave this world is close, so you would promise me you will take care of my children," whispered Sisika weakly.

Darkstar sunk back down next to Sisika and buried his head in her lap, this wasn't happening, why had he left her? "Please," she whispered, "Please promise me."

"I promise, your children are my children. They will live without fear from Black Eagle, I swear this," he said his face wet with tears as he looked into her beautiful eyes. He then bent to kiss her lips and she closed her eyes, looking peaceful and content. Darkstar felt the life dwindle from her and when he lifted his head, Sisika was dead.

He turned to face Tokala, and saw the boy's face crumple, Darkstar reached out for him and pulled him into his arms letting Tokala sob. They sat there for a long time, letting their tears fall together and then Catori started to cry. Tokala immediately pulled away from Darkstar and went to pick up his baby sister," she's hungry," he said and walked away to feed her some sweet gappin milk. Darkstar watched him go with a mixture of sor'srow and awe at how the boy was coping with all this.

"He had to battle his father to save his mother," said Wigolt suddenly as if reading Darkstar's mind. "He took his father's eye out and for that Black Eagle will have him killed if he finds him."

"He won't find him, he and his sister are coming back with me," said Darkstar.

"Careful my King, you cannot let your people know Catori is your daughter, there will be trouble if they find out," warned Wigholt.

"I cannot leave them here," argued Darkstar.

"No, I agree, but you could take them to Ragnar. He's gentle and kind, he will raise them well and teach them the ways of the mountain," said Wigholt.

"But so far away from the city, it's not fair to hide them away. Catori is my daughter and Tokala should be a king, it does not sit well with me," said the King trying to convince himself he could just take them straight to the palace now, but he knew deep down Wigholt was right. He couldn't just spring these strange children on his people, Lada would have a field day.

"Perhaps just for now let the Crystalites get used to seeing them, let them warm to the children of their own accord and we can see what comes from that," suggested Wigholt. "I have already sent a message to Ragnar, he knows they will be coming, he will be prepared."

"You seem to have organised everything," said Darkstar bitterly. "This is my child your making decisions for."

"I just want to keep everyone safe, surely you want the same?" replied Wigholt.

"Yes of course, I would have just rather been consulted first, or at least given some time to discuss it with Sisika," Darkstar sighed.

Wigholt did not respond to this, he just shook his head sadly, the Crystalite King was still blinded to the danger he was putting them all in. Wigholt could only hope that as his grief subsided, he would begin to see sense.

"If you are going to make it back to the city before daylight, you must leave now," he said more sternly than he intended.

"The city won't miss me for a day," replied Darkstar.

"Of course they'll miss you! You are the King! They'll have search parties out by mid-morning, you must go back," Wigholt was getting impatient.

Darkstar got to his feet, the weight of his grief almost too much to bear. He walked over to Tokala and pulled the boy up to face him, "I'll be back for you, I promise."

Tokala nodded, his eyes still moist with his tears. Darkstar leaned over and kissed Catori, then picked up his cloak.

"I'll let you know when they arrive at Ragnar's," said Wigholt firmly. "It will be within the week, until then, stay in the Crystal City."

Darkstar looked like he was going to argue for a second, but then his shoulders slumped and he nodded, "very well, one week," he said, then he climbed slowly up the steps back to the Silversands.

Wigholt sat with Tokala next to Sisika's body for hours until the boy's eyes started to droop. The Wizard uttered a small enchantment under his breath and Tokala laid down finally nodding off to sleep. Wigholt covered him with some furs and then looked down at Sisika's body. It was time to release her spirit, he cast a spell and a blue bubble appeared raising her up off the ground then floated her through a small tunnel to the underground stream where it laid her gently on the pallet. Wigholt put her right hand in the water then stepped back to start an incantation.

"Not yet Wigholt," came a voice he recognised. He turned to see Sirena surrounded in blue light, standing in a gateway to the portals.

"Sirena, my lady," he said and bowed low before her.

"Allow me to take Sisika and I will reunite her body with her soul," said the White Witch.

"That is a great honour," replied Wigholt.

"She has suffered enough, and I believe there are dark forces watching her, trying to steal her soul. I must protect her," she explained.

"I've felt the presence of these forces for some time now. Is it Draconan?" asked Wigholt.

"I believe so, Black Eagle has unwittingly invited him in, and his darkness is threatening to infect what's left of my beautiful Satiren. You must be alert my friend, if he gets too strong it will be the end," replied Sirena. "I haven't much time, I must not let the Overlords know of my presence here, allow me to take her, cast the spell using the moon magic then send her in the portal and I will take over."

Wigholt looked down at Sisika's lifeless face, still beautiful even in death. He held his hands aloft and started the incantation, almost immediately the air surrounding Sisika began to sparkle, and she was engulfed in potent magic. She opened her eyes and took her hand out of the stream then slowly got to her feet. Still surrounded by the magical aura of the moons she turned to Wigholt, "thank you," she said in a strangely distant voice.

Sirena held out her hand and the Mavaho Queen walked into the portal to join her, then darkness fell and they were both gone. Wigholt took a deep breath, so many things were changing in his world, the peace he longed for seemed more distant now. He should have died a long, long time ago, but he was still here, not ageing and wondering just how much more death and heartbreak he could endure. Now he had two children to take care of, and an unstable Crystalite King who was threatening to let his emotions get the better of him. It was a precarious situation, especially with Draconan's greedy eyes watching.

CHAPTER FOURTEEN

It was already daylight when Darkstar slipped back into the Crystal Palace, he was numb, unable to process what had happened. In the forefront of his mind he could only think that all this time he had selfishly been pandering to his spoilt, vain wife while Sisika was being brutalised by Black Eagle, and was almost too much for him to bear. If he had only known, he blamed Wigholt for that, it was the Wizard's interference in the first place that had driven them apart before Sisika could tell him she was carrying his child. If he had only refused to stop seeing her then things would have been different. But what could he have done? He had loved her enough to leave his city, they could have made a life for themselves in the foothills of the mountains, but now that choice had been taken from him.

Darkstar raged inside his chamber for the rest of the day, refusing to see anyone, even Atolin stayed away. Towards evening one of the Queen's consorts arrived to tell him that Lada insisted that he visit her and the baby. He angrily dismissed her, telling her to tell the Queen he had no interest in what she had to say. He felt no guilt when the frightened woman scurried off looking dismayed, he could not bear to look at Lada just now. She would only remind him of what he had lost.

He didn't sleep that night, fighting the urge to put on his cloak and go back to Wigholt's cavern. His mind turned to Catori, his baby daughter, now without her mother because of his foolish choices. How dare Wigholt suggest she be raised by Ragnar high in the mountains, why couldn't he have her here at the palace? He had done what Wigholt suggested once before and it had resulted in the death of Sisika, he would not trust that little blue Wizard to make decisions for him again. Darkstar then began to make his own plans for the children, Wigholt could send them to Ragnar, but they would not be staying there.

***

Ragnar heard the sweeping sounds of huge wings before he saw Wigholt's chariot heading towards him. The two desert bats lowered it to the ground in front of Ragnars cave, allowing their passengers to disembark before they took off back to the warmth of the desert. Wigholt was carrying Catori in his arms and Tokala followed him, shivering in the strange cold of the mountains.

Ragnar had been astonished by Wigholt's first message, he knew the legends of the little blue Wizard, but thought him long dead. He had journals written by his ancient ancestors over five hundred years ago that spoke of Wigholt of the Jacartans along many other strange creatures that once existed here on Satiren. Never in his wildest dream had he thought that Wigholt may still be alive and yet here he was, reaching out to Ragnar with a tiny baby in his arms.

"Bring them inside, the boy is shivering, he needs warmer clothes for the mountains," said Ragnar ushering them inside his cave.

The warmth greeted Tokala as soon as he stepped inside the cavern, he was feeling nervous and did not know what to expect. Ragnar took them over to the fire aware that Tokala was scrutinizing him closely, he smiled kindly at the boy then took Catori from Wigholt and sat by the fire indicating they should do the same.

"You didn't tell me they were from the Mavaho city," he said as he gazed down at the baby. "Though this child has paler skin. Is she not a Mavaho?"

"I didn't know if you knew about the Mavahos, but I expected you would," replied Wigholt ignoring Ragnar's last question.

"The animals know more about this world than you or I ever could, they tell me many stories of the Mavaho hunters on the desert sands," replied Ragnar getting up to fetch some warm goat's milk for Catori. He handed Tokala a cup also, "Here drink up boy, the milk will make your bones strong."

"My names Tokala," said Tokala stubbornly, he didn't like being called boy.

Ragnar laughed and tousled his hair, "Just what I need, another boy with attitude! I think you and Atolin will get on well."

"Atolin?" repeated Tokala.

"He is King Darkstar's son and is about the same age as yourself. I'm sure you will be friends, he comes here often and he'll show you around the mountains," replied Ragnar, then he turned his attention back to Wigholt. He had a lot of questions he wanted answered before he agreed to this.

"You mentioned that Darkstar knows about the children in your message, what should I tell the Crystalite people? I cannot keep them hidden up here indefinitely."

"I think you may have to leave that to the King, he has quite an interest in these children," replied Wigholt mysteriously and Ragnar narrowed his eyes thoughtfully.

He looked down at Catori's alert green eyes and her tufts of golden hair and recognition dawned on him, "Who is the baby's father?"

"I think you know the answer to that question, which is why it's imperative that the children be kept a secret until the time to introduce them is right," sighed Wigholt. "Darkstar has his own baby daughter to raise, he cannot show more interest in Catori, it will cause conflict within the city."

Ragnar stared at the Wizard for a second then said, "You know, don't you?"

"I'm not here to cast judgement, things happen for a reason, but you and Darkstar cannot simply switch daughters, things have gone too far now. You must be careful, and you must make the King see that he needs to tread carefully also," said Wigholt.

"What about the boy, I mean Tokala?" he said, recovering himself quickly when he saw Tokala scowl at him.

"I have promised my mother to keep my sister safe and I will not leave her side," he said stubbornly.

"We will do that together," promised Ragnar, wondering how he was going to stop Darkstar from doing anything foolish.

Wigholt stayed with them until the evening and then he summoned his bats. The chariot arrived after the children had gone to sleep, Tokala had already reluctantly said goodbye, he liked Ragnar, but he felt safer with Wigholt. The little Wizard promised he would keep an eye on them and at the first sign of danger he would come for them and this made Tokala more at ease with the situation.

During the next few days Ragnar kept Tokala busy, he taught him about life in the mountains, about the animals that lived there and the respect they must be shown. Tokala took care of the horses, while Ragnar took care of Catori. She was a healthy baby, bright and alert for her age and was already grasping onto his fingers tightly. He became quite enamoured with this strange looking child, then one day he awoke to find the moon snake Kai coiled around her crib. Ragnar jumped up in fright, but when he reached the crib, he saw the snake had gently laid its head on Catori's stomach and the baby was giggling in delight, he had never seen anything like it.

The snow eagles also showed a healthy curiosity towards the baby and visited more often than usual, taking it in turns to stand guard over the baby's crib.

When Ragnar asked them why? They communicated that the child was important and that she had a special healing bond with Satiren. It seemed that all creatures were drawn to Catori and were content just to sit and watch her.

Ragnar noticed quickly that Tokala was a bright child and realised he should really think about sending him to school as he needed company his own age, but for now the boy was still grieving his mother. Ragnar heard him cry himself to sleep every night and his heart was heavy, he knew Tokala was trying to be so brave for Catori. Then one morning when the Animal Wizard awoke, he found Solitaire sitting in his human form talking quietly with Tokala.

"Morning Ragnar, I didn't know you had guests," he said cheerfully.

Ragnar saw Tokala was smiling, "I'm sure you did know, but never mind, what are you two talking about?"

"Did you know that Solitaire can change into a cat?" said Tokala his eyes brighter than they had been over the last few days.

"I did. I also thought it was supposed to be a secret," replied Ragnar looking suspiciously at Solitaire.

"A secret that now Tokala is part of, I can't very well walk in here if the boy doesn't know," said Solitaire.

Tokala was captivated with Solitaire and spent the rest of the day with him, listening to stories of the Gods and the ancient warriors that fought their battles for them. Solitaire taught him how to use a sword which delighted the small boy and for the first time since he had arrived, Tokala went straight to sleep that night.

Ragnar began to wonder why Darkstar had not visited him yet, surely the King knew the children were here? Ragnar had expected to see him within a couple of days, but it had been a week and there was still no sign of him.

***

Darkstar was getting impatient. If the children were with Ragnar, surely the Animal Wizard would have brought them to the Crystal City by now, he couldn't hide them away forever. The King had been like a bear with a sore head for over a week now and Atolin was a bit bewildered by his father's temper. So, one morning when he had no school, the young prince got up and decided to ride up to see Ragnar. He would be much better company than his father was and he could play with the animals.

Atolin saddled his own small mountain pony, and snuck out of the city before either of his parents had got up. A couple of hours later he was approaching Ragnar's cave when he saw a strange looking boy with skin the colour of coal standing outside Ragnar's cave brushing a horse.

As he drew closer, Tokala turned when he heard the pony's hooves and the boys stared at each other for a minute, then Tokala said "Hallo?"

Atolin jumped down from Icicle, "Hallo, I'm Atolin," he said his eyes wide with curiosity.

"I'm Tokala, I'm staying here with Ragnar." He paused for a bit and then said, "I know who you are, you're the King's son. Ragnar has told me about you."

"He hasn't told me about you. Are you from the desert?" asked Atolin recognising Tokala from the description his father had shared with him when he described the people of Burning Towers.

"I'm from the Silversands, we came here a few days ago, I came with my sister, Ragnar is going to look after us," explained Tokala. "Would you like to meet my sister?"

"Yes, I would," replied Atolin and he hauled a bucket of oats over for Icicle then followed Tokala inside the cavern where Ragnar was seated feeding Catori.

"Ahh Atolin, so you've finally met," said Ragnar looking pleased. "I'm glad, Tokala needs a friend like you to show him the ways of the mountain people."

"Have you never been to the mountains?" Atolin asked.

"No, they haven't, their mother was dying and she asked me to take care of her children after she had gone, so they have come to stay with me," said Ragnar.

"I'm sorry about your mother," said Atolin and Tokala nodded sadly. Atolin patted him on the back, "do you want me to help you with the horses?"

Tokala nodded and grinned at his new friend, relief washed over Ragnar as he watched the two boys walk back outside chatting happily.

***

Darkstar awoke to find Lada sitting at the edge of his bed holding Kai in her arms. He was instantly irritated by her presence. "What brings you uninvited to my chamber?

Lada's eyes narrowed slightly but she kept her voice level, "I am just worried about you. You haven't seemed yourself lately, everyone in the palace is talking about it."

"You're worried? You've never worried about anyone but yourself for your whole life and everyone else needs to mind their own business," barked Darkstar throwing back his covers and hauling himself out of bed.

"I just thought seeing Kai would cheer you up. You haven't been to see your daughter for a week," replied Lada stung by his spiteful comment.

"Stop pretending when we're alone, we both know she's not my daughter. What is it you actually want Lada? A new dress? Some more jewels? Just make a list and leave me alone!" he barked.

"Don't you dare speak to me like that!" cried Lada. "Why are you playing this game? Pretending to everyone she is your daughter, when you don't give a damn about her."

"Not true my lady. I don't care about you, but she is an innocent child and is not going to suffer because of your infidelity. Just stay away from me Lada. Do not enter my chambers again, you are not welcome here!" Darkstar started to pull his clothes on ignoring his wife who was sitting there furiously biting her lip.

"You drove me to it Darkstar. You know you did. You never paid any attention to me! What was I supposed to do?" Lada started to cry.

Darkstar felt a little guilty over his harshness, "Look Lada, you are the mother of my son. For that I will always indebted to you, but there is nothing between us. You know that, you feel nothing for me anymore than I do for you. We keep up this pretence because that is what our people want. We don't need to hurt each other, you live your life as you see fit, and I will live mine. Please just leave me alone!"

Lada felt her whole-body tremble with rage, she would rather his anger than this dismissive way he was he treating her. She hated him, she wanted to scream and hit out at his arrogant face. No one had ever spoken to her in such a way, and she would make him pay. All she needed to do was bide her time, then she would find a way to have her revenge. She got to her feet and left Kai lying on his bed before storming from his chambers.

Darkstar sighed, he knew he had been cruel, but she had no idea what he was going through. He sat on the bed and picked Kai up, the baby smiled at him and his heart melted a little. She would be a good companion for his own daughter, if he could ever get Catori to the palace. He made up his mind, he would go and see Ragnar today, it was time that he paid a visit and saw Sisika's children. He played with Kai for a while before he carried her gently through to the nursery and handed her over to one of the nursemaids, then Darkstar headed out to the stables.

CHAPTER FIFTEEN

He heard the boy's laughter before he saw them as he approached Ragnar's cave. They were out grooming four mountain horses, who were all trying to nuzzle up to the boys to get their attention. Darkstar watched them from a distance, his heart swelling with pride as he saw how Atolin had befriended Tokala so easily.

"We were just coming to see you." Ragnar appeared carrying Catori in his arms. "I felt it was time to bring the children to the city."

"I was wondering what was taking you so long," replied Darkstar dismounting and taking the baby from Ragnar. She smiled up at him, her hypnotic green eyes looking directly into his and his heart skipped as he stared down at his daughter.

"Come and see the moon snake father," said Atolin grabbing hold of Darkstars arm. "She has been looking after Catori every day, hardly ever leaving her side."

They all went into the cavern and Atolin went to sit next to the great snake, who was curled up asleep next to Catori's crib. "Ragnar says Catori has a special magic and the animals recognise it, that's why they want to protect her."

"Does he now? Well she is still a tiny baby, I'm sure in time we will see if that is true or not," replied his father casting a disbelieving look in Ragnar's direction. The Animal Wizard smiled; he was used to Darkstar's reservations when it came to his ability to speak with the animals.

Darkstar turned to Tokala, the boy looked revitalised, his shoulders that were once slumped and carrying the weight of the world, were straight and strong. He was smiling happily and Darkstar wondered at Ragnar's ability to bring life back into the boy so quickly. Just then they heard the sound of another horse approaching the cave.

"I wonder who that is?" said Ragnar walking towards the entrance. As he did so Lada came running in and threw her arms around him sobbing aloud. She did not notice the others watching her from around the fire

"Why have you not come to see me? I can't bear Darkstar any longer! I hate him! He is so cruel to me Ragnar. I want to tell him Kai is yours, please Ragnar we could tell him together and watch his face. He deserves to know!"

Ragnar stood frozen in silence and the atmosphere in the cavern went icy as Lada lifted her head from his shoulder and gasped when she saw who was watching.

"Boys it's time to saddle up, we'll go to the city today and introduce Tokala and Catori to our people," said Darkstar, his face betraying no hint of emotion.

Atolin and Tokala didn't have to be told twice to go, and they both ran for the exit getting as far away from the situation as they could.

"Is that all you're going to say?" cried Lada, her face pale.

"Ragnar, do you have a travel cot for the baby, she can ride with me," Darkstar continued as if Lada was not there.

Ragnar did not reply, he could hardly face Darkstar, so instead he went to get the cot together.

Lada stared opened mouthed as Ragnar did what he asked, "Say something! Don't let him order you around like that!" she screamed.

Ragnar turned towards her, his eyes filled with pity and simply said, "Lada, he is my King."

The Queen's face had turned deathly white and her eyes grew cold and distant. She turned to stare at Darkstar who would still not look at her, and her heart turned to stone. She never moved from the spot as Darkstar carried the baby out past her to the horses, and she never moved nor spoke when Ragnar came back to her to tell her he that he would come to speak with her later. Lada never moved as they rode away leaving her alone, even the moon snake slithered out of the cave to escape her presence.

Then someone was beside her, his hand resting gently on her shoulders. She could not see him clearly but she could feel him feeding her malevolence and hatred, fuelling her need for revenge. His presence made her stronger, filling the voids that were opening inside her with a sinuous evil and giving her strength. Lada gave a nauseating smile and promised herself she would kill Darkstar along with all those he loved.

***

The descent to the city was quicker than the ascent, and there was an uncomfortable silence, even the boys said little to each other, aware of the tension between Ragnar and Darkstar. The King never mentioned what he had just witnessed, but remained focused on Catori as Ragnar's head was bowed in shame.

As they started to ride through the streets of the city people stopped in their tracks to stare at the strange looking boy riding alongside their King and young prince. The news spread quickly through the streets and people came out of their houses to watch them pass. Tokala felt afraid, but Atolin reached over and patted him on his back for reassurance.

When they finally reached the Crystal Palace, there was already a small crowd gathered awaiting their arrival. The Wizard Council had been about to conduct a meeting when news of Darkstar and the strange children was brought to them. They all went down to the palace forecourt making Darkstar irritated when he saw them, surely, they could have waited until he brought Tokala to them. He got down off his horse and lifted Atolin and Tokala off their ponies, then turned to face the inquisitive crowd.

"I hope this is a welcome party," he shouted angrily and some of the Wizards shifted around uncomfortably with embarrassment.

Garik, the Justice Wizard stepped forward. "I'm sorry Darkstar, news came of your arrival and we were curious. We have all heard stories of the desert people, but we've never set eyes on them."

"I've brought these 'CHILDREN' here to safety," he replied emphasizing the word 'children'. It's a request from the White Witch herself, she asked Wigholt the ancient one to take them to Ragnar for safe keeping," explained Darkstar. It was his first lie and Ragnar swallowed uncomfortably as he noticed Solitaire pad out onto the forecourt to watch what was going on.

"Why here?" inquired Egor, the Wizard of Education, stepping forward to the front of the crowd. "Why should we take them?" He was a miserable little man, an unpleasant teacher, taking joy in tormenting and finding fault where he could.

"Why not us? We are a peaceful people; we love our children and we would give these children a good and safe place to grow. They have been through terrible torment at the hands of their Chief. The people of the desert live under a brutal tyrant's rule and their mother was savagely murdered by his hands. He would have killed them also had they not been saved by Wigholt. But the ancient one cannot raise these children, they need fresh air, friends and love. Surely, we as a good people can offer them a home with us. They have nothing." Darkstar was appealing to their good nature.

"I've lots of baby toys and clothes my Gisella has grown out of. They would fit the baby," cried out one of the palace maids, putting everyone else to shame. Darkstar smiled and thanked her warmly then pulled Tokala over to stand in front of him. This is Tokala, he is the same age as Atolin and they are already friends. I have offered that they be schooled together here at the palace. Are there any objections?"

Egor was about to speak but Garik stopped him. "Tokala is very welcome here at the palace, I'm sure he'll be able to teach us many things about the great Silversands and we'll be able to show him how we live in the mountains."

There was a general murmur of agreement amongst the other Wizards and Egor stepped back into the crowd, his face was sour.

The palace maid who had spoken out asked Ragnar if she could hold the baby and so he gently passed Catori over. The maid looked into the bright green eyes, "Oooo she is so pretty." Within seconds the other palace servants had surrounded her so they could see the new baby girl.

"As it's so cold up in the mountains, Ragnar asked if I thought it would be better if Catori was cared for at the palace for now. She could share the nursery with Kai," suggested Darkstar knowing already he had the palace on his side. Ragnar sat speechless, this was not what Wigholt had wanted, but after Lada's revelation at his cavern he could not argue with the King. He had no idea what Darkstar was planning and when Lada found out what he was doing, there would be trouble.

The Wizard Council agreed this was a sensible suggestion, unaware of the tension between the King and the Animal Wizard. They retreated back to the meeting hall and Darkstar said he would join them as soon as the children were settled. Atolin took Tokala to his rooms and the palace maids took Catori to the nursery, cooing over her with every step. Ragnar turned to Darkstar, "I will have to take Tokala back with me soon. I want to get back before it's dark."

"Leave the boy here, he can start schooling with Atolin tomorrow," replied the King.

"Wigholt said it would be safer if the children remained with me. You know that Darkstar, is this your way of punishing me, by taking them," asked Ragnar.

"I have no desire to punish you, old friend. We have all made choices that have caused great misery. I am only trying to make things right and I do not believe Wigholt is thinking about what is best for the children. He interfered once, and that led to the death of their mother. From now on, I will make the decisions about what is best for them. What happened between you and Lada is not my concern. I have never loved my wife, you know that, I am grateful that you were able to give her what I couldn't. But don't try to interfere with what I have decided as you will not wish the Crystalites to know how you betrayed your King."

Ragnar stared after Darkstar as he walked into the palace, he could not ignore the threat in Darkstar's tone. There was nothing he could do, he would have to send a message to Wigholt, the ancient one would not be happy. He felt something brush against his legs and he looked down to see Solitaire looking at him. "I know, it's a mess. Can you watch over them all, I have to leave now." The cat bowed its large shaggy head and Ragnar left to collect his horse.

When he turned to leave he heard the sound of hooves enter the forecourt and he saw Lada riding in. He face was paler than he had ever seen it, she must have left her cloak behind at his cavern, and she seemed to be completely unaware of what was going on around her. He went over to help her off her horse, she had a strange look on her face and was freezing cold to touch. "By the Gods Lada, why have you travelled without your cloak, you are chilled to the bone."

She did not respond and Ragnar helped her into the palace calling out to the maids for some help. They appeared and flurried around her, taking her to her chambers, ordering a hot bath to be made. Lada's eyes were dead, she looked straight ahead making eye contact with no one and saying nothing. Ragnar felt sick to his stomach, what had he done?

CHAPTER SIXTEEN

Time passed peacefully at the Crystal Palace. Lada was ill for a number of weeks remaining in her chambers all of that time, she did not want to see anyone, not even her baby. Rumours began to spread about her mental health, but Darkstar was too pre-occupied with the children to listen. Tokala and Atolin were inseparable and the city got used to seeing them out and about on their ponies. They visited with Ragnar often, which brought some relief to the Animal Wizard. Wigholt was not happy when Ragnar had messaged him to tell him that Darkstar had moved the children into the palace, but agreed there was nothing that could be done about it now. Tokala seemed happy with his new life, although much to Atolin's amusement, it had taken him some time to get used to the cold.

Lord Arcos taught the boys sword skills, archery and combat which were their favourite lessons of the week. Atolin was already skilled with his sword, Tokala had only ever used one with Solitaire, but he picked it up quickly and it was not long before the boys were evenly matched. As for using a bow and arrow, Tokala's skills were far superior he even taught Lord Arcos a thing or two. He taught Atolin how to make a sling shot and the boys would compete with each other up in the mountains, soon Atolin was as good an aim as Tokala was.

They both hated their lessons with Egor, the sour-faced Wizard had no time for their friendship and often tried to humiliate Tokala in class. Atolin kept complaining to his father, but Darkstar simply said that sometimes in life you would meet disagreeable people, and you just had to learn to rise above it. That didn't stop Atolin putting an ice scorpion in Egor's desk one day, which only resulted in Tokala getting the blame, no matter how much Atolin tried to argue that it was actually him.

Egor kept company with the Queen these days. The 'Ice Queen' as she was widely known now amongst the staff in the palace had a strange group of friends that visited her regularly. They were an unpleasant bunch, all vying for the Queen's attention by any means necessary. The trouble was, it usually involved spreading malicious rumours about these strange children that had been brought into their midst and questioning why they were being brought up in the palace as if they were royalty. Lada continued to play the victim, unable to protect her own children from these mysterious outsiders.

She concocted her own versions of why Darkstar was so infatuated with the children and suggested he had been bewitched by the ancient one they called Wigholt. Egor informed the Queen that the people of the desert were once the enemies of the Crystalites, it was written in their history books. How could they be sure that Tokala was not sending messages back to his people?

Egor continually bombarded the Queen with stories of Tokala's insolent behaviour in class and how he had some sort of control over Atolin. Bit by bit, Lada's spiteful followers grew in numbers, and soon the rumours they created began to trickle out into the streets of the city, not so anyone would notice at first, not unless they were actively looking for a reason to dislike the children. However, the distrust started to filter slowly through the streets, their strange skin and the colour of their eyes was unsettling and many of the Crystalites did question why these children were living at the Palace as if they were Royalty.

Time went on and months turned into years, but still the rumblings of uncertainty spread. Darkstar did not help matters, he lavished gifts on the Mavaho children, Tokala became like a second son and many within the palace believed he paid more attention to Catori than he did to his own daughter. The queen watched on silently, fuelling the flames of doubt that were now well rooted. She was patient, her time would come, she would discredit Darkstar and get rid of these children once and for all.

Kai and Catori were both three-year old now, and shared the nursery happily together. Catori was a beautiful child with golden hair, emerald green eyes and olive skin, but her resemblance to Darkstar was uncanny, and becoming more noticeable as time went on. It was on one of her rare visits to the nursery that Lada finally noticed. She totally ignored Catori as she usually did, but on this particular day she was watching the child from afar, when she noticed familiar mannerisms along with the unmistakable shape of her jaw line. Then the realization dawned on her like a bolt from the blue, Catori was undoubtably Darkstar's child, she was sure of it.

Then everything seemed to fall into place and Lada started putting it all together in her mind. Of course, this was why he had brought them to the city, this was why he had ignored her for years and it explained his strange disappearances through the nights. He had been seeing a Mavaho woman, something must have happened to her? He said she'd been killed by their Chief. No doubt the Chief had probably found out about their affair, no wonder he wanted to kill the children. Lada left the nursery with her heart pumping with excitement, she summoned her friends to her chambers.

Darkstar was oblivious to the stories now speading around the city, but the Wizard Council were not. Garik was concerned it was causing a divide and he called a meeting to discuss the future of the Mavaho children. The Wizards, Sorcerers, Mage's and teachers filled the meeting room, never before had there been such a large number attending a meeting. Even Zebulon arrived and he looked grim as he took his seat at the council head table, alongside Zodiac and Garik. The others sat facing them, all were awaiting the arrival of Darkstar. When he finally marched into the room Zebulon could sense the anger burning within him and he sighed knowing that was not going to help matters.

Ragnar and Soliatire slipped into the room unnoticed, the Animal Wizard took a seat at the back. He hadn't been to the city for over a year, but Solitaire had remained in constant contact reporting on all the events surrounding the children and the cat had heard the rumours and accusations. Ragnar was worried, he had wanted to talk to Darkstar about taking the children back with him to Mount Solomite. But the Wizard Council had beaten him to it and he waited with bated breath to see what was going to be said. Ragnar had not spoken to Lada for years, she completely ignored him and he had no idea how she felt about the children however, he could take a good guess.

"I'm not sure I understand why you've called this meeting Garik?" Darkstar had taken his seat instead starting off the proceedings immediately without bothering to hide his displeasure at being there.

"Then you have not been aware of the rumours that have been spreading throughout the city. People are concerned that you are spending so much time with the Mavaho children that you are neglecting your own," said Garik coming straight to the point. "People are also questioning the decision to have them live at the palace and be treated as royalty. There are many in the city who believe you have been bewitched by them."

"Is that what you truly believe Garik!" cried Darkstar feeling his anger grow.

"It does not matter what I believe, I have the voice of the people, and they want to address this." Garik remained calm, he knew they had caught Darkstar off guard and he hoped the King would forgive him in time. He did not believe a word of these rumours, but many did and it was becoming a problem.

Darkstar turned towards the other dignitaries, "They are only children. I felt nothing but compassion for their plight when they arrived here and I wanted to help them. My son has formed a close bond with Tokala, they both learn from each other, it cannot be a bad thing."

"It can if Tokala is leading Atolin astray, and I'm sorry my King but I have watched him in his lessons, he has complete control over the prince," interrupted Egor.

"Nonsense!" butted in Lord Arcos. "They are both equally matched and firm friends. There is nothing sinister about their friendship."

Darkstar smiled gratefully at the Lord Warrior then turned to Egor, "You would find something wrong with a new born puppy if it suited your purpose. I know you hold court with my wife, and I know her feelings about me."

A deafening hush swept around the room at Darkstar's comment, no one had ever heard him talk about the Queen that way in public. They all knew that they lived separate lives and only tolerated each other, but Darkstar had never spoken about it openly before.

"Perhaps you could explain to us again how the children happen to be here. I for one, find the story a little flimsy in places," replied Egor not about to be silenced so soon.

"Perhaps Ragnar could tell us," interjected Garik. "I believe he was the one who brought the children here."

Ragnar shifted in his seat uncomfortably, he had no idea what else Darkstar was about to reveal, he had to choose his words carefully.

"As you were aware Wigholt the ancient one came to me to ask me for a favour. He had discovered the two children along with their mother who was gravely ill. He tried to care for her but she died, and he knew the children could not return to the Mavaho's, so he asked me to care for them."

"But why could they not return to their own people? Did he not give you a reason?" asked Zodiac.

"Tokala is the son of Black Eagle, the Chief of the Mavaho's. Sisika, his mother was Black Eagle's wife. The Chief is a brutal man as I have said before, and one day he was beating his poor wife when Tokala stepped in to protect his mother and in doing so, he took his father's eye out with his sling shot. They had to run, but Sisika was heavily pregnant and having already been beaten, she died shortly after giving birth to Catori." Darkstar had stood up to address them all, he knew he was taking a chance revealing so much to them.

"Why was she being punished?" asked Egor his eyes filled with sardonic glee.

"Because I am Catori's father." There was an audible gasp, and then a buzz of conversation as the council digested what their King had just confessed to them. "I never meant for this to happen, but I cannot turn my back on my daughter, surely you can see that. The Mavaho people are terrified of their

Chief and his men, he is a tyrant who rules by oppression and bullying. I could not send Tokala back, it would have been sending him to his death."

"Are you telling us that it was you who brought them here. This has nothing to do with Wigholt," said Garik trying to piece it all together.

"No, it was Wigholt who found them and it was Wigholt who convinced Sisika and I to stop seeing each other. We were putting ourselves and our families at risk, I had no idea she was carrying my child, and that is a burden I must bear. Wigholt sent for me when Sisika was dying, we made the plans together and I promised her I would take care of the children. There is nothing sinister about this, these children are simply victims."

"You have betrayed your people and you have betrayed the Queen. We cannot tolerate you fathering another child whilst you ignore your own wife," shouted Egor over the buzz of other voices.

"I would be careful with your accusations Egor. There is much you do not know," Zebulon's voice drowned out all the other voices and silence fell. "There is much to discuss. No one is as innocent in this as they may seem, including your Queen. Darkstar is correct, we are talking about children. There is no bewitching here, only lies and coverups that many of us are involved in, including myself. I was the one who gave Darkstar the ability to travel into the desert at night, to satisfy his curiosity. I had no inkling that it would lead to this, but what is done is done. I suggest we take some time to think these revelations through, then meet again tomorrow."

"I agree," said Kaeshia getting to her feet. The very tall, slim mage was a well-respected calming influence in the meeting room. "We cannot possibly decide the fate of the children when so much has been divulged. Let us take time, look to our hearts and find the right solution for this."

"Thank you Kaeshia, as always you are right. I will adjourn this meeting until the same time tomorrow. May you all take time in considering all you have heard, and please do not mention any of this to anyone outside of this room, and that especially means you Egor!" said Garik drawing the meeting to an end whilst giving Egor a harsh stare.

Darkstar was slumped in his seat as the council members left the room, Lord Arcos came over and laid a reassuring hand on his shoulder as he passed him by. Ragnar remained seated at the back of the room until everyone else had left, then he got up and walked over to the King.

"You were right Ragnar, I should have left the children with you. I may have put them in danger."

"It's become quite a mess, if Lada hears about this then I fear it will only get worse. I'm sure Egor is on his way to the Queens chambers as we speak," said Ragnar.

Soltaire stretched and a blue light engulfed him, then he changed into his human form. Darkstar watched on expressionless, he had always suspected that there was more to the strange cat than Ragnar led him to believe.

"Once again, I have been too long in that cat's body," said Solitaire stretching his limbs.

"It's time you met Solitaire," explained Ragnar. "He is a friend of the White Witch and he visits with me from time to time.

"Sirena has asked me to watch over the children, but I fear now that it may become unsafe for them to remain. I will have to go to her and tell her what's happened here. She'll be worried about Kai, if it comes out that you're not Kai's father then it will divide the city, Lada is not stable and I don't trust her."

"We can protect the children, nothing will happen to them, especially not Kai" argued Darkstar. "The Crystalites are good people, they will do the right thing."

"I fear you are blinded by your love for them, there is a darkness growing within the Crystal City, I have seen it and it will not take much for it to take hold. Already Draconan's forces are hovering, biding their time as they look for a way in," replied Solitaire.

"I don't understand what you are saying, there are no dark forces at play here, just a foolish King. I am ready to step down if that is the answer to a peaceful solution. I can take the children and bring them up elsewhere," said Darkstar.

"I'm sure the people will not accept that. I can only hope things smooth over, nevertheless, Ragnar I want you to send for Wigolt, he can watch over things while I'm gone. I would feel more comfortable with him here." Solitaire ignored Darkstar's reasoning, the King was refusing to listen to sense.

"I don't want Wigholt here, if it wasn't for him Sisika would still be alive," cried Darkstar.

"Rubbish, you're being foolish. You and Sisika got yourselves into this mess, Wigholt only tried to help you out of it. You need him here, Ragnar do as I say."

"Yes, my Lord," replied the Wizard and left immediately, feeling Darkstar's eyes burning into his back.

"Take some time, Darkstar, to think things through rationally. You are their King, they will hear you out, but if Lada decides to admit that Kai is not your child and it comes out that you've known this all along, then there could be trouble. I have an uncomforatble feeling about this." A blue glow appeared around Solitaire before Darkstar could answer and once more the white cat sat in his place. It turned and padded quietly out of the room, leaving Darkstar alone.

CHAPTER SEVENTEEN

As Ragnar expected, Egor couldn't wait to get to the Queen's chambers to share his news. Lada and her friends were already gathered, eager to hear how the proceeding had gone. The Queen listened open-mouthed as Egor told them how Darkstar had actually admitted he was the father of Catori.

"Enough is enough!" she cried, her eyes filled with victorious menace. "Egor, order the soldiers under my command to bring Tokala and Catori to the plateau on Mount Gloom. They will be judged the old way, spread the word amongst our friends in the city, we need an audience, and don't let Darkstar find out!"

Mount Gloom was so named as it sat between two giants, Mount Solomite and Mount Kracus, making it completely overshadowed, the sunlight never touched it. It was a table top mountain, its plateau made of solid ice, the edges of which dropped a thousand feet to the jagged rocks below. In years gone by it had been used as a place of execution for the Crystalite courts, those who committed the most vicious of crimes were sentenced on Mount Gloom, then thrown off the plateau to their deaths. It had not been used since Darkstar had taken the Crystalite throne, he did not believe in the old law of a life for a life.

Two hours later wrapped in white furs, Queen Lada stood in the centre of the plateau looking villainess. Crowds of people were beginning to arrive, bewildered by the rumours spreading throughout the city. Garik had also been summoned although he was reluctant to go at first, suspecting that something untoward was happening. But as it was a request from the Queen he had to obey. Garik decided it would be wise to bring Lord Arcos with him, the Lord Warrior could take charge if need be.

When he and Arcos arrived, they saw with disgust that Tokala had his arms bound behind his back and Catori was sobbing holding tightly onto her brother's legs. Atolin was standing pale faced next to his friend, unsure what to do. Garik strode over to them angrily, "Atolin, go get your father now!" he told the boy firmly and Atolin immediately ran off, grateful that he could get his father.

The Queen glared at the Justice Wizard and hissed under her breath, "do not try to interfere Garik."

"I suggest you untie the boy before Darkstar arrives, he will not tolerate this behaviour towards children," replied Garik, then he turned to Lord Arcos. "Untie Tokala and take him and Catori back to the palace."

"You will do no such thing!" roared the Queen and Lord Arcos hesitated, unsure what to do. "Garik I am in charge of these proceedings! You had your chance to do the right thing and you failed!"

There was a general murmur of agreement throughout the crowd and Garik turned on them, "this is what we have come to, terrifying small children because of some vicious rumours. I am ashamed of you all!"

People dropped their eyes as he glared at them and Garik prayed that Darkstar would arrive soon.

***

"You will be silent Garik or you will be held in contempt. This is an official court and your opinion has no place here!" roared the Queen.

She had brought along her own jury, all of which were low ranking palace officials, disgruntled by their lack of power and looking for quick promotions no matter at what cost. The Queen was in charge now, and Egor was in his element, after all he had brought the Queen the news she needed and he knew he would be rewarded well.

Garik had no stomach for the persecution of children, but he had no power to stop it. Lada was declaring this hearing an emergency, and everyone was already questioning the strange hold these children seemed to have over their King, so he listened on with a sour taste in his mouth as Lada addressed the jury she had put together.

"Look at the strange eyes of the boy, these are not human eyes, these are the eyes of a demon!" cried the Queen. "We all know Darkstar has been bewitched, and soon enough he will leave our city open to an invasion. These desert demons must have put this plan in motion years ago, helped by Wigholt, the Demon Wizard himself. What do any of us really know about him?" she cried with her voice echoing around the plateau.

Egor stepped forward with an old book from the palace library, it was open at a page that had a drawing of the little blue Wizard riding a yellow eyed dragon that was breathing fire out of its mouth whilst people were running for cover beneath them.

"What nonsense is this?" cried Garik marching over and snatching the book from Egor's hands. "This clearly states that Wigholt is the savior of the Crystalites. He brought us to the mountains to save us from the desert heat and slavery, this drawing was done depicting his power, nothing more!"

"You can clearly see that he is ready to attack our people, how can we believe Garik when the evidence is illustrated for all to see? Perhaps Garik and some of the Council members have been bewitched also!" cried the Queen ignoring the Justice Wizard's interruption.

"Everyone who has studied our history knows that Wigholt saved our people, you cannot change history to suit your needs" shouted Kaeshia, the Earth Wizard, suddenly appeared on the plateau. "I will not stand here and allow these children to be treated this way. The King will not tolerate this!" The crowd moved aside to let Kaeshia through and she marched over to the children and touched Tokala's bound hands with her finger, immediately the ropes dropped to the ground. The shivering boy stooped down immediately and picked up his weeping sister, hugging her close to him whilst Kaeshia removed her cloak and wrapped it around them.

"You will be sorry for your interference!" Lada threatened her then turned to Lord Arcos. "I demand that you get your men and arrest this woman. She has overstepped her authority!"

"Stand down Arcos," said Garik calmly. "We will not continue this until Darkstar arrives, it is only fair that our King is present."

"You fools! Do you think the King will listen to us when he has been so bewitched? He has already admitted that he is Catori's father, who was her mother? Where is she hiding?" There was an audible gasp from the crowd at Lada's revelation and Garik shifted uncomfortably. This was all taking a sinister turn and close by, high on a cliff above them, Draconan stood watching it all play out with a sinister sneer on his face.

The Queen knew she had everyone's attention now and she continued, "All the while I was left alone to carry our baby daughter, he was with another woman, an enemy of the Crystalites. He betrayed me and now is has lied to all of you!"

"Then let Darkstar answer for that!" demanded Garik. "This has nothing to do with these children!"

"It has everything to do with these children. Their mother lured him to the desert, who knows what magic she used on him. How do we know the truth? Are you asking us to believe the word of our bewitched King? How can we be sure that Tokala is not spying on us for Black Eagle?" Lada was winning them over; she was sure of it. "What sort of demons have we been harbouring and to what end? We must act now! These children, if that's what they are, do not belong amongst us. We must be rid of them to free our King from this madness. We must send them to their deaths on the rocks below."

"Madness! I have heard enough of your accusations here today. I will not stand for this a second longer, Darkstar will punish all who are involved here today and rightly so. Everybody go home! Lord Arcos, see that everyone returns to the city!" Garik had no patience left for this, the Queen was insane if she thought she could get away with this.

"You have no authority over me Garik, stand down Lord Arcos!" Lada's voice was shrill with madness and then before anyone knew what was happening, she ran towards Tokala and grabbed Catori attempting to pull the toddler from his arms.

Kaeshia jumped in front of the children and managed to fend off the Queen's attack, but Lada was furious and she lashed out at the Earth Wizard in a violent attack.

"Mother stop!" cried Atolin running down from the top of a ridge, he grabbed hold of his mother's cloak and attempted to pull her back. Kaeshia managed to remain with her arm around the children, but her face was bruised and scratched. " Mother, what are you doing? Tokala is my friend! He is not a demon!" wept Atolin as he held onto to her.

Lada spun around to face him, her insane eyes bearing down on him, "you have been bewitched also! Atolin, I will save you from these demons!"

"Mother your ill, please stop!" begged her son.

Garik turned to Lord Arcos, "Take the children and Kaeshia out of here, put a guard on them."

Kaeshia ushered Tokala who was still carrying his sister towards the Lord Warrior, keeping her eyes firmly on the Queen, in case she attacked again.

Lada was seething, her eyes wide and her teeth bared as she panted heavily, the people who had initially supported her, were in disarray as their Queen's madness was exposed for all to see. The jury, now embarrassed at their involvement, slunk off in different directions just wanting to get as far away as possible.

Lada turned on her son, "you little fool! Can't you see what's happening here?"

She grabbed hold of Atolin and shook him viciously, her fingers digging into his arms.

"LET HIM GO!" Darkstar's voice came booming over the plateau and everyone froze to the spot as they looked over to see their King looking positively murderous. The crowd parted as their King leapt down onto the plateau, followed by Ragnar. Lada screamed with fury when she saw him approach her, "You fools, stop him!" No one moved.

"Let my son go," growled Darkstar, his voice cold and threatening.

"You have no authority over me, you have betrayed all of us. I am the one in control here!" she hissed at him her arm tight around Atolin's throat.

"You are in control of nothing, even your own destiny is now mine to decide. Now let my son go!" demanded Darkstar his voice raised now.

"You care nothing for your son. All you are interested in now is Tokala and your child Catori. You deny even Kai your love," spat Lada venomously.

"Kai is not my daughter, as well you know," said Darkstar and the crowd gasped again.

"You see, he is bewitched. He thinks his own daughter is not his child. What did I tell you!" declared Lada.

"Kai is not Darkstar's daughter," said Ragnar.

"How do you know this?" asked Garik attempting to keep everyone calm. Atolin was going blue in the face, they had to get him away from Lada.

"Because she is mine. I have been a fool, but Darkstar in his wisdom agreed to bring Kai up as the princess to avoid scandal," replied Ragnar bowing his head with shame.

Egor slipped to the back of the crowd, no longer wishing to be associated with the Queen.

"Liar!" screamed Lada. "You are in league with Darkstar, you have also betrayed me! I will kill these children; I will free our people and then I will kill you!"

"You will kill no-one Lada. Your lies and games have come to an end. You will be taken to the ice tunnels underneath the city. The gates have not been opened for over thirty years, so you will have to wait while we pry open the entrance to your new home. But don't worry, I'll make sure you will have enough food and water to last you at least a few days, and if you're lucky you might even bump into Vulcan the Dragon, if he's still alive. If you do manage to survive then your pretty face will shrivel and grow old before its time, you'll wither and decay alone until death finally takes you, and no one will care." Darkstar was vicious with his words, he wanted to hurt her now as his hatred matched hers.

On the cliff top Draconan smiled, it was all coming together.

Atolin was confused by his father's vicious words, he had never heard him speak like that before and it frightened him. He was gasping for air and he tried to wriggle free from his mother's grip, but she was now standing as still as an ice statue, her arms still tight around his neck. Then, before he knew what was happening his mother suddenly moved with uncanny speed, dragging him to the edge of the precipice, dangling him dangerously over the edge. Atolin stared at her face in horror, it was unrecognisable, crazed beyond belief, she was snarling like an animal.

"Lada, he's your son, please stop!" cried Ragnar running towards her.

"One step closer and I will drop him," she warned.

"Darkstar, tell her you didn't mean it! Tell her you will help her!" yelled Ragner, but the King just stood there as if frozen in his hatred.

"Nothing he will say will save his son," spat the Queen and she held Atolin out further over the edge. The boy screamed and that seemed to awake Darkstar from his trance, and he threw himself towards them both with a roar.

But it was too late, Lada grinned hideously just before letting go of her son. Atolin fell backwards over the edge screaming "F F FAAAA THER!". His cry continued for what seemed like an age, and then there was silence.

Darkstar collapsed on the ground howling in despair, whilst Lada stood on the edge, triumph filling her crazed eyes, then before anyone else could move she turned and leapt after her son to her death on the rocks below. The only noise that filled the air was the sound of Darkstar's tortured howls. No one knew what to do or what to say and they turned weeping from the plateau heading back to their homes. Ragnar sat on the ice with his head buried in his knees and wept.

***

Wigholt watched the events on Mount Gloom unfold through his seeing Crystal. He had promised Solitaire he would not interfere, but even Solitaire would not have expected things to turn out this way. He prayed they would get to Atolin in time, but then watched in horror as the child was thrown from the edge.

Sending his bat chariot on ahead of him to the mountains, Wigholt waited until the plateau was deserted apart from Darkstar and Ragnar before using the power of the portal. He materialised on the cliff above the plateau and he made his way down to were Darkstar was still kneeling.

"I'm sorry Darkstar," he said sadly. "Your son was a brave child."

"I have nothing, nothing left now. First Sisika and now Atolin, everything I touch is destroyed," the King wept.

"Atolin was a boy any man would have been proud of, you must send out a search party for him, there is still hope I am sure. You must remember you are still a father, you have Catori and she will need her father now more than ever now," Wigholt reminded him gently.

"There is no hope for my son and as for Catori, she is better off without me. Wigholt you must take her and Tokala away from here before there are repercussions, I cannot protect them now, the city will blame them for Atolin's death" replied the King. He staggered to his feet, looking completely defeated as he turned towards Ragnar, his voice ragged and hollow, "take Kai and never come back to the city. I never want to lay eyes on her again, she reminds me too much of Lada."

Ragnar looked stricken and he glanced over at Wigholt, but when their eyes met the little blue Wizard simply nodded. Ragnar stumbled to his feet, he could say nothing, perhaps one day the King would change his mind, but right now he had to get his daughter out of the city. If the people were looking for someone to blame, they would turn towards him and Kai. Yet there was something still bothering Ragnar, in the back of his mind he could not help but question why Darkstar had not tried harder to save Atolin? Why had the King frozen when his son's life was hanging in the balance? He would never forget the look of betrayal in Atolin's eyes as Lada sent the boy to his death.

Wigholt waited until Ragnar had left then he turned back to Darkstar. "I will take Tokala and Catori back to the desert with me, but I will return in a few days. Please send a search party down to find Atolin, things are not always what they seem."

Darkstar did not respond, he collapsed back down onto his knees, staring out into the bleak, grey sky. Leaving him to grieve Wigholt stepped back through the Portal. His main concern now was to get Tokala and Catori to safety, he was sure the city would find it hard to forgive these children now. There would be blame cast in their direction as well as Ragnar's, and there was nothing he could do about it at present.

***

The loss of Atolin consumed Darkstar, guilt filled him with unbearable pain and torment, he could hardly breathe with the hurt that tore through him and his whole body shut down. He could no longer see a future and the past was too painful to remember, his life was over.

CHAPTER EIGHTEEN

The Crystal City was in chaos, people were arguing in the streets and hostility was spreading like an ugly virus right across the city.

Tokala and Catori were safe, Wigholt chariot had arrived in good time and had taken them back to the Wizards underground home miles away from the mountains. Tokala was quiet, he had hardly spoken a word since they had arrived and Wigholt tried his best to comfort him, but the boy had just seen his best friend thrown over the edge of a cliff. Atolin had been killed because he had tried to protect him and his sister. Tokala could not understand the hatred that had suddenly sprung around them, he had never experienced any hostility from the Crystalites before and his heart ached with the loss of Atolin. Wigholt brought him over a sweet herbal tea, "Drink this boy, it will help you sleep."

"I don't want to sleep, I want to go and find Atolin! " cried Tokala.

"I have told Darkstar to organize a search party, but we must be realistic, it's unlikely that Atolin will have survived the fall. If by some miracle he has, then we have to leave it to Darkstar, he should be searching for his son as we speak and you are not safe in the mountains any longer," replied Wigholt sadly.

"Why didn't Darkstar save him?" Tokala asked. "He was right there, but he didn't move until it was too late."

"I am not sure, perhaps he didn't believe Lada would kill her own son, but whatever the reason I am sure Darkstar will be torturing himself over the same question. Tokala you must try to rest now, Catori needs you, she doesn't understand what has happened and I don't think we will have heard the end of this."

***

Garik was pacing anxiously inside the meeting room, whilst a large crowd was gathering outside the palace looking for answers. Darkstar had still not returned from the plateau on Mount Gloom and the Justice Wizard was about to send Lord Arcos to go and find him. When the news of Atolin's death spread through the city, people were openly crying in the streets, but it did not take long for the tears to turn to anger. No one knew who was to blame, the Queen was mad but she had a point about Darkstar's infatuation with these strange children.

Ragnar and the Queen had betrayed Darkstar, so it was understandable that he had found love elsewhere. With Tokala and Catori safely out of their reach, the people turned their anger towards Ragnar and his daughter Kai, an angry mob formed and grew bigger as they made their way to the palace. If Darkstar did not return soon, Garik could not guarantee Ragnar's or Kai's safety.

The door of the meeting room opened and the Wizard Council turned to stare as Ragnar came in holding Kai in his arms with Lord Arcos at his side, "I've come to let you know I'm taking my daughter away from here to a place of safety."

"That may be wise Ragnar, but I don't see how you will get her past the crowd outside. Lord Arcos will have to escort you," replied Garik.

"Thank you, but I have Solitaire with us. I was the one who deceived Darkstar and the people, and I am prepared to take responsibility for that, but not at the expense of my daughter's safety. I must get her out the city first, Lord Arcos had agreed to create a diversion for us while we slip away."

"Where will you go? The people know where you live Ragnar, they will follow you to your home, you won't be safe there," said Kaeshia.

"Better to stay and explain yourself, there should be an investigation," butted in Egor.

"Yes, there should be! Perhaps you could tell us who told the Queen about Darkstar's child, sending her into an insane rage!" said Garik rounding on Egor with his eyes ablaze. Egor shook his head quickly then stepped back away from Garik's accusing stare.

"I will take my leave now, please tell Darkstar I'm sorry, I never meant it to end this way," said Ragnar. He looked at Kai who was staring at him with a puzzled expression and she reached up and brushed away a tear that escaped from his eye. Ragnar turned and left the meeting room followed by Lord Arcos, Solitaire was standing just outside the room in his human form waiting for them.

One of the palace maids came running from the nursery crying, "Please don't let anything happen to her?" she sobbed when she saw Ragnar.

"She'll be safe," promised the Animal Wizard wrapping Kai in a blanket, she was very quiet as if she understood what was going on. She clung onto Ragnar's neck while Lord Arcos picked up a small bundle that looked very similar to a small child wrapped in a blanket.

"Good luck old friend," said Arcos and watched as Ragnar stepped into the portal that Solitaire had created, carrying Kai along with.

The Lord Warrior had his men surround him as if they were protecting something and then they marched out in formation onto the palace forecourt where the mountain horses were already saddled and waiting for them. As they rode out of the palace the angry crowd tried to stand in their way, but Lord Arcos ordered the men forward and they split the crowd so they could ride through. A rock was flung after them and the crowd started to shout abuse hurling more rocks and stones. Lord Arcos kicked his horse into a gallop and he and his men sped through the streets.

"He's taking her to Ragnar!" someone cried. "Let's go the mountain!"

The crowd surged forward, marching towards the pathway that led to Mount Solomite and Ragnar's home. Draconan watched on revelling in the anger and confusion he had created. His dark menacing presence was feeding their anger, filling them with a blood lust as their minds cried out for vengeance. Yet even with his interference, there were many more who slipped back into their houses, suddenly afraid at how the anger in the city had escalated and not wanting to be part of it.

Solitaire had a firm grip on Ragnar as they exited the portal on the southern side of the city away from the crowd that followed Lord Arcos and his men. Ragnar was dazed from being in the portal blue light and took a minute to come back to his senses.

"Are you able to move?" Solitaire asked him after a short while. He was sitting on a rock with Kai on his knee playing with the feathers in his hair.

"Yes, I think so, I don't know what happened," replied Ragnar groggily.

"It's the blue light in the tunnel, its intoxicating to those who are not used to it, your head will clear soon, but we should really be on our way."

Ragnar got to his feet taking Kai from Solitaire and then started to descend down towards the lower slopes. They had only travelled for a short while when Solitaire suddenly announced that he had to leave them. "You should be safe for now but I must report back to Sirena. She will know what to do and where to take Kai."

Once Solitaire had gone it was only a short time later when they rounded a bend and stumbled upon a young goatherd from the city. He was on his way back with a number of mountain goats, and he recognised Ragnar immediately. The boy had been out with his goats for a few days and had not heard what had happened, so he greeted Ragnar like an old friend, offering Kai some goats milk. Ragnar declined the offer explaining that they had to keep moving so as not to be caught out by nightfall. The goatherd looked strangely at Kai, trying to figure out who the child was, feeling sure he had seen her before. Ragnar made no explanation, instead making a hasty departure leaving the young goatherd puzzled. The Animal Wizard cursed himself for being stupid enough to be seen and guessed that now it would not be long until the crowds came after them.

***

Darkstar remained kneeling at the edge of the plateau, he had been there for hours and the temperature had dropped way below freezing. All he felt was pain, his heart had been ripped into pieces and he no longer cared about his city or his people. He had let them down, there was no going back. Part of him wanted to follow Atolin over the cliff, but the only thing that stopped him from doing so was that Lada had made that choice before him. He wanted to tear her apart with his own hands, but she had robbed him of that pleasure, his hatred for her consumed him.

As he stared out over the mountains, he felt a presence hovering nearby that filled him with dread. He tried to turn his head, but found he could not move and he shuddered violently as an icy hand placed itself upon his shoulder.

"I feel your anger the hatred burns deep within you. Let me help you," hissed Draconan into Darkstar's ear. Still the Crystalite King could not turn to see who was speaking to him, nor could he answer, what was wrong with his body?

"I can take you from here, you can be with Atolin again and get the vengeance you are seeking. All you have to do is invite me into your world." The Dark Lord hovered, a black faceless entity looking for a way to finally step through the ghostly void into Satiren.

"*Atolin is dead. How can this be?*" Darkstar thought.

"He doesn't have to be dead; I can bring him back for you. All you have to do is swear allegiance to me and invite me in." Draconan was engulfing Darkstar with his essence and the Crystalite King felt as if he was being smothered.

"NO! get away from me demon!" Darkstar cried out in his mind. *"Why can't I move? What have you done to me?"*

Draconan's insinuous laughter filled his ears, "I have done nothing, you did this to yourself, let me in and you can be free."

"Never." Even in his grief, Darkstar could sense the evil surrounding him. He was not thinking clearly, he had to get free and return to the city. Wigholt was right, he should be sending a search party out for Atolin, how had he allowed this anger to overwhelm him in such a way?

It was dark on Mount Gloom now and as Darkstar stared straight out into the night sky he saw a light coming towards him. The light brought him hope for as soon as he saw it, he felt Draconan's evil presence trickle away. The Dark Lord left him alone at last.

The light drew closer and took shape in front of him. Sisika was standing there swathed in light, a shining bow slung over her shoulder and a quiver of silver arrows at her side. She reached out to him and the light fell on him, she was looking at him with so much love and compassion, he wanted to weep.

"My love, I am sorry this has happened to you," she said and kissed him gently on his cheek.

Darkstar could still not move, he couldn't understand what spell had trapped him like this.

"It is no spell," said Sisika sadly answering his thoughts. "You are no longer in the world of the living, your body has died and it is time for you to pass over. Let yourself go Darkstar and come to me."

"I'm dead?... That is why I cannot move?... I'm dead!" his mind cried out.

"Your body is dead, but your spirit is alive. Come to me Darkstar, I will help you," said Sisika holding her hand out towards him.

"How?" he thought.

"Just let go, release you anger and take a step towards me," she said, her beautiful eyes blazing into his frozen dead ones.

Darkstar became aware of his body, it was as Sisika said, a frozen dead shell trapping him within it. Her light was burning into his soul and suddenly he could see everything before him, the past, the present and the future were all one. His time was done and it was time for him to leave this world. He felt lighter, and he reached out with his mind managing to step out of his dead body. He was whole again, the light engulfed him as it did Sisika and she fell into his embrace. After a time, she took his hand and led him gently away, floating upwards into the night sky towards the heavens.

***

Ragnar could hear the sound of hooves from above him, they were coming after them, the goatherd had spread the news quicker than the Animal Wizard thought. His heart was thumping now, where was Solitaire?

He was getting tired carrying the child and Ragnar knew he should stop and rest, but he dared not lest they caught up with them. He had to get Kai to safety.

"Over here!" Ragnar heard Solitaire call from just above him on a ledge.

"Where have you been? They are almost upon us!" said Ragnar.

"I am here now, we had to decide where to hide Kai. It took time, but Sirena has found her a new home away from Satiren," said Solitaire.

"What do you mean away from Satiren? She is my daughter I'm not going to send her off somewhere unknown!" cried Ragnar.

"What choice do you have? You cannot live with a small child as an outlaw? She would constantly be in danger, have no friends, no proper home. Is that what you want for her? I will be with her and she will be safe and able to grow up in peace. You cannot deny her that," argued Solitaire.

There was a shout from just above them and Ragnar knew he was running out of time.

"You have to go with Solitaire," he said to Kai who was clinging onto his neck.

"No, I want to stay with you!" she cried as he prized her fingers from him.

"I know, but I will be watching over you and someday, Solitaire will bring you back to me," said Ragnar, his eyes wet with tears. "You will bring her back?"

"I promise I will keep the two of you in touch. Now Kai we must go, or Ragnar will be in terrible danger." Solitaire took her from Ragnar's arms and a portal opened immediately behind him, "Good luck old friend. You must run now and stay hidden, Darkstar will not be coming back to the city." Then Solitaire walked into the light carrying Kai in his arms and the portal closed behind them.

Ragnar stood shocked, what did Solitaire mean? What had happened to Darkstar? An arrow struck him in his shoulder knocking him backwards. He staggered to his feet and tried to run but another arrow struck him in the chest. The mob descended on him, pulling him roughly to his feet with blind fury in their eyes.

******

No one ever spoke about what happened to Ragnar, though the snow eagles watched it all. When the Crystalites arrived back in the city, they were no longer the same angry mob that had left. They looked tired and subdued, many were ashamed, others were shocked and horrified. They returned to their homes, and no matter how many of them Lord Arcos questioned, none gave any clues to what had happened to Ragnar, nor where his body was. However, they did all confirm that Kai was not with the Wizard, none of them had seen her. Lord Arcos could only guess that Solitaire had her and he prayed that she was safe. He should never have let them try to escape and he blamed himself for Ragnar's death.

The snow eagles had waited until all was quiet, then they flew in and retrieved their friend's broken body. They flew Ragnar to the top of Mount Solomite and laid him to rest, covering him with a mound of rocks, snow and ice.

***

The following day Lord Arcos found Darkstar's body on the plateau of Mount Gloom. He had frozen to death in his grief, and the Crystalites were left without a ruler. They all looked to Garik, but the old Sorceror knew he could not run the city. He would have to call a meeting once the mourning for their King was over. The Crystal City was in turmoil.

***

Wigolt heard the news about Ragnar and Darkstar and gently broke it to Tokala and Catori. The children yet again endured another painful loss and they wept together as the little Wizard wondered how many more deaths there would be, before peace resumed on the mountains. He told them that Solitaire had taken Kai away for her own safety, and they both seemed to accept that.

Wigholt did the best he could to cheer up the children, but it would take time to heal and he suspected they wouldn't have that much time left together. Things were changing on Satiren, and he was sure there was more trouble in the horizon.

CHAPTER NINETEEN

He lay there winded and was somehow aware in the back of his mind that his leg was broken, but he was too shocked to register the pain. As he had plummeted to what would certainly be his death, Ragnar's giant snow eagles had been ready, they could not hold his entire falling weight, but they hung onto him with their talons, slowing his fall and guiding him to a safe, flat surface. Even so, he hit the ground hard, his leg twisting and snapping underneath him.

Atolin pulled himself painfully up onto his elbows and dared to look down at his leg. Its bone had snapped and was protruding through his skin lying at an awkward angle. Atolin lay his head back down feeling defeated and his thoughts turned to his father, why had Darkstar not tried to save him before it was too late? He could remember the coldness in his father's eyes before he was thrown off the edge and he wondered what had happened to his mother? He lay there, putting the agony of his broken leg to the back of his mind and prayed that it would not take them long to find him.

The boy lay there for what seemed an age, before he knew he would have to move or risk freezing to death. Surely the eagles would tell Ragnar where he was, but he had no idea how long it would take them. He had never travelled to this part of the mountains before, it could take them a couple of days to get down there.

There was a small stream being fed by the many small waterfalls splashing down the mountain, so he took a deep breath and started to drag himself painfully along the ground towards it. Perhaps if he could soak his leg in the ice-water the swelling would go down and he could try to make a splint from the branches of the trees that were struggling to grow next to the stream.

He made slow progress, every movement sending shooting pains up into his body but finally, he managed to haul his broken leg into the cold running water, then he lay back as the water cooled the burning pain of his injury and he stared up towards the top of the mountain. Atolin had never felt so alone in his whole life, and he began to feel afraid. "*What if they didn't come?*"

When his leg was numb with the cold, Atolin dragged himself over to one of the small trees at the water's edge. He pulled out his short knife that he always carried on his belt and he reached towards one of the branches. He eventually cut down four long branches tying them together with slip knots using a cord he had in his cloak. He placed them around his leg and pulled the cord tight screaming with pain, but his leg straightened and using his belt he was able to strap it tightly. The effort and pain had left him exhausted, but now his main worry was the cold, there was no immediate shelter anywhere around, so he would have to make a fire with what wood he could find. There were enough trees, but the wood was alive and damp, it would take a long time to light, if at all.

It was almost nightfall before Atolin had managed to collect a sufficient amount of the damp wood. At least it would take a long time to burn, providing heat for longer if he ever got it lit. Using his flint, he set to work trying to catch some brush grass alight, but every time he did it burnt out too quickly for the wood to catch. An hour later, he knew it was useless, he would never get a fire going with the tools he had. He pulled his cloak around him and shivered as nightfall arrived, praying that someone would come soon.

"Allow me to help you," came a sinuous voice out of the darkness making Atolin jump with fright. Suddenly his fire sprung to life, burning with such an intensity that the heat penetrated him immediately. He looked around, but could see no one.

"Who are you?" Atolin called out.

"You will come to see me as a friend, for now just accept my gift," replied the unpleasant voice and Atolin shivered.

The fire continued to burn throughout the night without him having to add anymore wood to it, and eventually he managed to drift off to sleep. He was awoken by the pain in his leg and after a few minutes of registering where he was, he groggily pulled himself up to see that daylight had arrived. There was still no sign of a search party, so Atolin decided he would try to find some food. Ragnar had taught him enough survival skills in the mountains that he could fend for himself, though his broken leg would hamper his efforts. The fire had almost burned out, so Atolin piled on some more of the branches he had collected the evening before and waited until it crackled back to life.

Using one of the larger sticks to help him, Atolin got to his feet and painfully hobbled to the stream before collapsing down at its edge. He reached down to take a drink and noticed small fat Turtle fish swimming through the water. They were about the size of the palm of his hand, he and Tokala had spent hours catching these funny little perfectly round fish that lived in all the mountain streams. They competed with each other to see who could catch the most before they let them go again. This time Atolin was looking at a meal in front of him, and so he set to work. Half an hour later he had six of the fat fish, gutted and roasting on a stick over the fire. They sizzled as the fat dripped down into the flames and Atolin wolfed the delicious oily fish down in minutes.

After he had eaten all six, he set to work collecting and cutting down as much wood as he could for the fire. He could not afford to let it burn out, he did not know if his strange visitor would be back and he could not take chances. Surely his father would find him today, he just had to sit tight and wait.

Three days later Atolin watched his fire dwindle, there was no more wood for him to collect, he had stripped all the trees of their branches and now he would have to find some shelter, he could not afford to wait any longer. He had become more accustom to the pain in his leg now, and could walk a little further, so gritting his teeth he set out through the rocky paths, staying next to the stream as it was his only source of food and water.

He made slow progress and eventually a few hours later Atolin came across a small cave, not completely sheltered from the outside, but it would do, he could make it more comfortable. There was a new supply of wood now, and this time the kindling at the back of the cave was dry enough to burn easily and he soon had a fire going. That night it started to snow and Atolin was thankful for his shelter but decided he would have to make a screen of some sorts to stop the wind blowing in.

The next morning after catching more turtle fish for breakfast, he made some snares, hoping to trap some mountain Gripers. They were small furry creatures, about the same size as a mountain hare, but they had sharp claws and even sharper teeth and were deceptively fierce. However, they made good meals and Atolin had heard them scurrying around during the night. He kept himself busy, trying not to dwell on the reason that no help had come for him yet.

Once he had laid his snares, he spent the rest of the day weaving together grasses and twigs to create a screen for the front of the cave. He put it up just before darkness fell and that night he slept well, cosy inside the cave. The next morning, he had some luck, he had managed to trap a Griper, though it nearly took his hand off when he tried to grab hold of it. Killing it with his knife Atolin finally had a substantial breakfast of fresh, fatty meat and he ate until his shrunken belly was full.

Another two days passed and Atolin decided to try to explore further out, and leave messages for whoever came looking for him. Each day he hobbled for as far as he could go, but still there was no sign that anyone had been searching for him. He began to wonder if what his mother had said was true, his father had cared for Tokala more than him. Was that why no one was searching for him? He could still see his father's frozen expression as Lada had dangled him over the edge of the plateau, and Atolin's young heart ached with hurt and betrayal.

As the time went on, still no one came and Atolin's hurt began to turn slowly to anger. He started to remember all the times Darkstar had spent with Catori in the nursery, he hardly ever paid any attention to Kai. Then he remembered what his mother had said, that Catori was Darkstar's daughter, so that would make her his sister. Why had his father lied to him? Tokala had known, he must have, so even his best friend had kept that secret from him. And now they had left him down here to die alone, perhaps that's what his father had wanted, so he could have Tokala for his son.

The pain in Atolin's leg was subsiding, he had either got used to it or it was getting better, he wasn't sure, and it looked a mess. He could still see the bone through his skin but he was able to walk a lot further than he had before, though he had no idea where he was. He daren't leave his shelter to try to get back to the city as he didn't know which direction to take and he probably wouldn't make it.

On one morning he followed the stream a little way to see where it led, when he saw something lying on some rocks a little way up the slope. He managed to pull himself up to take a look but what he saw made him recoil in shock. It was his mother's dead, broken body, already feasted on by the Gripers and the crows. Atolin stared to sob inconsolably, then threw up his breakfast. Had Darkstar pushed her off the cliff as a punishment? She was ill, his father's treatment of her had made her insane, it wasn't her fault. Atolin had never been close to his mother, but she had never been unkind to him and he loved her for what she was. Finding the strength, he pulled what was left of her body off the crumbling rock ledge and set it next to the stream. He began collecting rocks and stones, and spent the rest of the day burying his mother's body. With each stone he laid, his anger grew, igniting a deep hatred for his father. By the time he laid the last stone, he swore that he would make his father and Tokala pay for their betrayal.

That night he listened to his stomach rumble as he lay inside his shelter, he had gone to bed hungry. Burying his mother had taken most of the day and he had no time to check his snares and it was too dark to catch turtle fish. Suddenly the fire started to burn wildly, lighting up the whole cave and Atolin could see a dark figure standing just outside the entrance. Atolin struggled up to see who it was.

"Just stay where you are child," said a hideous whispering voice he recognised from his first night alone here. "I am nothing more than a spirit and I cannot cross over to this world yet, but I can help you."

"Who are you?" Atolin was afraid, the dark shape did not move but he could sense a dark malevolence all around him.

"Names are not important, but allow me to help you. You are in great pain and you have been betrayed by those you loved the most. Let me ease that pain."

"Can you heal my leg?" Atolin asked.

"Not yet, but if you help me to get stronger, I will be able to."

"How do I do that?" Atolin shifted uncomfortably, he didn't like this dark creature, his skin was beginning to crawl with its presence so close to him.

"Swear allegiance to me, then everything you wish for will be yours," said the dark shapeless form.

"But I don't even know who you are?" cried Atolin.

"You will soon enough. For now, I have left you a gift. I must leave, but I will return when you need me most." The shape flickered as the fire began to die down, then it vanished and Atolin was left alone. The evil voice had been unsettling, but after all this time alone it was a relief to have some sort of company. He slipped outside his shelter and stood on something hard. He bent down and picked it up, and saw it was a wooden flute, similar to the one he played at home. There was also the fresh carcass of a mountain hare lying next to the shelter. Atolin gratefully started skinning the hare, he would feast well tonight. After eating he blew on his flute and the musical notes echoed around the cliffs. He began to feel better than he had done in days, not just from the music, but from the hope that his dark visitor had given him. He knew now that somehow, he would be saved.

Draconan watched the boy struggle with fascination, he had felt Atolin's anger grow each day, but today, when the boy had found the body of his mother, his anger had turned into something else. Something Draconan could feed on, something that tantalized his essence and stirred the darkness within him. Atolin would be his soon enough and then he would have a foothold in the mountains. Black Eagle was already his servant in Burning Towers and once he had a foothold in the mountains the White Witch would not be able to stop him descending on Satiren, then this world would be his for the taking.

CHAPTER TWENTY

Late in the evening Wigholt was sitting on the boulder that marked the entrance to his underground cavern gazing up at the stars. He was smoking his long pipe, puffing perfect circles of white rings watching them dissipate into the night air as he tried to fathom what his next move should be. Tokala and Catori were both asleep, they were already feeling the confinement of being cooped up underground even after a few days, but Wigholt could not risk to let them leave, even for a few minutes. If any of the Mavaho hunters who often rode this way saw them, then he would have Chief Black Eagle to deal with.

Wigholt could sense the darkness growing stronger on Satiren and he guessed there was a great evil steering some of the events that had transpired. It was ten days since they had found Darkstar's body, and things in the Crystal City were in turmoil. The Wizard Council could not agree on how to move forward, or who should replace their King, a meeting was being held at the palace in two days. Garik had sent a message out to Wigholt, asking if the little Wizard would attend, but keep himself hidden during the proceedings. The Justice Wizard wanted to talk to Wigholt about the children, and Wigholt realised that Garik probably thought he had Kai alongside the other two.

He knew his reception in the city would be hostile, so he decided to use a spell that would render him invisible to those who were not actively looking for him. Only Garik would know he was there. It meant he would have to leave the following night if his chariot was to get him there under the cover of darkness, then he could slip into the city.

Late the next evening he left the children making Tokala promise that they would not leave the cavern. Tokala was desperate to know if they had found Atolin yet, he wanted Wigholt to ask if they would let him help with the search. Wigholt assured him that they would be out looking for him already, but it was safer if Tokala and his sister remain hidden just now. Having convinced Tokala to remain where he was, Wigholt left them in his cavern wondering what had actually happened with the search for Atolin. He had not had any news, had they just assumed the boy was dead? Surely Lord Arcos had taken a search party out by now to retrieve Atolin's body if nothing else?

The next day as Wigholt entered the city, he could feel the tension in the air. People were avoiding each other, keeping their eyes to the ground as they went about their business. There was bickering and unpleasantness everywhere he went, he wondered how these peaceful people had turned so aggressive towards one another in such a short space of time? He finally reached the Palace entering the meeting hall completely unnoticed by anyone. It was already beginning to fill up, he could see Lord Arcos standing next to Garik, they both looked sombre as they spoke to each other quietly. Wigholt had expected to see Zebulon, but the ancient Overlord was noticeably missing and he wondered why? Egor was holding court with about six others at the rear of the hall, however his antagonistic whiney voice was drifting across the room.

Garik was leading the meeting and he stood up to call everyone to order. "We are here to discuss a number of issues, not least of all who will stand in for Darkstar. This has been a turbulent time for us and it will depend on this meeting whether we can resolve these issues and bring harmony back to our people."

Egor got to his feet and coughed. "I think you are avoiding the question that is on all our lips. It seems obvious to me that Wigholt has to take responsibility for what happened. He brought the Mavaho children to us, and he has now taken them away. Was this some sort of plan to destabilise us? We should be looking out for a Mavaho invasion, I and many others think that Lord Arcos should have his soldiers guarding the city."

"There is no proof Wigholt meant any harm to our people. He has fought for the rights of the Crystalites many times in the past, he strives only for peace on Satiren. You are too ready to cast blame where it does not belong," said Zodiac from his chair. "His dark intense eyes were fixed on Egor and the little man squirmed under his gaze.

"I'm sorry but I have to agree with Egor," said Pinto getting to her feet. She and her twin sister, Piro, were young, strange elemental Wizards, who had only just been promoted to attend the Wizard Council. "How do we know what the Mavaho's have planned for us. If Tokala and Wigholt were innocent, then why have they disappeared at the first sign of trouble?"

"I think the answer to that is obvious," said Kaeshia interrupting. "Look what happened to poor Ragnar and Princess Kai. Our people have lost control and have a lot to answer for. We should have held proper proceedings after Mount Gloom, but everyone decided to takes matters into their own hands. Now we are left with a population that feel ashamed, angry and betrayed. I do not blame Wigholt for removing the children away from here. It is not safe for them without Darkstar here to protect them."

"But that is the point," interrupted Egor. "Our King was bewitched by these children, he put them before his own children, we could all see that. We should have listened to the Queen she recognised what was happening."

"Are you trying to imply that Darkstar was a traitor? Be very careful Egor," warned Lord Arcos the threat in his tone unmistakable.

"I am just saying that Darkstar did not know what he was doing. He was showing Tokala all our secrets, the boy could lead a Mavaho army to us any day now," argued Egor knowing he had the backing of his friends.

"That is nonsense!" roared Garik angrily. "Tread very carefully Egor, Lada's actions were that of pure madness, she murdered her own son because of her hatred towards Darkstar and I am still not convinced that you were not to blame with all your mutterings."

"He drove her to it," responded Egor. "He treated her appallingly."

"You have no proof of that. Only the ravings of a self-centred and power-hungry woman. Are you saying she had a right to murder Atolin?" Garik's eyes were blazing with fury.

"No, of course not……I just mean't……"Egor sat back down with everyone's eyes on him. He realised he had gone too far and it had sounded like he condoned what Lada did. Garik had led him into a trap, he sat scowling in silence as the meeting continued.

The doors to the meeting room flew open and Zebulon entered, his power radiating around the room. Wigholt felt relief wash over him and he watched on curiously, the Overlord was saturated with magical essence and Wigholt wondered what he had been up to.

Zebulon turned his gaze towards Egor and the other younger Wizards that surrounded Wizard of Education. "I have been forced to listen to your ravings once again Egor. You are striving for power you ill deserve, there are many older and wiser Wizards who are in this room that have earned the respect they ae entitled to. You have earned nothing Egor, you spend your miserable life sidling up to those you assume would give you a more prominent status here in the palace. You are no longer entitled to your place here amongst the Wizard Council, from now on you are banished from the palace. Leave now, but be warned, if I hear any more of your poisonous words around the city, I will have your tongue removed from your head."

The room turned deathly silent as Egor's hauled himself to his feet with his face burning red. He looked for a moment as if he would argue and he turned to get support from his friends, but they had their heads bowed, avoiding eye contact with him.

"Egor, Zebulon has told you leave, pray do so for I no longer wish to look upon your face," said Garik breaking the silence.

Egor pulled his cloak angrily around himself then made for the door glaring menacingly at Garik as he passed, he didn't look back but slammed the door shut behind him. No one moved for a few seconds and the younger Wizards sat back quietly in their chairs looking sheepish.

"There is no room in the Crystal City for the likes of him, if anyone else feels the same way, then leave now," said Garik, but no one moved.

Zebulon turned towards Wigholt, "Hallo old friend, I suggest you take your cloaking spell off, we have lot to discuss."

Wigholt bowed his head slightly then stepped up next to Garik and removed his spell, a surprised buzz filled the room then Wigholt spoke. "I was invited to attend by Garik, I will help in any way I can."

"Well I'm glad you're here Wigholt, now we can really try to get to the bottom of things," said Kaeshia.

"I think if any blame is to be had, then perhaps it should be directed at me," said Zebulon. "It was I that gave Darkstar the ability to move at speed across the Silversands at night. I found his curiosity endearing and did not see any harm in helping him fulfil his curiousity. However, I did not realise he'd met Tokala's mother and fallen in love until it was too late, perhaps you should continue from here Wigholt."

Wigholt took up the story, "They met when Tokala had run away from his father and got injured in the process. His father is Chief Black Eagle of the Mavahos, and they live in a great walled city in the Silversands desert that they have named Burning Towers. Darkstar often spied on them in his nightly adventures, and came to learn of Black Eagles cruelty to his people. Tokala's mother, Sisika was forced to become Black Eagles wife, but she hated him and he was exceptionally brutal to her. Sisika escaped to Darkstar most evenings and they found comfort in each other's arms. I recognised the danger it may bring so, one night I came to warn them that they were being foolish and they agreed to part for the sake of their people. Neither Darkstar nor I knew at the time that Sisika was pregnant with Darkstar's child. When she could hide it no longer from Chief Black Eagle, he lost control knowing he was not the father and he cruelly punished Sisika, then ordered to have her killed. Tokala, although just a small boy managed to save his mother with some help from their friends. I found them in the desert having escaped the city, but by then Sisika was already too ill for me to save. She gave birth to Catori and died soon after. I had to let Darkstar know he was the child's father and he wanted the children brought to the Crystal City where it was safe. There was no conspiracy with the Mavahos, just a father trying to help his child."

When Wigholt finished the room became noisy as everyone seemed to be in agreement that Wigholt was not responsible, then Zebulon stepped forward once again.

"That is not the only news I have for you. I have come from Odysseus himself, he is unhappy with events here on Satiren. The Dark Lord Draconan has been hovering around this world making contact with those he can corrupt, hoping to claim Satiren as his own. He has already corrupted Chief Black Eagle bringing despair and misery down upon the Mavahos. With all this unrest in the mountains the other Overlords have sensed Draconan's presence, if he is allowed to manifest onto Satiren they will have to destroy it or risk their own worlds getting infected with his evil."

"How can we stop this from happening?" interrupted Garik. "We can try to supress the rumours that are running throughout the city, but there are always those, like Egor, who thrive in causing trouble."

"The White Witch wants Tokala to return to Burning Towers, she believes that once he takes over as chief, he will bring peace back to the Silversands. In doing so, he would establish a firm friendship between the Mavahos and the Crystalites making a positive force that would eject Draconan from this world."

"While Chief Black Eagle is in power this will not be possible," said Wigholt. He is an evil man, and will kill Tokala as soon as he sees him. I will not allow the boy to go back to Burning Towers."

"I was not suggesting he should, certainly not at first," replied Zebulon. "But if an envoy of Crystalites visited Burning Towers and suggested a trade between them and the mountains, it would be a start of communication. I don't believe that Chief Black Eagle would harm a delegation from the mountains, he is too greedy for power and his curiosity about the Crystalites in the mountains will lead him to try to invade the Crystal City. He will attempt to establish a friendship with the Crystalites, while he puts a plan into place. Once he leaves with his army for the mountains, Lord Arcos and the Crystalites will be waiting to defeat him and put Tokala back in Burning Towers as Chief."

"I'm not so sure," remarked Wigholt. "There are very little things that Chief Black Eagle cares about, except ultimate power to rule as he sees fit. I think a delegation would be riding into danger, he has no regard for human life, it means nothing to him and once he learns of the Crystal City he will simply torture his visitors to get its location."

"I will go," said Lord Arcos, "I'll take a few of my best soldiers with me and we'll find a way to escape if things turn sour."

"I'm not sure arriving at Burning Towers looking like the great warrior you are will set their minds at ease. You need to be more of a diplomat, perhaps create a disguise so you do not look threatening," suggested Zodiac to the nods and approvals of the rest of the room.

Wigholt shook his head, he was still not convinced but the rest of the council seemed to be swept up with the idea, and it looked like it was going ahead. He understood why Zebulon was so concerned. No one on Satiren except for Wigholt knew that Zebulon had once been the Overlord to the planet Earth. He watched Earth fall into darkness as Draconan took hold unable to save it from its fate. Zebulon helped Sirena bring the people of Earth through the portals to Satiren, and had remained here ever since. When the Mavaho's killed the Ne'shuwa , Zebulon felt responsible and promised himself he would do everything in his power to stop it following in the footsteps of Earth. Yet Wigholt was filled with a sense of dread, Chief Black Eagle was not a reasonable man, they had no idea what they were walking into.

The meeting continued until it was finally agreed that Garik would go to Burning Towers, along with Lord Arcos and his best soldiers. They would travel under the guise of tradesmen selling mountain jewellery and furs, then establish contact to try to get an idea of how the Mavaho people felt about Tokala. Perhaps they would find some support for the boy and could build on that. It was decided they would set off the next day and the council meeting was adjourned until their return.

Soon there were only Garik, Wigholt, Zodiac, Kaeshia, Lord Arcos and Zebulon left in the room. "I am very worried about this Garik, we could be putting the Crystalites in terrible danger. Chief Black Eagle will try to squeeze information from you, especially if he learns about Tokala. He is not a stupid man and I fear he will guess that his son has been hiding out here in the mountains. You must be alert at all times," said Wigholt.

"Garik is aware of the danger and I will make sure he carries enough magic to protect them all if things turn ugly," sighed Zebulon, he was not going to allow them to back out now.

"Very well, I just wish there was another way, I must return to the children now but I will be watching your progress and pray that you'll be safe my friends," replied Wigholt.

"You said the children? Do you have Kai with you?" asked Kaeshia hopefully.

"No, I don't have Kai, but rest assured she is safe. Solitaire took her to a place of safety before Ragnar was attacked, only he and the White Witch know where she is now. You needn't worry about her for now."

"I just miss her that's all," whispered Kaeshia sadly.

CHAPTER TWENTY-ONE

"Why did you let them go? My father will kill them, we must stop them!" cried Tokala angrily.

"I am as worried as you are, but I cannot interfere, I've done too much already. The Crystal City is divided, many rumours are spreading that you and your sister were sent by the Mavaho's to spy on them. The Wizard Council believe that in sending Garik, he will be able to find out what Black Eagle is up to. Lord Arcos is accompanying them, he'll protect them." Wigholt tried to offer up some sort of explanation but in truth he also felt that the decision was a mistake. He looked over at the boy and saw tears of frustration forming. "Just hold on Tokala, we'll know soon enough and perhaps things have changed at Burning Towers. It's been years since you were there."

"Unless my father is dead, nothing will have changed," replied Tokala stubbornly then walked off to play with Catori. The boy was right and Wigholt knew it, they were walking into terrible danger, he should have tried harder to stop them.

***

They had ridden for two nights across the Silversands, sleeping during the daylight hours under canopies to protect themselves from the fierce sun. Garik was finding the journey harder than he imagined he would, his old bones were aching and he hated the thought of getting back on his horse each evening. He had been wise enough to bring healing tonics with him, they helped, but only just.

Lord Arcos had decided to bring four of his best soldiers with him, it was the most he could bring without it looking threatening. Lisle and Anya were two of his best bow women and they had dressed in female Crystalite clothing instead of their usual uniforms. He had also brought Cnut and Tanj with them, they were strong, excellent with their swords and well trained in combat. They had all been briefed about the dangers in Burning Towers and told not to mention Tokala. Even so, the soldiers were excited about going on such a dangerous mission, the Crystalite army trained hard, but had never been in any sort of direct altercation with an enemy. None of them had ever killed another man in fact, this was the closest they had come to a possible conflict.

As morning approached on the start of the third day, they finally saw the flaming torches lighting up the city of Burning towers and so they continued on through the daylight towards the city. It was an impressive sight standing alone in the middle of the red desert, with its one huge tower penetrating the skyline.

Some of the Mavaho's were leaving the city gates to go and work in the fields when they saw the unusual group of riders approaching. They stared in surprise at the strange pale-faced people on horses and shouted out a warning to the warriors at the gates. The Crystalites kept their faces passive and friendly as they approached the gates where already a large group of Mavaho's had started to form all vying to get a look at the pale strangers.

"Good day Mavaho's of the desert, we've been travelling a long way and are looking to find somewhere we could rest," said Garik trying to sound light hearted.

"You would need to get permission from our chief," said one of the bare-chested warriors looking at them warily.

"Very well, we will wait," said Lord Arcos and he winked at a small child who was staring up at him open mouthed from behind his mother's legs. The child grinned and Anja pulled out many brightly coloured strings of crystal beads from her saddle bay and threw one over to the child. "We have many gifts from the mountains," she said with a cheery smile on her face.

The child picked up the string of beads and before long more children were stepping forward to collect gifts for themselves. Everyone was smiling and Lord Arcos began to relax a little at the warm welcome they seemed to be getting.

Then suddenly there was the sound of many horse's hooves heading in their direction and the crowd dispersed, many running off back into their cabanas to hide. Lord Arcos and Cnut instinctively put their hands to their swords that were hidden under their cloaks.

About twelve Mavaho warriors came riding at speed up the street towards them, led by a magnificent black stallion that was mounted by a huge muscular man wearing a spectacular feather headdress. The man had one eye covered with a black patch and Garik guessed correctly that this was Chief Black Eagle. The Chief pulled his horse up to a skidding halt and eyed the Crystalites suspiciously.

"I can tell from your fine stature that you must be the Chief. I would like us to introduce ourselves, we are traders from the mountains, looking to find some hospitality and perhaps some trade with the Mavaho's of the Silversands." Garik spoke a little uneasily as the Chief regarded him with coldly.

"I am Black Eagle, Chief of the Mavahos," he said riding in closer to look at Garik and the others. Up close Garik could see a vicious scar that ran down the Chiefs face from his covered eye, while his other golden eye was narrowed in distrust as he surveyed them. Wigholt had been right, this man wreaked of evil and Garik shifted uncomfortably, the tension was mounting and he was not sure how to proceed.

Then, in an instant Black Eagles demeanour changed and his face transformed into a warm, friendly smile, "please forgive me, I was taken aback by your strange appearance, we have never come across mountain people before, please let us welcome you."

The other Mavaho's started to shift around and smile nervously, Garik felt a sense of relief wash over him.

"You can come to the castle, there will be rooms ready for you. I'll have baths and food arranged for you, and your horses will be cared for I our stables, then we can talk, you must be exhausted after your long journey," said the Chief.

Garik was a little overwhelmed by Black Eagle's generosity and he and the other Crystalite soldiers thanked the Chief gratefully, all except Lord Arcos who remained seated on his horse in stony silence. He was being openly hostile towards Black Eagle and Garik felt irritated, this was not supposed to be the plan, they were supposed to be making inroads with the Mavahos, not enemies. He cast Lord Arcos a warning glance, it did not go unnoticed by Black Eagle however, the Chief maintained his smile as he turned to lead them to the castle.

The Mavaho's came out their cabanas to stare at the strangers, Lord Arcos noticed the fearful faces with haunted looks behind their eyes, there was something not right in this city, he had felt it as soon as he arrived at the gates.

Lisle and Anja produced many strands of the string beads made from colourful mountain crystals and once again started to hand them to the children that lined the streets. The children started to crowd around them to receive their gifts but then Black Eagle's voice roared over the top of them, "get back to your homes!" Parents grabbed hold of their children and dragged them away back into their cabanas, within seconds the streets were completely cleared.

Lisle looked guiltily over to Lord Arcos, she too felt uncomfortable in the presence of these warriors. He grimaced back at her and she put the rest of the beads away inside her pack.

Once they rode into the castle forecourt stable hands came running out to help them with their horses. "I prefer to see to my own horse," said Lord Arcos firmly and once again Garik frowned a look of warning to him. However, the Lord Warrior paid no attention following the stable hands to where they kept the mounts, he wanted to be sure he knew where their horses were should they need them. Chief Black Eagle simply laughed it off not in the least bit offended and he clapped Garik on his back in a friendly manner before leading him and the others into the castle where immediately they thankfully found it to be much cooler.

When Lord Arcos got to the stables, one of the stable hands came to show him where to put his horse. The small man had a calming way with the horses and helped Arcos stable his horse. The Lord Warrior thanked him and then asked his name, wondering if he could perhaps strike up a conversation with him.

"I'm Yumi and if you don't mind me saying you and your people need to be careful, do not trust Black Eagle, he's very dangerous."

"I got that feeling when we arrived. Thanks for your warning," replied Lord Arcos.

"I'll help you if I can, I'll make sure your horses are taken care of, but if I were you, I'd make your stay a short one," Yumi continued. "And don't tell him where your people live, you would be putting them in danger."

"We'll be careful, I'll warn the others," replied Lord Arcos. He thanked Yumi again, making up his mind that he would come back and ask the stable hand about Tokala before they left. He left to join the others, he had a really bad feeling about Black Eagle, he had done since the minute he laid eyes on him and Arcos intended to keep his sword close to his side.

They were all taken to separate rooms that had already been arranged for them, they could bathe and food was left out. They were told to rest as a welcoming feast was being prepared for later in the evening, where they would be entertained as Chief Black Eagles guests. After bathing the Crystalites snoozed on comfortable beds for the rest of the day, all had their weapons close at hand, ready should anything happen. Lord Arcos did not rest, he sat by the window watching the comings and goings in the castle forecourt, it did not take him long to establish there was a hierarchy in the castle, and the servants all lived in constant fear.

When the sun finally went down the castle servants knocked on their doors and told them it was time for the feast. They all met each other in the hallway on route to the great hall, Tanj and Cnut had also worn their swords as did Lord Arcos which made Garik visibly annoyed, he felt it was an antagonistic gesture towards their hosts.

"Please stop your hostility," whispered Garik to Lord Arcos. "I can sense it from here."

"I don't trust their Chief, you should be more wary," replied the Lord Warrior grimly and Lisle nodded in agreement.

Garik ignored them, he had come to do a job and so far, it seemed to be going well. When they arrived into the great hall and Wizard of Justice forced a smile onto his face. The great hall was on the ground floor running alongside the castle forecourt, with huge windows that reflected the flaming torches that lit up the room from along the walls. There were long stone tables situated at the sides of the room, already filled with the chosen Mavaho elite, all of whom were curious about their strange guests. The Crystlites were taken to be seated to the left of the elevated head table at the back of the hall where Black Eagle sat between two beautiful Mavaho women and four of his warriors. As soon as the Crystalite's sat, they were bombarded with limitless amounts of food and drink that was put down for them to enjoy.

"Eat up, tonight is a celebration!" announced Black Eagle to his guests. Garik helped himself to a plate of meat and nodded to the other Crystalites to follow suit. Lord Arcos did not help himself to any food or drink, Lisle and Cnut abstained from eating also until Garik hissed at them, "Stop insulting our hosts, we are here to befriend him!" They reluctantly picked at their food and sipped their wine, but still Lord Arcos consumed nothing. Black Eagle did not seem to notice as he spoke freely, asking them many questions about the mountains.

Garik was guarded with his replies, but he told Black Eagle a little about the Crystal City and the people who lived there. He played his role well, telling his attentive audience that he owned a store in the city and had decided to see if the Mavahos were interested in his wares. Black Eagle was fascinated by his descriptions of how readily available precious gems were in the mountains and how jewellery was an important status symbol amongst the Crystalite people. All the time Lord Arcos watched on quietly, now beginning to be a little puzzled at how open Garik was being.

His soldiers, even though they had taken no more than a few sips of their drinks also seemed to be getting confused. Arcos noticed their speech was becoming slurred and their eyes looked clouded. Garik felt his head become fuzzy, and he shook it to try and clear the haze, but it only got worse and then he heard Black Eagles voice questioning him from what seemed to be a distance away.

"I have to say Garik, I have enjoyed your company this evening but one thing puzzles me. Why would the Crystalites wish to trade with us? You know nothing about us, your furs and jewels hold no value to us here in the desert and we have nothing we could offer you that would suit your mountain needs. I think it is time you told us your real purpose behind this visit."

Garik could not focus on anything else except Black Eagles voice, it was willing him to reply and he felt he had no option but to obey.

"I am Garik, the Wizard of Justice from the Crystal City. We have come here to help Tokala regain the trust of the Mavahos, and return him to become their Chief. Black Eagle must be held accountable for the evil he has brought to this world, we have to stop him for the sake of all Satiren."

Lord Arcos had his hand on his sword hilt, he looked over at Lisle, her head was on the table, she and his other soldiers were drugged, they would be useless. Why had Garik insisted they consume the food? They had been trusting fools and now Garik had compromised everything.

"So, Tokala is still alive. I can't tell you how much that pleases me. I'll be able to have my revenge at last," replied Black Eagle rubbing the scar on his face.

"He and his sister have been accused of bewitching our King and causing his death. We are here to prove otherwise," Garik could not stop himself from talking. He felt like a fool, and prayed that Lord Arcos could escape and warn the others.

"So, Sisika had a daughter, did she? Tell me, is my wife still alive?" asked the Chief clearly enjoying himself.

"No, Sisika died after giving birth to Catori, that is why Wigholt brought the children to the mountains, Darkstar is Catori's father," replied Garik, his voice slurring as he tried to regain control from whatever spell he was under.

"Darkstar?"

"He is our King, or was our King. He is dead," said Garik and Lord Arcos swore under his breath then jumped to his feet. He was instantly surrounded by five Mavaho warriors, all had their long knives drawn ready.

Garik's head was beginning to clear a little and he could start to focus on the room. He looked over to Lord Arcos, "Go," he mouthed.

"I would like you to tell me where Tokala and his sister are now," said Black Eagle enjoying the mockery he was making out of Garik.

"No, I won't," rasped Garik struggling against the spell.

"So, the truth spell is wearing off already, that's a shame, perhaps we need to use a little more next time. Take them all to the dungeons, and believe me Garik, by the time I've finished with you, you'll have given me the location of my son and this Crystal City of yours. It sounds as if you need a new King!" said Black Eagle triumphantly.

Lord Arcos drew his sword before anyone saw him move and cut down three of the warriors in an instant. The other two made a feeble attempt to attack, but Arcos also dispatched them in a flash.

"GET HIM!" roared Black Eagle getting to his feet and drawing his own long knife. His warriors rushed towards Lord Arcos, but they were no match for this powerful Crystalite, and the Lord Warrior cut through them with ease as he made his way towards the exit.

"You'll never escape the city!" cried the Chief staggering over the bodies of his dead and injured men.

"The next time you see me it will be at the head of a great Crystalite army, and I will personally tear you in two for what you have done to shame my friend Garik," Lord Arcos shouted across the hall.

"Brave talk for a man who is about to have his head and entrails displayed on my wall," Black Eagle roared back at him, furious that he was unable to reach him.

Arcos left the great hall and sprinted down the passageway towards the outer doors. He knew he couldn't help Garik, the old Wizard had known that, he had to get back to the Crystal City to warn them. When he reached the large wooden outer doors, he found them closed and barricaded with a bar from the outside, he could not budge them. Lord Arcos was trapped, he turned with his sword ready to face the men he could hear heading in his direction. He was prepared for might possibly be his last battle, but he was determined he would fight to the death. Then a hand came out of the darkness and pulled him through a hidden doorway behind one of the giant wall tapestries. It was Yumi, the stable hand who had warned him earlier.

"I've a horse ready for you, follow me," he whispered and ushered Lord Arcos through a small opening that led out of the castle. "Your mountain horses do not have the speed you need to get across the desert, so I have saddled Chaser for you. He is the fastest horse in the stables, he'll carry you with ease."

"Why are you doing this Yumi? You're putting yourself at great risk?" Lord Arcos was aware there were eyes watching them as they ran across the forecourt to the stables.

"I was hidden and could hear what was being said in the Great hall, Tokala is still alive, is that true?"

"Yes, he's alive and a good, strong boy," confirmed Lord Arcos.

"Then we have hope. Many is the city live in fear every day, the Chief is cruel, he punishes the people for his own amusement but now we know Tokala lives, we have hope and that will give us strength. You must leave now, but promise me you will give Chaser to Tokala. Black Eagle is not fit to own such a horse, it should belong to the boy," said Yumi. "You must leave now I can hear them coming."

Lord Arcos mounted the magnificent stallion, "Thank you Yumi, I will protect Tokala, have no fear and we will be back, now stay safe!" Chaser took off at the slightest nudge and Lord Arcos found himself flying through the city, Yumi had already arranged for the gates to be opened and soon the Lord Warrior had sped out into the Silversands, the ground sparkling beneath them as they flew off into the night.

Chief Black Eagle came marching into the stables, he grabbed hold of Yumi by his neck and held him high, his legs dangling as he turned blue from Black Eagle's vicious grip. Then the Chief threw him across the yard, howling with fury as he did so. "You don't deserve a quick death! I will make an example out of you that will leave you screaming for mercy."

"You don't frighten me," coughed Yumi rubbing his throat. "Your time is coming to an end I can feel it. Tokala will defeat you and return to Burning Towers and then the people will rejoice singing and dancing over your bones. There's nothing you can do to me now that will stop this from happening, your days are numbered Black Eagle."

"Take him and nail him to the city gates for all the town to see. Keep him alive long enough so the people can understand what will happen to them if they disobey me," ordered Black Eagle and Yumi was hauled to his feet and dragged down the streets towards the city gates.

Draconan's ghost manifested in the stables and watched Black Eagle pace for a while, before stepping out of the darkness. "Stay calm my son, it will soon be daylight then you can take your warriors and go after the Crystalite warrior, but first you must discover the whereabouts of Tokala and the Crystal City." The

Dark Lord laid his cold bony hand on Black Eagle's shoulder and whispered into his ear, "Remember you still have the others, make Garik tell you all you need to know and soon you will be ruler of all Satiren."

******

The Crystalite soldiers awoke in a damp, stinking cell deep beneath the castle. They had been stripped of most of their clothing and their hands and feet were chained together. Garik was in the cell next to them, he was already awake when he heard them move around.

"I am sorry, I should have listened to Lord Arcos," he called through to them. "We will never give up the whereabouts of the Crystal City, I promise you that."

"How can we stop Black Eagle's magic? We need to do something now Garik!" said Cnut furious at being caught so easily. He thought of Tanja and his daughters, he should not have left them and now they were all in danger from Black Eagle."Garik, you must use your magic, we cannot give Black Eagle the location of the city!"

They all heard the sound of metal grate on the floor and Garik turned to see the loathsome face of Mavaho Chief sneering at him.

"Did Lord Arcos esacpe?" Garik asked.

"No, I killed him myself," replied Black Eagle and Garik smiled. They all knew the Chief was lying, Lord Arcos had got away at least they could be sure of that.

"If you want to save your friends in the next cell, you will lead to me to the Crystal City" said Black Eagle.

"No Garik!" cried Lisle and Anja unison.

"Garik, we know what must happen. We're prepared for what you must do," said Tanj through the bars. The Crystalite soldiers all nodded at each other resigned to whatever their fate would be.

"You've had your fun with me Black Eagle, but you're no longer in control here," replied Garik his eyes fierce.

"It was not so difficult to loosen your tongue last time, if you insist, I'll have more of the potion poured down your throat. Surely it would be easier for you if you just gave up," snorted the Chief holding up a bottle of liquid and shaking it menacingly in front of Garik's face.

Garik was unmoved, he closed his eyes and started muttering words that made no sense to the Chief and immediately a strange humming noise started to filter through the walls. Black Eagle stared at him suspiciously then started to laugh, "is this supposed to frighten me?"

Garik ignored him and continued with the incantation, the humming became louder and Garik opened his eyes, they were pure white and a haunting look spread over his face, Black Eagle started to feel uncomfortable. The cell had become icy cold, the Chief reached out to shake Garik roughly trying to make him stop, but the humming continued and Garik now seemed to be in a deep trance. A blue light started to glow in the cell and as it reached out and touched Black Eagle's skin he recoiled in fright as it made his skin tingle. He stepped away from the light and out of the cell slamming the door shut on Garik, then saw that the light was not only coming from Garik's cell, but also from the cell that the other soldiers were in also. The haunting humming sound continued from all around the dungeon, getting louder and more high-pitched. Black Eagle put his hands over his ears unable to move as he watched the light engulfed Garik and the other Crystalite soldiers. Their chains fell to the floor as their bodies rose up from the ground and then in an instant, there was silence the light vanished leaving only darkness in its wake.

Black Eagle's eye had to adjust to the blackness surrounding him, he grabbed a torch and called for his guards to open the cell doors. But it was too late, Garik was gone, there was nothing left of the old Justice Wizard. He moved to the other cell and as he expected the Crystalite soldiers had also vanished. Black Eagle cursed his own stupidity, he should have stopped Garik when the old man started that spell. Now he had nothing and he had not discovered where Tokala and his sister were hiding, that more than anything else made him furious.

The Chief crashed out of the dungeons, he needed to get his army together. They could not catch Lord Arcos when he was riding Chaser, but he did not want to give the Lord Warrior any time to prepare. He would lead his men to the mountains, Draconan would show him the way to the Crystal City and he would defeat the Crystalites. He would bring them all to their knees, then he would find his son and break the boy's spirit. It would give him great satisfaction to see Tokala beg for forgiveness every day of his young life. As for the child Catori, he would kill her on sight.

CHAPTER TWENTY-TWO

Chaser ran like a hurricane through the Silversands, Lord Arcos clung on for dear life he was not used to a horse that could travel at such speed, the mountain horses were nimble and sure-footed, but not particularly fast. Daylight arrived and the hot desert sun burned into his pale skin like a blizzard of fire as they rode, but it did not affect Chaser and the horse managed to keep up his pace throughout the day. Then the horse veered off suddenly, he seemed to know where he was going and Arcos prayed it was to a waterhole he was so parched. Then he saw Wigholt and Tokala waiting for him and Chaser came to a sudden halt.

"Lord Arcos, I think you both need to rest," said the little blue Wizard, "you can warn the Crystal City tomorrow."

"You know what happened?" croaked Lord Arcos his throat was red raw.

"Yes, we watched in Wigholt's crystal," said Tokala. "You should never have gone there."

"Enough Tokala, what's done is done. Let's get you inside Arcos, your skin is badly burnt and we need you to be at full strength, I have something that will help," said Wigholt. He and Tokala led Arcos down into the underground cavern where Catori was playing with a young fox cub, she squealed with excitement when she saw him. Wigholt told him to sit while Tokala took Chaser to rub him down and get him some fresh water and food.

Catori climbed on the Lord Warrior's knee. "Is your face sore?" she asked reaching up and stroking Arcos's raw cheek.

"It's ok," he replied, he was so relieved to see her. Tears welled up in his eyes as his thoughts turned to Garik for the first time since he had left Burning Towers, the old Wizard would be so happy to see how well the children looked.

Wigholt appeared with a lotion and started to administer it to Arcos's face and hands, the burning sensation stopped and almost immediately it started to feel better. "I can't stay here for long, I have to get to the mountains and warn them about Black Eagle, I'm sure he is not far behind me."

"You have time, I will send you to the Crystal City in my chariot, you'll be there within three hours, plenty of time to prepare," replied Wigholt.

"You should come with me, he knows Tokala is alive and if he interrogates Garik further he may discover where he is. He'll hunt him down, I'm not sure if Garik will be able to stop him from finding out all he wants to know," warned the Lord Warrior.

Wigholt looked at him sadly "I'm sorry Arcos, Garik ended his life and those of your soldiers before Black Eagle could question them. In doing so, he has protected Tokala and the city and has bought you time, I don't think he felt he had any other choice."

Arcos put his head in his hands as he let Wigholt's words sink in. "I shouldn't have left them," he whispered to himself, "It's all my fault."

"It's no one's fault but Black Eagles! Garik and your soldiers knew it was a difficult mission, they all chose to end their lives for the sake of their families and friends. What could you have done? You would have been tortured alongside them, and there would be nobody left to warn the Crystal City. Stay focused Lord Arcos, there is much to be done," said Wigholt beginning to lose his patience. "The Mavahos are tired of Black Eagle and his army of vicious warriors, now they know that Tokala is still alive they have a flicker of hope that things may change in Burning Towers. The majority of Black Eagles army are being forced to fight, if they were to come across Tokala at the head of the Crystalite army, asking for peace, then I believe the tides will turn and Black Eagle may be forced to back down."

"How can you be sure?" asked Lord Arcos already doubting this would work.

"No one can be sure, but I've seen the misery in Burning Towers. Yumi is just one of many who would stand against Black Eagle. The Chief ordered him nailed to the city gates and left to die after he helped you escape, but he never reached the gates. Black Eagle was so caught up in organising his army he never knew that the people helped Yumi to escape, he is now being hidden by friends. There are many who feel like this, it will not take much to topple Black Eagle." Wigholt saw the cogs in Lord Arcos's mind turning as he spoke.

"If I take Tokala back to the city with me and tell them Garik is dead, I fear I would be putting the boy's life in danger. People in the city are not yet convinced of Tokala's innocence after what happened on Mount gloom. It will take time to convince them, and from what you say we don't have time. We need to meet Black Eagles army before he reaches the mountains, I cannot have him find the Crystal City," replied Lord Arcos.

"Agreed, which is why I'll have Tokala meet you and your army on the lower slopes. He can take Chaser. I can put a speed spell on the horse and as you know Tokala is an excellent rider. You go to the city, tell them what has happened and get your men organised then set off for the Silversands as soon as you can. When you finally meet up with Tokala, it will be easier for you to convince your soldiers to accept him rather than trying to argue it out with the entire Wizard Council, you don't have time for that," said Wigholt.

Lord Arcos turned to Tokala who had said nothing up until now, "How do you feel about this? Are you up for facing your father again?"

"It was my idea," replied the boy. "I want to save my people, and I want my father to pay for what he has done. There should not be a war between our people, from what I have seen we all hold the same values."

Lord Arcos was moved by Tokala's words, the boy's insight was so advanced for his years and Arcos looked at him with a mixture of pride and worry. He was too young to have all this placed on his small shoulders, yet Tokala seemed to have accepted what he must do. Lord Arcos stood and placed Catori down at his feet, "very well, let's do this, I think we have talked enough Wigholt, how soon can I leave?"

"The chariot is ready and waiting, come," said the Wizard and there was a rumble as the giant boulder moved once again uncovering the entrance to the cavern. They went outside, it was almost dark already and Arcos saw what looked like a roofless carriage just sitting in the sand. "Get in," instructed Wigholt.

The Lord Warrior opened the door to the carriage and climbed aboard, there was a seat and a pile of furs. On each corner of the chariot was a firm, tall pole with a metal ring attached to the top of each of them. He turned and looked at Wigholt with a puzzled expression and Tokala laughed. "Sit down Lord Arcos, they won't come while you're standing."

"Who won't come?" asked Arcos looking around nervously as he lowered himself into the seat. Then he heard a whooshing of giant wings flapping above him and he looked up in time to see four huge bats descend towards him at speed. He put his hands over his head thinking they were attacking but they stopped suddenly, hovering just above the chariot and each grabbed hold of one of the metal rings, the next second he was airborne before he had time to say goodbye. The bats flew with such a speed he could hardly catch his breath so he lowered himself deep inside the chariot and pulled the furs over him. Lord Arcos had never experienced anything quite like this, he had never thought himself afraid of heights but this whole experience was unsettling and he was eager to get his feet back onto solid ground.

***

Just before sunrise the next morning Tokala was getting prepared for his journey when everything inside the cavern started to shake. Dust flew around, and the ground trembled beneath his feet.

"What is it?" he asked Wigholt who was sitting calmly smoking his pipe.

"It's the Mavaho army, they are above us sooner than I expected, Black Eagle must have made them travel through the night. You'll have to leave soon my boy."

"I'm ready now, but they'll see me if I overtake them," said Tokala.

"No, they won't, I've a spell that will protect you, but first you have to dress the part, these Crystalite clothes will not endear you to your people. You must look like a Mavaho Chief, here change into these," said Wigholt handing Tokala some gappin skin pants with a thick leather belt that held long knives hanging from either side of his hip. He put on an embroidered jerkin to match and Wigholt also handed him a magnificent feather head dress that fitted Tokala's head perfectly, trailing down his back. "Now you look the part."

"Wow, can I try it on," asked Catori staring in awe at the head dress. Tokala laughed and handed it over to his sister. "I'll save that for when we meet the Mavaho army, it might frighten the Crystalites if I wear it now."

Tokala went to get Chaser, the horse was well rested and eager to get going. It stamped its feet with excitement and Tokala patted his flank. "We'll be off soon," he promised and the huge horse nodded its head.

Wigholt was standing by his desk going through a dusty old spell book that he had, "Ah, here it is, this will give Chaser the speed you will need. When you pass your father's army all they will see is a ball of dust, but remember to slow Chaser down when you reach the mountains. He cannot be charging up these dangerous mountain paths at high speed or he will get injured."

Wigholt strolled over to the horse reaching up to lay his small blue hand on his front leg, then muttered an incantation. The horse whinnied nodding his head excitedly as Wigholt finished and stood aside. "Up you go Tokala, Chaser is ready. Keep yourself safe and come back to us."

Tokala mounted Chaser and Wigholt opened the boulder once again, and they climbed the stairway up to the surface. Far in the distance they could make out the thick dust cloud from Black Eagles huge army.

"Will you be back soon?" Catori asked, she the same height as Wigholt now.

"I'll be back very soon," promised Tokala and blew her a kiss. Then he turned Chaser and nudged him gently, the horse took off and Tokala felt a surge of power flow through him. It had been a long time since he had ridden a horse at speed like this, but he had never forgotten how. Exhilaration flowed through him as they travelled over the desert and soon enough, he came upon his father's great army. They were closer to the mountains than he had anticipated, Black Eagle was riding them hard. The army saw nothing except an odd cloud of dust over take them as Tokala sped onwards taking only a couple of hours to reach the yellow dried grassy meadows of the lower slopes. They started to climb, Tokala slowed Chaser down with difficulty, the horse was charged with energy and eager to keep sprinting. But as they reached the narrow pathways and the air grew cooler, he started to calm and allowed Tokala to lead him with care up through the rocky mountain slopes.

CHAPTER TWENTY-THREE

Arcos had arrived at the Crystal City a few hours before and even though Wigholt had been against it, he called an emergency meeting immediately. Everyone attended, the city had been in turmoil since he and Garik had left, the Wizard Council were finding it hard to keep the citizens calm. There seemed to be a growing element of disruptors in the city, and there was trouble wherever you went.

The news of Garik's death brought a hushed silence to the Council as they listened to the descriptions of what had happened in Burning Towers. The news that a Mavaho army was on its way to invade the Crystal city caused alarm across the room and it was the general consensus that the plan to go to Burning Towers had been a bad one.

"How many soldiers do you have to protect the city from Black Eagle?" asked Kaeshia. She had taken on a more prominent role within the Council since Garik had left.

"Not enough, but Wigholt has a plan that may help," replied Lord Arcos.

"Not Wigholt again!" cried Piro getting to his feet. "Is he not the orchestrator of all our problems, or are you all ignoring that fact."

"The fact as you call it, is that Wigholt has done nothing but protect us. He was against Garik going to Burning Towers from the start and if we had listened to him we wouldn't be in this mess. Wigholt would never hurt the Crystalite people, he has been our friend for centuries," snapped Kaeshia as Piro quickly sat back down on her seat. "We have to listen to Lord Arcos and then we can decide what we must do," she continued.

Lord Arcos told the Wizard Council of Wigholt's plan, he described the suffering and despair within the Mavaho city and how hope was spreading through its people now they had found out that Tokala was still alive.

"So perhaps it was not a wasted journey after all." Zebulon appeared looking grave. "I'm sorry about Garik and your soldiers, their bravery will not go unrewarded in the afterlife. Whatever happens now will change the destiny of

Satiren, and it is up to you to decide whether it will be for good or evil. Wigholt's plan is a good one and Tokala has already reached the mountains ahead of the Mavaho army. No more time can be wasted here, you must go and meet the boy Lord Arcos."

"Are there any objections to this?" Kaeshia casting an unnerving glance towards Piro and Pinto, but the young elemental Wizards remained quiet. "You must get prepared Lord Arcos, how soon until you leave?"

"We'll be underway within the hour," he replied.

***

Tokala was sure he had the right track, but there seemed to be something unnerving about it. His eyes scoured the sides of the cliffs and then he realised too late what was wrong. There were a number of thick rope-like vines uncoiling their was down from the cliff tops and they seemed to have a life of their own. One hit the back of his head just as Tokala tried to duck to get away from it, but it snaked its way around his torso in seconds and he was held tight. Chaser shrieked with fright as more vines came tumbling down wrapping themselves tightly around his legs and neck so that before long, he and Tokala were trapped unable to move.

A shrill, high pitched screaming echoed around the cliff face and Tokala managed to turn his head just a few centimetres in time to make out some black creatures scurrying down the vines towards them. They were long limbed, adapted for climbing, with short bodies covered in thick black course hair. Their faces were elongated with large widely set black eyes and rows of nasty sharp looking teeth protruding from their mouths. With ear splitting screeches they wrestled each other in excitement as they tore down the side of the cliff to land in front of their quarry, then a few of the braver ones started to tug at the vines trapping Chaser's legs. It was a stupid move as Chaser's front legs came loose and he reared up bringing his hooves down on one of his attackers, crushing the creature's skull. The horse was furious now, rearing angrily to free himself from the rest of the vines. The creatures ran off screaming in fright just as Tokala managed to wriggle his arm free to grab hold of his knife, he then started stabbing at the vines that were holding him and the strange plants immediately let go of their grip, squealing and hissing as they coiled quickly back up the cliffside.

The hairy creatures were regaining their courage and started to throw rocks and stones down on them and with no shield to protect them they could only hurry along the path trying to find shelter from the rocks raining down on them.

"Is this how I find the Chief of the Mavaho's? Getting beaten up by a bunch of Trolls!" cried Lord Arcos laughing. He had been riding ahead hoping to come across Tokala before the others did.

Some help please!" Tokala shouted back and Lord Arcos raised his bow and shot one of the Trolls off its ledge. The others screeched and immediately ran off back to where they had come from.

"I could have done that," said Tokala grumpily. "I just couldn't get my bow out."

"Well I won't tell anyone if you don't," laughed Arcos, relieved to see Tokala had made it unscathed. Trolls could be nasty when they attacked in large groups. "The other will be with us soon enough, how far behind is your father's army?"

"They haven't reached the lower slopes yet, but it won't take them long," replied Tokala.

"Are you sure you're ready for this?" Lord Arcos asked him, his face had become serious now.

"I'm more than ready, I've waited for this day for three years,"Tokala assured him and the Lord Warrior found it hard to believe that he was talking with a small boy.

They waited for the rest of the Crystalite soldiers to catch up and then continued down once again to the lower slopes. The soldiers seemed pleased to see Tokala again, chatting to him easily asking if he had been well and how Catori was. Any doubt that Tokala had when he was riding up to meet them vanished, he was proud to call them his friends.

They reached the lower slopes and saw the huge Mavaho army approaching, the Crystalites were outnumbered at least five to one, but the well-trained soldiers showed no fear as they stood guarding the way to the mountains. The Mavaho army were not all trained warriors, many were just young men and women who had never held a sword let alone a bow. They were field workers, bakers, blacksmiths, just everyday people who had been forced by Black Eagles men to ride into a battle they did not understand. Fear began to fill them as they approached the magnificent looking warriors in shining armour who stood at the foot of the mountains.

Black Eagle smiled maliciously when he saw the numbers of the Crystalite army that faced them, but his men were not so comfortable, they had seen

Lord Arcos fight, he had taken down eleven trained Mavaho warriors before he had escaped the castle. The Crystalites may be few in numbers, but they stood tall and powerful looking in their protective armour with their enormous long swords in hand. Black Eagle rode forward flanked on either side by one of his warriors. As he drew closer Lord Arcos rode out to meet him, "Turn around Black Eagle, take your people home, you are not welcome in the mountains."

"There seems to be little you can do to stop me, your army is outnumbered, surrender to us now and we may let you live," he sneered.

Lord Arcos raised his hand and the Crystalites moved apart slightly to allow a rider on a black stallion through. Tokala charged down on Chaser, passing his father and Lord Arcos, then he rode alongside the breadth of the Mavaho army to make sure they could all see him. The Mavahos started shouting and crying out with joy when they recognised Tokala looking so strong and well. He had remembered to wear the Chief's head dress that Wigholt had given him making him all the more impressive as he rode Chaser. Once he was sure they had all recognised him, he steered the stallion back to finally approach his father.

Black Eagle looked murderous, his hand twitching on his long knife as his son drew closer. "I wouldn't," warned Lord Arcos watching the Chief closely.

"So, you survived," said Black Eagle, then he nodded towards the Crystalites, "Though this is strange company to be keeping."

"How is your eye? It must have been painful," replied Tokala, determined to provoke his father.

"You'll know that pain soon enough boy!" snarled the Mavaho Chief and his men laughed.

Tokala ignored them instead turning to the Mavaho army who shifted uncomfortably. He called out to them "It's time to lay down your weapons my people, there is no battle to be had here. The Crystalites are good people, they came to you in peace because I told them that you needed their help to get rid of my father and his followers. They know you are good people and do not wish to fight you, but they will protect the mountains. The choice must be yours!"

"Prepare for battle!" snarled Black Eagle and he turned his horse back towards the Mavaho army. "Pick up your arms!"

As he and his men rode back to join the army, Tokala suddenly overtook them on Chaser to ride once again the breadth of the army shouting out to them and this time his voice carried further, "Black Eagle has corrupted you with fear. He has murdered your families and friends as you have stood helplessly by. I watched him beat and torture my own mother and I was too young to help her, but I am no longer too young, and it is time that Black Eagle paid for his crimes. We can stand together and get rid of this tyrant and his followers, we deserve to live in peace! Lay down your arms!"

There was a faint murmur of agreement coming from the army, but they seemed confused and Tokala knew he was asking a lot. Then Black Eagle drew his long knife and turned his horse in a bid to charge at his son, but Lord Arcos was there in an instant, disarming the Chief and holding his mammoth sword at Black Eagles throat. "Let the boy speak!" he ordered.

"Many of you have been forced to come here and fight, but there does not need to be fighting. Lord Arcos and his people gave me a home, they cared for my baby sister when our mother died. They have been kind, they are good people and if you choose to fight them, then you will find that I will be on their side, fighting against you. It doesn't have to be this way, let us return home to Burning Towers with new friends in the mountains and a new Chief." Tokala spoke clearly and this time there was more of a response from the Mavahos.

"I will not fight you!" shouted a woman squeezing through to the front, she threw down her weapon. "Me neither!" cried someone else and then there was more shouting as the rest of the Mavaho army followed suit. The sounds of cheering and of weapons clattering to the ground echoed around the hills.

"Pick up your weapons you cowards! Do you think this boy can defeat me? I know your faces and you will all be punished for this!" screamed Black Eagle as he pushed Arcos's sword away from his throat spinning around quickly with his long knife and stabbing the Lord Warrior deep in his shoulder. Lord Arcos managed to get his sword around to defend himself as Black Eagle bore down on him in a furious attack. But it was what Arcos had been waiting for, he wanted his revenge for what happened to Garik and his soldiers and now he would have it. He met Black Eagle blow for blow, ignoring the searing pain in his shoulder as he fought with super human strength pounding the evil Mavaho Chief again and again until Black Eagle eventually fell on his knees trying to fend back the blows from Lord Arcos's sword.

"Arcos stop!" cried Tokala, "Don't kill him!"

"He deserves to die!" panted Lord Arcos his sword poised ready to strike again.

"No, he deserves to be punished by his own people, the people he has wronged for so long. Let the Mavaho's decide his fate, it is they who have suffered the most," said Tokala.

Black Eagle spat at the ground and pulled himself unsteadily to his feet, hatred oozing out of his every pore. Lord Arcos still held his sword aloft, he would like nothing better than to ram it down Black Eagle's throat, but he knew Tokala was right and so he shouted over to his men, "Bind him so he cannot escape." Two of his soldiers came forward and pulled Black Eagles hands behind his back tying them tightly.

The Chief stared menacingly at Tokala then spat some blood from his mouth, "You think you have the power to rule Burning Towers? My men will destroy all of you!"

"Your men seem to be in hiding, but they will not remain hidden for long. The people know who they are and they will also be punished," replied Tokala unfazed by Black Eagle's threat.

The air around them suddenly turned cool and they saw a portal started to open inbetween the two armies, blue light poured out of the gateway as everyone fell silent and watched the White Witch step through. It was the first time in years that Sirena had set foot on her beloved creation and she walked towards Tokala smiling with her white cloak billowing out majestically behind her.

"You have done well Tokala, your decisions here today have restored peace to Satiren and for that the Overlords applaud you." Her voice carried easily throughout both armies as if she were talking directly into their ears.

Black Eagle has been infected by Draconan, his own cruelty made him an easy target for the Dark Lord and I want him off my world. I will take him to Dhurgon and I will take great pleasure in gifting him back to Draconan myself. You may punish his followers as you see fit, but I will not tolerate his evil soul on my Satiren any longer."

Tokala was confused, "but will he not be punished?"

"Oh Tokala, trust me he will endure a life of misery, Dhurgon is a planet of torment, it exists in darkness and the people there must fight each other every day just to survive. Draconan takes pleasure in their suffering, just as your father took pleasure in torturing his own people. He should feel very at home, but I suspect he will loathe every minute of it," reassured the White Witch.

"Now Lord Arcos, you have neglected to send a search party out for Atolin, the boy still lives but he is badly injured and needs your help," said Sirena.

"He is alive! I must go to him!" cried Tokala.

"No, you must take your people home Tokala, you are their Chief now and they need guidance and that is your job. Lord Arcos will take his men to the foot of Mount Gloom and rescue Atolin, for he also will need to step up. The Crystalites also need a new ruler, perhaps in time the two of you will meet again, but for now there is much work to be done rebuilding trust and peace within your people," said Sirena.

Black Eagle staggered towards the Mavaho army and cried out in disbelief, "You're going to let them do this to me?" he cried. "My people, don't let this happen to me, I have given you so much!"

Black Eagles warriors hid their faces from him and sunk back into the crowd, but the other Mavahos knew who they were, their day of judgement was yet to come. Sirena walked over to Black Eagle and put her hand on his shoulder, he instantly fell silent losing control of all his movements. He had no choice but to obey her and she clicked her fingers as he watched with horror the portal open once more.

"Lord Arcos, go find Atolin, he is at the bottom of Mount Gloom not far from here," she said as she stepped into the light. Black Eagle walked after her, unable to resist her pull and within a second the portal closed and they were gone.

Tokala turned to Arcos, "Please tell Atolin I'm sorry, I never wished for any of this to happen."

"I'll tell him, take care Tokala and look after your sister for me. You are one of the bravest young men I have ever met and I hope one day not too far off, we can meet again.

BOOK 3

EVIL VS GOOD

CHAPTER TWENTY-FOUR

Eleven Years Later

She became aware of her hand in the water, her fingers felt numb and cold so she pulled her hand out to try and get some feeling back. She was on her own, Wigholt must have been out organising the chariot. At least she knew what to expect now, she had seen the giant bats already in her visions of the past. Kai had mixed feelings about what she had discovered, her parents were both dead, she had been told that all her life anyway, but somehow now that she knew them it affected her more. She was eager to find her brother and see the Crystal City for herself, there was something inside her telling her she must hurry. Getting to her feet Kai went back out into the main cavern, the boulder entrance was open and so she climbed the steps up to the surface to find Wigholt sitting by the chariot, obviously waiting for her to appear.

"How do you feel?" he asked puffing out a cloud of sweet-smelling smoke.

"A little strange, and a little sad. I had no idea and these visions are not my own memories. I wish that Sirena had not taken those from me."

"She thought she was protecting you. I think along the way we have all made mistakes, but perhaps you are here to fix everything," replied Wigholt.

"So I've been told, yet I don't see how. I must see my brother, then perhaps things will become clearer. So this is the chariot, shall I leave now?" said Kai opening the door climbing inside eager to be underway.

"Wait a minute, we haven't decided where you should go yet? You told me that the White Witch was sending you to Tokala, perhaps you should go to Burning Towers, I can't imagine why, but she usually has a good reason." Wigholt had been thinking about this when Kai was dreaming, there must be some reason why Sirena didn't want Kai going to her brother. He had not heard anything from the Crystalites for years, truthfully he had not bothered to find out. After Tokala had come to collect Catori from him all these years ago, Wigholt had hidden himself away, he no longer wished to play a part in the lives of the

Mavahos or the Crystalites. It seemed that every time he did, people were killed and there was nothing he could do about it. Wigholt had had enough of living and he prayed that whatever curse was upon him would soon be lifted and then he would be allowed to move onto the afterlife to join his wife and the other Jacartans.

"There is nothing for me at Burning Towers and I've a very strong feeling that whatever is happening in Satiren, it permeates from the mountains. Solitaire will find me there, you know that. I must see Atolin," argued Kai, she was determined now.

"I tend to agree with you, but perhaps I should take some time to consult my crystal and see what is going on in the Crystal City before you arrive unannounced."

"We don't have time the White Witch made that clear and I have already been delayed. Will you help me Wigholt? I must leave now," replied Kai.

"Very well, but I don't think you should fly into the city, it will cause an uproar and the sun has come up now so you will be seen arriving by everyone. I'll get the bats to take you to the start of the path up to the Crystal City, you'll be able to walk from there but firstly you need to change into appropriate clothing for the mountains, I've some here for you."

Kai climbed back into the chariot minutes later, she was dressed in warm grey skin leggings with a matching tunic tied tightly in the middle around her waist. Wigholt produced some fur lined boots and a heavy woollen cloak and then he handed her a sheathed dagger to tuck into her waistband along with a small pouch, "This is explosive powder, it scares off the trolls should you come across any. Just take a pinch between your fingers and throw it at them, it will make a loud bang and a lot of smoke, but it won't harm them."

"Thank you Wigholt, you've saved my life and I won't forget it," said Kai looking fondly at the strange little blue man.

"One more thing, if your brother does not welcome you, search for Lord Arcos, he's a good man and he will help you. He has always regretted not being there to save your father," said Wigholt then he clapped his hands and looked towards the sky.

"Bye Wigholt!" Kai called out as she heard the great wings whoosh down towards her. As she had seen Lord Arcos do in her visions she sat down and pulled the furs over her just as the bats appeared, each grabbing hold of a metal ring then lifting the chariot off the ground with great speed. The wind struck her face as she dared to peer over the edge, she could see the sun was starting to come up over the mountains in the distance.

They only travelled for a couple of hours and the sun was already high in the sky when the bats arrived at the lower slopes that led up towards the mountains. Thankfully the air was fresher here than it had been in the desert, Kai had found it stifling inside the chariot dressed in the mountain attire that Wigholt had given her. They flew onwards and soon enough they started to fly over steep rocky mountain slopes towards a small plateau. The bats lowered the chariot onto the plateau allowing Kai to climb out as they hovered in the sky above her. Once she had disembarked, they flew back down collected the chariot then flew off back towards the Silversands, leaving Kai alone at the start of the mountain trail.

***

"Wigholt, I know you can hear me! We need your help this time, it's important!" Tokala called out. He wasn't sure if he had found the right boulder it had been years and boulders tended to look pretty much the same.

Then there was a familiar rumbling and the huge rock started to shift, revealing the entrance to Wigholt's cavern. "I think the whole desert can hear you!" shouted the ancient little Wizard as he stepped out onto the desert sand to find that Solitaire and Catori were both with Tokala.

"Oh Wigholt," cried Catori running over and throwing her arms around him. She now towered over him and he wriggled away from her.

"Bah! Get off me, I can't be doing with that nonsense." Catori burst out laughing and he had to smile back at her, admitting secretly to himself it was good to see them both again. "The pair of you have grown, Tokala look at the muscles on you! And as for you Catori, your beauty outshines the rest of Satiren."

"It's good to see you after so long, why wouldn't you allow us to visit?" she chided him.

"I don't think we have time for that discussion right now," replied Wigholt. "I presume you're here to find Kai?"

"You've seen her then," said Solitaire with a sigh of relief. "Is she down with you in your cavern?"

"No, I've sent her on to the mountains, she wanted to see her brother," replied Wigholt and could tell instantly from all their faces it was the wrong thing to do.

"She's not supposed to go to Atolin, it's too dangerous for her. How long ago did she leave? Will we be able to catch her?" asked Solitaire.

"No, I sent her on my chariot, she's been gone half a day now no doubt she'll have reached the mountains already. I was prudent though I told my bats to drop her on the mountain trail, I didn't want them to take her to the city in case the people there recognised my chariot. I'm not sure how the Crystalites view me in the Crystal city these days. If you leave now you may be able to catch her before she reaches it," explained Wigholt then he shook his head with frustration. "I guessed something was not right when she said that you were taking her to see Tokala, but it did not make any sense."

"Atolin is no longer the boy we once knew Wigholt, things changed him after he fell. He is very dangerous and I don't think he'll be pleased to see Kai," sighed Solitaire. "I should have told her more before I tried to bring her here."

"Well that is one thing I did do right, believe me when I say that she has learnt a great deal already. I did not want to send her out alone without having some idea of who she was. She knows what happened here and she strikes me as a wise although maybe slightly stubborn young woman," said Wigholt.

"This is not the same Kai we are talking about. The Kai I know is impulsive and angry most of the time, Odysseus knows what she will do when she meets Atolin," replied Solitaire.

"What can we do?" interrupted Tokala. "Chaser and I can reach the mountains in a couple of hours with the speed spell, but Catori and Solitaire will have to find another way."

"We can take my chariot when it returns. Perhaps if we go to Ragnar's old cavern up on Mount Solomite, we could see what's going on in the city from there. Solitaire, could you transform to your cat form and have a look around while Catori and I remain hidden. If Tokala reaches the mountains the chances are he will catch Kai before she gets to the city, she is walking. Then he can bring her to meet us and we can decide from there how to proceed."

"Do you think you can catch her?" Solitaire asked Tokala.

"Yes, we'll catch her," assured Tokala patting Chaser's neck. "Can you give us the spell Wigholt."

"I'll fetch my book, and pray we're not too late. I should have just stayed underground," he muttered as he went back down to his cavern to collect his spell book.

***

Kai felt strangely at home amongst these high cliffs and rocky passageways, there was an inkling of familiarity in the back of her mind, but nothing she could grasp onto. The pathway got steeper and she was reliant on the small map Wigholt had drawn for her. There was only one direct route to the Crystal City, but the pathway often split into different directions, thankfully Wigholt's magical map seemed to know exactly which way to go at each junction she came to. Kai was making good time and gaining confidence the higher she went, but as she got to the top of a small incline, she was suddenly stopped dead in her tracks. In front of her was a steep precipice, too wide for her to jump but she could see that the path continued on the other side.

Kai swore aloud in frustration, the precipice looked the same width in both directions, she would somehow have to find a way across if she were to continue. Just as she was tryng to figure out what to do there was some rustling and what sounded like high pitched laughter from somewhere above her, she turned quickly her hand reaching for the small pouch of explosive powder that Wigholt had given her. Kai looked around the high slopes and cliffs that surrounded her, she thought she saw something black scurrying up there but she couldn't be sure.

She turned her attention back to the gap in front of her, surely this couldn't be the end of her journey, there had to be another way over. Kai stepped to the edge and peered down, the drop was steep and she couldn't see the bottom. A voice spoke clearly in her head. Actually, it was more of a feeling than a voice, but it was so strong an emotion that Kai felt as if someone was talking directly to her. *'JUMP!'*

Kai frowned as an overwhelming surety took hold of her that everything would be fine if she just jumped across. Her head was telling her that she would be killed, but the voice in her head was insisting that it was the only way across. There were more rustling sounds both behind and above her but still she could see nothing there. *'JUMP NOW! TRUST IN YOURSELF."* Kai looked at the gap, it was too wide and if she didn't make it, she would undoubtably fall to her death. Her head felt like it was exploding inside as she tried to battle against the urge that was pushing her forward, but instead she gave into it and ran forwards leaping out into the air. She closed her eyes her immediate thought was '*why did I do that?*' then she became aware that she was not falling and she blinked open her eyes again in surprise to find was sailing through the air landing gently on the other side of the precipice. Not understanding what had just happened, Kai managed to pull herself together and tentatively continued up the path.

Soon enough the way became more of a climb than a hike and Kai was hauling herself over jagged rocks squeezing through narrow passageways. This was the area where Wigolt had warned her about the Trolls, they lived in these steep cliffs, hunting for food and caused havoc with travellers. She was ready with her explosive powder as she heard more and more shrieks coming from high above her.

Looking up continuously searching for Trolls left Kai blinkered and before she could stop herself, she found she had walked into the coiling vines without thinking. As soon as she touched them, they wrapped themselves tightly around her trapping her arms and legs. She swore at herself for not remembering the vines that had trapped Tokala in her vision as the screeching grew louder. Kai saw the long-limbed black creatures descending the slopes heading directly towards her. She was completely ensnared in the vines and she struggled helplessly as a pair of black beady eyes from a snarling Troll appeared right in front of her. His was slavering and his breath stunk, then two more of the ugly beasts dropped down next to her. They seemed a little afraid of touching the vines, and were shrieking excitedly as if waiting for something.

"*Think, use your power!*" The same feeling swamped her mind once again and a sense of calm washed over her as she surveyed at the vines that held her. They were living creatures, and living creatures could feel pain, she bit down hard on the closest vine to her. It exploded with yellow sticky substance and gave a high-pitched hiss as it let go of her snaking its way back up the cliff. Without hesitating Kai bit down on another, and another and soon she was able to move her arm and retrieve her dagger, she lashed out at the vines and they let go their hold, recoiling back to where they had come from.

Kai turned to face her attackers just as an enormous black ugly Troll landed next to her on the path. He was much larger than any of the other beasts and he shrieked at her with his slavering jaw wide apart revealing rows of deadly looking teeth. Without thinking Kai grabbed a handful of the explosive powder and threw it down in front of him, the bang was deafening and the explosion sent Kai flying off her feet to land hard on the ground. Then there was chaos, the Trolls were in complete disarray screeching and screaming as they fled panicking back up to their hideaways in the cliffs. The large Troll was lying on the ground, he was still alive but his fur was smouldering and he was in shock. Kai stepped over him carefully, he made no attempt to attack her, so she just carried on climbing up the path. Perhaps she had used too much powder,

Wigholt had said to only use a pinch, *"Oh well, I guess I won't have any more problems with the Trolls now,"* she thought.

As she climbed Kai noticed the sun was going down already which was strange, she had not been travelling for a full day it should be hours until nightfall. Within a few minutes, darkness fell and Kai felt a strange sensation throughout her body making her turn to look up at the three moons of Satiren. There were only two.

CHAPTER TWENTY-FIVE

Tokala arrived at the foot of the mountains as the sun went down, he also noticed that one of the moons were missing, it was a clear sign that he would have to find Kai quickly and he urged Chaser onwards, this time for the Trolls and their creeping vines.

***

Kai travelled swiftly now, the power from the moons had energised her and she could see as well as an owl in the darkness. *'STOP!'* Kai stopped in her tracks and looked in the direction she was being drawn to. There was a cave entrance about fifty feet from her that she would have probably passed unnoticed if she had not been drawn by the strange presence in her mind

Something about the cave was important and then she remembered the vision of Satiren the White Witch had given her in the portal, she had seen the same cave entrance then. Kai left the path and climbed over to the cave, slowly she entered and found it was much bigger on the inside than she had first imagined. The walls were covered in a thick layer of ice, although the floor was soft with dried vegetation, she stepped further inside and saw the top of a set of stone steps leading downwards. Kai knew that Wigholt would not be happy that she had left the path, but a very strong feeling was urging her onwards.

She started to descend the stone steps, they were steep and seemed to go down forever deep into the mountain, the air was damp and icy cold and Kai could hear water trickling up ahead. Her foot slipped on the step, but she managed to regain her balance, the stone steps were now covered in slippery black ice so she had to take each icy step carefully. Eventually she could see the bottom the walls were now glistening with crystals under the ice as she passed. Eventually stepping off the last step her foot hit the ground and there was a sickening crunching sound. Looking down Kai could see the ground was littered with bones, small animal bones and some larger ones she did not recognise and did not want to try to guess what they were. Tentatively she carried on walking trying not to think about the ground crunching under her feet. It was some sort of animal graveyard, probably left by the Trolls and she had to swallow back the bile that had begun to rise in her throat. Up ahead was a very large gate made of thick metal bars, it was blocking her way. There was a sign on the gate and she scrubbed off the ice to see what it said. 'THE LAIR OF VULCAN. DO NOT ENTER.'

"Who is Vulcan? Wigholt never mentioned him," she wondered. There was no way she would turn back now, something was drawing her in, but there was a huge padlock locking the gates preventing anyone from getting through and Kai rattled it with frustration. She pulled out her dagger, she could try to pick the lock, but the blade was too wide to fit in the keyhole and she had nothing else that would suffice. Perhaps she could smash it with a rock, it looked really old and the cold may have weakened it. She found a large sharp-edged rock and smashed it hard onto the metal padlock continuing to strike until eventually the rock broke in two, she tossed it aside in disgust.

Then Kai remembered the explosive powder, she took a small handful out of the pouch, threw it at the padlock leaping backwards at the same time. The bang was deafening and Kai was flung to the ground once again, she waited for the smoke to clear then tried the padlock, it hadn't budged and she laid her head on the bars feeling defeated.

"Don't give up Kai, or you'll not survive in this place," said a woman's voice from behind her. Kai spun around and came face to face with a striking woman with intense golden eyes.

"Sisika?" Kai recognised her from her vision.

"Yes, I'm Sisika. I'm here to help you Kai," replied the Mavaho Queen.

"Can you get me through this gate?" asked Kai.

"I cannot, I'm no more than a spirit in this world, but you can do it yourself. You have the power to wield the magic of the White Witch, she gifted you with her magic when you were born. The Overlords are watching her closely, she cannot be seen interfering in the outcome of Satiren, but you can use her magic here."

"So everyone keeps on telling me, but I can't even get past a stupid gate!" replied Kai sounding exasperated.

"Of course you can, take the padlock in your hands and imagine it's made of ice," instructed Sisika.

Kai took hold of the padlock and tried to imagine it made of ice, but she had a hundred more questions for Sisika and she couldn't remain focused. "It's no use, I can't concentrate!"

"Yes, you can, close your eyes and feel the heavy metal of the lock in your hands. Rub it gently with your thumbs and imagine it turning to ice under your touch. Focus only on your thumbs and how the metal feels."

Kai started to rub the padlock as Sisika instructed and suddenly felt her hair start to tingle as energy flowed through her body, she focused harder imagining the padlock freezing in her hand. With her eyes closed Kai could not see the faint blue light wrapping itself around her hands however, she did feel the padlock turn ice cold and a few seconds later it shattered into a thousand pieces.

"I did it!" she cried, opening her eyes to find that Sisika had gone and she was alone once more. Sighing with disappointment, she pushed the gate open, it was stiff from lack of use and it raked noisily across the frozen ground. Kai walked through a short tunnel that opened up into a larger cavern which had a number of tunnels all leading in different directions. Kai counted six in total and she decided to just choose one at random as they all looked very much the same. Then worried that she may not be able to find her way back out, she picked up a rock and scraped scuff marks onto the wall to leave a trail she could follow back if needs be. It was only when she had been walking about ten minutes that she noticed that all the other tunnels led back into this one.

The tunnels themselves were as dark as the blackest night but Kai could still see where she was going as she descended deeper and deeper into the mountain. She began to notice a loud scurrying sound echoing all around her, as if hundreds of rats were making their way through adjacent tunnels all around her. Kai hated rats and she prayed that she was wrong. Every now and then there was also a deep low rumbling that shook dust off the walls followed by strange grunts like the pigs she used to see at the farmers markets back on Balon. For the first time since she had arrived here on Satiren she began to wish she was back there.

A few minutes later Kai saw lights up ahead and found herself in another large cavern lit up with flaming torches that were imbedded into the walls. She saw dark shapes scurrying in the shadows and realised that there were also Trolls down here underground. Pulling out her pouch of explosive powder and this time taking only a pinch, she threw some in their direction. There was a loud bang and flash, then there was a lot of smoke and she found herself coughing with her eyes stinging. Perhaps using the powder in a confined space was not such a good idea. There was shrieking now all around her and as the smoke cleared, she saw she was surrounded by what seemed like fifty or so angry Trolls whilst more were squeezing through cracks in the walls. The eyes of these creatures were ghostly white making them look even more grotesque and unnatural than their counterparts out on the mountains. It seemed to her that the walls were opening up letting more and more of these revolting creatures appear, they were packing themselves onto high ledges and peering out of small crevices high up in the cavern walls. Kai grabbed a torch from the wall and held it out in front of her just as one of the beasts ran towards her. She swotted it with the flames and it ran off screeching. Another ran at her from behind and then another and another, soon Kai was swinging the torch around wildly as the Trolls descended on her from all sides.

Then there was a loud banging, like many drums being struck at once, the noise bouncing off the walls and confusing the Trolls. It was followed by roar and a rag tag group of Crystalites came running into cavern, all carrying flaming torches and spiked clubs. The Trolls shrieked, running for cover as they were swatted and struck and almost as quickly as they had come, they were gone and silence prevailed.

A small pale boy grabbed hold of Kai's hand and dragged her with him down the tunnel they had appeared from. They were all running and Kai kept pace as they descended even deeper into the labyrinth, she would not find her way back so easily now.

They slowed down as they reached another torch lit cavern leading her inside. Kai caught her breath while looking around to see at least seventy or so Crystalites eyeing her curiously. They all looked half-starved and dirty, their clothes were ragged and some of them looked very ill.

"Who are you people?" she heard herself ask.

An old man stepped forward, he was almost bent over double leaning heavily on his stick and kai had to duck slightly to see his face. She saw he was blinded in one eye and his hands were horribly crooked, as if he had broken all the bones and they had not set right. There was something horribly familiar about him and as he drew closer, she bent low to get a better look at his face. This was not the face of a very old man that stared back at her, this was Lord Arcos.

"Lord Arcos, what happened to you?" Kai staggered back in horror.

"You don't know?" he responded sounding puzzled. "What was your crime my lady? Why have you been sent to the ice caves of Vulcan?"

"I came here on my own, I found the entrance and I was curious," replied Kai.

"That is impossible, the entrance is sealed, no one can pass through," said the broken warrior twisting his head up with difficulty to get a better look at her.

"It's a long story but I think I was led here to help you," replied Kai, now sure that was the reason she was here.

"Ask her who she is Arcos," said a tall woman wrapped in a grey cloak. She had very dark rings under her eyes and looked extremely ill, but Kai recognised still her.

"You're Kaeshia, I've seen you before, I don't understand why are you all imprisoned down here?" she asked then saw the confused look in their eyes. "I'm Kai, I think many of you will remember me from when I was a small child. I've returned to Satiren to find my brother, but I did not expect to find this."

"Are you telling us the truth girl?" asked Lord Arcos twisting his head around to get a better look at her.

"Why would I lie?" she replied.

"She speaks the truth." Another voice filtered through the Crystalites, Kai looked over to see a very old man lying in a makeshift cot. She walked over kneeling down beside him, it was Zodiac. He smiled weakly up at her, "I would recognise you anywhere child."

Kai laid her hands on his fore head, his skin was like ice and she felt an over whelming sense of pure raw emotion pulse through her. Then without even trying to focus a blue light sprang to life from her hands and Kai experienced another rush of the potent energy flowing through her. Zodiac's face began to glow and he closed his eyes smiling peacefully. The light faded and he opened them again and then slowly got to his feet. "Thank you I don't know how you did that, but I feel much better," he said looking around at all the awe-struck faces.

"Can someone tell me why you are all imprisoned here?" Kai asked.

"I think firstly you should tell us how much you do know and then perhaps we can fill in the gaps," replied Zodiac.

"Very well, that makes sense," agreed Kai and so she told them of her journey to Satiren and of her meeting with the White Witch. How she had been on her way to meet Solitaire and Tokala when she was knocked off course and saved by Wigholt. From there she had learnt what happened in the Crystal City and at Burning Towers all these years before, but more importantly she discovered who she actually was. From there she had taken the decision to find her brother, Wigholt helped her get to the mountains and she was making her way through the mountain paths when a strange sensation led her here.

The Crystalites listened quietly until she finished speaking, but Kai didn't miss the sneaked glances they made to one another at the mention of her brother.

"Would I be right I saying you know nothing of what has happened here in the last eleven years?" asked Lord Arcos.

"Yes, you would be right, which is why I believe it's your turn now to tell me what happened," replied Kai.

CHAPTER TWENTY-SIX

Someone helped Lord Arcos hobble across to a jutting ledge and he lowered himself down on it painfully, taking a deep breath he began his tale.

"When Atolin was thrown off the plateau at Mount Gloom the snow eagles tried to save him, but they were not strong enough to slow his fall completely, when he landed, he shattered his left leg. Everyone assumed he was dead and we left him down there, and for that mistake, I take full responsibility, I should have sent a search party out immediately."

"You weren't to know Arcos, all of us should have shouldered that responsibility," Kaeshia interrupted. "We were all distraught and not thinking clearly."

"Nevertheless, the boy managed to survive using skills he had learnt from Ragnar, Tokala and Darkstar. It was a miracle that he managed to survive at all, it took three weeks for us to finally go and find him. When I first saw him, I got the impression he was not altogether pleased to see me, there was definitely a flicker of anger in his eyes, but I couldn't blame him for that. We had neglected him badly and to make matters worse his leg had reset itself without proper treatment leaving him horribly crippled.

On our journey back to the Crystal City he said very little about his time there, and when I finally broke the news about Darkstar's death he said nothing, there was no reaction at all. He rode the rest of the way with a cold haunted expression on his face that left me feeling very unsettled.

Even when we arrived at the Crystal City and the people came out in the streets to welcome him, he remained expressionless and did not acknowledge anybody. He simply rode straight ahead to the palace then took himself off to his rooms without a word to the palace staff.

The healer, Little Coodle, went to see him with her bag of magic and tried to do what she could for his leg, but in the end, he was still left with a prominent limp. He stayed out of sight for a month while Coodle attended to him daily then eventually he began to leave his rooms. When I first saw him, my heart was left cold, this was no longer the wide-eyed playful boy I had taught, his eyes were hollow and cold and he had no interest in what he had once loved.

Atolin always had a huge amount of love for the animals of the mountains, so I attempted to take him to Ragnar's cave on Mount Solomite to check on the creatures that Ragnar once cared for. He refused, he wouldn't even visit Icicle, his own beloved mountain pony.

According to Crystalite tradition Atolin could not be crowned until he was fifteen years old and so the Wizard Council governed the city in the absence of a King or Queen. In the meantime, Atolin attended his studies as he should, but his behaviour was causing concern amongst the Wizards. He was often seen skulking around the palace, eaves dropping on conversations, even those of the servants. When he was invited to attend Wizard Council meetings he refused, yet one day he was discovered listening in from behind one of the panels. He did not wish people to look at him and his strange behaviour was causing concerns in the Council room, but again we all dismissed it due to his horrific experience and the shock of the death of both his parents. We should have paid more attention, but it was easier to just let things be.

When Atolin finally started to make friends outside of the palace we all thought this was a good sign. But his new friends were bully boys, wild and rebellious, terrorizing others in their wake, spurred on by their friendship with the future King.

Yet again we did not take a firm hand with this behaviour, we told ourselves they were not particularly mean spirited but just boyhood pranks, but then they started to harass old people, terrorise girls and young women and intimidate the other children.

As they continued to be ignored, their numbers grew and they became a very real problem in the streets of the Crystal City. It was no longer a safe place to stroll through, and I spent a lot of my time rounding up these rebels and taking them back home to their parents, who were completely losing control of them.

Atolin always seemed to be at the centre of the worst violations, and one day I pulled him aside to talk to him about his behaviour. He listened to me without interrupting, but I could see I was wasting my breath. He was smirking and clearly ignoring everything I said, when I finished, he went straight outside to join his friends.

Because of his behaviour the Wizard Council held a vote and decided they would hold off on crowning Atolin as King. When he heard this, he flew into a crazed rage threatening anyone who came near him. However, a few hours later he seemed to calm himself and methodically set about correcting his behaviour. He organised a meeting with the Wizard Council where he apologised for his recent loss of morals, blaming it on the fact he had felt so lost after what had happened. He promised to change his ways and for a while he did just that. He became a model student, courteous and kind to those around him. He no longer went out into the streets, he stayed away from his thuggish friends and worked hard at his studies paying a great deal of attention on how to run the Crystal City. Before long the Wizard Council said he was ready and Atolin was crowned King. I still had my own reservations, there was something behind his eyes that didn't sit right with me, but again I let it go.

His first action as King was to move all his friends from the city into the palace and make them his bodyguards and advisors. The members of the Wizard Council who had initially opposed him and had stood in the way of his coronation, mysteriously vanished over the next few weeks. As you can see for yourself, many of them ended up here.

The people were outraged and started to protest in huge demonstrations outside the palace walls, but soon the leaders of these demonstrations disappeared also and when their families and friends came looking for them, they also vanished. I had all my powers stripped from me and one of Atolin's friends took over the title of Lord Warrior. I should have fought back then, but I'd had enough over the years, no one could replace Darkstar and if I were to be honest, I still hadn't forgiven the people for what they did to Ragnar, so I decided to leave them to it. In hind sight it was a cowardly thing to do, I should have taken control of the city from Atolin there and then.

I first toyed with the idea of going to find Tokala and Catori, but the desert is not a good place for a Crystalite, so instead I went to live in Ragnar's cave up on Mount Solomite. I have to admit the peace of the mountains was a blessed relief from what had been happening in the city and I had no desire to return. But more and more people soon came to join me in my seclusion, many were running for their lives as Atolin hunted them down, punishing everyone who stood up against him. They told me the city lived in terror, every day brought more public floggings or imprisonments down in the ice caves. Darkstar had closed off these ice tunnel prisons years before calling them barbaric, but Atolin had decided to re-use them. His followers ran amuck throughout the city doing exactly what they wished with no regard for the citizens.

Eventually I decided to travel back down to visit the king for myself and see if there was anything I could do. As I was packing up my horse for the journey, I heard hooves approaching and then there were shouts of warnings coming from my friends. Upon leaving the cave I walked straight into an ambush, ropes were thrown over me and I was bound tight along with the others who hadn't managed escape in time.

Atolin was there, seated on his horse wearing his crown looking every bit the tyrant that had been described to me. He told me that Darkstar had been announced as a traitor to the Crystalites, and all those who had served under him were to be tried and punished accordingly. He was unrecognisable as the Atolin I'd once known, his eyes that had been so hollow when I found him, now shone with pure festering evil. I became angry asking Atolin what unnerved him about his father so much that he had to label him a traitor. Perhaps it was because he could never hope to live up to his father's good name within the city.

This provoked a response I hadn't anticipated, I was thrown to the ground and attacked by twelve of his men, all of them kicking me repeatedly breaking many bones throughout my body. They were relentless and I eventually must have passed out because when I awoke I found myself tied over the back of a horse being taken back to the Crystal City. I was barely alive when we got there, but my suffering was not yet to end. They put me in a small metal cage and hung me in the centre of the city for everyone to see. The only person allowed to attend me was Little Coodle and she did the best she could, but I was already so broken. The cage itself was only four feet square so I could not straighten my body and as you can now see, I became crippled. The air at night in the mountains is cold even for a Crystalite and although Coodle brought me blankets I wasted away in that cage for a full year. If it were not for the kindness of brave citizens who dared to bring me hot drinks and food when the city was asleep, I would have certainly died. During the day the people would not dare make eye contact with me for fear of reprisals from Atolin's men, and when the King and his men rode past, they would hurl rocks and stones at me, causing me a number of injuries."

"I can't believe what your telling me Arcos, how could anyone be so wicked," cried Kai, her eyes wet with angry tears.

"Eventually after a year was up, I was put down here along with Little Coodle, who refused to work for Atolin. This is where I found the others had been put, Zodiac and Kaeshia had been here for two years already along with most of the other Wizard Council members. Piro and Pinto arrived here shortly after myself, they had been in hiding but were betrayed by Egor, who once again is living in the palace. Zebulon seems to have left us and of course Ragnar and Garik are both dead. We expected to be eaten by Vulcan by now, we have heard him roar from time to time, but he has stayed away from us. Piro was able to use her elemental magic and making us fire for warmth and light, whilst Coodle knew what mosses and fungi we could eat. Although there is an underground lake with some fish, we have still been forced to eat troll meat from time to time, but we have managed to survive, only just."

Kai was appalled and sick to her stomach as she looked around at the people who had suffered so much at the hands of her brother. All she had ever seen of Atolin in her visions was a sweet loveable boy, who cherished all life, surely it was Draconan that was behind this. She would undoubtably be walking straight into danger if she went to the Crystal City alone, now she understood why Sirena was sending her to Burning Towers. Any dreams of an emotional family reunion were shattered, she was going to have to find a way to remove Atolin from the Crystalite throne, but from what Arcos had just told her that would be almost impossible.

"It seems as though I would be foolish to go to the Crystal City without some sort of plan. I'm going to have to meet up with Tokala and Solitaire as the White Witch wanted me to do in the first place. Atolin needs to be stopped and you Lord Arcos along with everyone else here, are all going to help me. The gate is open and we can all leave this place."

"All I can do is advise you Kai I am too weak to make it out of these tunnels now. I still know people in the city if they are still alive, they'll help you if they can," Arcos replied.

Kai walked over to Lord Arcos looking down at his broken body and sad blue eyes. She reached down and grabbed his twisted hands, "Stand up for now Arcos, let me try something."

Arcos struggled to his feet while she held both his hands in hers and smiled, "Can you feel it?" she said as a tingling sensation spread between the two of them. Arcos went to pull his hands away but Kai held on to them tightly as the power surged through her with more strength than any of the times before and she gasped as it transferred from her into Arcos. He became engulfed in a bright blue light as Kai closed her eyes envisioning him as he had once been, young, tall and strong, standing in his magnificent shining silver blue armour with his white hair falling down his back and his bright violet eyes glowing with vitality in his chiselled handsome face. She remembered his strength when he had fought Black Eagles warriors and then Black Eagle himself, and the memories of these battles flowed through her hands into his body. Kai could feel his hands shake but she held on tightly refusing to let go too soon.

At first the energy was hot, seeping through him and easing the pain away from his shattered bones. Every hair on his body was standing on end as he felt the heat pour into him, then the energy turned ice cold in an instant and what Kai had thought was shaking was in fact an involuntary shiver. He could feel his bones straightening, mending themselves as he slowly began to straighten to stand upright again. The bones in his hands snapped back into place and he felt them regain their strength as he held onto Kai's hands tighter than before. His vision started to return and he could see out of both his eyes once more as the energy continued to flow into him. Lord Arcos felt his strength and power return as he suddenly was engulfed with memories of the past, of when he had defeated Black Eagles men and the strength that had taken. He felt stronger, charged with more power than he had ever felt before in his life. Then abruptly Kai let him go and she staggered backwards, her energy depleted.

Lord Arcos reached his hands up to his face, it felt smooth and whole, the scars had gone and he turned to face his fellow prisoners, he had been completely restored to how he had been eleven years before, a young strong warrior ready and willing to fight for them once again. He helped Kai to sit down. "I don't know what sort of sorcerer you are Kai, I have never seen anything like this. I am totally in your debt."

"I am no sorcerer, the White Witch gifted me with magic abilities and I am only just learning how to use them. You look wonderful Lord Arcos," she said tearfully. Her strength was returning quite quickly now and she turned to face the other Crystalites in the cavern. "I don't have the strength to heal you all just yet, but we are going to get out of here. All those who can, must come with us now, those who are too weak we will send help for you soon, that I promise."

"But where shall we go?" asked Kaeshia.

"Firstly, we need to get back to the gate that I opened, it's the way out but I can't remember the way. Does anyone know it?" Kai looked around hoping for a positive reply.

"I do," said a little boy who looked around nine or so, Kai recognised him, he was the one who had dragged her from the troll cave. He looked so pale and thin and she wondered how long he had been trapped down here.

"What's your name? Can you lead us?" she asked.

"This is Togs, his mother was put here just before she gave birth and died soon after. He has been here all his life, he knows the tunnels better than any of us," said Lord Arcos ruffling Tog's hair.

"Well lead the way Togs, it's time to get you out of here," said Kai.

Togs was glowing with pride as he took hold of Kai's hand and began to lead her out the cavern. There was a brief discussion going on behind them, and around thirty of the Crystalites followed on, the rest were too weak choosing to remain and wait for help.

They made their way quietly through the tunnels and caverns, looking out all the time for trolls but none came near. Then all around them there came the same deep rumbling sound that Kai had heard throughout her journey in these tunnels, "is it Trolls?" she whispered to Lord Arcos.

"I don't think so, let me lead," replied the Lord Warrior and he drew his sword and went up front. The noise grew louder and Togs began to look confused. "The tunnels don't seem right, they keep changing," he said.

Lord Arcos took the lead, there was only one way to go and it led them to a huge cavern, so gigantic and wide that it was impossible to see how far it went. Kai knew she had not come this way before, they were standing on the banks of a lake that seemed to fill the cavern.

"I don't recognise this place," whispered Togs to Kai looking worried. "I don't know how we came to be here I've never seen it before."

"I think there is magic involved here Togs, it's not your fault," Kai reassured him.

The rumbling started again and the lake that had been as still as glass a second before started to splash around violently at its banks, then there was a roar that sounded like one of the great mountain lions, except it was louder than any lion they had ever heard before. It was followed by explosive splashing coming from somewhere in the lake, as if something massive was striding through the water towards them, but still they could see nothing.

"Let's find another way out of here," cried Lord Arcos over the roars, but before he could move his sword flew out of his hands and embedded itself in the ice wall at the side of the lake. He ran over to try to free it as the terrified Crystalites were trying desperately to locate a way out. Then silence prevailed once more, whatever was heading towards them was no longer moving.

Kai stared out into the darkness and could make out an enormous shape standing in the middle of the lake. A grotesque, innately evil laughter echoed all around them.

"Did you really think that leaving here would be that easy?"

CHAPTER TWENTY-SEVEN

Tokala was making slow progress, he was having to lead Chaser on foot as the horse was nervous amongst the high cliffs and narrow rocky passageways. He had found the remnants of a small explosion with blackened cliffs and a number of these dreaded vines hanging down lifeless. Wigholt had already told him about the exploding powder he had given to Kai, and he suspected she must have used it. At least she wasn't caught up in the vines like he had been, he cringed as he remembered.

The track was getting more difficult for Chaser, but Tokala did not want to leave his horse out here alone in the open, not with the cliffs teaming with trolls. Eventually they arrived at the precipice that separated the path and Tokala wondered how Kai had managed to get across. It was too wide for him to jump, but Chaser would probably manage it. He remounted and led Chacer back a little way then with a small amount of encouragement, he nudged Chaser on, his sleek black stallion ran at full speed and leapt over the drop with ease.

He stayed mounted for a time, it seemed to comfort Chaser but then his eyes were drawn down to the left and he could make out the dark outline of what looked like a large cave. For no other reason than just an overwhelming urge, he rode Chaser over to the cave and found it was wide enough for them to both enter. Drawing his long knife in case they had stumbled across the home of a sleeping bear, they stepped inside but the cave was thankfully deserted.

Tokala knew Kai had come this way, he couldn't explain why, he just did, so he turned to Chaser, "You're going to have to remain here boy, I'll be back." The horse nodded its head snorting and stamping its foot angrily.

Tokala made his way tentatively into the darkness, it was very cold and he was glad of the thick cloak Wigholt had given him for mountains. He felt the walls to discover they were covered in ice and as he went in further, he found he could no longer see particularly well. Stumbling along in the dark he arrived at the top of the stone staircase, he had no idea how far down it went and it was now so dark he could barely see the shape of his hand in front of him. Tokala hesitated, he knew he would be a fool to attempt the descent when he was virtually blind in the darkness and he wondered how Kai had managed it, for he was sure she had.

The walls around him started to glow, he looked down at his feet and saw a small round glass orb burning with a bright blue light, lighting up the cave around him. Tokala bent down and picked it up, "What sort of magic is this?" he said aloud, but realised he was speaking to no one.

Holding the orb aloft he started to descend the slippery steps that led him deep down into the mountain. Eventually arriving at the bottom, he stepped out as Kai had done onto the hundreds of strewn skeletons of small animal. Making his way over them he eventually arrived at the iron gateway that was now standing prised open. He read the sign before slipping through the gate only to find himself staring at a number of tunnels leading in different directions. What now? He had no idea which way Kai had gone, he held his orb aloft and inspected each tunnel entrance trying to find some sort of clue, a footprint or something. Then he saw on one tunnel wall some scratch marks and realised she must have marked it. Impressed by her clever thinking he followed the tunnel finding similar scratches marking the way as he continued.

***

The beast in the middle of the lake was thrashing around once more, this time they could all see its massive body coming towards them, the Crystalites were terrified. He moved slowly and methodically through the lake, even though the deep water only came up to the top of his thighs. His colossal head was covered in horns and dangerous looking spikes and his wicked flaming eyes glowed fiery orange just above a long snout that smouldered smoke from its nostrils. When he spoke, his mouth flickered with dancing flames revealing enormous deadly sharp teeth and a red, glowing forked tongue.

"I am Vulcan, last of the dragons and you're all my prisoners as well as my food when I see fit, you will not leave my domain." The dragon lowered it mammoth head to look at them, his thunderous voice had shaken the cavern and rocks were falling down from the roof.

Kai boldly stepped forward as Arcos continued trying to free his embedded sword from the rock. She called out to Vulcan, "I didn't know that dragons lived underground. Why are you locked down in these caverns? Are you not as much of a prisoner as we are!"

"Silence, you dare to address me girl!" The dragon roared angrily with flames flowing from his mouth and cascading across the roof, more rocks stared to crumble away and the Crystalites ran for cover. Kai remained where she was facing Vulcan who was watching her curiously.

"We thought you were nothing but a made-up story to scare the children, Vulcan the scary dragon! Why have you not escaped? she continued to badger him and the dragon eyed her thoughtfully.

"You're brave and intriguing girl, but I won't rise to your bait. Draconan has not abandoned me he has promised me that one day soon I will rule the skies of Satiren once more and my dragons will rise again with me as their leader."

Zodiac managed to cast a small incantation on Lord Arcos's sword and between them they managed to release it from the wall. The Lord Warrior started towards the dragon but Kai stopped him, "Get the others out of here while I distract him, you won't defeat him on your own with just a sword."

Kai stepped towards Vulcan, "So you are a servant of Draconan? It seems the Dark lord has many servants he is making promises to. I have already heard Draconan promise this world to my brother, King of the Crystalites. How can this be? Are you sure he will keep his promise to you?"

"How easily these lies fall from your lips girl. Draconan would not betray me for a mere Crystalite!" roared Vulcan and Kai could feel the heat of his breath on her face. "I will tear all the Crystalites apart, limb from limb."

"How do you know I don't speak the truth? You have been trapped down here for how long? Centuries. You have no idea what has transpired on the surface. Why do you not leave and see for yourself?" she shouted.

Lord Arcos had found his way back to the tunnel entrance and was quickly ushering the others out of the cavern unnoticed by Vulcan, "Zodiac, take them onwards, Togs lead the way, I'm going back for Kai. Don't stop for anything!"

"Centuries mean nothing to me, I sleep through mere centuries. What is an eternity for you is but a few days in my life. I can no longer live in the sunlight but Draconan is bringing the darkness and soon I will be free."

"He has lied to you. Draconan has no power on Satiren, the darkness he has promised you will never come and you'll be trapped here forever. You have been a fool!" Kai taunted him.

Vulcan raised up his head and roared, flames spread over the roof of the cavern and Kai had to run for cover as flaming rocks and debris came crashing down all around her. The dragon was furious now charging through the water towards her and Kai guessed it was probably time for her to escape also. She turned and ran towards the tunnel but suddenly felt her body lifted from the ground by some invisible force and she was spun around in mid-air to find herself face to face with a grotesque cloaked figure standing by the water's edge.

"Master," hissed the dragon as he stopped and bowed his great head. "I am here to serve."

"You have allowed this girl to poison your mind Vulcan. Have I not told you the time is near, why do you doubt me?" hissed a sinuous voice from beneath the hood of the cloak. All Kai could make out were pinpoints of white lights where his eyes should be, his face looked like nothing more than a shadowy skull half hidden under his hood while his long skeletal bone fingers curled and moved grotesquely as if he were playing an instrument of some sort.

"Master, the girl confused me for a moment, but I knew you would not betray me," replied the Dragon who had seemed to have shrunk in size under the gaze of this hooded figure.

"So, I'm guessing you must me the infamous Draconan then, the scary Prince of Darkness himself no less," said Kai, keeping her voice light and airy. She saw Arcos sneak back in the cavern, but she wasn't sure what they could do right now. She was still hanging limply in mid-air, maybe if she just concentrated. She closed her eyes and willed herself to be free of the force that held her, instantly she could feel the dark force struggling against her power then suddenly she dropped to the ground, landing in an ungracious heap. She pulled herself to her feet quickly as the hooded figure descended on her.

"Who are you to challenge my power?" demanded Draconan. She could see his face more clearly now, the skull was covered with a thin layer of skin, he had no nose or lips, just a gaping dark hole where his mouth should be. His sinister white eyes blazed with an intensity that made Kai shiver, but she didn't back away.

"I am someone who is going to stop you by any means necessary," replied Kai sounding a lot braver than she felt.

Draconan was silent for a moment, then still staring at Kai he flicked his skeletal hands in Lord Arcos's direction and the Lord warrior came flying out of his hiding place landing with a crash next to Kai. "I want to know who you are?" hissed the Dark Lord.

Kai stood silently she would not answer him.

"Then die!" said Draconan and he flicked his wrist once again and a red flaming arrow came flying from his hand straight towards her heart.

Everything before Kai turned to slow motion and the speeding arrow instantly became a small flock of harmless blue moths.

"What is this!" hissed Draconan before flinging a volley of flaming arrows at them both, but all the arrows again turned into moths.

"I told you, I will stop you!" cried Kai with her confidence growing. She wasn't sure how that had just happened, but she there was no point dwelling on it. Something was clearly on her side. "While the moons still shine here on Satiren, you have no power to harm me or the ones I protect. Leave this world now!"

Kai had no idea why she had just said that, but it seemed to have the desired effect as Draconan started to back away.

"You carry the power of the White Witch but it will only protect you for so long. Your moons are already dying and I am getting stronger every hour that passes. Soon I will bring the darkness with me and you will bow down to me as my slave." Draconan's appearance became distorted, and he started to fade, but before he disappeared, he cried out to the confused dragon, "Vulcan, Kill them!"

The Dragon raised his head, flames flying from his mouth and then he charged. Kai held up her hand as red-hot flames threatened to incinerate them both, but instead they bounced off an invisible shield leaving them unharmed. Vulcan roared again before descending on them in a fury, he intended to rip them to pieces.

***

Tokala could hear the dragons roars but he also heard voices and whispers coming from up ahead, drawing his long knife he followed the sound and came across a group of rag tag Crystalites, being led by Zodiac whom he recognised immediately. The old Wizard looked confused when he first saw him. "Zodiac, it's me Tokala, don't you recognise me?"

"Of course, it's you," said the old Wizard relief washing over him. "Have you come to help us?"

"Yes, have you seen Kai?" asked Tokala.

"She's back fighting the dragon, she told us to get out. Lord Arcos is with her," replied Zodiac just as another blood curdling roar rang through the tunnel. Zodiac pointed, "that way! It will take you directly to them."

"Wait for us at the cave entrance. My horse Chaser is there, I will get them out," cried Tokala as he sprinted off down the tunnel. The roars from the dragon were terrifying and he prayed he was not too late.

Turning around a tight bend he found himself running straight into what seemed like an inferno of fire and smoke, he could just make out Arcos jumping over the ledges above the head of a huge serpent like creature that was lashing out with its barbed tail. Then he heard a young woman's voice cry out, "Arcos you need to cut out its tongue, it's the only way to kill him!"

The dragon charged at Kai furiously, she leapt out the way as it crashed down on the rocks where she had stood a second before. Tokala drew his bow then fired multiple arrows at the dragon's head, but they bounced off, not even scratching the surface of its skin.

"Aim for his eye!" cried Kai when she saw him.

Tokala aimed again and this time his arrow struck its target, embedding itself in the dragon's eye. The dragon roared again and flames shot towards Tokala as he leapt behind a rock to escape them.

The distraction was all Arcos needed and he jumped from the ledge and landed on Vulcan's head, narrowly avoiding the sharp spikes. He hung onto the horns of the dragon for dear life as it shook its head violently trying to throw him off. Lord Arcos's sword was raised but the dragon crashed his head against the cavern wall and sent Arcos flying. Kai ran in front of Arcos just in time to save him from being incinerated.

Tokala ran from his hiding place and started to clamber up the back of the dragon discovering his long knife was useless against the thick hide of the beast. The dragon became aware of him and turned from Arcos and Kai to try to throw Tokala off. It was all the distraction Lord Arcos needed he ran forwards again sprinting up the side of the wall and launching himself back onto the dragons's head. Vulcan threw his head back opening his colossal mouth sending a stream of fire up to the roof with his tongue protruding just enough for Arcos to leap forward, take aim with his great sword and swipe clean through it.

The fire in the dragon instantly petered out as it staggered back into the lake, its huge head crashed down into the water causing steam to erupt and fill the cavern. Arcos managed to jump clear before the dragons head hit the water, landing clumsily on a rocky ledge at the side of the lake. They all stood staring at each other as an eerie silence filled the cavern.

"Tokala?" Lord Arcos's voice made Kai jump.

"Hallo, old friend, looks like I saved your ass again," replied Tokala grinning from ear to ear.

Kai suddenly felt a little self- conscious, she should remember Tokala but she couldn't, and it made her uncomfortable. He was very tall, almost as tall as Lord Arcos, with wide powerful shoulders and muscular arms. She watched quietly as the two warriors greeted one another, forgetting she was there for a time. They had been close; she could tell that as she listened to them talk and banter with one another.

"I think it's time you met Kai," said Lord Arcos suddenly pulling her forwards.

Kai felt herself blush as Tokala's intense golden eyes turned to regard her, "Do you remember me Kai?" he asked.

"I know who you are, but my memories were taken from me, so I'm afraid not," she admitted regretfully.

"I'm sorry for that, but we haven't time for catch up," he said a little more abruptly than he intended. "I've come to stop you; you cannot go to the Crystal City."

"I think the Crystal City is exactly where I should be going. I have seen what Atolin has done to his people and he has to be stopped," she snapped back.

"If you walk into the city, Atolin will have you imprisoned or killed before you even reach the palace," replied Tokala irritated by her response. He didn't know what to expect from Kai, but he had not anticipated her arguing with him.

"Perhaps we need to talk about this once we're out of these ice caves. It's been a while since I've seen the sky and I'd like to join the others," suggested Lord Arcos attempting to break the icy atmosphere that was forming between them.

Agreeing, they left the steaming body of Vulcan behind and made their way back through the ice tunnels with Tokala leading as Kai followed on behind them both at the rear. They didn't speak much and Kai wondered if that was her fault. She hated being told what to do, it had always been one of her problems, but she was not about to back down. The White Witch had entrusted her with this power so she was perfectly able to take care of herself.

They finally reached the iron gate that led to the steep icy steps, they made their way up to join the others who were waiting for them in the shadows of the cave. It was dawn outside and the sun had just risen, but the Crystalites were struggling with the brightness after being locked away in the darkness for so long. Chaser stamped his feet excitedly when he saw Tokala, and the Mavaho chief went to greet him while Kai watched on with interest at how affectionate he was with his horse.

"As I was trying to explain in the ice caves, Wigholt and Solitaire suggested I came to find you and bring you to Mount Solomite where your father's cave in. They have gone on ahead and are waiting for us there, so we can formulate a plan together," said Tokala, speaking slowly as if Kai was stupid and couldn't understand.

"You didn't explain that!" said Kai defiantly. "You just told me I couldn't go to the Crystal City. If I had known this then I wouldn't have argued with you, so don't treat me like an idiot."

"Look, we're getting off on the wrong foot. They just asked me to come and find you, I'm not trying to make you do anything, but I do think it's a good idea if we go to Ragnar's cave first," sighed Tokala.

"It makes sense Kai," said Lord Arcos hoping these two would drop the animosity soon.

Kai had to agree, she really hadn't any other plan in place and was still trying to come to terms with her brother's cruelty and treatment of Lord Arcos and the others. Tokala was right, it would be too dangerous to just ride into the city and announce herself. "What about everyone else?"

"It will take some time for our eyes to adjust to daylight, we will have to remain here for a few hours at least. We could follow on when nightfall comes, I know how to get to Ragnar's cave from here," said Kaeshia.

"We can send Wigholt to help you, just stay put for now until you hear from us, you've all been through so much, I don't want any of you risking the chance of being seen yet," said Tokala taking charge again much to Kai's irritation.

"We'll need mountain horses if we are to reach Ragnar's place any time soon," suggested Lord Arcos. "I know where we can find them, that's if Atolin has not enslaved them all."

Having formulated what seemed like a simple plan, they left the other Crystalites minutes later following Lord Arcos in the search for some mountain horses.

CHAPTER TWENTY-EIGHT

Lord Arcos knew where he was going, he enjoyed every step he took with his new strong body and made good time as he led them to a natural thermal milky blue pool that was being fed by water from an ice glacier. Steam rose as ice cold water splashed down into the bubbling pool and Kai could feel the warmth radiate off the surface. All around the pool the rocks were covered in a strange lime green moss, and eating the moss were around nine or so horses. The horses looked up nervously as they approached. "It's not so long ago that these horses would have come over to greet us, but since Atolin has been King they have been abused by his men and they no longer trust us. I'm not sure if they'll allow us to mount them," said Lord Arcos as he slowly approached, but they backed away watching him suspiciously.

"Let me try," said Kai and she walked around Arcos towards the horses, they stared at her with more curiosity than fear. Kai found she could sense their uncertainty as she drew closer and was particularly drawn to a pretty white mare with black feet. Kai recognised the apprehension in the mare so she stopped moving remaining still where she was. After a moment the mare took a step towards her and then another, then slowly walked over to where Kai was standing. *"It's alright girl, I'm your friend,"* she projected her thoughts towards the horse and suddenly it was at her side allowing Kai to stroke her.

"You really are your father's daughter," remarked Arcos, "He's the only person I ever knew who had that connection with the horses."

"You must tell me what he was like, I can't even see his face in my memories," said Kai sadly stroking the pretty mare, "she will take us up the mountain along with her son." As she spoke a handsome black and white stallion trotted over to them proudly shaking his very long black mane.

Chaser snorted with disgust and shook his own mane, "are you telling him who's boss?" Tokala laughed at his jealous horse. As he turned, he saw that Kai was smiling also, it transformed her and he swallowed hard as his heart started to beat a little faster. Her eyes were a shining lilac and her skin was glowing pink in the cold mountain air, her white hair was streaked with blue and braided loosely down her back. She was tall and athletic, and he could sense the strength within her, she was no simpering female like her mother had been. Kai caught him staring at her and he quickly looked away, embarrassed.

Lord Arcos was busy making friends with the horses, "We're going to have to ride bareback, will you manage Kai?"

"I should think so, we won't be galloping through the mountains anyway," she replied whispering something into her horse's ear before leaping up onto the animals back. "Her name is Kyte," said Kai, "and Arcos your riding Gusto, are you both ready to go?"

The ride up to Mount Solomite was thankfully uneventful, Lord Arcos led them away from the city so they could approach Ragnar's cave from the other side of the mountain. They stayed alert in case they came across anyone, but the paths were clear and apart from the odd screech from a troll, they were safe.

Lord Arcos passed the time by telling Kai stories about her father and Darkstar, they had all been friends when they were younger, exploring the mountains together and getting into all sorts of scrapes. Tokala was silent as he listened to Arcos telling his tales of fighting trolls and playing with bear cubs before having to escape their raging mother. He couldn't work out if Kai was ignoring him, or if she just didn't like him as she didn't seem to notice he was there. She was so wrapped up in Lord Arcos's stories he was feeling like a third wheel and he found himself feeling irritated with her again. Why was she having this effect on him?

Catori was sitting on a rocky ledge acting as lookout, she called down to them,"finally, we were worried something had happened!" Then she stood up and ran backup to Ragnar's cave to tell the others they had arrived.

"That can't be Catori," said Lord Arcos looking mesmerised.

"It looks like the only person that hasn't aged any is you," replied Tokala. "That is my sister."

They arrived at the cave to find Solitaire and Catori outside waiting for them. Lord Arcos and Tokala jumped down from their horses to embrace their friends, everyone seemed to be talking at once. Kai suddenly felt like an outsider, they all knew each other so well, she was a complete stranger. Tokala looked back to see her still seated on her horse so he went to help her down.

"I can manage myself," she snapped at him then instantly regretted it. She didn't know why she was being like that towards him, he hadn't done anything wrong. "I'm sorry, I didn't mean to sound so harsh."

"Forget it!" he said coldly and walked back over to join the others. She looked over and saw Solitaire watching her with raised eyebrows. She still wasn't used to seeing him in his human form and she gave him an indifferent shrug, before sliding off Kyte. Instantly she found herself caught up in a pair of arms as Catori jumped on her, "Kai, it's really you, I missed you so much when they took you away!" she cried.

Kai immediately felt awkward, she only remembered Catori from her visions of the past, and she felt robbed. "I know you don't remember me, but I have enough memories for the both of us," said Catori suddenly pulling away from her. Kai was completely overwhelmed and to her horror suddenly became aware that tears were forming in her eyes. Catori noticed and hugged her again and then led her quickly into Ragnar's cave before anyone else noticed. "It must be so hard for you, come on, Wigholt's in here and he always makes things feel better."

It was strange for Kai being in her father's cave, she had seen it in her vision but it seemed bigger now she was here. She looked around, Wigholt was presiding over some bubbling pots hanging over a fire, there was the huge white moon snake curled up asleep in one of the alcoves, and she wondered if it was the same snake she had been named after by Atolin. It made her weepy again when she saw it, so to hide the tears that threatened to fall she went over to play with the small, agile mountain goats in a make shift corral at the back. There was something very calming about the atmosphere and Kai took a deep breath trying to stop the tide of emotion that threatening to overwhelm her. She was finally home, yet instead of feeling relieved and like she belonged, she felt like a stranger.

"Well young lady, you did well," said Wigholt not even bothering to look up from the pot he was stirring. Kai was grateful, if he had behaved any other way she might have crumbled. "It seems I made a mistake sending you to the Crystal City. I had no idea that Atolin had become so black hearted, I could have sent you into danger."

"Well if you insist in locking yourself away for decades at a time, then it makes it very hard to fill you in with what's actually going on," said Solitaire striding into the cave, followed by Lord Arcos and Tokala.

"Perhaps if you had all been more truthful to me at the start, then I would have been able to make my own choices," said Kai, she wasn't going to let Wigholt take all the blame.

"We've all made mistake," interrupted Tokala, "if I had known Atolin was struggling so much I would have tried to help him. He was my best friend, I still find it hard to believe the things he has done."

"I think Draconan has a lot to do with it," said Kai. "We saw him in the ice caves, he is determined to make Satiren his and he is manipulating Atolin to make it possible for him. Perhaps if I try to talk with Atolin alone, I could make him see that he's being used as Draconan's puppet. Maybe the shock of my return will waken him up to what is actually going on."

"I fear he is too far gone for that. I have seen that boy change into something unrecognisable over the years, and I'm ashamed to say I stood by and let it happen. After all he had been through after the fall and losing his parents in that dreadful way, we all gave him too much freedom. Instead of counselling him and teaching him, we let him do what he wanted, I should have taken a stronger hand," said Lord Arcos sadly.

"You weren't to know," said Catori taking his hand. "I'm sure you would have laid down your life for him, no one knows what happened to him after he fell. It must have been awful, he must have felt so abandoned, but no one is to blame, no one could have foreseen any of this."

Lord Arcos shuddered as the touch of her hand sent his blood racing through his body. Never had he seen anyone so beautiful, and when she drew her hand away, he had to resist the urge to grab it back.

Wigholt started to hand out cups of hot herbal tea and they all sat around the fire to try to configurate some sort of plan. Kai suggested that Lord Arcos tell the rest of them what had happened to him and the others in the ice caves, it would give them a clearer picture of what they were dealing with. The Lord Warrior told his story while the others sat in shocked silence, never in their wildest dreams had they expected this. He told them that the inhabitants of the Crystal City lived in fear, no one knew who to trust and most of the inhabitants stayed hidden in their homes when they had finished their working days. Catori burst into tears when he told them of his cage, unable to process that level of cruelty. When he finally finished all remained silent for a while, staring into the flames letting his words sink in.

"The Crystal City is just how Burning Towers used to be under Black Eagle, a place of fear and hatred. The only way to fix Burning Towers was to get rid of Black Eagle, but I still find it hard to think of Atolin in the same vein as my father," said Tokala eventually.

"He is not the Atolin you remember, there is nothing of that sweet, animal loving boy left in him," replied Lord Arcos.

"Whatever we do, we have to do it quickly. I think we have only three days left for me to find the Ne'Shuwa and try to put things right. The moons are dying and when they do the sun will never rise on this world again. If Atolin is behind it, then I'll have to face him, there is no choice," said Kai.

"I knew you were going to say that," said Solitaire. "I'll be going with you, in fact perhaps we should all go?"

"No, there are too many of us, if we ride into the city as a large group, they will perceive us as a threat, we must play it another way," said Lord Arcos.

"I have an idea," said Tokala. "What if Kai and I ride into the city just before dark, we can ask to be brought to Atolin and attempt to talk with him."

"But why would that work?" asked Catori not liking the idea.

"Well from what Lord Arco tells us, it wouldn't, but it will keep Atolin and his men occupied. Then Arcos and Solitaire can go into the city after dark. You said there are still many who would stand up against Atolin living within the city, if they see you restored to health as you are, then they will follow you if you ask them to. Gather up as much support as you can and make the city ready to over throw Atolin. In the meantime, Wigholt and Catori can take some mountain horses and supplies down to help the Crystalite's at Vulcan's Ice caves. Catori can use her healing magic and those who are able can come to join us stand against Atolin in the city."

"But what if Atolin just kills you on sight?" asked Catori, still not convinced.

Tokala shook his head, "he won't, if he's anything like my father he will want to make an example of us to show off his power. He will try to humiliate us first and that will buy us time."

"It seems like the best idea we can come up with," agreed Kai, and Tokala raised his eyebrows in surprise at her approval. Kai had only just found her family and friends; she didn't want to lose them now.

"I don't like riding horses," said Wigholt suddenly. "I'll take the chariot if you don't mind."

Tokala and Kai both looked at each other and started to laugh. "We'll leave that to you," said Tokala. "If we're going to reach the Crystal city by nightfall, we'll have to leave soon."

They were on route to the city fifteen minutes later riding back down Mount Solomite a little way together as a group before Catori split off from them and headed towards the other side of the mountain and down towards the ice caves. Lord Arcos was not happy about her being alone, but Tokala wasn't worried. "Catori can take care of herself, she's as proficient with her bow as you are with your sword."

Finally they rounded a bend and Kai caught her first glimpse of the Crystal City, it was stunning but nothing seemed familiar to her and she was filled with disappointment. Lord Arcos and Solitaire decided to remain where they were, waiting for darkness to fall before heading onwards, so Kai and Tokala rode on alone. Kai was beginning to feel anxious, but she was determined to see it through, she looked over at Tokala and found him watching her. Instead of turning away he smiled, his eyes reassuring her. She smiled back giving him a small nod, they didn't need to speak to know what the other was thinking. Soon they would come face to face with Atolin, they would have to keep their wits about them and Kai had never been so glad to have someone watch her back before.

CHAPTER TWENTY-NINE

Scared, suspicious faces peered out of windows as Kai and Tokala rode slowly through the quiet streets of the Crystal city. A couple of street vendors that were packing up for the night stopped what they were doing to stare open-mouthed at the strange couple. Tokala was an impressive sight sitting straight backed on his magnificent black stallion oozing an air of superiority. He looked strong and muscular, his black skin radiant and his long braided hair was decorated with brightly coloured feathers. His striking golden eyes were taking in everything as he passed by.

In startling contrast kai was seated on her white horse, as pale skinned as Tokala was dark, her long white hair streaked with blue falling loosely over her magnificent navy cloak. She was a beautiful Crystalite woman, tall, strong and glowing with vitality. No one could fail to be impressed at the sight of them.

Kai could hear whisperings as they rode on towards the castle, many of the older inhabitants recognised Tokala and the news of his arrival was spreading like wildfire. By the time they started to ride up the main stretch to the palace the street was lined by crowds, all vying to get a look at the newcomers. Kai could see fear behind their eyes as she turned and smiled at them, they averted their gaze as soon as her eyes fell upon them and she guessed sadly that no one wanted to be seen befriending them.

"The atmosphere here is nothing like the Crystal City I remember," said Tokala quietly so only she could hear.

"They all look terrified," she replied, "What are we walking into?"

"I think we're about to find out," said Tokala nodding towards the palace where a group of men had just appeared at the gates. "That's Atolin."

Kai looked ahead at the men who were stood awaiting them and recognised Atolin immediately, he stood right at the front wearing a contemptuous sneer on his face. As they arrived two of his men stepped forward to take hold of their horses, but Chaser reared in anger and the man who had reached out to grab him stepped back looking fearful.

"Well if it isn't Tokala! This is strange surprise, I have to admit I didn't expect you to show your face in the Crystal City again," said Atolin walking forwards and Kai noticed his limp. He had a handsome face, but it was twisted with such loathing that it made her shudder.

"I thought it was about time I visited my old friend," replied Tokala, his voice was strong and determined and Kai took strength from it.

"You really didn't expect a warm welcome, did you?" Atolin's icy laughter echoed around the crowds who watched on quietly. Tokala remained seated on Chaser watching Atolin with sadness in his eyes.

"I've have come to learn that you're now incapable of a warm welcome for an old friend Atolin. Your reputation has spread far and wide and the people in this city live in fear of being either robbed, beaten or never heard from again. I didn't want to believe that my best friend had become this monster, so I've come to see for myself and my heart now aches, for I see it's true."

"Save your speeches Tokala, who do you think you are? This is my city, I run it as I see fit," snorted Atolin, it was clear that he was getting angry now. "Who is this? Why are you riding with a woman from the mountains, why have I not seen her before?"

"You have seen me many times brother," said Kai staring down at him.

There was an audible gasp from the onlookers and Atolin narrowed his eyes as he stared at the young woman on horseback. He suddenly turned his back on them and strode back towards the palace barking orders to his men, "take them, bind their hands and bring them to me in the throne room. I'll continue their interrogation there."

Without another word Atolin disappeared into the palace as Kai was roughly pulled from her horse. She didn't bother to struggle instead twisting round to see how Tokala was faring, he was dismounting Chaser himself, his eyes staring threateningly at anyone who dared to approach him, and no one did. Kai smiled slightly she couldn't help being impressed. Her hands were tied tightly in front of her and she saw Tokala lazily offer the men his two hands so they could be bound.

Suddenly there was a loud whinny and Chaser started rearing and kicking out as one of the Crystalite soldiers tried to lead him away. The angry stallion broke free of his grip, "Go to Lord Arcos!" shouted Tokala and the horse turned and ran back through the streets vanishing out of sight. At the mention of Lord Arcos the crowd all started to speak at once and Tokala could feel their excitement spreading.

Kai and Tokala were led into the palace forecourt and through the palace doors. It was a spectacular building with high ceilings sparkling with crystals and intricate carvings on shiny granite walls and pillars. They were taken to what Kai recognised as what was once the council meeting room, but now the interior had changed. The circular seating for the Wizard Council was gone, replaced by an empty auditorium with one spectacular jewelled throne set upon a podium towards the back wall. Seated on the throne with a crown on his head was Atolin awaiting their arrival.

"Am I to believe you are Kai?" asked Atolin as soon as they had entered.

"I am Kai," she replied as she was forced to stand in front of him.

"Why have you come here? You must know you will be killed. Your father was a traitor," said Atolin completely emotionless.

"I came because our people need my help Atolin."

"And how are you going to help? You won't be alive long enough to even get to know your people," laughed Atolin nastily, affronted by her boldness. One of his men went to his side and whispered something in his ear. Atolin's eyes widened slightly then looked confused, he turned to Tokala. "Broc tells me you sent your horse to Arcos. How can this be?"

"I'm sorry did I forget to mention. Lord Arcos is healed and is gathering an army as we speak, in a very short time you will pay for what you did to him and the other Crystalites who stood against you," said Tokala.

Atolin's eyes betrayed his thoughts, he was clearly shaken by this revelation, surely it was impossible that Arcos was still alive. "It seems you have a lot of information for me, and I will take great pleasure in extracting it from you."

"Your cruelty knows no bounds brother, but this time we shall stop you," said Kai. "What you did to Lord Arcos was wicked, and for that alone you'll be punished."

Atolin started to laugh again, but this time there was an edge of nervousness attached to it. "Believe me, I'll think up something much more interesting for your ending, you are after all, the daughter of a queen. I'm not foolish enough to think you've arrived here without some sort of plan, but whatever it is, you'll not succeed. Take Tokala to the ice cells, a few hours in these freezing temperatures will loosen his tongue," Atolin ordered. "As for you Kai, we have much to discuss and I have a feeling you'll tell me what I need to know very soon. Take her to my rooms!"

Tokala snarled angrily and pulled hard at his bindings, the flimsy knots the nervous soldier had tied fell apart and he started forward to grab a sword from one of Atolin's men, "Tokala No!" cried Kai. "We must stick to the plan!"

Tokala stopped on the spot, wondering what part of the plan involved him getting locked up in the ice cells away from Kai, but one look from her told him she had an idea. So, he stopped and allowed the Crystalites to bind him once more, this time much more rigorously, he would not escape so easily. Atolin watched on, curious at Kai's control over the Mavaho chief, but no matter, soon enough she would be singing her secrets to him.

Tokala was marched off and taken down to the ice dungeons below the palace, another new creation of Atolins's. Darkstar would have never considered a throne, he always seated himself at the same level as the rest of the Wizards to discuss matters. He certainly would not have allowed cells of torture to be built underneath his palace. The cells faced outwards over a steep cliff that would be impossible to climb, therefore the back of the cells had no walls or bars, they just stood completely open to the elements with a sheer drop beneath them. Tokala was taken into one of the cells, the walls were solid ice with chains embedded in them to which his feet were chained and his boots removed. The icy breeze made a low whistling as it blew directly into his cell and Tokala had already begun to shiver before the door was slammed shut on him. He hoped that Kai knew what she was doing, he wouldn't last long in this cold.

Kai was led to Atolin's chambers where her hands were untied and rebound again, but this time tightly behind her back, making her shoulders ache. She was left alone to await Atolin's arrival and she surveyed the rich décor and many jewels that were hanging on the walls and sewn into the tapestries. The chamber was void of warmth and life and Kai could sense a dark presence that she recognised. Draconan had been here, she was sure of it, his dark essence was lingering all around the room. She wriggled her hands to see if she could loosen the bindings but they were on tight, so instead she focused her mind hoping to loosen them with magic.

"I could probably untie them for you," said Solitaire and Kai jumped around startled to see the ancient warrior lying on Atolin's bed with his legs crossed and his head propped up.

"How did you get here? Your supposed to be with Lord Arcos," she said slightly bewildered.

"What and miss out on all the fun. I don't know if you realise but a cat can get into almost anywhere," replied Solitaire grinning annoyingly.

"Well make yourself useful and untie me," said Kai refusing to rise to his bait.

"Now what good would that do? You still wish to talk to Atolin, and now is your chance. You can have one more attempt at trying to turn him back to the light before…."

"Before what?" asked Kai.

Solitaire sighed and sat up on the bed with a serious look on his face, "before you have to call the Ghost Council."

"The Ghost Council? Is this something else I should know about?" asked Kai.

"I wish you didn't have to, but Sirena thinks you may have no choice. It's a dark magic created by Zebulon many, many, years ago. He was once one of Odysseus's greatest Overlords and he worked tirelessly for peace in the Universe. As a reward Odysseus gifted him a world was known as Earth, a world similar to Satiren in many ways," explained Solitaire.

"I heard a little about Earth from Wigholt's story," said Kai.

"Earth was an ancient planet but it's power and technology was beginning to rival the magical power of the Overlords themselves. Earth was led by Warlords, men and women hungry for power and riches with no thought to those who struggled to survive around them. The Gods and the Overlords were forgotten, becoming nothing but children's fairy tales and Zebulon could only watch in despair as his beautiful world was destroyed bit by bit.

Odysseus stepped in, he had to take control before Earth infected the rest of the Universe and helped Draconan's power to grow. The Dark Lord fed off hatred and greed, so in a desperate attempt to save his beloved Earth, Zebulon created a spell that would summon a Ghost Council, an apathetic force of reapers who cast judgement on all those found wanting. When the ghosts found a dark corrupted spirit, they would drain their life force and send their souls onto Dhurgon. Zebulon believed it would cleanse Earth of all its evil and those left could begin again. However, Zebulon was too late, the Overlords had already decided on Earth's fate and his world was destroyed before he could act."

"So, Sirena wants me to summon the Ghost Council here on Satiren?" said Kai.

"Only as a last resort. We know Zebulon hid the summoning enchantment in the Wizard Council meeting room when Darkstar died. He was concerned then that they may have to use it, but it was avoided when Sirena took Black Eagle away. We would have to retrieve it first, perhaps I can help with that seeing as your hands are tied," replied Solitaire.

"Very funny, in the meantime I'm supposed to stay here and endure whatever kind of torture Atolin throws at me?" said Kai.

"He can't hurt you, you have the White Witch's magic," replied Solitaire.

"Well I can honestly say that's good to know, but what about Tokala, will he be safe in these ice cells?" she asked.

"That, I can't answer you, he's strong though and once I find the enchantment I'll go and find him. He may have lost a few toes and have a few icicles growing from his nose but I'm sure he'll survive," said Solitaire then realised by the look she gave him that Kai was not amused by his flippancy. He chuckled, "I won't let anything happen to him, I promise."

***

Tokala was angry with himself, he should never have let them take him so easily. He tried to release the chains imbedded deep in the walls of ice, but they would not move, he really was trapped and extremely cold. His teeth were chattering involuntarily and he could not feel his finger or toes, this was not his idea of a warrior's death, being frozen in some ice cell.

Just then the door to his cell swung open and Atolin casually walked in, looking smug and still wearing that ridiculous crown upon his head. Tokala snorted and shook his head in disgust at the sight of him, then watched with disbelief as Atolin gestured one of the guards to bring in a chair into the cell for him to sit on. Atolin straddled the chair facing Tokala and smirked, "I'm curious Tokala, why would you come back here? You must have known you would not be welcomed."

"As I said before I came to see if the stories are true. The son of Darkstar, the one who I called my friend could not possibly be the monster I see before me."

"I am no monster! I have simply cleansed this city of the memories of a traitorous King and a weak pathetic council. Your fate was sealed as soon as you set foot in the city and the only reason you are still alive is because I want to know how you found Kai. I spent years trying to guess what Ragnar had done with her, was she with the Mavahos this whole time?"

Tokala regarded the young man who called himself Atolin with distaste, he wasn't going to answer any questions so he remained silent.

Atolin laughed, "You think your silence will unnerve me? I have taken down bigger men than you, it will give me great pleasure to watch your face when I deal out my punishment to Kai. I will give what's left of her to my soldiers and if she is alive after that, then she can join the others in Vulcan's ice prison. Its where all the traitors are sent, and her father was a traitor, he took advantage of my mother whilst betraying his King."

"Darkstar adored you Atolin, you were his only son, his pride, his heir and his reason for living. Losing you destroyed him, he could not go on without you. If he saw you now, he would be ashamed," stammered Tokala through chattering teeth.

Atolin got to his feet abruptly and his chair went crashing over. "Darkstar was a weak, unworthy fool! He drove my mother to insanity and he made his own son subservient to the children of an outsider. I regret every day that I ever had to call him my father!"

"Don't you see, your hatred has taken control of you. Your actions are destroying our world as you allow the darkness inside of you to take hold. Your mother was an insane, greedy woman, she wanted power, she didn't care about you, for Odysseus sake Atolin! She tried to kill you to hurt Darkstar," argued Tokala knowing deep down it was pointless.

"Darkstar stood watching me being thrown to what would have been my death, even Ragnar tried to save me, but my own father did nothing. I will never forget the look on his face as he just stood and stared at my predicament, and where were you, my so- called friend? I protected you, but you left me to die," Atolin spat into Tokala's face. "When I have finished with Kai you will be taken to Mount Gloom, and there you will face the same fate as I did, but this time I doubt the Snow Eagles will be able to bear your weight, you will die."

"You are as insane as your mother," replied Tokala.

Atolin drew his knife pressing it against Tokala's throat causing a trickle of blood to run down its edge. "I will show you just how insane I am, in a matter of hours Tokala you will regret those words and there will be no one left to challenge me for the Crystal City throne."

"You're a brave man Atolin, threatening me while I'm chained to a wall. But you haven't thought this through, what about Catori? Is she not Darkstar's daughter also, and your sister? Does she not have a claim to the throne?" said Tokala deliberately taunting the Crystalite King.

"Liar! Catori is not Darkstar's child!" said Atolin but his eyes were betraying his doubt.

"So, they never told you, that's interesting," replied Tokala feeling Atolin's knife slice deeper into skin.

Suddenly Atolin backed away, "I'm not playing your games Tokala. If Catori were to come to the city she would suffer the same fate as you are about to."

"I doubt you will ever get a chance to meet her, our world is dying Atolin, because of you. Have you not seen the moons, only two remain, we have a few days left at best."

"More lies and trickery, I'm tired of this. The next time I see you will be at your sentencing," said the Crystalite King and he banged on the cell door to be let out.

Tokala watched him go, he needed to get out of these chains and get to Kai, she was in terrible danger.

CHAPTER THIRTY

The door leading into Atolin's rooms started to rattle and Solitaire jumped off the bed instantly transforming into the huge white cat, then he sped away to hide behind one of the jewelled tapestries just as the Crystalite King walked in carrying a tray with a jug and a glass on it.

"Oh, you haven't made yourself comfortable, here let me help," he said setting down the tray and roughly pulling her over to a hard chair. He pushed her down and she sat perched on the end of it watching Atolin closely as Solitaire took the opportunity to scurry unseen out the room.

"What have you done with Tokala?"

"I would be more concerned about what I'm going to do to you," replied her brother maliciously.

"I'm not scared of you Atolin, all I see before me is a spoilt brat playing at being King," she replied unimpressed.

"You'll change your mind when your screaming for death to come and take you, but first I want to know where you came from. You will tell me all I want to know."

Kai thought back to her vision of Black Eagle, he had made a similar threat to Garik, but achieved nothing. Now her brother was behaving in the same way, Kai was thankful that her memories of him as a boy had been taken from her. This monster making these threats could not possibly be her brother.

Atolin picked up the jug and poured some amber liquid into the glass, he approached Kai then reached out grabbing her hair roughly tilting her face upwards to face him. He put the glass to her lips forcing some of the amber liquid into her mouth. Kai spat it out, coughing and spluttering but he just continued to force more of the foul-tasting liquid in, and she knew she had inadvertently swallowed some of it.

"I only need a small amount to loosen to your tongue, you will be feeling the effects already," he said letting go of her and pulling up a chair so he could sit facing her.

Kai could feel her mind grow foggy and her eyes began to lose focus, so she closed her eyes and reached out for the magic within her. She felt the blue light of power burn inside her and after a moment she reopened her eyes to find her vision was clear. Atolin had a pathetic smirk on his face and his eyes shone with triumph, "now you will tell me where you came from Kai?"

"From a place far from here, somewhere you have never heard of," she replied and smiled sweetly at him.

Atolin looked confused, surely the drug had to be working, but Kai could tell he was uncertain.

"Where is Arcos just now?" he asked.

"Lord Arcos is somewhere that you will never find him," she replied calmly.

Her brother swore out loud and got to his feet shouting, "are you toying with me?"

"I'm not sure how I'm supposed to answer that, haven't you given me some sort of drug to make me tell the truth? It doesn't seem to be working," replied Kai.

Atolin grabbed the jug once again and filled up the glass with more of the nasty drink, this time he slammed the glass into her mouth pinching her nose shut and forced her mouth open, he poured the entire contents of the glass into her mouth. Kai choked bringing most of it back up but she could feel the drug attacking her consciousness. Again, she closed her eyes reaching out for her magic and once again the blue light diminished the effects of the potion, soon enough the drug was gone from her system.

When she opened her eyes Atolin was scrutinizing her closely, "It didn't work," he cried then was suddenly possessed by a fit of fury throwing the jug at her head, she managed to duck but it smashed on the floor next to her sending glass flying everywhere. "I am going to have to think of something else, don't think this is over."

***

Solitaire padded through the palace unnoticed eventually finding his way into what had once been the Wizard Council's meeting room. It was in darkness but even so Solitaire could see it had changed since his last visit. The floor space was enormous with only Atolin's huge throne furnishing the room. Solitaire changed back to his human form and the room instantly sensed an occupant and the crystals in the ceiling above him started to glow to light up the room. He began to search the walls, it had been years since Zebulon had shown him the secret panel that all the ancient scrolls were hidden behind, and he cursed himself for not paying more attention. It was a big room with many panels, it might have been easier for him if the lay out of the room had been the same as before.

It took him more time than he intended but eventually he found the loose panel and opened it up to reveal rows and rows of old magical scrolls. Now he would have to go through them all to find the right spell and there had to be about forty or so. He had only just stared unravelling them when he heard the entrance door swing open and three soldiers strode in, they were dressed in Atolin's elite colours and had their swords drawn.

"Looks like we have another strange guest for the King," said one of the soldiers as they spread out to surround Solitaire. The ancient warrior sighed deeply then stood up straight and drew his own magnificent sword, "Do you really want to do this?" he asked in a bored tone.

"Drop your weapon now and we'll spare you," said a soldier pointing his sword level with Solitaire's face.

Solitaire moved so fast they had no time to register his attack and he had disarmed two of them before they could blink. He floored them both then lay a hand on their heads and they both found they could neither move nor utter a sound, they just lay there frozen to the spot. The third man attempted to run at him, but Solitaire simply grabbed the end of his attacker's sword with his hand, pulling the stunned man towards him and sweeping his legs out from under him. Within seconds the third soldier was on the ground as immobile as the other two. It had taken less than a minute leaving Solitaire able to return to the hidden panel to search through each of the scrolls one by one.

***

Atolin struck Kai's face again, sending her crashing to the floor. He grabbed her viciously pulling her backup to the chair, but not before Kai managed to grab a piece of glass. "You are nothing but the offspring of a mad woman and a traitor. What makes you think you can ride into my city and make demands of me?"

"Your city? The people hate you Atolin! How can you not see that? You have made them all live in fear for their lives!"

“I have had to be firm, but I have cleansed this city of all its corruption, the people worship me and everyone knows their place,” he told her.

“Can you actually hear yourself? You have tortured and imprisoned people, those who dared to oppose you were sent to Vulcan’s ice caves. For the love of Odysseus you actually sent children there! You are as insane as our mother!”

Atolin pulled her out of her seat up to face him, his face only inches from hers. ”How do you know who I sent to the ice caves? How do you know so much?”

“I’ve been there, I’ve seen for myself and I have freed them all. You’re going to have a reckoning Atolin, things are completely out of your control now!”

Just then there was a knock on the door, Atolin gathered himself and stepped outside, Kai could hear men’s voices talking in low whispers she twisted the glass in her hand and started to saw at the bindings around her wrist. Atolin was suddenly aware she may be listening, so he reached back in the room to grab the door handle shooting her an icy look as he slammed it shut. Kai was left alone in the room wondering what could have happened that was more important than questioning her. She could feel a sticky substance around her fingers and knew it was her own blood, but she continued sawing on her bindings.

***

Solitaire finally found the scroll, closing off the panel he stepped over the men lying sprawled motionless on the floor. He opened the door carefully, but closed it over again quickly as a group of palace guards marched past, the palace was alive with activity they were clearly searching for someone. He heard Atolin’s voice barking orders, and guessed they were trying to locate the three men he had disabled. Even if they did find them, it would be another few hours before the spell wore off and they could talk about what happened. Solitaire changed into the white cat, picked up the scroll in his mouth then trotted unnoticed once more through the palace back to where Kai was being held. There was a guard outside her room, this posed a problem he couldn’t transform back to human form and risk being seen before he gave Kai the scroll, but he couldn’t walk through walls, nor open doors as a cat. He slipped behind a tapestry and waited, thankfully he didn’t have to wait long, there was an angry shout and Solitaire guessed they must have found the men in the meeting dome. Then sure enough minutes later Atolin came striding angrily up the corridor towards Kai’s room, the guard immediately jumped out of his way as Atolin opened the door and Solitaire bolted from behind the tapestry flying into the room unnoticed by either of them.

Kai was on her feet, her hands were untied though they were covered in blood as Atolin slammed the door shut behind him, "Who is in my palace?" he cried bearing down on her, seeming to not notice that she was free.

Kai pushed him away, "I told you, your time is coming to an end!"

He grabbed hold of her furiously raising his hand as if to strike her, but was suddenly grabbed from behind and hurled across the room.

"You took your time," said Kai.

Solitaire noticed at her bruised face and swollen lip, "Are you alright, what did he do to you?"

"Nothing I couldn't handle, I guess the protection magic doesn't work all of the time," she grimaced.

Atolin staggered to his feet, "It's you! I've seen you before! Your Solitaire!" he cried trying to remember.

"A long time ago boy, when you were worthy to say my name," replied Soltaire looking at Atolin with distaste.

Atolin screamed, "GUARDS, IN HERE NOW!"

"No one can hear you, I've put a charm on the door" said Solitaire then he handed Kai the scroll. "Are you ready for this?"

"Ready for what?" yelled Atolin and he attempted to grab the scroll from Kai's hands. Solitaire pushed him away with little effort.

"Sit and remain silent, you're not the one in control here any longer."

"Is this the only way?" asked Kai sadly.

"Time is running out, only one moon has risen tonight, the power on Satiren is fading and Draconan is waiting in the shadows," replied Solitaire.

Kai opened up the scroll, she looked over at Atolin who stood simmering with humiliation and rage and she knew that Solitaire was right. She could not reason with her brother, he was too far gone, the darkness had spread throughout him and was infecting everything. She looked down at the words printed out on the paper in front of her and they began to glow as she read aloud.

LO, I call to my father Lord Odysseus hear me

LO, I invite the Ghost Council to the realm of the mountains on Satiren

LO, In the name of the Overlord Zebulon
May the Ghost Council seek those of courage and pure of heart
LO, let those brave souls live forever in the halls of Odysseus
May the Ghost council find those who have lost their way

LO, put them back on the path to purity and honour
May the Ghost Council seek those tainted by evil
LO, remove those unworthy souls from our world and gift them to the darkness of Dhurgon
LO, I call upon the Ghost Council to cleanse this city of all evil
Let judgment commence.

CHAPTER THIRTY-ONE

Lord Arcos arrived along with Solitaire at the city just after dark, they stayed hidden in the shadows as he made his way to his old friend Gustav's house and once there, Solitaire left him to go onto the palace while he banged on the door. Although the plan had been to initially stay together, they were both eager to discover what had happened to Kai and Tokala, so agreed that Solitaire should go on ahead to find out what was going on.

Gustav had been one of the senior ranking soldiers at the Crystal palace before Atolin became King but when Lord Arcos was dismissed from the position of Lord Warrior, Gustav left also. He opened the door slowly with his sword in his hand ready to defend himself and his family, then stepped back open mouthed when he saw who was there.

"Odysseus be praised, how can this be? I was sure you were dead!" Gustav cried then he ushered Arcos quickly into his home, before they were seen.

"Things have changed here my old friend. The balance of power is changing and I'm healed as you can see. It is time we got our city back," said Lord Arcos.

"Odysseus be praised," said Gustav falling to his knees, his eyes filled with emotion. "I was being watched Arcos, every day you were in that cage. I had a young family and I couldn't risk putting them in danger. I've lived with the guilt of my cowardness every day since, can you forgive me."

"There's not a cowardly bone in your body Gustav, you protected your family, I expected nothing less. Now is the time for action, are you willing to join me?"

"You don't have to ask, they're many others who'll wish to be part of this. You're the answer to our prayers," replied Gustav.

In a matter of minutes, Lord Arcos explained the plan and Gustav sent his son out to tell their friends to come to his home immediately. Before long, his house was filled with people of all ages, all filled with new hope at the sudden arrival of the Lord Warrior.

The city was already on high alert after the arrival of Tokala and Kai, now Lord Arcos was here people were ready and willing to rise up against Atolin and his oppressors. Lord Arcos told his eager listeners what had happened down in the ice caves, and how Kai had helped free all those imprisoned there. As he was regaling his story a young boy ran in the front door with his eyes as big as saucers yelling at them to look outside.

Venturing out the door warily in case it was a trap, Lord Arcos went first and his eyes were immediately drawn to the sky where two huge fire balls were descending at speed heading straight towards the city. A few seconds later they struck right in the square at the centre of the city and blue flames erupted sending a pulse of energy throughout the streets, penetrating the houses making the Crystalite people feel disorientated and confused. Lord Arcos pulled everyone back inside closing the door, he didn't entirely understand what was happening but he suspected they would all be safer inside the house together.

The fireballs had split into ten flaming blue pillars that stretched high into the sky, then out of these pillars stepped ten tall frighteningly thin figures who stood facing each other in a large circle, then all at once they turned around so they were all facing outwards in different directions. They were indistinguishable in appearance, identical bodies with long elongated limbs and when they moved it was in a strange prancing manner almost as if they were dancing. The creatures were hairless, the skin on their faces looked as if it had been stretched over their skulls leaving a gaping hole for their mouths. They had no noses but deep sunken sockets where their eyes should have been glowing with unnatural blue lights. They were grotesquely misshapen moving at odd angles, human like but not human at all. Unearthly howling sounds came from their gaping mouths as they began to bounce and leap through the city. One by one they descended on the homes of the Crystalites to cast judgement on those who lived there, skipping through solid walls as if they were simply fresh air. No one escaped their scrutiny and terrified screams could be heard echoing all over the city as judgement was passed on all.

Lord Arcos felt the air grow ice cold and everyone became silent, fear spreading throughout the house and then the ghostly spectre stepped in. It bowed its hideous head from side to side as it began to survey the room, a woman fainted from her fear, everyone else stood still in sheer terror as they felt invisible icy tendrils start to crawl all over their bodies. It seemed to last forever, and then the creature turned its head almost comically nodding at them as if it were thanking them, before it leapt back through the wall leaving them shaken and alone. They all looked with questioning eyes to Lord Arcos not understanding what had just happened, but even he could not explain it. He just felt an overwhelming sense of relief.

***

Solitaire held Atolin firmly up against the wall, the Crystalite King had attempted to escape but it was no use. They all felt the energy pulse as it raced through the palace and now they could hear screaming coming from all around the city.

"What did you do?" whispered Atolin.

"What I had to," replied Kai sadly. "I'm sorry Atolin, I wish things could have been different."

Solitaire released his hold on Atolin snarling at him as he did so, "are you going to stay put?"

Atolin flopped down on a chair and put his head in his hands, "You know Kai I really did love you. Things could have been different, but they didn't even search for me. They left me to die alone, I was only a boy!"

"They were wrong, they should have looked for you but that is no excuse, you survived against all the odds Atolin. You should have been proud of that achievement, instead you turned on everyone who ever loved you," replied Kai her face showing no pity.

"I only lived because Draconan helped me! I wouldn't have lasted the first night if it were not for him, you cannot condemn me for being angry!" Atolin was shouting now, his fear bubbling to the surface as the screams from outside drew closer and closer.

"I condemn you for the pain and suffering you have inflicted on your people since. You have no excuse for your evil, you turned away from the light the moment you accepted Draconan into your life," said Kai unmoved by his excuses and wishing she could drown out the screaming.

***

Tokala was shivering uncontrollably when he saw the fireballs falling through the sky and landing somewhere above him in the city. The ripple of pure energy tore through his cell and the chains that held him to the wall fell to the ground instantly, he was free. He stood up rubbing his arms and hands trying to get feeling back into them, then he started to jump around to get his blood flowing. Suddenly, impossibly, the room grew even colder and Tokala froze as a terrifying skeletal figure pounced through the door towards him. He couldn't move and he didn't know if he was trembling with fear or just with the cold as the unsettling head of the creature bent at an impossibly hideous angle to look directly into his face, its blue lights penetrating deep into his soul. Then as quickly as it had come, it turned and leapt back through the door.

Tokala realised he wasn't breathing and he gasped for air greedily as he tried to make sense of what he had just seen. He could hear the screaming throughout the city now so he ran to the door and found it unlocked. Tokala slipped unseen out of his cell, all that remained of his guard was a dusty, crumbling skeleton that disintegrated as soon as Tokala stepped over it. He found his way back up to the palace, passing many skeletal remains on his way and fear began to grow inside him. He wasn't sure where Kai had been taken and as he started to search the rooms, he discovered a serving girl hiding behind the door of one of them.

"Do you know where Atolin took Kai?" he asked her.

She nodded, her eyes were wide with terror and Tokala wondered if she had been visited by the strange creature also. "She's in his chambers, down that way," she pointed.

He ran in that direction and arrived at some double doors at the end of a corridor with a crown carved in each of them and he tried to push them open but they wouldn't budge. Tokala put his shoulder to them and slammed hard, but still the doors wouldn't move. Then he heard a crazed, petrified scream come from inside the chambers, it was Atolin.

***

Atolin stared in horror when the skeletal entity leapt in through the wall making him shrink back against the window but there was nowhere else for him to go. It pranced around the room, tilting its head hideously from side to side, its long fingers reaching out as it twisted its head around oddly to look at Solitaire before letting out a primal, high pitched screech that reverberated around the room. Kai put her hands over her ears as the sound vibrated through her and Atolin moaned in terror as the creature moved away from Solitaire turning its attention on Kai. She felt cold, icy tendrils creep over her body and she tried to close her eyes but she couldn't move. Kai found herself staring deep into the blue lights shining from the creature's eyes, they gazed deep inside her, she had never felt so exposed in her life. Soon enough it turned away from her and pranced over to Atolin.

The Crystalite King was trembling uncontrollably as the creature reached out to him, he felt its ice-cold tendrils penetrate his soul and suddenly he saw his life spread out before him, being dissected bit by bit. He saw his himself riding through the mountains with Darkstar and he also saw the love his father had for him. He saw himself in Ragnar's cave playing with Kai the moon snake, then he saw his baby sister for the first time. Atolin gave an agonising scream, "make it stop!"

Then he saw himself fall, being caught by the snow eagles and he felt the pain, hunger and despair all over again. Then Draconan came to him in that weakened state twisting his mind and turning his innocence to wickedness. Atolin was shown glimpses of the people he had killed and tortured, of Lord Arcos hanging broken and defeated in his cage, of Kaeshia and the other Wizards being dragged from the council room and brutally flogged, before being taken to the ice-caves.

What seemed like a lifetime took only a few seconds, there was nothing hidden and when the entity put its bony fingers on Atolin's head the young Crystalite King screamed again for the last time. His flesh withered disintegrating into dust leaving only his decaying bones, then the entity turned prancing over the floor in a sickly jovial dance before disappearing back through the wall.

Kai collapsed in a heap and started to sob, she had not expected to feel so devastated by her brother's demise, but it was too late now, he was truly gone.

The door burst open and Tokala came flying in, he took in the room in one glance, and saw the dusty bones by the window and Kai's distraught face. She was bruised and cut and her eyes were red from crying, Solitaire also seemed to be in a state of shock. He turned towards Tokala looking grim and worried.

"Is that Atolin?" the Mavaho Chief asked.

"What's left of him," replied Kai tearfully.

"He has been taken from his mortal life, but his spirit still exists," said Solitaire

"What do you mean?" asked Tokala helping Kai to her feet. His experience with the Ghost council had left him feeling bereft and empty, like he had a gap to refill with goodness and light just to feel whole again.

"The Ghost Council take the souls of the damned and leaves them on Dhurgon, where they will spend eternity in torment, always fighting to survive while serving Draconan."

"I wish there had been another way," Kai whispered.

"You must put that out your mind now Kai, I need to go to Sirena now and report to her what has happened here. Remember, you have the Ne'Shuwa still to find Kai and there is not much time," said Solitaire changing into his cat form as soon as he finished speaking.

"But I have no idea how to do that?" cried Kai after him, but he had already left the room.

Tokala put his arm around her shoulder hugging her to him, he could feel her pain as he felt it also. Atolin had been his best friend, Tokala had also hoped they may be able to get through to him eventually, but that option had been taken from them now.

After a while Kai pulled herself together and they left Atolin's chambers heading out of the now deserted palace, there were dusty skeletons littering the courtyard as they went to the stables to get Chaser and Kyte. The horses were all wide eyes and anxious, the screams were still ringing out over the city, along with the terrifying screeches of the ghostly spectres. Chaser stamped his foot pleased to see Tokala, and they slowly led the horses out into the deserted streets of the Crystal City. Kai looked up, there was only one moon left in the sky and its brightness had started to diminish.

"I think we may be out of time," she said quietly.

"Don't lose faith Kai, the White Witch sent you for a reason. We'll find Arcos and the others then decide what to do," replied Tokala and they mounted their horses and rode in silence through the empty streets of the city.

******

Wigholt was waiting for Catori when she reached the entrance to the ice caves, he had already found the other Crystalites still recovering inside the cavern. Zodiac had gone back into the ice caves to help the others who were too weak to leave, having been healed by Kai he was doing his best to make them more comfortable. Wigholt had gone to join him, bringing a magical healing tonic that enabled the other Crystalites to finally leave their dark prison.

Catori had packed food and more healing tonics on two horses, so while the Crystalites helped themselves to a decent meal she set to work restoring their eyesight so they could finally venture outside.

Wigholt already had a magical fire blazing in the cavern filling it with warmth and the grateful Crystalites were already feeling better, with their strength was returning to them slowly they planned to leave the next morning. There was a shout from outside the cavern and a few of them saw the fireballs plummeting down from the sky, they heard the crash as the fireballs landed from somewhere high above them. The energy pulse did not escape them either and when they felt it they looked bewildered at Wigholt as if waiting for some sort of explanation. The small Jacartan was not sure what had happened but he suggested that they should all return inside the cave until morning. They were ill-prepared for what was to visit them that night. The creature pranced in through the cave entrance descending on them one by one, judging every one of the Crystalite's and leaving them feeling violated and empty. They all survived the judgement, but their spirits were low and it took daylight to arrive before Wigholt could convince any of them to leave and head for the Crystal City.

They started to make their way slowly up the mountain tracks, the warm sunshine making the day seem a little better although they were all afraid about what reception they might receive in the city. Wigholt assured them that things had changed now, and their lives would be returned to them once more, all the while praying he was right.

***

Arcos heard the sound of horses coming up the street and he stepped outside, the sun had risen now but there was a peculiar haze to the day, like there was something heavy in the atmosphere. "Is that Tokala?" asked Gustav who joined him.

Kai and Tokala rode up as people began to come out of their homes onto the street. "You're alright, thank Odysseus," said Lord Arcos. "What of Atolin?"

"He's gone, along with all his followers, the ghost council took them," replied Kai and there was a buzz of confused chatter from the crowd.

Lord Arcos grabbed hold of a crate and pulled it over then stood on top of it holding his hand aloft, "Everyone quiet please! Listen to me!" he called out at the growing crowd that surrounded them.

"Atolin and his followers have gone and we are now free to choose our own leaders. This is Kai, most of you will remember her as a child, she saved me from the ice caves along with the rest of the Wizard Council. They are making their way back to the city as I speak, things will change for us now and you will all have a hand in making this city the great place it once was."

Kai watched the crowd, they were still confused and shaken from the Ghost Council, but they hung onto every word Lord Arcos said and she felt a spark of hope begin to grow. Then the crowd parted allowing Zodiac and Kaeshia to stride through leading the rest of the Crystalite prisoners from the ice caves. People started to clap and soon the euphoria caused by their sudden arrival started to build, filling the hollow void that had been left from the judgement the night before. The cheering and clapping grew louder, faces began to smile and Kai turned to Arcos, "You're a born leader," she said.

"I am no King," he replied.

"You have the strength and authority that these people need right now," interjected Zodiac. "Kai is right, you must lead us."

"I will take control until the people are ready to vote for their new King," said Lord Arcos and he turned to the crowd once again. "I have been asked to take over the city while we rebuild the Wizard Council and the trust of our people. Zodiac will take Gariks place as council leader until the city is ready to vote for themselves."

Zodiac spoke, "There are many of the old council that are no longer with us, we are depleted but we are strong and recognise the work ahead of us. I have been informed that all of Atolin's followers were taken by the ghost council, this city will no longer be a place of fear and whispers, we will not allow the likes of Egor to poison and exploit the weak minded, we are free to live as we please."

There was a deafening cheer from the crowd, and Kai felt someone squeeze her hand. She looked down from Kyte and saw Catori beaming up at her. "You did it, Kai," she said.

Kai jumped off the horse and pulled Catori away from earshot of anyone else, "No, I haven't, I still have to get the Ne'Shuwa to return and I have no idea how. The world is getting darker, I don't know if there is any going back."

"What can we do?" asked Catori. Tokala spotted them and moved over to join in the conversation.

"I think I have to go back to Ragnar's cave. I have a feeling that there is a portal there that I can access, if I can open it then we may have a chance," replied Kai.

"We'd better leave now," said Tokala looking up at the sky. "It looks like this will be the last time we'll see daylight on Satiren if we don't."

CHAPTER THIRTY-TWO

"It's seems you failed me," came a rasping voice he recognised. He could not make out Draconan's features in the shadows, but that voice he could never forget. "No matter, in a few hours Satiren will be mine, perhaps I shall return you to rule King Atolin. I would hate to think the years I spent blackening your heart were a complete waste, it would be a shame to let all that evil flitter away and to be honest if it wasn't for you, Satiren would still be a glowing star in the heavens."

"What do you mean?" said Atolin, his voice sounded echoey and strange. He looked down at his hands, they were translucent, ghost like and he wondered if this was what it meant to be dead.

Draconan stood up stepping into a thin ray of light making Atolin recoil from the grotesque face of the Dark Lord. "You are mine now, my slave to do with as I see fit. I did not for see the arrival of your sister, she has created some difficulties, but even she has run out of time. The Overlords have given me Satiren, and soon I shall descend on that world with you, and Black Eagle at my side."

Atolin's recognised Black Eagle's name, he was the father of Tokala, an evil monster by all accounts. But who was the evil monster now? Kai had been right, Satiren was dying and it was his fault. A strange emotion washed over Atolin and for the first time in a very long while he let go of his anger only to find it was replaced with guilt. He had taken things too far, he had allowed Draconan to fuel his sense of betrayal and find a way into Satiren. Atolin knew he had hurt many of his true friends doing so and standing here in front of the very essence of all evil, it was as if he could see himself through Kai's eyes. He had tortured and mutilated all those who had tried to help him, it had given him pleasure, but he had never been happy since the day his mother threw him off that cliff. He had destroyed his world and now he had been judged and would be a prisoner of this monster for ever. He was trapped and there was nothing he could do about it.

"When the last moon leaves the sky, I will return you Atolin and you will take your men and feed me the souls of all those who survived the judgement. I will allow you to inflict much suffering on your people as you wish, once you have turned each of their souls to the darkness, you will offer them to me."

Atolin felt sickened, he could not reply, what had he done? Then he was aware of another entity in the room with them. He looked around to see another apparition of a tall man that he recognised although he had never seen him before. He could have sworn he was looking at Tokala except this man's face was contorted in evil, he had a missing eye and an ugly scar that cut deep down his cheek.

"But what about me master? You promised me I would be returned to Satiren. I have earned my right for vengeance!" cried Black Eagle.

"Silence, you dare to tell me what your rights are. You have been rewarded already, have I not given you power over the slaves of Dhurgon? It is Atolin who has set this path in motion and for that he should be rewarded. He proved himself to me time and time again, his evil was unprecedented, even you did not have the imagination Atolin had for punishments."

Shame consumed Atolin as he listened to Draconan's words, had he really been that evil? Yet even asking himself that question, he knew in his heart it was true.

"I only ask that you allow me to have my revenge on Tokala. I have waited for so long to repay my son, do not deny me that," begged Black Eagle.

"I am sure Atolin will give you that privilege, you need only ask him," answered Draconan seating himself back on the throne.

Black Eagle turned to look at the stricken Crystalite King. Atolin shook his head in despair, "you may do as you wish with Tokala, I'll not stand in your way."

His answer seemed to please the monstrous being seated in front of them, but his soul was crying out to be released. The darkness that had consumed Atolin was now seeping away and he only wished he could see Kai one more time to tell her he was sorry.

"But first I have a task for you both. Your sister Kai is trying to find the Ne'Shuwa. If she succeeds in this then she will still have a chance to restore Satiren. I want you to find her, kill her and then kill the remaining Ne'Shuwa. To do this you will need to enter the portals and I will restore your bodies to mortal form. The Ne'Shuwa live in the tunnels, but be careful they are more powerful than they seem and to kill them will be difficult in their own domain. But be warned, if you fail me and Satiren is restored, I will leave you both to the mercy of the inhabitants of Dhurgon. You will have a thirst for blood that will never be quenched and you will have to fight to feed everyday of your existence." Draconan's threat was unmistakable but Atolin was beyond caring, he was consumed in guilt and that was torture enough.

"We will not fail master," replied Black Eagle then he looked over at Atolin expecting him to speak.

"We will obey you," said Atolin pulling himself together and hoping he sounded convincing. If he was to help Kai, then he would have to watch Black Eagle, he would not allow the Mavaho Chief to kill her or the Ne'Shuwa.

A shrieking sound suddenly cut through the darkness, "AAAAATTTOOOOLLLLIIINN!" An entity flew past his head screaming out his name. Atolin tried to cover his ears to stop the sound from penetrating him, but his hands had no substance and were useless to him. The ghost floated in front of him and he recognised the madness in its eyes, he was looking at what was left of his mother.

"ATTTTOOOLLLLIIIINNN, IISSSS HEEEEE DEEEEEEEAAAAD? DDDAAARRKKSSTTARR, DDIIDD YOOOUUU KKKKILLLL HIIIMMMM FFFFOOORRR MMEEE?" the ghost of his mother howled.

Atolin stood shocked, after all these years she was still consumed with hatred for his father. "He's been dead for fifteen years!" he cried out to her.

"DEEEAAADDD DDDEEEEEEAAAADDD!" the crazed ghost shrieked in delight then her ear-splitting laughter echoed all around them as she floated away.

Draconan watched with a repellent look of satisfaction on his skeletal face and Black Eagle reached over to lay his hand on Atolin's shoulder. It felt strange, Atolin knew it was there but there was no weight to it.

"It's time to go," said Draconan and he waved his bony fingers. Atolin started to feel the physical strength return to his body, he began to feel whole again. As the feeling returned, he felt what seemed to be the hilt of a sword in his right hand. He looked down to see he was holding a huge sword that glowed fiery red in the darkness. Atolin noticed that Black Eagle was similarly armed and the old Mavaho Chief was staring right at him with a menacing sneer on his face.

"You will need some warriors, take these men with you, if you succeed, they will be rewarded for their effort," rasped Draconan. Atolin saw a group of eight half-starved Mavahos step out of the darkness and gather around the light of the portal that Draconan had just opened.

"Kai has entered the Portal already, I believe your son Tokala is with her Black Eagle. Your vengeance will come sooner than you expected," hissed the Dark Lord.

The blue light emanating from the portal illuminated the darkness and Atolin could see all Draconan's malformed skeletal features clearly for the first time. "Do not fail me," the Dark Lord warned once again. Without hesitation Black Eagle stepped into the light followed by his men, and then Atolin followed close behind.

CHAPTER THIRTY-THREE

They arrived at Ragnar's cave to find Solitaire there waiting for them with news. The White Witch had seen Draconan's slaves in the portal tunnels, they were already hunting the Ne'Shuwa and looking for Kai.

"Perhaps I should go alone?" suggested Kai.

"Why would you say that?" asked Tokala frowning, he had no intention of letting her do this by herself.

"It's the Ne'Shuwa, they are very nervous and if they find me with a Mavaho warrior, then I'm sure they will flee. Remember, Wigholt showed us that it was your ancestors who hunted the Ne'Shuwa for their wings."

"I'll be careful, I won't approach them and I'll keep my weapons hidden, but it's not safe for you to be alone. Solitaire has just told us that Draconan has sent warriors in after you, You'll need me to be there to watch your back," replied Tokala.

"He's right," said Solitaire standing up from the pot he was stirring over the fire and stretching lazily in a cat like manner. "Kai everything hangs in the balance now, if you find the Ne'Shuwa you cannot get distracted. You must persuade them to return to Satiren while Tokala keeps watch, it's for their protection as much as it is for yours."

"Very well, but what about the light, it's so easy to get lost in it," said Kai remembering her first time in the portals.

"Which is why I've made you both this tea to drink, it will keep you grounded and focused," he said handing them a cup filled with a purple coloured tea. They both took a sip and both pulled a face of disgust at the same time. "It's not supposed to be tasty, it serves a purpose, now drink it down and stop complaining."

They downed the nasty tea then followed Solitaire out of the cave, he led them up a narrow path through some rocks and out onto a rocky ledge where a portal doorway was already standing open. "Ready?" he said.

"As ready as we'll ever be," replied Kai and Tokala nodded. They took each other's hands and after one more glance at Solitaire, stepped through into the light.

Tokala felt the blue light bathe him and a sense of euphoria raced through his body making him grin stupidly. Kai recognised the look on his face and shook him hard, making him focus on her. He blinked then shook his head, clearing the fogginess that threatened to take control.

"It's potent in here," he said feeling more himself as he focused.

"It takes a little while to get used to, you have to will yourself to move forward and you'll find you are being lifted from the ground. It's a strange feeling but you'll get the hang of it, take my hand and imagine flying through the tunnel," said Kai.

Sure enough, Tokala felt his feet leave the ground and he found himself floating forward. Kai grabbed his hand to pull him along and soon they were speeding through the portal tunnels aimlessly, neither having any idea which way they should go. Tokala was gaining confidence by the second and he let go of Kai's hand so he could speed past her.

"Show off!" she called out after him.

They searched tunnel after tunnel, speeding their way through miles and miles of the magical light but meeting no one. Each tunnel began to look the same and Kai could not swear that they weren't turning back on themselves, when suddenly she felt something whizz past her head. She called out to Tokala to slow down and as he did so he was struck by an arrow in his shoulder. He fell to the ground and Kai landed next to him just as another arrow narrowly missed her.

"Get behind me!" yelled Tokala yanking the arrow from his shoulder, then he drew his own bow while he looked around wildly to see where the arrows were coming from. He spotted a group of figures coming towards them in the distance and then another arrow sped by dangerously close. Tokala shot off a volley of arrows in their direction and everything went quiet for a second or two before a voice he thought he would never hear again cried out to him.

"You have a good aim Tokala, I wouldn't expect anything less from a son of mine, however you are outnumbered, lay down your bow and I'll reward you with a quick death," roared Black Eagle through the tunnel.

Tokala responded with another volley of arrows then he turned to Kai, "Get out of here, find the Ne'Shuwa, I'll hold them off!"

"But I can't…" she cried.

"You must or everyone I love will die. Now go!" he yelled.

Somewhere deep inside Kai knew he was right, but it wasn't easy leaving him. She leapt into the air and started to fly once more, speeding away from Tokala and their attackers. She had to find the Ne'Shuwa but where were they?

She turned another corner and flew straight into netting of some kind. She tried to wriggle free but was caught like a fly in a spider's web.

"Well well what have we here?" said Black Eagle stepping out into her line of vision. "You flew straight into our trap, I'm disappointed, this was all a bit too easy."

Kai stopped wriggling to stare at Black Eagle, he was uglier than she remembered.

"Cut her down!" he ordered and some ragged looking men brandishing knives started to hack at the netting that held her. Soon they pulled her down so she could stand on her feet and they spun her roughly around to face Black Eagle who was grinning maliciously.

"Well if we don't have Kai, the Crystalite Princess and sister to that gibbering idiot," he said nodding over to a man curled in the corner making strange noises.

Kai looked over and saw Atolin, he was consumed by the light, it had taken over his senses and he was completely lost in it.

"What have you done to Tokala?" she asked.

"My men are keeping him busy but I will deal with him soon enough, first I have something to show you." Black Eagle grabbed hold of her wrist and hauled her forward.

She saw a huge hessian sack on the ground, it was moving, "Who is that?" she asked fearfully.

"Not who, but what my dear, it seems we found the Ne'Shuwa before you did."

Kai stared at the sack in disbelief then a pitiful cry came from inside it wrenching at her heart strings. Another cry answered it's call from somewhere up ahead and Kai guessed the other Ne'Shuwa must be close by, "You are a monster," she choked out in despair.

Black Eagle smiled, "I don't have to be," he said pulling her close to him and grabbing her hair with one of his hands. He turned her head up to his and he leaned forward kissing her hard. Kai fought like a wild cat to get loose, she had not expected this she would rather die than have him touch her that way. She kneed him hard in the groin, it had the desired affect and he let go of her crying out whilst doubling over in pain, but his men were there in an instant and two of them caught hold of her between them so she couldn't move. There was another cry from the sack and Kai felt helpless.

"I always wondered what a Crystalite woman would taste like, I could grow to like it, but first I have a proposition for you," said Black Eagle recovering quickly.

"I don't want to hear anything you have to say," cried Kai.

"That's a shame, it would be beneficial to us both," replied Black Eagle. "What if I were to release the Ne'Shuwa on Satiren? I have no desire to see my world destroyed and I have no intention of allowing Draconan to take control."

"You would betray the Dark Lord?" said one of the men holding Kai.

"Think on, we could return to Satiren as rulers, Kai would become my wife, that would appease the Overlords and get rid of Draconan for good, he has no power outside of Dhurgon," replied Black Eagle.

Kai stared at him incredulous. "Are you completely delusional? You cannot just take the Ne'Shuwa there, they have to want to go and that won't happen. As for becoming your wife, you are as insane as Tokala said you were!"

Black Eagle struck out in fury, punching the side of her head and sending her reeling across the ground. She staggered to her feet with her head was spinning but no one had hold of her anymore. Before she could move Black Eagle was back on her, he grabbed her by her throat and lifted her off the ground shaking her violently. She was choking now, her head felt as if it would explode and she began to drift in and out of consciousness.

Atolin was trying to focus, he had been lost in the light, everything was good there and he felt free, but then he heard Kai's voice somewhere in the distance. He heard the anguish hidden in her words and he felt an overwhelming urge to protect her. The more he focused the more the power of the blue light began to subside and his vision started to return. There in front of him he saw Black Eagle murdering his sister and suddenly he had absolute clarity. Atolin jumped to his feet launching himself at Black Eagle and knocking the evil Chief to the ground. Kai fell down barely conscious gasping for breath.

"You were to leave Kai to me!" roared Atolin furiously as he pulled Black Eagle up to his feet.

"So, the Crystalite King has finally regained his senses," sneered Black Eagle. "Do you really think I would ever follow your orders? You will be bowing to me before this day is out!"

Atolin drew his sword and pointed the tip at Black Eagle. "You have more gall than I expected, but you are a fool if you think you can defeat me."

Black Eagle drew his own weapon and launched a vicious attack on Atolin, but the Crystalite King held his own, even with a lame leg Atolin was a skilled swordsman.

Kai struggled to her feet and watched in dumbstruck fascination as they fought and then in a split second Atolin looked towards her and yelled, "Kai, get out of here, do what you can to save our world!"

Snapping back to reality she looked over at the hessian sack, it was being guarded by two of Black Eagles men, but she had to free the Ne'Shuwa. She dug deep to find her power, but before she could act, she saw the Mavahos lift their bows to take aim at Atolin.

Black Eagle was tiring, he had not expected Atolin to out master him in battle, but he was taking no chances. "Now!" he cried and a volley of arrows struck Atolin in the back, he fell forward and Kai screamed with outrage. She ran over to his side and found he was still breathing, she gathered him up in her arms laying his head on her lap.

Atolin could hear Kai speaking to him, but she seemed so far away, she was saying sorry, but why was she saying sorry? Wasn't it him who had destroyed their world and murdered so many of their people? She looked so like his mother, but her eyes were softer and he smiled, it felt so good to really smile again. He couldn't speak but he squeezed her hand with the last of his strength and she seemed to know he was sorry. He felt one of her tears hit the side of his face, then from behind her appeared a large figure of a man, he was glowing in white light and holding his arms out, beckoning Atolin to come to him. Atolin slipped out of his body and his spirit drifted over to the waiting man, his father had come to save him at last.

Kai watched Atolin's soul leave his body and she could see Darkstar step forward to claim him. Her eyes were wet with tears, but Black Eagle was already descending on her so she jumped to her feet. "Is Atolin dead again? Who will mourn for him now I wonder?" sneered Black Eagle.

"He fought for his people in the end and he was brave, unlike the coward you have proved yourself to be!" Kai stooped and picked up the sword Atolin was carrying, she felt for her power and the sword began to glow in her hand. Black Eagle watched her curiously, a little reluctant to step towards the glowing sword in her grasp. Kai backed away from him and made her way over to the sack that held the Ne'Shuwa and Black Eagle's men nervously moved away, something about Kai's demeanour scared them.

She swept the glowing sword down and sliced through the ropes that held the sack shut and the Ne'Shuwa sprang out, its great metallic wings blinding them with their brightness as they reflected the blue light of the portal. It cried out once again, regarding Kai with its huge black oval eyes, then it majestically stretched out its wings and flew off in the direction of its waiting family.

Kai turned towards Black Eagle still holding the glowing sword as he and his men surrounded her.

CHAPTER THIRTY FOUR

Tokala had killed three of Black Eagles men, but now there was no sign of his father. He had become disorientated and was speeding through the tunnels having no idea which way Kai had gone. It was a maze of blue light and he felt like he was getting more and more lost so he decided to stop for a while. As he settled onto the ground he thought he could hear something.

Sure enough, there was a strange inhuman cry coming from up ahead and it sounded as if it was getting closer. Then he saw them, it was the flash of their wings that drew his eyes at first but as they got closer, he could make out their true breath-taking shape and size. There were four Ne'Shuwa heading in his direction and he jumped aside just in time pressing himself against the portal wall as they sped past. They disappeared as fast as they appeared and he found himself choked with emotion as their essence immersed itself into him. Should he follow them? Perhaps they would lead him to Kai?

He was about to go when he saw another figure approach him, dressed in silver armour with her shiny black hair falling in tight braids around her shoulders. Her golden eyes melted into his and he opened his mouth to speak, but no words came as he gazed into the eyes of his mother.

"I'm here to help you Tokala," she told him and he reached out to her but she shook her head sadly.

"I'm only a ghost in these portals, the White Witch has sent me here to lead you to Kai, time is running out," said Sisika .

"But how is this possible?" he managed to whisper his throat tight with emotion.

"My spirit travelled on to serve the White Witch, and I was able to observe you and your sister grow into the wonderful people you are. There has never been a mother as proud as I am," she told him. She was every bit as beautiful as he remembered and his heart pounded with pride. "We must not waste any more time," she reminded him. "Kai is in danger."

At the mention of Kai, Tokala regained his focus. "Let's go!"

Sisika nodded and pointed in the direction he should travel. He started to fly at speed through the light and at every turn his mother was there to direct him, it was only a matter of minutes before he descended on an ugly scene.

Kai was surrounded by Black Eagle and what was left of his men, she had a sword drawn and was holding her own but was seriously outnumbered. Tokala arrived bringing down two of Black Eagles men before they even noticed he was there.

"You managed to escape my men, I was looking forward to dragging you back to Satiren and finally paying you back for my eye, but it makes no difference to me boy, I can kill you just as easily here," said his father before Tokala could move again.

The young Mavaho Chief looked at Kai, her lip was split and bleeding again and she was struggling to hold the huge sword aloft, "Get behind me," he whispered to her but she stubbornly stood her ground next to him. Black Eagle's men all had their bows aiming straight in their direction.

"Put your swords down, it will be easier in the end," said Black Eagle sounding bored with the situation.

"Why don't you fight me father?" asked Tokala, "That's what you want isn't it?"

"Kill them," ordered Black Eagle and his men let loose their arrows but this time Kai was ready. The men gasped in horror as the arrows turned into flowers falling harmlessly to the floor. "What sort of magic is this?" Black Eagle roared.

Kai was summoning her power and her strength was growing as Tokala lunged towards his father and another sword battle erupted. Black Eagle's men drew their own swords and attacked Kai but she was ready for them, the sword in her hand moved as if she had always been an expert swordswoman and soon, she had floored two of her attackers. Tokala was blocking Black Eagle's attack at every turn, the old Mavaho Chief was already depleted of energy from his battle with Atolin and it would not be long until Tokala finally took him down. Then suddenly there was a wave of dark energy that swept through the tunnel throwing both Kai and Tokala to the ground. As they lay there, both a little dis-orientated they saw Black Eagle grinning at them maliciously, his strength and energy had been replenished and he sprung on his son, inserting the blade of his sword deep into Tokala's thigh before he had a chance to roll away.

Kai could see Draconan's entity standing behind Black Eagle, feeding him the strength he needed to finish the battle and she jumped in front of Tokala to defend him, but was once again was thrown to the ground with dark energy. She could hear Draconan's rasping laughter echo throughout the tunnel.

Black Eagle's evil face contorted into some sort of malformed smile as he descended on his son to take the final blow, but before he could act there was a flash of white light and there in front of him stood Sisika, her magnificent armour shining and her eyes alight with fury.

"You will not touch my son!" she cried.

Black Eagle stumbled back in horror as Sisika took advantage, stepping towards him and embedding her sword deep into his chest. She watched with satisfaction as Black Eagle howled in agony and then disappeared in a cloud of dust.

Kai looked around for Draconan, but he too was gone, the Dark Lord's men had been defeated.

Tokala was trying to stem the flow of blood from his wounded leg, he looked at his mother, "How?" he asked.

"Draconan broke the rules, as soon as he interfered in the portal's, he sent the balance of power back to the White Witch and I could become mortal to even things out," explained Sisika. "I must leave now though, Draconan had fled back to Dhurgon and so I must return. I love you Tokala, take care of Catori and Kai."

Sisika was radiant as she smiled, kissing Tokala on his forehead for the last time before she disappeared into the light.

"Can you walk?" Kai asked him as soon as they were alone.

Yes, I think so, but you'd better find the Ne'Shuwa without me, I'll slow you down," replied Tokala. Kai was unwilling to leave him but knew he was right, she leapt up into the light without another word and soon she was speeding through the tunnels willing herself to find the Ne'Shuwa. This time she seemed to know which direction to take, all the time flying faster and then she saw them, she drew level with the one at the rear and flew alongside it. The Ne'Shuwa screamed out a warning to the others and they turned their heads and saw her, then flew faster in panic.

Kai's power helped her to keep up, she called out to them, "Please I just want to set you free! All your enemies are gone, come back to Satiren, I promise you will be safe!"

But the Ne'Shuwa kept flying as if they didn't hear or understand her, so Kai tried again, "You will be worshipped and revered, the people of Satiren await your arrival, they wish to show you how sorry they are," she called out again.

The lead Ne'Shuwa slowed a little turning its head to regard her and the others followed suit. He recognised Kai as the one who had freed him from the sack.

Kai dug deep again for her power and she began to shimmer with magic making the Ne'Shuwa even more curious and eventually they stopped. Their huge shining wings beating slowly to keep them aloft as they stared at her twitching their strange heads from side to side.

"The White Witch sent me, we have removed the evil from Satiren and now we need you to restore our beautiful world. Do you remember how happy you were there before the strangers came, it can be like that once more. You can make your home there, have your children and finally be at peace. No one will ever hunt or harm you again. Please, I beg you, we await your arrival, come and save our world."

The Ne'Shuwa antennas seemed to be flickering at speed and Kai guessed they were talking with each other, so she waited patiently. She didn't wait long, the Ne'Shuwa all cried out with their strange sound and flew off once more. Kai had to struggle to catch them up, "Where are you going?" she cried.

They cried out this time with a haunting trumpeting sound and suddenly they vanished through the opening of a portal and Kai went flying through after them. She crashed down in a clumsy heap on the ground. Getting to her feet she looked around and found she was back near the summit of Mount Solomite. Then she heard the Ne'Shuwa calling out across the mountains and she got to her feet looking up at the sky, she could see them flying over the snow-covered peaks, their huge wings glistening in the sunlight, the Ne'Shuwa had returned to Satiren.

"You did it," said Solitaire coming over to join her.

Yes, we did," said Kai then her face grew concerned. "I've left Tokala in the tunnels, he's injured!"

"I have him Ragnar's cave, Sisika came to me and told me where he was, he's safe," replied Solitare and Kai threw her arms around his neck and hugged him for the first time as a human.

CHAPTER THIRTY-FIVE

The Ne'Shuwa trumpeted joyously and the sound reverberated around the mountain tops. The snow eagles flew down to their landing perches to watch in wonder as these strange magical creatures took over their sky.

Huge waterfalls erupted from bare rocky cliffs on the mountain sides crashing down into the valleys below filling up the old dried out riverbeds. The rivers ran wildly, foaming and racing towards vast empty craters and falling once again in spectacular waterfalls to refill the craters and form the great lakes that had once been the source of life on Satiren.

As the water flowed down from the mountains, fresh lime green grass spurted to life on the higher slopes and pine trees grew at a phenomenal rate, soon dense green forests were rising again, their sweet pine scent a foreign but pleasant smell to the Crystalites on the mountain.

The cry of the Ne'Shuwa rang out once again and the lower slopes sprung to life, with large oak trees appearing that looked ancient beside the fruit trees covered in blossom and meadows filled with colourful wild flowers.

Then on to the Silversands they flew, and the twisted dead tree stumps started to unravel themselves and rise up towards the sky. Buds appeared in seconds then the trees exploded in lush green leaves bringing life and colour to the once dry and rocky terrain. Great swathes of desert landscape collapsed in on itself creating deep canyons exposing the underground lakes to sunlight once more.

The Ne'Shuwa trumpeted in delight, their haunting melody echoing all around Satiren signalling all their creations to spring to life.

The Mavahos in Burning Towers were afraid at first, they saw dark rain clouds forming in the sky and they could not understand what they were. As the first drops of rain fell, they ran for cover in terror thinking the world was coming to an end. But a curious toddler went out into the rain unseen by his mother. When she heard his laughter, she panicked and ran out after him to find him jumping in puddles of water grinning from ear to ear. His older brother ran out to join him and soon the street was filled with children all playing in the rain and the puddles.

The older Mavahos came out of their shelters feeling a little foolish at their fear and they turned their faces towards the sky allowing the cool water to soak them through to their skin. Whatever was happening here was no threat to them.

The rain stopped after a time, the clouds parted and the sun shone brighter than it ever had done before. The Silversands was sparkling with rain drops hanging from the new growths of plants, bushes and trees. They opened the gates to the city and tentatively left the confines of the wall and wandered out into the new world that surrounded them. The perfumes from the fruits and flowers filled their senses and they were filled with both joy and wonder.

The Ne'Shuwa sang out to the heavens, as insects and small creatures broke out of their cocoons, the ground began to tremble as great herds of buffalo, antelope and all manner of grazing animals arrived through the portals to find a new home on a rich and fertile Satiren.

The lakes, now full, sprung to life with fish and water mammals, as great oceans formed to separate the land bringing back a weather system that Satiren desperately needed.

The Crystalites watched the world change from the city and as nightfall came the sun finally went down and the three moons returned, albeit hidden from time to time behind clouds.

The White Witch watched her world return to its former glory and Solitaire put his arm around her, she reached up and kissed him. They could be together now for the foreseeable future. Satiren was in good hands.

CHAPTER THIRTY-SIX

It had been a week since the Ne'Shuwa returned and Tokala was almost fully recovered. Kai had stayed at his side for much of the time as being out and about in the Crystal City still felt strange to her. People were overly friendly, showing their gratitude and complimenting her wherever she went and she often found herself overwhelmed and lost for words.

Lord Arcos was busy establishing a new government, it was not something he had ever thought about before and it was turning out to be more complicated than he thought. Everyone was so eager to please him that he felt as if he wasn't being challenged enough and couldn't be sure the decision's he made, were actually the right ones. The only one who questioned him was Catori, she had taken a great interest in the running of the Crystal City and Arcos knew he would be lost without her. She was after all, Darkstar's daughter, and the Crystalites had grown to love her in a very short space of time. Lord Arcos was sure when the time was right, that Catori would be crowned the new Queen, but he kept that to himself for now. His heart would beat a little faster every time he saw her, he loved the way she smiled and how intense her green eyes looked when they were discussing aspects of the city.

He tried his best to hide his feeling for Catori from everyone, but it did not escape Kai, and she could see that Catori felt the same. She toyed with the idea of telling them but decided she would just watch it play out instead. Catori would need time to grow into her role here amongst the Crystalites, she had already made it clear that she wished to stay in the Crystal City when Tokala went back to Burning Towers and her brother agreed. He would miss Catori but as Kai had decided to accompany him back to Burning Towers, it made it easier to accept.

Ten days after the return of the Ne'Shuwa they left for Burning Towers. The ride was so different from before, they rode through thick green forests that smelt beautifully intoxicating as it led them out onto grassy flower covered slopes. There they followed the banks of a wide, fast flowing chalky blue river that was inhabited with large jumping fish. This brought many strange creatures to its shores to fish and feast on the endless supply of fresh food. The first night they camped under a canopy of stars looking up at the three blue moons of Satiren burning brightly in the sky.

Chaser and Kyte munched on the new shoots of green grass as Tokala made a fire and they cooked some of the fish they had caught from the river. Kai had never as relaxed and happy as she did now, away from the crowds of the city and totally free, she wondered what this feeling meant. Was she destined to live alone?

A bright light started to glow close by and Kai recognised that a portal was opening. Sure enough, Sirena, the White Witch emerged from within the portal with Solitaire at her side. She looked radiant as she smiled happily at them both, "I came to thank you," she said. "And Kai I have something to give you, something I should have given you a long time ago as far as Solitaire is concerned."

Solitaire grinned then winked at Kai, "I love it when I'm right!"

Sirena rolled her eyes then approached Kai, "I'm going to return your memories," she said and light sprung from her hands as she laid them gently on Kai's head. Kai closed her eyes and suddenly a million pictures flew through her mind at once and she staggered, Tokala jumped up to catch her.

Sirena looked concerned but when Kai opened her eyes and they were filled with tears of pure joy, "thank you," she wept. The White Witch bowed her head then took Solitaires hand and the two of them entered the portal and vanished.

Kai couldn't speak, she closed her eyes and remembered Darkstar and Ragnar as they had once been to her when she was a small child. She remembered her nursery and playing with Catori, but most of all she remembered Atolin and how much she loved her brother.

Tokala brought her some tea, and made her lie down, guessing correctly that her emotions were overwhelming and he left her alone to wander to through the recesses of her mind.

The next morning, Kai felt brighter and they set off making their way through what had once been the Silversands desert. It was now a lush landscape, humming with the sound of insects busy pollenating the plants and birds singing from up in the trees. This was not new to Kai, she had grown up on Balon and was used to greenery and insects, but Tokala was like a child every time he spotted something new. The horses kept stopping to munch on some fresh sweet grass and they hadn't the heart to stop them, so they made slow progress. Tokala's endless curiosity about the new world around him was endearing and Kai found herself wishing that this journey would never end.

The day was almost coming to an end when they came across a small piece of land that still looked like the old desert and Tokala immediately recognised it. "We're at Wigholt's home," he shouted jumping down from Chaser's back. Kai followed suit sliding off Kyte while Tokala went over to the giant boulder that normally covered the entrance, except it was now lying open. "That's strange," he said frowning and started to make his way down the steps to the cavern below.

The torches in the cavern were burning low, "Wigholt!" shouted Kai but she couldn't see him, so they searched the adjoining caverns ending up finally in the one with the little stream running through. Wigholt was lying in a small cot next to the water, his pet fox was lying with its head resting on the little Wizards chest and Kai sensed immediately something was wrong as she ran to his side. Wigholt looked so old and frail, he smiled weakly as Kai leaned over him and rested her hand on his forehead.

"Wigholt, what's happened to you?" she asked gently as Tokala crouched next to them.

"Something that should have happened a long time ago, I'm finally dying," said the little blue Wizard softly.

"No! Wigholt you can't die!" cried Kai then she looked helplessly at Tokala. "Get a blanket, I'm going to try my healing magic."

"No child, please let me be," said Wigholt, his voice faint. "It's way past my time and I've waited for this moment for centuries. My beautiful world has been restored and I now I can finally go to join my wife and children."

"But I need you Wigholt," sobbed Kai. Her memories had only just been restored to her, she didn't want to lose him now.

"No Kai, you're strong, this is your time to shine, I see many adventures ahead for you. You must become the protector of Satiren now, you have the power. Take my books and learn all you can, but now you must promise to let me rest, for I have lived too long," replied Wigholt.

Kai sat holding his hand for a time, Tokala sat with her until eventually Wigholt turned his head a little to offer them a faint smile. Then the last Jacartan closed his eyes for the last time.

***

Losing Wigholt hit them both harder than they could have imagined and they decided to stay on in his cavern for a few days. They buried Wigholt next to the magical stream and then spent their time sorting through his belongings. Kai packed away all his magical books, filled with spells, stories and history of Satiren. Tokala found a hidden store in one of the tunnels and they put all the books inside. One day she would return and retrieve them, but for now they would remain safe.

Four days later they continued onto Burning Towers, when they arrived, they saw the city gates were wide open, everyone was outside exploring their new world. Paco was delighted to see his best friend and a little mesmerised by Kai.

That night they all feasted in the great hall of the castle, Tokala introduced Kai and told the Mavahos all that had happened in the mountains. It was a night of celebration, everyone was glad to see their young Chief back, though disappointed that Catori was not with him.

Kai was quiet, she watched on smiling as they all laughed and danced, Tokala was home but she was not. She had never felt so alone, her memories were back and with them a dreadful feeling of loss. She had missed out on so much growing up on Balon, she felt like an outsider to everyone, even in the mountains.

The next morning while the Mavaho's slept, Kai went to get Kyte from the stables. As she led her horse quietly out Tokala appeared rubbing his eyes, still groggy from the night before.

"I thought you might try something like this. Where are you planning on going?" he asked.

"I'm not sure yet," she replied honestly. "There's a lot of world out there to explore, and I need to do that."

"But now, so soon?" he asked looking hurt and confused.

"Tokala this is where you belong. I don't know where I belong yet," said Kai.

"Then let me come with you," he said. "Paco would love a shot at being Chief and I've never really wanted the job anyway. My people are happy now, that was all I ever cared about."

Kai looked into his pleading golden eyes, she had really enjoyed their time alone together, it was the happiest she had ever been. But she couldn't ask him to leave his people to come with her?

As if reading her thoughts, Tokala pleaded his case. "For years I have gone through the motions of being Chief in Burning Towers, but I was never fulfilled. I knew there was a world out there and now the Ne'Shuwa have returned, I want to explore it. Even if you left without me, I would not remain Chief here. Kai let me come with you, let's make our own adventures and see what this world has to offer us."

"Are you sure?" she said already knowing the answer.

Tokala grinned and clicked his fingers, Chaser trotted over itching to get underway. Tokala wrote a message and stuck it to the door of the stables, then the pair of them slipped out of the city and headed into a green new world.

EPILOGUE

The Ne'Shuwa lazed in the warm sunshine on a ledge overlooking a spectacular waterfall that flowed into the valley below. The return to Satiren had been bittersweet and although the planet was restored to its former glory, it only served to remind them of the friends they had lost. It would take time for them to trust the humans again and for their numbers to grow. Already the first of their seven eggs had hatched and it was almost fulltime job feeding just one hungry larva. When the others hatched there would be no time for sunbathing, the next few years would be a busy time for the five surviving Ne'Shuwa as they raise their new family.

Down below they could hear the sound of riders approaching, and instinctively they went and hid amongst the thick branches of surrounding trees. They recognised Kai with her Mavaho companion riding along the banks of the river, but still they stayed hidden, it was safer that way.

The Ne'Shuwa knew if they continued to follow the river, they would eventually find themselves at one of Satiren's three oceans. The Selkies had re-emerged after centuries of being cocooned underground, they had already made the coastal regions their home now and the Ne'Shuwa wondered how they would react to these strange land dwellers. They were a fearsome species of water beasts who could transform into humans once out of the water, and now they were back in the ocean, they would guard their home no matter the cost.

Throughout Satiren, different races of magical beings were slowly returning having been in a state of self-induced hibernation for centuries. The return of the Ne'Shuwa had awoken them and once they had re-established themselves back in their homes, they could go back to resuming their very different lifestyles, but all these magical beings had one thing in common. They would not allow their homes or their families to be threatened ever again.

Notes From The Author

I've walked through steamy rainforests whilst parrots and black cockatoos screeched down at me.

I've rafted down raging rapids whilst pythons hung overhead on the branches of trees over the river.

I've trekked through a red-sand desert withstanding the searing heat of the relentless sun whilst being attacked by blizzards of desert flies.

I've slept underneath a canopy of stars, their brilliance shining down on me undeterred by the artificial light from cities hundreds of miles away.

I've stood on mammoth snow topped mountains, recognising their majesty and bowing to their splendour.

I've climbed cliffs and watched the magnificent golden eagles take flight over barren mountains in search of food.

I've stood on ancient glaciers and marvelled at the waterfalls, milky torrents spurting from the ice down to wide chalky aquamarine rivers.

I've sailed in boats across the sea and been soaked by rogue waves as I dared to stand at the bow of the ship.

I've dived in coral reefs, felt the shells of giant clams with my hand and watched them close at my touch.

I've stood and looked over the edge at Niagara Falls and been soaked by the spray from these colossal waterfalls.

I've swum in oceans next to sharks, octopus and tropical fish of every colour you could imagine.

I've sat hidden in yellow barley fields in the sunshine with my friends, chewing on the stalks of the golden barley.

I've walked along deserted beaches, paddling in the waves that spread across the shore then sat and watched the seals play and sing to each other amongst the rocks.

I've heard the thunder and watched the lightening dominate as tornados formed and started their descent from the sky.

I've lived a life in awe of our wonderful planet. I have travelled and seen things that will remain with me forever.

Now I live in fear that we will lose all these wonderful places. My Grandchildren and their children's children will not get to sit in the barley fields at the end of summer, because summer will be eternal.

You, the young people of today, you know the stakes, we have to act now to save our planet.

About The Author

Alison Hill lives is a Scottish author who lives in Edinburgh. Her books include: *Seal Lodge of Kintyre*, *The Ghost of Glencoe*, *Road to Lag* and *The Fires of Cruden Bay*. They are all historical Scottish ghost stories and this book, *Kai*, is her first novel aimed at children.

Alison is a retired chef and spends a lot of time researching unique historical characters, and spending time with her five children and five Grandchildren. She is often found walking her dogs in the Pentland Hills finding inspiration for her next novel.

Available worldwide from Amazon

---

http://mtp.agency

http://facebook.com/mtp.agency

@mtp_agency